UP
AT
THE
COLLEGE

Also by Michele Andrea Bowen:

CHURCH FOLK
SECOND SUNDAY
HOLY GHOST CORNER

UP
AT
THE
COLLEGE

Michele Andrea Bowen

GRAND CENTRAL
PUBLISHING

NEW YORK   BOSTON

Grand Central Publishing
Hachette Book Group
237 Park Avenue
New York, NY 10017

Visit our Web site at www.HachetteBookGroup.com.

Printed in the United States of America

First Edition: April 2009
10 9 8 7 6 5 4 3 2 1

Grand Central Publishing is a division of Hachette Book Group, Inc.
The Grand Central Publishing name and logo is a trademark of
Hachette Book Group, Inc.

Library of Congress Cataloging-in-Publication Data

Bowen, Michele Andrea.
    Up at the college / Michele Andrea Bowen. — 1st ed.
        p. cm.
    ISBN 978-0-446-57775-5
    1. African American Congregationalists—North Carolina—Durham—Fiction.
2. African American churches—Fiction. 3. Durham (N.C.)—Fiction. I. Title.
    PS3552.O8645U6 2009
    813'.54—dc22

                                                            2008026066

Book design by Charles Sutherland

This book is dedicated in loving memory of my godbrother,
Eric Alphonzo Haskins (aka Broskie)
April 8, 1948, to August 22, 2007
We miss you, with your grinnin' self!

Acknowledgments

Wow!!! I can't believe that I have been so blessed as to reach the point where I am writing the acknowledgments to *Up at the College*. Readers, you all have been so sweet and supportive, and patient. I am so thankful for you, your love, and your prayers.

With any book, there are a lot of people to thank. And while I can't put everybody in this acknowledgment, know that I appreciate and love you all.

First, thank you Grand Central Publishing. Karen Thomas, my editor, Latoya Smith, and Linda Duggins—thank you for your help and support. To the gentleman who so graciously creates my beautiful book jacket artwork—thank you one more time. I love this cover!

Thank you, S. B. Kleinman. Your copyediting was "on the money" and enhanced the quality of this book. Plus, shout-outs to the publicity team—Tanisha Christie and Nick Small. I appreciate all of your help.

Pamela Harty, my agent. Girl . . . we've been through what some folks would refer to as "trills and trybulayshons." Thank you, from my heart.

I want to give a shout out to my "big brother," Coach Joe Taylor, head coach of Florida A&M University's (FAMU) football team, and play cousin, FAMU's former head basketball coach, Mickey Clayton. Your input helped with the construction and development of the characters Head Coach Curtis Parker and his assistant coach, Maurice Fountain. Plus, Beverly Taylor, my good friend of over fifteen years, really schooled me on life as a coach's wife. *Whew*—never knew that it was so akin to being the first lady of a church. My hat goes off to both you and Mrs. Clayton.

Thank you, Elaine Cardin, owner of Lakewood Hairquarters in Durham. It was so much fun writing you in as the character who gave Yvonne her fabulous makeover.

To my girls—Jacquelin Thomas and Victoria Christopher Murray—almost a decade that we have been in this business together. And God ain't thru' with us yet.

My church, St. Joseph's African Methodist Episcopal Church in Durham, North Carolina, along with my choir, The Inspirational Singers. Love you much.

My pastor, Reverend Philip R. Cousin Jr., and First Lady Angela M. Cousin. You two are mighty people of God and a blessing to the AME Church.

Ken and Ava Brownlee—y'all know I cannot write an acknowledgment and not put you all in it.

And my family. My mommy, Minnie Bowen, is always there for me and my babies, Laura and Janina. What would we do without MaMa? My grandmother, DaDa, my Uncle James (Bishop Nelson) and my Aunt Bessie (Mother Nelson), along with my aunts, uncles, and cousins. Love to all of you.

But most importantly, I thank and praise the Lord in the name of Jesus. None of this would have been possible without the Lord, who is my everything.

I will bless the Lord at all times; His praise shall continually be in my mouth. My soul shall make its boast in the Lord; The humble shall hear of it and be glad. Oh, magnify the Lord with me, and let us exalt His name together.

Psalm 34:1–3 (NKJV)

Michele Andrea Bowen
June 4, 2008

UP
AT
THE
COLLEGE

PROLOGUE

Yvonne sat on the floor, surrounded by the boxes crowding up the living room, wishing she had said "Yes" instead of "No" when her parents asked if she wanted them to come up to Richmond and help with the packing. The movers were coming in three days and Yvonne felt like she could use six.

She didn't want to move out of her home. But she had to because Darrell, her soon-to-be ex-husband, had threatened to fight her for custody of their two daughters if she didn't take the girls and get out of their home by a certain date. Nobody who heard this story could believe that a man would put his wife and children out of their own home based on the bogus assumption that this house was his simply because Yvonne was an at-home mom when they bought it.

The doorbell rang.

"Who is it?" Yvonne spat out, and then kicked a half-filled moving box, hurting her toe.

The doorbell rang again, this time followed by loud and insistent knocking. Didn't this person hear her say "Who is it?" Yvonne thought as she snatched the door open, ready to flip off on whoever was on the other side. Her angry glare met the bewildered expression of the young lady cradling a crystal vase filled with three dozen velvety pink roses.

"Mrs. Copeland?" the young woman asked in a kind and soothing voice.

"Yes?" Yvonne said, her voice a whole lot softer.

"These are for you."

"Me?" Yvonne raised an eyebrow, wondering who thought she needed a vase full of expensive pink roses when her budget was so tight.

"Yes, they are for you," the young woman answered and put the vase in Yvonne's hands.

"Come on in," Yvonne said over her shoulder, as she put the vase on top of the white baby grand piano and turned to sign for the flowers.

"You have a beautiful home, Mrs. Copeland."

All Yvonne could do was nod. The house was very beautiful. But it was not her home anymore. She said, "Do you have a pen?"

The young woman reached into the bag on her shoulder and put a pale pink envelope into Yvonne's outstretched hand.

They are not paying me enough for this, she thought, watching Yvonne trying to figure out what in the world was going on.

"These flowers are not from the florist. My boss, your husband's lawyer, was instructed by Dr. Copeland to deliver your separation agreement and these flowers to you."

Yvonne couldn't believe Darrell. Today was Valentine's Day and he knew how much she loved Valentine's Day. It was like he was doing everything in his power to hurt her as badly as he could. She felt the weight of the envelope and tried not to admire the exquisite, fine linen stationery in her favorite color. *Valentine's Day*, Yvonne kept thinking as she whispered, "Why me?"

"Mrs. Copeland, are you all right?"

"Yeah, I'm fine," Yvonne answered, as she struggled to blink back hot tears. She had been prepared for hurt, surmising that she couldn't get through a divorce without some casualty of the heart. But she didn't know it would be this bad.

The young woman had never met Yvonne but she knew that in her worst moment, Mrs. Copeland had never done anything to be treated like this by her husband and the father of her children.

Tears streamed down Yvonne's cheeks as she stared into the kind blue eyes of this unlikely bearer of bad news.

"Mrs. Copeland, I could get fired for saying this to you. But you have to know that any man who treats you with such disregard is not worth your tears. I pray that the day you leave this house, you will step out on faith, trust God, and never look back."

Yvonne sat down on one of the moving boxes. She put her face in her hands and sobbed. The young lady sat down and put her arm around Yvonne's shoulders.

"I know you might not feel this right now, but God is on your side, and He will see you through this storm."

Yvonne nodded. *See her through.* How many times had she heard those words in the past few months? As far as she was concerned, God seeing her through this disaster was a pretty tall order. Here she was, a well-educated, forty-three-year-old black woman with two daughters, unemployed, forced to leave a home she didn't think she'd ever be able to buy again, and crying on the shoulders of a blond, blue-eyed white woman who looked like the worst problem she'd ever had was being a day late paying her rent simply because she had forgotten to post a reminder on her calendar.

The young lady reached into her bag and pulled out a baby blue suede Bible. She turned to the first chapter of Luke and found verse thirty-seven.

"You know," she said, "it says right here that '*nothing is impossible with God.*' Not only is He going to see you through all of this, He is going to create for you cause to give a wonderful testimony about the glory of the Lord. And whenever it feels like it can't get any worse, you just remember that nothing, absolutely nothing is impossible with our God."

"Thank you," Yvonne whispered, thinking that she was experiencing one of those "it can't get any worse" moments right now.

"I'll let myself out," the young lady said as she got up and walked to the door.

By the time Yvonne's three days were up and February seventeenth, moving day, rolled up on her, Yvonne was ready to transform this season in her life into a "gone are the things of the past" event. She walked through the house, making sure that all of her boxes were in place, and came upon the last unsealed box, pulled back the flaps, and peered inside at the worn white satin wedding album. It was obvious that Darrell had tossed the album into the box, apparently hoping to convey that he did not want any reminders of her in this house.

"I wonder if he plans on tossing the girls in a box, too," Yvonne mused. She pulled the wedding album out of the box and stared at Darrell's thin, solemn face on what was supposed to have been one of the "happiest days of her life," wondering why the boy had ever formed his mouth to ask her to marry him. Even during their best times together, Darrell always found something wrong with Yvonne. Throughout their marriage, he lectured her relentlessly on what he contended was her "tendency to act like a simpleton, marred even more so by her country ways and mannerisms."

She stared at herself a moment, wondering why the pretty twentysomething in the picture, with yards and yards of delicate lace trailing behind her, didn't have the sense to bunch up that dress and run. She couldn't help but think about the day Darrell came home and announced, "After much contemplation, relentless journaling to soothe my endless vexation with you, tai chi, acupuncture, and colon cleansing to rid myself of the impurities brought on by my anxiety over this situation, I have decided that I must find my way back to my original self through a wrenching detachment process some refer to as a *divorce*.

"And *please*, turn off that clamor," he snapped, referring to the music on her CD player. "I can barely hear myself think above all of that rump-shaking, bass-thumping garbage."

"Darrell," Yvonne said evenly, "this is a Jonathan Nelson CD, and he is a gospel singer."

Darrell snorted in disgust. He disliked gospel music even more than he did hip-hop and rhythm and blues.

"You want to sit down?"

"No," he answered. "I prefer to stand."

"Okay. Suit yourself."

"That's the problem with you, Yvonne," he snarled. "You are so simple. I mean, look at me. I've spent years earning a PhD in Exotic Agricultural Studies, done postdoctoral studies all over the world, and I continue to expand my intellect in every way possible. But you"—Darrell snorted in disgust—"you are content to walk around grinning over the smallest and most insignificant matter. You are enamored with R&B and gospel music, but rarely do you want to listen to anything that expands your mind. I have yet to walk into this office and hear something worthwhile like the Brahmin Folk Shamans."

Yvonne was not going to dignify that comment with a response—even though she had plenty to say on the matter. The one time she tried to listen to a song by that group just to please Darrell, the leader's voice, which was weird, gave her a splitting headache. He sounded just like Chewbacca from *Star Wars*. She stared at Darrell for a moment and thought about going off on him and putting him out of her office. But she heard a soft voice in her spirit whispering, "Get still and be quiet."

Neither said a word. The longer they were silent, the more peaceful Yvonne became, even though her husband's agitation escalated with each passing second. When Darrell finally spoke again, he was so mad for a moment he literally forgot how to unclench his teeth. His words came hissing out.

"We've been together a total of sixteen years and it feels like an eternity spent betwixt and between Heaven and Hell. I want you and the girls out of my house seven weeks from today. And here are the terms of our pending separation," he said as he tossed a heavy envelope at her feet.

Yvonne was stunned. She didn't know that her husband, her babies' daddy, felt this way about her. Oh, she knew that Darrell was going through something—he was *always* going through some kind of dramatic episode. But this? This was something beyond the usual "Darrell is going through something or another." This was a carefully planned *kill, steal, and destroy* mission.

When Darrell stormed out of her office that day, it was the end of her marriage and life as she'd known it over the past decade. Yvonne remembered sitting at her desk staring at the ocean screen saver on her computer until she got bored enough to initiate the excruciating process of putting her shattered life back together.

Even now, Yvonne marveled at all the things she didn't do or didn't say. Whenever she relayed the story to family or a close friend, they all said the same thing.

"Girl, you mean to tell me that he said all of that and you didn't yell, get to cussin', cry until snot ran down into your mouth, put sugar in his gas tank, smear his car with creamed corn, send nasty e-mails to his boss, or open up a bunch of magazine subscriptions in his name?"

"Nope," was all Yvonne had said. As much as she had wanted to do all of the above and then some, she had not been able to do anything but ask the Lord to provide her with protection in the midst of this raging storm—a Holy Ghost umbrella that wouldn't bend back and be ripped out of her hands by a particularly harsh and bitter wind.

Yvonne dropped the wedding album on the floor, stepped on it, and then kicked it across the room. She sealed the box and went through the house one last time before the movers were scheduled to arrive. When she was sure that all was in order, Yvonne went into the kitchen and made herself a big, fat, *simple*, *country*, and ghetto-licious sandwich with the bologna she bought specifically for this day. She washed out the empty mayonnaise jar in the sink and filled it up with red Kool-Aid. She wrapped the sandwich in a piece of wax paper, grabbed the jar of Kool-Aid, and went and sat on the kitchen chair she'd put on the front porch to sit in while she ate this sandwich. She swallowed the last bite right before she saw the nose of the moving truck rolling up the street. It was the best meal she'd ever eaten at this house.

ONE

Yvonne's oldest daughter, D'Relle Copeland, sneaked and turned the car radio from her mother's favorite station, the old school Foxy 107, to her favorite, 102 Jamz in Greensboro, then turned the radio off right before Yvonne walked out of the house.

"You know she is going to turn it right back to her station. She always does."

"Shut up, Danesha," D'Relle snapped at her younger sister. Sometimes Danesha acted like her calling in life was to tell and comment on everything.

Danesha rolled her eyes at her sister, mumbling, "You are such a butt-head."

"God don't like ugly."

"Then He sho' don't like you. 'Cause whenever I look up the word 'ugly' in the dictionary, all I see is a picture of D'Relle Lenaye Copeland."

"Middle schooler."

"Yo' mama," Danesha shot back, and then shut up when Yvonne opened the car door and it dawned on her that she was talking about her own mama, too.

"*Middle schooler,*" D'Relle said as she licked her finger and wrote an invisible score in the air. Danesha, an eighth grader, hated that she had to wait another year before she could go to Hillside High School with her older sister.

Yvonne slid into the driver's seat, buckled her seat belt, and turned on the radio. One of her favorite older rap songs, "Just Walk

It Out," was playing: "East side walk it out, west side walk it out . . ." She knew D'Relle had rigged the radio and wished something her old school ears couldn't stand to listen to was on so she could flip the switch on her smarty-pants fifteen-year-old. But she opted for an even better comeuppance for Miss Thang.

"D'Relle, you go and sit in the backseat with your sister."

"But, Mama, you drop me off first."

"So what's your point," Yvonne replied, knowing that D'Relle was working hard to think of a reason to stay in the front.

D'Relle got out of the car and went and sat in the back with Danesha, who snickered and then said, "Mama, D is breathing on me and rolling her eyes just 'cause she has to ride in the backseat like she is in *middle school*."

"Stop breathing on your sister."

"But, Mama, I look like a chump sitting back here like this, losing cool points."

"Then get up and get moving and don't miss your bus again," Yvonne told her, not caring if she never earned a so-called *cool point* ever again. "And from now on," she continued, "every time your lazy butt misses that bus, you will ride in the back for the entire day. 'Cause I get tired of driving you to school when I don't have to."

"I ain't never heard you complain about driving *Trog* to school, just me," D'Relle snapped at her mother, and then rolled her eyes to add to the effect.

Yvonne drove back up into the driveway, put the car in park, and got out. She opened the back door and reached for her oldest child.

D'Relle grabbed the passenger-side seat belt strap in a feeble effort to stay in the safety zone of the car. But when her mother began to climb into that backseat, D'Relle started to cry and whimpered, "I'm sorry, Mama. I didn't mean it. Okay, Mama? Okay, Mama?"

"D'Relle, if you ever take a mind to talk like that to me again, you are going to need the SWAT team to get me up off of you. Do you understand me, *little girl*?"

"Yes, ma'am," D'Relle said, sheer relief pouring all over her when Yvonne finally retreated from the backseat.

Danesha was still and quiet, hoping to fade into the seat upholstery. The last thing she wanted was for her mama to break off a piece of what she was about to put on D'Relle and then give it to her. But her plan to remain unnoticed wasn't foolproof. Yvonne's keen *mama eyes* bore into Danesha with greater precision than any laser.

"And you better watch your step, too, missy. I have plenty left over of what I was planning to give your sister. Do I make myself clear?"

"Yes, ma'am," Danesha whispered.

"Now let's see if we can do what we've been trying to do all morning—leave this house and get you two to school," Yvonne snapped, and then turned the radio to the Light gospel station. She hiked up the volume on what she secretly knew D'Relle and Danesha believed was the countriest gospel song ever written in modern history. She tried not to laugh when she saw the sisters try to sneak and roll their eyes when the words "Jesus is my doctor, He brangs me all my medicines . . . in the room" blasted out of the car windows for *eerrbody* to hear.

D'Relle started praying under her breath, "Lord, PLEASE end this song before we get to the turn light for Hillside."

Yvonne waved at Danesha and pulled off from her last school stop, Durham School of the Arts Middle School entrance, and gave a sigh of relief. If those two weren't getting on her last nerve this morning, she didn't know who was. Yet irrespective of the "lil' negro chirrens show" the girls had put on this morning, life was more pleasant and peaceful than it had been in years. And to add to her joy, Yvonne couldn't even describe the relief she'd felt when Darrell called to announce that he was going on an academic sabbatical in Vietnam.

Six whole months without having to lay one eye on Darrell Edward Copeland and his wifey-to-be, Dr. Bettina Davidson, was the best news she'd heard in a very long time. Darrell was pompous and difficult. But that Bettina? The heifer was sneaky, mean, and always trying to take a shot at a sister from somewhere in the cut. Six whole months without those heathens in her life was enough to make Yvonne want to get out of her car and do the Holy Dance right out here on Highway 751.

Yvonne turned the radio to Foxy 107. An old Keyshia Cole song was playing. She turned the radio up, so as not to miss one note of one of her favorite songs. "I remember when my heart broke, I remember when I gave up loving you . . ." Yvonne could practically feel those words, sung to such a lovely melody with the smoothest jazz piano solo tinkling in the background.

Yvonne remembered the day her heart broke—felt as if it would never be made whole again. She used to wish, in the most painful moments, that there was some kind of Krazy Glue from Heaven she could apply to all of the fragments of her heart and put it back together. And sometimes it seemed as if nobody understood what she was going through. It was in those moments of the worst pain that she realized Jesus understood and He had everything she needed to put her heart back right. The day she gave up loving Darrell to Jesus was the day Jesus took her heart in His hands and healed her.

She was glad to be at a stoplight—it gave her some time to enjoy the beautiful blue sky, made even lovelier by the fluffy white clouds, and the warm sunshine bathing her face. It was a wonderful day and Yvonne was glad that her heart was free and full of joy. Folks just didn't know how heartache and too much struggling could dim even the sunniest day. But to be able to pray those clouds back and bask in God's love was something wonderful, and Yvonne didn't take it for granted.

"Thank you, Lord, for all that You've done for me," she said out loud, glad the DJ decided to really go old school and do an "instant replay" of the song. Sometimes, you just needed to hear one of your favorite songs more than once. Yvonne knew that God had been so good to her. She had a wonderful home in Cashmere Estates, and the perfect job as a designer and adjunct professor in the Department of Interior and Exterior Design at Evangeline T. Marshall University, or Eva T., as the school was called by most black folk in Durham County.

Yvonne turned left onto Okelly Chapel Road and then turned left again when she reached the entrance of the university, which was located where the Durham and Chatham County lines intersected. She drove down the narrow street leading to the Daniel

Meeting Building, where she worked, eyes scanning the area for a parking space. There was a shortage of decent parking spaces on campus, and if that wasn't bad enough, just across the road stood the brand-new Athletic Department with more spaces than they needed or ever used during working hours. She wished somebody could get through to the athletic director, Gilead Jackson, and persuade him to let her department use some of those spaces.

But Gilead was the kind of negro who loved having something other people wanted. And it made his day every time he stood in his picture window and watched folks from other departments driving around and around the campus looking for a decent place to park. When asked why he was so mean and stingy, Gilead said, "Those parking spaces are mine, and I can do whatever I want to do with them. If I choose to let them sit there empty, then that's just the way it is going to be."

The departments in close proximity to the Athletic Department's parking spaces, like Yvonne's building, decided to go over Gilead's head when he issued that bold, ugly, and callous statement during a faculty senate meeting. But they soon found out that those efforts were in vain because their president, Sam Redmond, was prone to looking the other way when Gilead Jackson was the subject of his faculty's concern. A few folks decided that they would just up and out-bold Gilead and parked in those spaces anyway. That rebellion was quickly put to rest, after everybody's car was towed to a barbed-wire-fenced lot in Chapel Hill with pit bulls running all over the place.

The faculty was furious, especially when they heard about those mean guard dogs standing watch over some folks' prized Mercedes and Lexus cars. They threatened Gilead with a boycott of all Athletic Department activities at the next faculty senate meeting. His response?

"This is a historically black institution of higher learning. Do you honestly think that I believe all of you black people are going to give up football, basketball, track and field, tailgating parties, homecoming, butt-jiggling cheerleaders, and the Battle of the Bands competition over some parking spaces? Y'all negroes best get up on out of my face before I honor my well-earned reputation as a Class A, Division I Butt-Head."

Yvonne had been at that meeting. She could not believe Gilead had gotten up at a university meeting and talked like he was a thug on the corner, getting ready to throw down. But she had to remember that they were at an HBCU, and there were some behind-the-scenes black people shenanigans occurring that boggled the mind and would run a white person crazy. Black people. She loved her people and she loved and cherished black institutions. But sometimes . . . black folk were something else.

She spied a decent parking space and eased her brand-new, sea-blue metallic-colored Infiniti FX45 SUV into it. Yvonne and the girls loved this car. The day they bought it, they rode all over Durham smiling and laughing, having the time of their lives, and hollering out the windows at anybody they knew. But this car was just the icing on the cake of the many blessings God had poured into their lives once Yvonne released her old life into His hands, and the divorce became final.

She had a year-to-year position in the Department of Interior and Exterior Design at a decent salary, along with a lovely 2,100-square-foot cottage, for the price of a modest two-bedroom apartment, in Cashmere Estates. It was nothing but the Lord who led Lamont Green to lease the home out to her for 850 dollars a month, in exchange for her upgrading and designing it for the virtual tour of cottage homes on the community's website. Yvonne also served as the in-house consultant for upgrades and changes to all homes in Cashmere Estates.

She got out of the car and went around to the back to get her bag filled with floor samples, paint samples, and swatches of materials for the furnishings needed for the university's newly rehabbed building for the alumni, boosters, and trustees. Yvonne set the bag on the ground, closed the back of the SUV, and headed inside. She set the bag down one more time, and was about to pull at the heavy door when her eyes lighted on Tangie Bonner, one of the university's assistant managers for food services, getting out of Rico Sneed's car. Rico was married to her friend Marquita Robinson Sneed, and didn't have a semblance of a job at Eva T. If her memory served her correctly, Rico worked at UNC in Chapel Hill. It was almost nine o'clock in the morning, and if what she knew about most state jobs was correct, old boy should have been on the clock about an hour ago.

She watched Tangie leaning down and sticking her head into Rico's window, butt twitching back and forth, like whatever was being said *sho' was sounding good* to her. Yvonne felt a stab of pain in her heart. Marquita was a sweet person and didn't deserve to be disrespected by either of them. Even though Rico had never been one of Yvonne's favorite people, she'd never pegged him to be a liar and a cheat. She always believed that he was a trash-talking and opinionated braggart—but not a cheat, and especially not with a cheap trick like Tangie Bonner.

Plus, Tangie should have been ashamed of herself, considering the many times she had been to Marquita's house, soliciting her help with a special catering job at the school that food services wasn't equipped to handle. Not to mention how many times the girl had been at the house stuffing her face with some of Marquita's good food, or bemoaning the loss of one more man who Tangie had previously claimed was *the one*. And there were absolutely no words to describe a man who would tap some tail off a woman who had been all up in his wife's house.

Yvonne could hear Rico laughing and wished she couldn't imagine what that negro looked like sitting in that red Cadillac STS, grinning and talking trash. Because she knew exactly what he looked like—had seen him countless times whenever they were around Marquita and her family. It was a good thing for those two that Yvonne didn't have her nail gun down in that bag, or else she would have shot out all of Rico's 350-dollar tires.

She went into the building, momentarily refreshed by the song playing over the department's sound system. Elder Jimmy Hicks's "I told that ole' devil to get on out of my way, he's got to move," was playing. Yvonne loved that song. It said exactly what the saints felt when the enemy was standing in the way causing trouble. There were two gospel musicians who could get you going good in the morning, as far as she was concerned: Elder Jimmy Hicks and Keith "Wonderboy" Johnson. Their earthy, down-home songs always told it like it needed to be told.

One of the best things about working in this department was that it was staffed by saved, sanctified, and Holy Ghost–filled folk. That was rare. Most times there were a few saved folks in the cut, but never like this. And it was a beautiful thing to work with people who loved the Lord and worked hard to live and work in line with the Word of God.

Yvonne unlocked the door to her office, which was more like an office/workshop. The room was about the size of a large family room in a good-size home. The walls were painted a soft and soothing shade of gray, with charcoal on all of the wood trim and molding. Her door was brick red, as were the wooden blinds and her desk and shelves. There were large plants in charcoal- and brick-colored pots placed along the windows, which practically surrounded the entire room. Industrial steel lighting hung from the ceiling, and there were two large steel cabinets at the back of the room that were full of rolls of upholstery fabric, area rugs, paint, and a host of interesting tools and items. There were also two ebony-colored wood tables, surrounded by brick stained steel chairs, with charcoal- and brick-colored tile flooring. Yvonne had decorated her own office, which was the envy of many of her colleagues.

She flipped on her computer, typed in the password, and then began her morning ritual of opening the blinds and checking on her plants. The phone rang just as she was about to stick her finger down into the soil of one of the plants.

"Do you ever answer your phone on time?" her cousin Maurice's wife, Trina Fountain, asked.

"I answered it on time this time," Yvonne responded defensively.

"Quit lying," Trina told her. "You know that you got to the phone on time by accident, and you probably wasn't even concerned if you got to it on time or not."

Yvonne didn't say anything. Trina was right. She didn't care if she didn't get to the phone on time. All she had to do was check her voice mail, and then call whoever it was back. What was so bad about that?

"Uh . . . huh . . . your butt always gets quiet when you get called out," Trina told her. "So, are you still coming to the house for dinner this evening?"

"I think so—have a lot of work to do today," Yvonne answered.

Trina blew air out of her mouth, exasperated. "You know something, Yvonne? It's high time you got a life, so that you can be out where the right man will be able to find you. He'll find you out there working and having a full life."

"Well, I am trying to have a full life. But I really don't know what there is that I can do about the man. I mean, if the brother is going to find me, it shouldn't matter what I'm doing. God will help him find me, don't you think?"

Trina was quiet a moment. Yvonne did have a point. God could do anything. If the Lord decided the man He had for Yvonne was supposed to find her while she was walking through her neighborhood in those old ratty-looking sneakers she loved to wear, that is exactly how the brother would find her. Nonetheless, Yvonne really did need to schedule more time to have fun and be in the mix of things a bit more. As far as Trina could tell, the poor thing didn't even know the art of light flirting. A brother approaching Yvonne better be prepared to get looked at like he was crazy, or figure out a way to draw her out into some conversation.

But then, she really couldn't fault Yvonne too much on that account. How could she know how to flirt when she'd been married most of her adult life to an old stick-in-the-mud? Plus, the girl had met very few brothers worth her time. And lately, she had been approached by some interesting *specimens*.

Why did the brothers who needed to keep walking always have to be the first ones to get in a sister's face when they discovered that she had been dumped by a man? Did they really think she was so desperate for a man that she was *game* for an encounter with them? To date, poor Yvonne had been hit on by a permanent part-time security guard at Durham Regional Hospital, who kept his wife safely hidden in South Carolina, a preacher who called her house late in the midnight hour on his way home to his wife, and a broken-down curmudgeon twenty-nine years her senior, who was what Yvonne referred to as "just a boll weevil lookin' for a home."

"So you're still coming to the house, by yourself, without the girls, to hang out with me and Maurice, right?"

Yvonne didn't answer Trina, because right now she was absorbed with watching Tangie Bonner and Rico Sneed. That girl was still hanging over in the window of his car. And were they kissing on campus in the daytime in front of the Athletic Center of all places? That had to be one of the busiest spots on campus.

"YVONNE!" Trina yelled into the phone. "Are you even listening to me?"

"YES!!! It's just that I am standing at this window watching Tangie Bonner and Rico Sneed acting like they go together."

"Because they go together," Trina told her. "I thought you knew that. Tangie's building is very close to yours, and she and Rico haven't been all that discreet. About the only person who doesn't know is poor Marquita. I know I shouldn't say this but what did she ever see in that dumb, think-he-got-game negro?"

Yvonne shrugged and then said, "I dunno" when she remembered that Trina couldn't see her. "Girl, do you know that this trick has some tissue paper hanging right out of her shoes? What kind of bama mess is that?"

"Are those some yellow pumps?" Trina asked.

Yvonne pulled the blinds up so she could get a better look at the shoes from her office window. Thank goodness she was on the first floor. "Yeah, she does. How'd you know that?"

"'Cause she had those things on when me and Maurice ran into her trying to act like she wasn't out with Rico, when we went to that Jill Scott concert over in Raleigh. I could not believe she was all dressed up on a date with another woman's husband, with some ugly yellow patent leather pumps from the Big Lots clearance bin on her feet. And if that weren't bad enough, the trick had some Kleenex hunched down at the front part of the pump, where the top of the tissue was hanging over that hump in the middle of your foot."

"A hot ghetto mess is what that sounds like," Yvonne said, and then asked, "So is yellow now the new black this season?" She stared out the window some more. "How did you know she got those shoes from Big Lots?"

"Saw them when I was there looking for some inexpensive plant pots. The bin was right next to a row of some pretty pots."

Yvonne started laughing. "Girl, let me get out of their business, get off of this phone, and get some work done, so I can relax and enjoy myself at your house tonight."

"So this means that you're coming, right?"

"Yeeessss," Yvonne answered.

"And, Yvonne."

"Yes, Trina."

"Rochelle is staying with the girls, right?"

"Yes, my little sister is staying with the girls—how else will I be able to come by myself?"

"So we're set, right?" Trina asked again. She knew Yvonne, and she knew that girl would start thinking about work and cancel to go off and mix up a special color of paint.

"Yes, Trina," Yvonne exclaimed in exasperation. Trina was really working her over about this.

"Okay, then . . . uh . . . please don't come to my house in your work clothes."

"But it's just your house and just you, me, and my cousin. Why would I need to change?"

"You need to get out of those clothes and into some cute jeans and a top" was all Trina said.

"Well, okay. I'll wear some 'cute jeans and a top' to make you happy. Now can I get myself off of this telephone and get to work?"

"Bye" was all Trina said right before she hung up.

TWO

Yvonne spun around in the middle of the kitchen. She said, "So, does this *ensemble* meet your approval, Mrs. Fountain?"

"Umm-hmm," was all Trina said as she dipped several pieces of fresh trout in her special homemade batter and then dropped them in a hot cast-iron skillet. It didn't take long for the fish to turn a golden brown, the batter making it all crispy. She turned the fish over and got some more pieces ready to put in the skillet.

Yvonne's first cousin, Maurice Fountain, came in from the back carrying a tray of vegetables he'd just taken off the grill. "What up, Cuz?" he said, while putting the tray on the counter and then going right back outside.

"Hand me that plate with the paper towels on it," Trina told Yvonne as she started scooping out pieces of trout. She pulled the oven door open and checked on the crispy-baked home fries. "Answer the door for me."

"The door?" Yvonne said. "I didn't hear the door."

"You hear it now" was all Trina said when the bell rang again. She hadn't heard it the first time either. Just knew that Curtis, who was very prompt, would be at the house about this time.

"So are you going to help me out a bit and answer the door?"

"Uh . . . yeah," Yvonne said and went up front.

Trina just shook her head to herself, thinking, "The baby is so goofy at times. But that is what makes you love her." She couldn't wait to see Yvonne's face when she came back in the kitchen with

Curtis Parker trailing behind her, trying to sneak and look at Yvonne's booty when he knew she wasn't watching him.

The doorbell rang a third time and was followed by heavy knocking. Whoever this person was sure did want to get into Trina and Maurice's house awfully bad. "OKAY," Yvonne yelled, before peeking out of a side panel to see who was on the other side.

Curtis Parker saw Maurice's cousin peeking at him and wished the girl would open the door—he was hungry and ready to eat. He stared back at her and rang the doorbell one more time for good measure.

"Just hold your horses," Yvonne hollered out and finally opened the door, stepping back almost three feet when Curtis Parker stepped inside and got too close for comfort. That good-smelling whiff of his cologne was enough to make her want to move back even more. But she didn't want to appear rude, or act as if she found the man offensive in any way—far from it.

"Hold my horses? Been a long time since I've heard that one, girl," Curtis said, laughing, secretly marveling at how tiny Yvonne Fountain felt standing next to him. He was a very muscular six foot four, which wasn't all that tall by today's basketball standards. He moved a foot closer to where Yvonne was standing. He noticed that she moved some more, so he moved closer to her again, just to get a rise out of her. This was fun. It had been a long time since he'd had that kind of effect on a woman, and he found it refreshing.

Yvonne moved some more and smiled up at him, then looked away. What in the world was wrong with her, smiling at Curtis Parker like that? She was a grown woman raising two daughters on her own and should know better than to be grinning up at a man like that.

"Trina done with that fish?" Curtis asked, now anxious to get back in the kitchen and get some food in his stomach. It had been a long day, full of meetings and more than enough paperwork. Folks always thought that being the head coach of a basketball team was all about what they saw happening on the court. But that was only a fraction of the job. If he didn't do all of what had to be done behind the scenes, there would be nothing to see on center court. He had to parent, raise money, pay bills, do budgets, train, administrate, recruit, schedule, meet, and advocate, and this often happened before he got to his job description—coach.

Yvonne bobbed her head yes and started walking back to the kitchen. Curtis followed behind her at a leisurely pace, so that he could enjoy the scenery. Maurice's cousin was fine and putting a hurting on those snug-fitting lowriders she was wearing. Few women could look that sexy in a pink T-shirt, blue jeans, and pink Timberlands. That pink was shimmering against Yvonne's cocoa-colored complexion. And those large round chocolate-diamond-colored eyes sparkled when she flashed that wide, full mouth into a heartwarming smile. Coupled with that firm, round butt, it was enough to make him want to ask the girl if they could "go together."

Curtis looked at that booty bouncing in those jeans some more. It was taking considerable restraint to resist the urge to pull a quarter out of his pocket and find out just how far it would go after it bounced off Yvonne's behind.

Yvonne had the uncomfortable feeling of heat bearing down on her backside, and decided to take a seat and get her butt out of the line of fire when she caught Curtis studying her with his head tilted to the side and a crooked grin on his face. Why did this negro have to be so cute? He was long and muscular, deep dark chocolate like a Mounds candy bar, and had eyes that lit up with merriment when he smiled. She thought his eyes were his best feature.

Yet, as cute and engaging as Curtis Parker was, Yvonne had to remember that he had yet to express any kind of interest in turning in his player's card. Plus, he always had some woman hanging on his arm whenever she saw him outside of a basketball game. Come to think of it, this was one of the few times Yvonne had seen Curtis without a woman trying to hang all over him.

"My man," Maurice said when he walked through the door with some more grilled vegetables and hush puppies.

"Man, did you just take those hush puppies off of the grill?" Curtis asked.

"Something Trina tried out on me and it worked. They are very good. You only put them on the grill for about a minute and a half, and man!" He picked up a fat hush puppy and held it out to Curtis. "Here, taste it."

Curtis chewed, and then fanned his mouth. "It is good but hot. I need some water." He picked up a hush puppy and turned toward Yvonne. "Here, baby. Taste this."

Yvonne held out her hand, but Curtis just walked over and put the hush puppy in her mouth when she opened it to say something back to him. She chewed and then fanned at her mouth.

"Whew . . . This is good but it is real hot!"

"Just like me, baby," Curtis said, grinning. "Good but real hot."

Yvonne gulped down some ice water to cool her mouth down and give that Curtis some time to cool down, too. He was just too grown for his own good. Maurice shook his head at his head coach and boss. Curtis was so wrong, and he knew he was being wrong and was enjoying every minute of it. Maurice noticed that Curtis had the exact same expression on his face as the one he had when one of the players stole the ball during a game, and nobody had seen it coming.

Maybe that is what his cousin needed—a man who knew what to say to get past what appeared to be an impenetrable wall of protection. But then again, Maurice understood why Yvonne was like that. She had not encountered any man worth her time, and didn't have any patience for foolishness from brothers who knew good and well they were of substandard quality where she was concerned. And it wasn't because his cousin was a snob—far from it. It's just that she deserved better than those rotten scraps he'd seen some brothers have the audacity to throw Yvonne's way.

As much as Maurice wanted his cousin to have a man in her life, he knew that this man had to be right—he had to be a brother whose heart and mind were turned toward Jesus. Curtis Parker was the only man who came close to fitting the bill. And even he was short a few credentials, since he needed a serious overhaul where his relationship with Jesus was concerned.

Curtis was enjoying messing with Yvonne. She was so sweet and unworldly, and it tickled him that he could get to her with the basic rudiments of flirting. He had grown accustomed to hardened women who fancied themselves to be more cosmopolitan and sophisticated than they were—women like his latest girlfriend, Regina Young, who was a staff attorney for the university. Yes, Yvonne was definitely a breath of fresh air, even if she was way too tight with Jesus for his taste. Curtis wasn't so sure he'd know what to do with the kind of woman who would tell you that she loved Jesus, and you knew that she meant it.

Trina put some more fish on a platter, took the home fries out of the oven, and started making a colorful arrangement of the grilled vegetables. She mixed some fresh lime juice, melted butter, and crushed red peppers in a bowl before giving it to her husband.

"Baby, go back out and baste the corn."

Maurice took the bowl and told Curtis, "Man, grab those cigars laying next to my laptop and come on outside with me."

Curtis picked up the cigars and then hesitated for a moment. He was enjoying Yvonne's company and wanted to stay inside with her.

Maurice opened the back door. "Come on, man, we can get a few good puffs in before dinner's ready."

"Yeah, Curtis," Trina said while making a pitcher of iced tea. "You and Maurice better go outside with those funky-smelling cigars. 'Cause I know you don't think that I'm going to let you sit back and puff on those things in my house. It already smells like trout. What do you want? You want it to end up smelling like butt, too?"

"Trina!"

"Don't Trina me, Maurice Lester Fountain. You know good and well that the trout and those cigars will make this house smell like some old wino's butt."

Yvonne wrinkled up her nose and pointed toward the back door. She had never had the "privilege" of being close enough to a wino to get a whiff of stank wino behind. But she'd gotten her fair share of glimpses of the back of some winos' unwashed pants. And she could tell just by looking at the way the pants dropped down past the contours of their behinds, that the last thing you wanted your house to smell like was how those pants seats looked.

THREE

Maurice picked up the basting brush and lathered up those ears of corn real good.

"Man! That smells good," Curtis said as he cut the end of his cigar and ran it under his nose. "I've been waiting to try one of these."

"Me, too" was all Maurice said. "Been saving them for the two of us."

"Where did you get these?"

"Charles Robinson," Maurice told him. "Charles wanted to thank me for putting in a good word for him with Veronica Washington."

"Robert Washington's ex-wife?"

"One and the same," Maurice answered and cut off the tip of his cigar.

"But why would a big-time player like Charmayne Robinson's brother, Charles, need you to put in a good word for him with any single woman in Durham County? Rumor has it that he has all of the free booty in the Triangle on lockdown," Curtis said and lit up his cigar. "Plus, isn't Veronica real serious about her relationship with the Lord? Wouldn't think she'd be all that appealing to Charles."

"Well, think again," Maurice said and lit his own cigar. "Old boy has it bad for Veronica. He has been checking her out ever since Robert left Veronica for his woman, Tracey Parsons."

"But, Maurice, Charles owns Rumpshakers Strip Club."

"Gentlemen's Club," Maurice corrected. "It's Rumpshakers Hip-Hop Gentlemen's Club."

"Okay, Gentlemen's Club," Curtis said. "But every time I've gone there, I always see women strutting their stuff in some stilettos to get some extra tips. And Veronica, on the other hand, owns a public relations firm and represents only Christian writers, actors, and musicians. So Charles doesn't foresee a conflict with those two businesses being at opposite ends of the lightness-and-darkness scale?"

"I don't know what he foresees, Curtis. All I know is that he has it bad for Veronica Washington and is glad that her divorce from her knucklehead husband Robert is almost final."

"Well, it seems to me," Curtis said, "that Charles doesn't have it bad enough to crack open a Bible and look for the Sinner's Prayer in Romans."

"Now, is this a case of the pot calling the kettle black?" Maurice chided Curtis before taking a puff on his cigar.

Curtis frowned. Maurice didn't have to go there. Maurice knew that he had said the Sinner's Prayer many years ago.

As if reading his mind, Maurice said, "You said the Sinner's Prayer and have been on milk ever since." He didn't care one bit that Curtis didn't want to hear this—too bad. But Curtis had yet to be weaned off of spiritual milk long enough to have a hunger for the bread of Heaven.

"Okay," Curtis conceded, when it was clear that Maurice was not going to back down on this one. "I could do better about reading my Bible."

"Just your Bible, dawg?" Maurice asked him. "Seems to me like you need a complete overhaul where your relationship with the Lord is concerned."

"Charles Robinson and me, too, huh?"

"Well, actually, Curtis, you are a couple of steps ahead of Charles Robinson. You may be on some milk but that boy can only take a few ounces of formula right now."

Curtis started laughing. Maurice was right. Charles owned the premier exotic-dancers establishment in the Triangle. He was making money like it really was growing on trees. That was a lot of money because trees and forest land were plentiful in Durham County—dense, uncultivated land was everywhere, even in the hood. He imagined that it would take a miracle to convince somebody like

Charles Robinson to let go of all of his worldly goods to go off and follow Jesus. Because truth was, running Rumpshakers Gentlemen's Club and living boldly for Christ was not going to work.

But then again, maybe someone who was as anchored in Christ as Veronica Washington, was the perfect incentive to make Charles think long and hard about the benefits of serving the Lord. There was nothing like a saved, Holy Ghost–filled woman (who was also fine) to get a brother to thinking about the potential benefits of turning his life over to Christ. Some folks might not think that was the best way to find your way to Jesus. But for men like Charles Robinson and himself, it could possibly be one of the most compelling reasons.

Curtis almost stopped breathing when it occurred to him the path this kind of thinking was leading him down. Because like it or not, he was only a few yards shy of his very own prototype of a Veronica Washington. There was no denying it, both Yvonne and Veronica were some seriously *fo' sho'* Proverbs 31 sisters—a brother couldn't find anything more old school than a woman replete with virtues that were outlined in the Old Testament.

Yvonne opened the refrigerator and took out a bowl of olive-green scuppernong grapes. She loved these wild grapes, which were native to North Carolina and tasted like you were getting a squirt of some homemade wine when you took a bite out of one. She tried her best to sneak a peek on the deck to see what Curtis was doing without being noticed by Trina, who rarely missed a thing. When she caught Trina watching her intently, Yvonne popped a grape into her mouth and then mumbled, "I'll be glad when dinner is ready 'cause I'm hungry."

Trina just looked at Yvonne trying to be slick and on the low, trying to watch Curtis and act like he wasn't getting next to her. *Humph*, Trina thought and then whispered to herself, "*Rochelle was right when she said that there ain't nothin' like a new negro to inspire you in all the right ways to get over and done with the old negro.*"

"You say something, Trina?"

"Not really—just thinking out loud. And speaking of thoughts, I didn't miss that little sniff-and-inhale number you were doing when Curtis walked past you."

Yvonne couldn't believe Trina had seen that. She was almost as bad as Rochelle. But she couldn't help it—Curtis was wearing Chanel for Men and it smelled good on him.

"Awww snap," Trina said, grinning. "Miss Thangy-Thang got a little crushy-crush on the coach. Who woulda thunk it? Sweet lil' Yvonne Fountain sniffin' and inhalin' on the big, bad Curtis Parker."

"Shut up, Trina," Yvonne hissed, hoping she wasn't blushing, even though her cheeks were warm and getting warmer by the second. She hoped that Curtis would stay outside for a few more minutes, and wished that he'd bring his butt back in the house. Last thing she needed was for a skilled player like Curtis to discover that she was blushing and sniffing up on his cologne.

"Girl, take a chill pill," Trina told her, hoping that the men would hurry up and finish with those cigars to come back in and hang out with them. Curtis of all people needed to relax with some good company—especially the company of a good woman like Yvonne.

As far as Trina was concerned, Curtis spent too much of his precious time *boo-boo kittying* with the wrong kind of women. And maybe they weren't just the wrong kind of women. Perhaps they were the worst kind of women.

Ironically, not a one of Curtis's women could *technically* be branded as a *skank, hoochie, skoochie,* or even a *skeezer.* If only it were that easy. No, these sisters were those well-dressed, educated, stuck-up old sticks-in-the-mud who thought more highly of themselves than they should. They were like those dry clouds Jesus accused the Pharisees of being—so many promises, so little action, so empty and dry and useless, their very presence a sin and a shame.

Trina believed that Yvonne was a blessing waiting to happen as far as Curtis was concerned. It was pretty clear that Curtis thought the girl was fine. Not to mention the way he smiled and chuckled at just about everything that little negro had said so far this evening. Every time Miss Yvonne said a little quip about something, all she heard from Coach was "Ha . . . ha . . . hahahaha, ha . . . ha . . . ha-hahaha." Yvonne was funny. But that negro wasn't *that* funny.

Curtis Parker wasn't the only one who was thunderstruck. Yvonne was just as taken with him as he with her. But Yvonne was in the hole with regard to cool points, so she was working overtime to try and hide her attraction to him. Trina knew the girl would rather die a thousand horrible deaths in consecutive order than have Curtis discover he was getting next to her. Yet, the best thing that could happen to Yvonne was for Curtis to be an eyewitness to the beautiful ruby blush that spread across her cocoa-colored cheeks, lighting up those sparkling chocolate-diamond-colored eyes, simply because of the sparks bouncing back and forth between the two of them.

It was time for Yvonne to have a good, handsome, and decent man to take notice of and appreciate her. When Yvonne was married to Darrell, she worked overtime to get along with that boy and keep the marriage intact. It was amazing. Darrell had earned a PhD in biology from Stanford University, and yet he acted as if he were mentally challenged whenever Yvonne tried to talk to him about the problems in their marriage. No matter what she said and how she said it, Darrell just didn't get it.

Darrell didn't want to understand that it was inappropriate for a woman from his department to call his house and hang up whenever Yvonne answered the phone. He didn't get it when Yvonne told him that Bettina was rude and nasty whenever she came to the house, and that perhaps he needed to get her straight.

Yvonne had tried and tried to explain, petition, and help Darrell understand the problem—but always to no avail. It was as if she had been speaking a remote foreign language. But once Yvonne rededicated her life to the Lord, went back to her home church—Fayetteville Street Gospel United Church—and dived headfirst into the Word of God, she told Trina that the Lord blessed her with an answer to that problem.

It had been on one of those hard nights, the ones when the reality of being divorced got to you. Yvonne was on her knees doing a bang-up job with the divorce thing—crying uncontrollably, hollering, flinging snot, hanging all on the bedpost, calling out, "Whyyyyyy,

God, whyyyyyy" in that raspy, gravelly, annoying pity-party, crying voice. She was on a roll with that thing and threw in some real good, desperate, and pitiful-sounding "Why me," "What's wrong with me, Jesus," "Why You let this happen, Lawwwwddd, You da' Alpha and da Omega," "Why come he gets to have all the fun, Lawd," "Jesus, what is taking You so long" and "Why, Lawd, why."

That night Yvonne ranted and raved as if she'd lost all of her brain cells. And the good Lord let Yvonne cut the monkey fool until she was exhausted, her eyes were swollen shut, and her voice was gone. At that point, while she was lying on the floor too tired to move, face wet and practically plastered to the rug, a calm came over her, warming her heart and giving Yvonne a peace that transcended her ability to understand how the Lord had calmed her completely down after all of that craziness.

When Yvonne was calmed down enough to get still enough to hear the Lord speak, she felt the words from 1 John 4:4–6 being whispered deep in her heart.

"But you belong to God, my dear children. You have already won your fight with these false prophets, because the Spirit who lives in you is greater than the spirit who lives in the world. These people belong to this world, so they speak from the world's viewpoint, and the world listens to them. But we belong to God; that is why those who know God listen to us. If they do not belong to God, they do not listen to us. That is how we know if someone has the Spirit of truth or the spirit of deception."

Those words came home to Yvonne with such force that she hopped up off of that floor and starting shouting, her voice returning with each increase of praise. God had let her know that there was no way that anybody, Darrell included, could hear and receive a word of wisdom if they didn't know the Lord, didn't care if they knew the Lord, and weren't trying to know Him, if their very lives depended on it. The Darrells of this world couldn't and wouldn't hear a thing because the spirit of deception that operated through them made it impossible for them to do anything but do their best to scheme, trick, plot, and contrive.

Trina believed that Yvonne wasn't the only one in need of attention from somebody with some sense. Curtis, in spite of his reputation as a playah, was long overdue to meet somebody like Yvonne—a woman who would make him laugh, be his best friend, pray for him, pray with him, have his back, understand him, jack his tail up when he needed to tighten up on a few things, and love him the way God called a woman to love a man. But most important, Curtis needed a woman for whom Jesus was Lord of her life. A woman who loved the Lord like that knew how to love her man right. Because she would do what the Lord told her to do where he was concerned.

Trina peeped through the blinds at Curtis and Maurice puffing on those expensive cigars. It always tickled her to no end to watch Maurice lean back and take a real long puff, then ease back up while blowing the cigar smoke out of his mouth like he was really doing something.

FOUR

Curtis liked to take short puffs of his cigar so he could taste the tobacco better. He puffed a few more times, looking up and smiling at the twinkling stars in the velvety, midnight-blue Carolina sky. Curtis loved himself a Carolina sky—especially on a warm fall evening like this one. It felt good to look up and see evidence of God watching him tonight. Because Curtis desperately needed evidence that God was watching, and better yet willing to help him. If the past couple of practices were any indication of the team's state and readiness, he might as well go back to the office right now and clean out his desk. And if his boss, Gilead Jackson, had had anything to do with it, Curtis would have been kicked off campus right after they lost the first two games of the season.

He unclipped his phone from his belt and pulled up the team's last season stats. He shook his head, shut down the Internet, and turned the phone off. Team stats, team needs, team issues, and team problems. It seemed as if that was all he and Maurice dealt with. He closed his eyes and felt these words from 1 John 2 being spoken directly to his heart.

"Stop loving this evil world and all that it offers you, for when you love the world, you show that you do not have the love of the Father in you. For this world offers only the lust for physical pleasure, the lust for everything we see, and pride in our possessions. These are not from the Father: They are from this evil world. And this world is fading away, along with everything it craves. But if you do the will of God, you will live forever."

Curtis didn't know why he was remembering, word for word, this scripture his grandmother had e-mailed him a week ago. Gran Gran was very concerned that the things of this world held way too much appeal to him over the things of God. He tried to deny that claim. But now, sitting here consumed with wanting to beat out all of the other teams in the Southeastern Negro Athletic Conference (SNAC), he knew that his mind and heart were completely absorbed with the things of this world. Curtis sighed and looked up at the sky, blinking back tears that came from the double-edged sword of conviction from the Word. What was wrong with him—a grown-tailed man sniffling up like a lil' wimp.

"So," Maurice said, eyeing Curtis curiously and wondering what had caused this level of sorrow to come up on him like that. "Are the stats for the mighty Fighting Panthers so bad I should dust off the old résumé?"

"I can't believe you, the man of God, are talking that mess, Maurice," Curtis admonished.

Maurice, like his boy Lamont Green's brother James, was a brother strong in the Word and strong in faith in the Lord. And Curtis always depended on him to see the problem through those lenses that most praying, faith-filled saints viewed the world through. Curtis's grandmother was like that. No matter what was going on, Doreatha Parker, or Gran Gran, always took the problem to God, left her problem at the altar, praised God for his blessings in her life, and waited in perfect peace for the answer to that prayer to become manifest.

Now here was Maurice, standing right in his face, blowing cigar circles out of his mouth, and acting like he didn't need to be combing through his Bible searching for a Word from the Lord about this dilemma.

"What is your problem?" Maurice asked, now just as calm and content, despite the stats and impending doom coming from a messed-up team and, even worse, a mean and crazy athletic director.

"My problem?" Curtis asked.

"Yeah," Maurice answered. "Your problem. Look, Curtis, I love the Lord. I trust the Lord. But I'm faithful, not perfect. Every now and then, I am going to have a moment, even if it's only for a moment."

"But you walk by faith and not by sight, man," Curtis told him.

Maurice could not believe this boy. He said, "Of course I walk by faith and not by what I see with these things"—Maurice pointed at his eyes—"but what about you, Curtis? What are you walking by? And why do you lean so hard on my faith instead of getting in the Word and building up your own self in faith and trust in God? Honestly, I don't know how you can stand to live life without total dependence on Jesus."

"'Cause I'm a man. I believe in working and fighting hard for what I believe in."

"So, Jesus, the one you are called to put your trust in, wasn't a man, a man's man to be exact? 'Cause I don't think a roughneck like Peter, and a smooth thug like Matthew, would have been following and chilling with Jesus if He'd been all wimpy and punkin' out on some brothers.

"You think those brothers whose money tables Jesus threw over were happy with Him? Don't you think that at least one of them got riled up and ready to throw down, but something, namely Jesus, made them think twice about doing that? I've seen plenty of hard-core thugs in my day. But I've never seen any of them roll up on somebody who gave the clear indication that they were not the one to mess with."

Curtis couldn't argue against that point. There was nothing in the Word that indicated Jesus had any problems, discussions, or pending altercations following that bodacious confrontation. He knew from coaching all of these years that any brother bold enough to throw down like Jesus did in the temple had better be able to back that up. There were some rough folks back in the Bible days. But it was pretty clear that you didn't just take a mind to roll up on Jesus. A few Pharisees tried but they got their feelings hurt.

"Okay," Curtis said with his hands raised in concession, "you have a point."

"You daggone skippy I do," Maurice said. "When did a person not have a point with the Word? It's a—"

"I know," Curtis replied, irritated. "It's an infallible, double-edged sword that does not return void. So what else is new?"

Maurice wanted to kick Curtis's butt. He was his boy and he loved him like a brother. But doggone it, if that negro didn't try the patience of Job. And Maurice knew he was nowhere near a Job, so his patience was shot. He said, "Why does this have to be so hard for you, Curtis? It's the Lord. He is a mighty, loving, gracious, and awesome God. Why do you persist in running from Him and your blessings?

"Don't you know that when you submit to the Lord, He is going to show you, show us, exactly what to do with this team? And there won't be a thing that Gilead Jackson and his flunkies Kordell Bivens and Castilleo Palmer can do about it. We just don't know how He is going to do it. And that's okay because we don't need to know all of that. Jesus ain't never worked on a need-to-know basis with anybody. Okay?"

Curtis knew that Maurice was right. But he wasn't willing to give his life completely over to the Lord because there were some things that he wanted to keep doing that he knew the Lord did not approve of. For starters, he'd have to relinquish what Trina referred to as his "stash of booty-call boos"—the women he could call to get his needs met without explanation or commitment of any kind. They would have to be the first thing to go. Just the thought of letting go of all of that ran his pressure up. What was a brother supposed to do to relieve some tension? Get married?

Next he would have to kick his so-called *head boo*, Regina Young, to the curb. Curtis knew better than any of his nay-saying friends that Regina, an agnostic, was not the one. She looked good on his arm and didn't give him a hard time about his other women. Regina liked the prestige of being the coach's public girlfriend too much to complain to him about things a woman like Yvonne would have checked faster than she could blink her eye.

But being with a woman like Regina Young got old real fast because women like Regina had little or no substance. While they may have had the look of a treasure, they were no more than a cheap piece of cubic zirconium. And women like Regina didn't even know that they were not jewels. They believed the hype about themselves and thought that their looks, education, airs, and so-called skills in the bedroom really and actually made them somebody.

Once a man got a good dose of Regina Young, he found himself longing for a simple, honest woman who didn't backstab, harbor secret agendas, or have unreasonable demands. It helped Curtis understand why a wealthy brother like Metro Mitchell, the owner of Yeah Yeah, Durham's hottest hip-hop store, was so enamored with his ghetto-fabulous baby mama, Dayeesha Hamilton, who worked at the Kroger on Martin Luther King Jr. Parkway. The girl was as ghetto as she could be sometimes. But she was good people. Dayeesha was honest, dependable, a good cook, kept a clean and orderly home, wasn't greedy, and was a hardworking young woman.

Thinking about how happy Metro Mitchell had been the last time he ran into him with Dayeesha on his arm was enough to make Curtis give serious consideration to canceling out his playah's card. But all of that was a whole lot easier said than done because Curtis wanted to remain in control of everything. It scared him to think about giving the Lord such complete control of his life. Plus, if he gave over that kind of control, he'd also have to step back and let God do the talking where women were concerned. He liked to be able to select a woman based on his perception of a need that had to be met. And Curtis knew that if God started picking his women, first off there would not be any *women*, just the good lil' Christian girl the Lord saw fit to place in his path.

Maurice snuffed out his cigar on the railing and sat down on the deck bench. He stretched his arms across the back and glanced upward, lips moving but no sound coming out. He didn't know how they were going to make it through the season going like this.

Curtis was bound and determined to run from the Lord the way Maurice wished some of those players would run down that court to score some points. Every victory and every defeat this season would be riding on what Curtis did or didn't do regarding getting close to the Lord. Folks didn't get it that your walk with the Lord directly affected how you went about your business from day to day.

They were just coming out of the early part of the season and had yet to win anything. They had gotten beaten so badly in an exhibition game with North Carolina Central University, a MEAC Conference school, that Maurice dreaded having to drive down the part of Fayetteville Street where NCCU was located.

That had hurt real bad. There was fierce rivalry between the two schools. NCCU, or Central, was pretty much down the street from Eva T. It had been founded a good decade and a half before Eva T. It had produced many of Durham's black movers and shakers, and the students, alumni, and faculty alike never failed to remind Eva T. that NCCU was the *real* black college in Durham.

The last thing Maurice had wanted to hear at that game was the buzzer of the final quarter sounding off with a final game score of 78 to 20. Central beat them by fifty-eight points. And that had only happened because one of NCCU's star players fouled out, another one was on crutches, and a third was sitting on the bench nursing a swollen eye with an ice pack.

If that spanking had not been bad enough, this game was played on Eva T.'s home turf. Eva T.'s president, Dr. Samuel T. Redmond, had sat through the game looking so mean and evil until there was a moment when Maurice could have sworn he was filling out pink slips. And the worst part was that this game paid both teams—$55,000 to the victor and $18,000 to the loser, if they didn't allow the winning team to keep more than a ten-point lead. In the case of the final score, Eva T. Marshall was eligible for a measly $3,000. That chump change would barely feed the members of the entire team entourage. The cheerleaders alone ate like they were all active members of an NFL team.

The season was relatively new, and the sinkhole they were in just kept getting deeper and deeper. And if that was not bad enough, Curtis's stubborn behind was stuck on being stupid and resisting getting right with the Lord. Gran Gran had told Curtis that he could expect to walk in some serious valleys if he kept playing "you can't see me" with God. And now they were standing in the middle of the valley, it was starting to rain, they didn't have any covering, their feet were sinking down in the mud, and Curtis remained intentionally clueless concerning what he needed to do. About the only hope Maurice had at the moment was that Gran Gran had offered to bring her prayer group, The Prayer Warriors, to practice to lay hands on and anoint the team.

But that wasn't working because Curtis, with his proud and hard-headed self, kept hemmin' and hawin' about the offer. He was just plain scared and punkin' out over letting his grandmother, Lamont Green's aunt Queen Esther, and their girls pray over him and the team. What did he think was going to happen—that he was going to hop up and start prophesying and speaking in tongues to the crowd during the halftime show at a game?

Those prayers were going to help the team. It wasn't something that could be seen, or explained, or proven. It just was. Carnal thinking was a trip and there were times when Curtis Parker, with his excessively carnal-thinking self, practically drove Maurice crazy.

Maurice sighed heavily and said, "Jesus, what us gone do?"

"It can't be that bad, can it, dawg?" Curtis asked, now concerned about his best friend and most valuable coach for the team. There were three assistant coaches working with the basketball team—Maurice Fountain, Kordell Bivens, and Castilleo Palmer, who'd just earned his master's degree in sports administration from Eva T. But as far as Curtis was concerned, there was only one real assistant coach. Those other two really didn't need to be on the payroll, sucking up precious resources and doing absolutely nothing but getting on everybody's (including the players') nerves.

Kordell Bivens was the kind of negro who was fiercely loyal to those he considered a friend—namely his boy and partner in crime Rico Sneed, who was around the basketball team way too much lately. Other than that, Kordell could not be depended on to do what was right and honorable—especially where Curtis and the team were concerned. He was dishonest to a fault. And he hid it behind a solemn, silent demeanor that made most people think he was just personality challenged and weird. Kordell Bivens was the type of negro who could be a guest in a person's house and turn around and bite them with betrayal like a rabid dog, as his own special way of saying "thank you."

And then there was Castilleo Palmer—a wannabe player with

the erroneous assumption that he was a gift to behold. Castilleo acted like he had the capacity to add something worth anything to the lives of the women he was involved with. About the only thing Castilleo ever did that was worthwhile was to break it off with his nicest girlfriends. And he couldn't even do that right. The boy was so mean and ugly-acting when he broke off from a woman that she never wanted to have another thing to do with him. In fact, once one of Castilleo's exceptionally beautiful ex-girlfriends was standing beside a flat tire at the Southpoint Mall parking lot in a thunderstorm. When he offered to help, she said, "No thank you. I'd prefer to be assisted by that man over there."

She then proceeded to point to a man who was standing at the bus stop singing the theme song from the 1970s version of the movie *Shaft,* dancing like Michael Jackson on one of his best songs from the famed *Off the Wall* album, and picking and eating boogers, when he appeared a tad bit tired and famished.

Castilleo Palmer and Kordell Bivens—the assistant coaches from the pit of Hell—with their ever-present, annoying, and so unnecessary sidekick, Rico Sneed. Curtis had inherited those two jokers from his predecessor when he became the head coach of the basketball team. And the only reason he had not chased those two jokers out of his department with a sawed-off shotgun was that he had needed to hire Maurice. Curtis knew that firing Kordell and Castilleo would make his boss, Gilead Jackson, mad, and make it hard to get Maurice on staff at the right salary.

It had seemed like a good plan at the time. But now, having to deal with all the stress, drama, and backstabbing that came with having Kordell and Castilleo as employees let him know he had not exercised any kind of good judgment concerning this matter. He wished he would have followed Gran Gran's admonishment to trust God, fire those two, and let the chips fall where they may.

Maurice's eyes were closed and his lips were moving in a silent prayer. Curtis asked him again.

"Man, is it really that bad?"

"Worse," Maurice answered.

"So, what do we do about June Bug Washington and DeMarcus Brown?"

"Bench 'em, Curtis. They are nothing but trouble, and I'm tired of fooling with those two spoiled, bratty pimp daddies just because Bishop Sonny Washington's son is one's pappy, and Reverend Marcel Brown *sired* the other."

Curtis started laughing. "Dawg, you make old boy sound like a rutting stag. Sire? If that ain't some old school mess from what century?"

"Well, it's true, ain't it," Maurice said with a chuckle. "Heck, you and I both know that DeMarcus's daddy is still pimpin' and he what . . . seventy-nine, eighty?"

"I think Reverend Brown is seventy-seven," Curtis said. "Reverend Harris told me that her dad, Bishop Simmons, was seventy-five, and I think Reverend Brown is a couple of years older than Sharon Simmons-Harris's father."

Maurice looked toward the back door to make sure Trina wasn't in earshot in the kitchen before he said, "Sharon is fine."

"Yes, Lawd," Curtis said and held out his fist for some dap. "Umph, umph, umph. And Lawd knows I shouldn't be talking like this about a preacher. But baby girl is tight—chocolate, tall, slender, with those hips and that butt." Curtis curved his hands as if he was drawing the shape of Reverend Harris's butt in the air.

"I know," Maurice said, taking care to keep an eye on the door. "And those legs? Where did that sistah get those legs?"

"She got 'em from her mama," Curtis answered, grinning. "You know Mother Simmons is fine and has some big, pretty legs. Lawd knows Bishop Simmons has his hands full keeping negroes off those two."

"Three," Maurice corrected.

"Three what?"

"Those three. You said two. It's three."

"Well," Curtis said, "who is number three? I know that Sharon has a younger brother, Theo Jr."

"She has a younger sister, too. Linda Simmons Bradley."

Curtis rubbed his chin. The only Linda Bradley he knew of lived in Atlanta, and other than being short and red, she did look a whole lot like Sharon Harris. He said, "Reverend Bradley's wife, Linda, is Sharon's sister? Reverend Bradley, the pastor of River of Life Gospel United Church in Atlanta?"

"Yep," Maurice answered.

"Small world. But you know she and Sharon favor a lot—especially those legs."

"Yep," Maurice answered. "Linda Bradley has a set of legs on her, too. I've heard that Reverend Bradley has had to roll up on more than a few negroes about his wife—especially when they go to the Annual Conferences."

"I can understand why that would be the case, Maurice."

Maurice nodded. His baby Trina was fine and he didn't know what he'd have to do if he had to deal with fine-woman issues as a preacher. At least folks expected coaches to cuss and fight and act crazy. But preachers were another story. He didn't envy them—not one bit.

"Curtis, hurry and do something about June Bug and DeMarcus because I don't want to be bothered with them this year. They need to sit out until they bring those grades up and quit ho-hoppin' in the dorms. I know that June Bug has had two pregnancy scares since school started. And DeMarcus came this close"—Maurice held up his hand with his thumb and forefinger less than an inch apart—"this close to getting pistol-whipped by Mr. Chandler, the head of the mail center on campus, for being at his house with his wife when he wasn't home."

"Why was that boy over at Dave Chandler's house like that? Is he taking a class with Pauline?"

"Yeah. And the dummy is failing it with flying colors. That's why he was over there—getting some tutoring. At least that is what he told Dave right before he got tossed out of the front door without his new 250-dollar shoes."

"What is wrong with Pauline Chandler?" Curtis asked, agitated. "You know one of Kordell's campus women, Prudence Baylor, told her not to marry Dave Chandler when she started chasing him five months after his wife died. Prudence said that spending a night with

Dave was worse than standing in a long line at Wal-Mart on Black Friday. Whatever he *thought* he was doing took forever and got on your nerves something terrible."

Maurice started laughing. Real life at an HBCU could give any reality TV show a good run for its money—and that included his favorite reality show, *Flavor of Love.*

Curtis said, "We have more problems than we need because DeMarcus decided to help Pauline get out of the Wal-Mart line."

"Yeah. That is part one of our problems," Maurice went on. "There's a part two. Dr. Redmond will not override Gilead Jackson's refusal to let LeDarius Johnson, Earl Paxton Jr., Sherron Grey, Mario Lincoln, and Kaylo Bailey get cleared to serve as the starting lineup for upcoming games."

Curtis ran his hands over the stubble of his close-cut hair and banged his hand on the deck railing. "Do Dr. Redmond and Gilead Jackson want to win any games this season? Heck, with a starting lineup like that, we have a chance to take the conference title—even with the losses we've already sustained. Those brothers are the best players on the team, and the only ones, in spite of June Bug and DeMarcus's talent, with a chance of being scouted for the NBA. Maurice, when was the last time Eva T. sent anybody to the NBA?"

"Nineteen-ninety-three."

"You're joking?"

"Nope. And it's not because we haven't had any NBA-quality players. But they all transferred to bigger schools, with better basketball programs, and more television coverage when it became clear that the last coach wasn't going to play them right."

"WHY?" Curtis practically shouted, and then calmed down. This was almost criminal. If this wasn't his own team, he would have reported them to the NCAA for unethical practices.

"Not quite sure. But I know that some of the players that were allowed to start had parents with pockets deep enough to buy their non-basketball-playing sons a prime spot on the team. Or Gilead is sleeping with somebody's mama and has to do something to pacify the girl and keep her from acting crazy on campus, or worse, going and telling his wife."

"Are you telling me that Delores doesn't know what her husband is doing? Gilead ain't got that kinda play in him."

"You ain't never lied, dawg," Maurice said with a smile spreading across his face. "Gilead doesn't strike me as the type of brother who can run with boo and then come home and tighten up everything all right and good with wifey."

"Naah, Maurice. He ain't coming home doing nothin' but lyin'. Gilead don't have that kind of stamina. You've seen how the brother has to walk with those old bad and stiff knees. Give him a few rounds with one of his women, and a blue tablet wouldn't even be able to help that negro."

Maurice shook his head in disgust. He was all man—a guy's guy if there ever was one. But he never had and never would cheat on Trina. For one, the loving was just too dang good. And two, he'd better sleep with one eye open, if she found out. Because she'd do some serious damage to his person, not to mention his body parts.

Thirdly, he wanted to set a good example for his two sons, even if they never ever saw him tipping out. He'd read enough books on spiritual warfare to know better than to do anything that could give the enemy a reason to attack his home because the head had gone weak and left a crack in the wall for the Devil to wreak havoc in their lives. Cheating on your wife was just wrong—there was no excuse for it. The Word made that clear in no uncertain terms. And Maurice wasn't doing anything that would interfere with his prayers being answered. 1 Peter 3:7 shot straight from the hip when it stated, *"In the same way, you husbands must give honor to your wives. Treat her with understanding as you live together. She may be weaker than you are, but she is your equal partner in God's gift of new life. If you don't treat her as you should, your prayers will not be heard."*

Maurice loved Peter. He was a trip—just as crazy, impetuous, and gangsta as he could be. But Peter loved him some Jesus. And Maurice did, too. Plus, Maurice wanted to see the team win the conference title. He didn't have time to be out there laying up with some trash and not getting his prayers answered. And it wasn't because he didn't have any offers. Women threw coochie offers at him all the time. Maurice Fountain was definitely easy on the eyes—six-five, built like a diesel truck, honey complexion, and dark, curly mingled gray hair—a welcome sight for the women who admired him from afar on campus.

"And I'm beginning to get concerned that there is another hidden reason, Curtis. But what I keep thinking is just as crazy."

"Aren't you the one always telling me that the Devil is just as crazy?"

Maurice smiled and nodded. That was one of his famous Mauriceisms: "The Devil is just as crazy." He said, "Sam Redmond and Gilead Jackson want a new coach. And it's something about this coach that is going to get them a whole lot of money—not money for the department. This is change they'll drop right into their pockets."

"Winning the conference title and playing your way to a seat at the dance during March Madness is a sure way to boost revenues, and even raise salaries," Curtis told him.

"I know. But it goes further than that. That's all I know right now."

"That's enough, man. I see why you stay on your knees. If I kept getting info from Jesus like that, I'd be on my knees, too. That's scary, man. Something that has better revenues than a straight-up conference win."

"It is scary, Curtis, if you don't have the Lord on your side. But with God, none of these weapons formed against us—no matter how big, sinister, and well-planned—can and will prosper. That's why you have got to quit playing and get your life straight. I mean it, man. You are the key."

Curtis didn't want to hear that. He knew Maurice was right but was having a hard time receiving that truth to his heart. He said, "Man, I will work hard, make whatever sacrifices—"

"This is about obedience and submission, not sacrifice, Curtis. God prefers obedience any day over sacrifice."

Maurice stopped talking and took a deep breath. Why couldn't this negro just admit that he couldn't handle this by himself? Pride—nothing but pride. Curtis wanted to get all of the credit for putting this thing right. But that wasn't going to happen—not this time.

Help this boy, Jesus, Maurice thought. He trusted the Lord. But trusting God while going through struggle was very hard to do—especially when it involved your mortgage, the light bill, the car note, and everything else where money, a job, and a steady source of income were the prerequisites to making this all work. And when you added in food to the equation—especially the way his two boys could plow through a meal—he might as well throw in the towel.

FIVE

Trina scooped the last piece of fish out of the deep fryer and began putting all the food on the table. She tapped on the window for Maurice and Curtis to put out those cigars, gather up the corn, and come in and eat.

"Yvonne, look down in that cabinet and get out my good paper plates."

Yvonne smiled. Leave it to Trina to have a section in her cabinet for the "good paper plates."

Trina opened the door so that the aroma of the food would lure Maurice and Curtis into the house. It worked. Maurice plopped the corn on a platter and the two of them came back in the house smelling like Fuente Hemingway cigars. Trina inhaled deeply when Maurice passed by her. She loved the mixture of his Cubans and Eternity for Men cologne. She picked up a paper towel and tried to convert it into a decent fan.

"Hot flashes," Trina told Yvonne.

"Yeah . . . right," was all Yvonne said.

"I do, too, have hot flashes. You know I'm going through this menopause thing."

"You having a hot something but it ain't got a thing to do with a *flash*," Yvonne said, and took a long sip of the iced tea Trina had just put on the table.

"Go on and tell us what has you flashing heat all over the place," Maurice said, grinning, delighted that all of this heat talk had everything to do with him. He knew that Trina always had a "flash"

when she smelled his cigar intermingled with the scent of his cologne. This was definitely turning out to be a good evening. Maurice
couldn't wait for the finale after everybody went home.

"Boy, please. Nobody thinking about you" was all Trina said.

"Maurice," Yvonne said, "when is the next game? Trina gave me
the schedule but you all made some changes after it was printed up
and the games aren't posted on the website, either."

Curtis raised an eyebrow, knowing full well that Maurice was
holding on to that new schedule. He said, "Our next game is with
Bouclair College."

"Well then, that explains it all," Trina said. "My baby hates it
when y'all have to play Bouclair College."

Maurice shook his head in exasperation at just the thought of
having to deal with those thugs in basketball uniforms. Playing Bouclair College set his teeth on edge. Bouclair was next to impossible
to beat. Few teams in the league managed to pull off a win against
that school. Most of the players were thugs, and their head coach,
Sonny Todd Kilpatrick, always managed to buy off a few referees to
guarantee a win.

"We win the game or we win the fight—you choose," Yvonne
said.

"Huh?" Curtis said.

"Lawd, ha' mercy, Curtis Parker," she told him. "I cannot believe
that you don't know what I'm talking about."

"Then school me, baby. School me good," Curtis told her with
just a taste of *tight* lingering around the edges of his voice.

Oh no he didn't, Yvonne thought. She said, "I know you have to
know Bouclair College's off-the-record motto. They've had it ever
since Coach Kilpatrick took over as head coach. And they mean
every word of that motto because they are nothing but a bunch of
criminals dressed up in some basketball uniforms. "I don't know how
that coach gets away with so much cheating, bullying, and mess."

"He's won the conference title ever since becoming the head coach
at Bouclair. They never won anything before he took over, and that
alone gives him a lot of leverage. Plus, he's a crook and knows how
to bend the system to his will," Maurice told them, trying not to get

upset over the mere thought of that man. He'd been studying Sonny Todd Kilpatrick all during the first semester. He was determined to figure that man out and find a way to kick his little narrow Barney Fife–looking white behind. It didn't make sense that this racist white boy had beat out several good coaching candidates—black and white—for that position at Bouclair College.

"Okay, Cuz," Yvonne said, "I know your position on Barney Fife. But I asked Coach Parker."

Curtis couldn't believe that Yvonne Fountain was clowning on him like that. *What does she know*, he thought. She wasn't even a real faculty member. She was listed as adjunct faculty. She spent all of her time on campus in the Department of Design mixing paint colors, painting furniture, sawing on wood, and figuring out what kind of flooring went where. What did that itty-bitty adjunct construction worker instructor know?

Trina had not missed any of what transpired between Curtis and Yvonne. Pride. There wasn't anything wrong with that boy but he was puffed up with pride he didn't need—especially since that pride wasn't helping the team win any games. She said, "Yvonne, you were at that first game with Bouclair College, right?"

Yvonne nodded.

"Did you see the fight?"

"Which one?" Yvonne asked. "The one where one of the players' gangsta grandmothers pulled out a switchblade and started swinging at everybody in Eva T.'s black and red? You know there was more than one good fight, right? Danesha kept count, and she said there were six."

"Seven," Maurice corrected. "There was a fight in our locker room involving two of their players and three of ours."

"Did we win?" Trina asked, hoping in vain that those three boys whipped some Bouclair College behind.

"Heckee naw," Maurice said in disgust. "They let those boys beat them like they were some hos on the wrong corner, and the resident hos had to teach them a lesson about encroaching on the wrong hos' territory."

"Well, I don't know about what was happening behind the scenes during that game," Trina said, laughing, trying to ignore Maurice cutting his eyes at her. "But what I do know is that they better be happy that they didn't have to face off with that octogenarian gangsta in the electric-blue satin jogging suit. That old lady, with those electric-blue highlights in her shoulder-length wig, cleared those bleachers out with a simple flick of her wrist."

"Yeah, she sliced that switchblade through the air right next to President Redmond's wife, Grace," Yvonne added.

"You lyin', Yvonne. That OG didn't mess with Grace?"

"Naw, I ain't lyin', Trina. That original gangsta wanted to put something on Grace Redmond's mind and it worked, too. Because the second time she took a swing at Grace, slicing off a chunk of that expensive weave, Mrs. Redmond took off faster than a running back on Super Bowl Sunday, and in a pair of black-and-red Manolo Blahniks, too. I didn't know that stuck-up heifer had it in her like that."

Maurice and Curtis started cracking up. They would have loved to have seen that. Curtis used to kick it with Grace before she married Sam Redmond back in the early 1990s. She was a lot of fun back then. But she turned into the "stuck-up heifer from Hell" when Sam was put at the helm of Eva T.

Curtis often wondered how Sam Redmond managed to pull that one off. He never liked Sam Redmond because he didn't act like a man with too many scruples. Sam had spent his entire career at Eva T. brown-nosing, serving as some high official's henchman, and being rewarded for this behavior by moving from one administrative position to the other—each one a step up the career ladder. But that kind of behavior must have carried more weight at Eva T. than actual administrative, corporate, academic, and scholarly capabilities. Come to think of it, their university had more than its fair share of Sam Redmonds. And that was most unfortunate for an institution with as much to offer as Evangeline T. Marshall University.

About the only decent thing Curtis could say about Sam Redmond's administration was that it raised a lot of money. Dr. Redmond had raised more money during his three-year tenure as the university's president than his predecessor had done in the entire ten years he'd been running the school.

Eva T. was established by the second pastor of the original Fayetteville Street Gospel United Church in 1933. It had always been viewed as the "farm school" or the "rural college" when juxtaposed next to the more urbanely placed North Carolina Central University, a mere twenty minutes northwest of Eva T. Whereas NCCU was conveniently placed in the heart of Durham's historically black community, Eva T. was located in what had once been the country, or the lush farmland right outside the Bull City's traditional urban limits.

Eva T. alumni always wondered why Central folk were so hard on them. Because the truth was that Eva T. had top ratings and had earned the distinction of offering the best education for a reasonable amount of money. Evangeline T. Marshall University may have started out as a little country college for "farm negroes" but it wasn't that anymore. And now, with the ever-increasing growth and development occurring on the Durham side of Chatham County, it was rapidly losing its rural identity to a more suburban persona.

The school was positioned several miles southeast of where Fayetteville Road intersected with Highway 751, not too far from Okelly Chapel Road. It was the most scenic campus in the Triangle, once described as the best-kept secret in Durham, North Carolina. And the university had experienced a growth spurt in the past five years, causing it to return to its glorious heyday of the mid-twentieth century, when it had attracted the best and the brightest of black high school students from across the state.

The school's newest programs were fast-growing and rapidly garnering national recognition. The Building, Construction, and Interior Design Program, along with the School of Entrepreneurial Studies and the Crime Scene Investigation Training Program, were innovative twenty-first-century programs. Some of Durham's most imaginative and financially successful entrepreneurs had matriculated through one of these programs. Unbeknownst to most Bull City residents, Metro Mitchell, owner of the Yeah Yeah Hip-Hop Store, was one such graduate. He was in the first class of graduates from the School of Entrepreneurial Studies, and their valedictorian.

Eva T. boasted pretty dorms, lush landscaping, and good food, much of it grown by the students earning degrees in the Agriculture Development Program. Its graduates came out well trained and had their pick of jobs, as well as graduate, law, medical, and professional degree programs. But the one department that made the university stand head and shoulders above all other schools in the area, including the big three (Duke, Carolina, and N.C. State), was its Department of Architecture, which had been built almost single-handedly by one of the most prestigious early twentieth-century black architects in the country, Daniel Meeting. And the school was now earning a top-notch rep with all of the great things happening in its Building, Construction, and Interior Design Program, an offshoot of this program.

Trina finished tossing the salad and drizzled a heaping helping of homemade bacon ranch salad dressing in the bowl. Yvonne inhaled—Trina's bacon ranch dressing with fresh peppercorns in it was the best.

Maurice ran his finger over the dressing on top of the salad and licked it off. "Mmmm, baby. I don't know what you do to that dressing to make it so good."

"I put my butt in it," Trina said, laughing.

"You know your self is just as crazy, Trina Fountain," Yvonne said. "But I don't know. You may have stuck your booty or feet or toe jams or something in that salad dressing to make it taste so good."

Curtis shook his head, smiling, and started putting some of that delicious-smelling food on his plate. He was starving and couldn't wait to finally dig in to the meal he'd been waiting to eat all evening. He took a seat next to Yvonne and picked up his fork, ready to dig in.

"Hold up a second, Curtis, man. We need to bless the food," Maurice said as he slid into his seat at the head of the table.

Trina put the pitcher of tea on the table and sat down. Maurice reached out his hands. Trina took one and Curtis took the other, and then reached out and wrapped his large hand, which could palm a basketball effortlessly, around Yvonne's.

Yvonne knew that boy had big hands but she didn't realize just how big they were until she felt her own lost in the warmth and security of Curtis Parker's. Curtis wanted to squeeze Yvonne's hand but feared he'd hurt her because it was so tiny and delicate. But then again, it was also a very strong and sturdy little hand—the kind that cared for babies, cooked delicious meals, trimmed hedges, painted, stripped wood floors, washed cars, and did a host of busy-bee types of things.

Curtis marveled at how this tiny and delicate hand could hold such strength, and yet contain such delicate sweetness. He knew that Yvonne Fountain had been "going through" as his grandmother and her girls would say. But for a woman to come through a crisis, remain strong, *and* stay sweet was something worth praising God about. Because Curtis was certain that the only way anybody could come through like this was by the grace and favor of God, and with faith in God.

He took a chance and squeezed Yvonne's hand gently, allowing their palms to touch. What he felt in that second set his heart on fire. He couldn't believe the power of this woman's touch. It took a considerable amount of restraint to refrain from lifting her hand up to his lips and placing hot kisses on Yvonne's fingertips. What an experience that would be—to feel her fingertips on his lips, and then have the pleasure of witnessing the girl's reaction to him when she felt all of that heat searing through her entire body.

Curtis smiled at that thought, and before he could stop himself, slipped his fingers through Yvonne's. His smile broadened when she blushed. It felt so good to behold a woman's simple and honest re-action to the feel of his fingers sliding through hers. Curtis closed his eyes for a second. How had his life become so sophisticated, of the world, and jaded that he'd forgotten how heartwarming such a straightforward response to him could be?

"Lord," Maurice began in a voice that sounded like he was get-ting revved up for a very long prayer, "we are some blessed people. And we just wanted You to know that we know it. We also know that everything we have comes from and will always come from You. Thank You, Lord."

"Yes, thank You, Lord," Curtis said hurriedly, hoping that this would push Maurice to focus on blessing the food so they could eat. He was hungry.

Maurice ignored Curtis. He could wait. "And, Lord," Maurice continued, "I just want to thank You for this basketball season. I want to thank You for the victory You have in the wings for us. I can't see it but Your Word has given us permission to call things that have not yet come, as if they are already right here in our midst. So, Lord, I'm calling for a victorious and blessed season in spite of what I see. Because Your Word does not return void. Thank You, Lord, in Jesus's name, amen."

"In Jesus's name," Trina and Yvonne said together.

They all sat there waiting for Curtis to say something to affirm that he was in agreement with them. When Curtis remained silent, Maurice frowned at him and said, "You need to get in that Word and come back to church. God just gave us a victory but He is not going to bless you in a tangible way, dawg, if you're not in line with His Word and will for your life. We've been hanging in there by God's grace. And I'm sure the only reason you and I are still employed at this university is because God wants us there, and He has kept us there so that you can get it together, so that He can bless you and the team. But, dawg, I hate to tell you this—God doesn't leave those windows of opportunity open forever. He does close them after a season."

Curtis acquiesced and said, "In Jesus's name." He then let go of everybody's hand, picked up his fork, and dug in to his food, stuffing a hefty piece of fish in his mouth. Curtis couldn't believe Maurice had clowned him like that—even though he knew in his heart that Maurice was right. Still, it hurt like heck to hear it, and especially in front of Trina and Yvonne.

"Baby," Trina said, "we've been praying so about the team and winning, I'm thinking that we might want to say a word lifting up the cheerleaders. 'Cause Lawd knows those little girls need somebody praying over them." She shook her head. "You know," she continued, "I almost hate to see them coming, when they bust up in the Sheraton Imperial at Eva T.'s fall reception, sashaying up to everybody who thinks they are anybody in black Durham."

"No, not all of black Durham, all of the black Triangle," Curtis said, his mood on the upswing after that Holy Ghost–inspired smackdown from the Lord. Maurice would have never spoken to him like that and especially in front of others unless he himself had received a nudge from the Lord to handle some heavy heavenly business. "'Cause y'all know," he continued, "that every *ed-u-mu-kay-ded* individual with visible African ancestry will be at that reception."

"True dat," Maurice said and scooped up a hefty forkful of salad, stuffing it in his mouth. "You know something, I'm sick of those little girls, and in particular that ShayeShaye Boswell and her partner in crime, Larqueesha Watts. I'm sick of having to deal with all of the mess they keep going with my players. *Always* something up with those two heifers."

Maurice finished chewing and then stuck some more salad in his mouth and proceeded to start talking again, as if the food in his mouth were helping with his ability to hold a dinner conversation. "You know, about the only thing I can think about lifting up on their behalf is that not a one of those baby skeezers in training gets knocked up by June Bug Washington or DeMarcus Brown this academic year."

Curtis shook his head in disgust. He said, "I've never seen young men act the way they do. In fact, other than Kordell Bivens and his boy Rico Sneed and *dem*, I really don't think I've seen any other brothers acting like those two overprivileged thugs. It's like they are running in some kind of *pack of hos* like they are in a pack of wolves."

"Who are the men running around with Kordell and Rico?" Yvonne asked, feeling bad that Marquita's husband was out in the streets embarrassing her and making a mockery of their marriage.

"Larry Camden, Castilleo Palmer, naturally, and Paulo Yates," Curtis told her.

"Are you kidding? Paulo Yates is in the ho pack with them?" Yvonne asked.

"Umm . . . hmm" was all Curtis said.

"But . . ."

"But what, Yvonne," he responded sternly. "You thought that because Paulo has a family and is on the usher board at the church that he was okay?"

She really wanted to say "Yes," but didn't want to let on that she was that naïve.

"I thought so," Curtis said evenly. "You and half of the folks who don't pay enough attention to people like that thought the exact same thing. But just ask Mr. Tommy, the head usher at Fayetteville Street Church—he'll tell you all about them."

"Okay, so now we all know that Paulo and the rest are out there ho'in' themselves out," Yvonne said. "But seems to me that they would want to ho alone, not in a pack where folks know way too much about your business."

"Okay, Cuz," Maurice said patiently. "First off, Paulo, Larry, and Rico are all married. They can't just up and go out without some kind of cover or excuse. They need that ho pack to get out of the house."

"All married to some good women who look a whole lot better than those scuzzleducks they out there in the streets with," Trina added.

"Baby, have you ever seen their women? We don't know that they look like scuzzleducks. They probably do. But we don't know that, baby," Maurice said.

"Maurice, you know good and well that tricks like that don't look like much. Even if they are *technically* cute, the way they live is bound to show up and make them looked used and hard—like scuzzleducks."

"And kinda ugly, too," Yvonne added.

"Plus, Mr. Tommy told me when I was talking to him after church that he saw pictures of those women, and that they didn't look like nothing."

"Trina," Curtis asked, "I know Mr. Tommy gets around. But when did he see those women?"

"At the new IHOP in Apex. Mr. Tommy said that he ran into Rico, Kordell, Larry, Paulo, and Castilleo at that IHOP. Said they were all huddled up over Rico's new laptop pretending like they were admiring it but what they were really doing was looking at those women. Mr. Tommy told me . . ."

"Baby girl, at first I was going to just stop by their table and say hi. Even though I ain't got much use for them, I believe in speaking to people. So I went on over to their table. But those fellows were so deep into what was on that computer screen they didn't even notice that I was hovering around. So, you know me," Mr. Tommy said, his eyes getting big like they do when he's giving you the 411. *"I just kinda eased over closer and looked, too. And Lawd, those girls weren't nothing but some cheap nothings. They were the kind of women who get up from laying up with a man, and then spray themselves with perfume instead of going somewhere to take a decent bath."*

Trina wrinkled up her nose.

"Uh . . . huh . . . I knew you know what I was talking about," Mr. Tommy said, and scratched at his head for a moment. *"I almost blew my cover and told them that I hoped they took some rolled-up newspaper with them when they met up those gals. 'Cause they were going to need plenty of it when those mutts started acting like the untrained dogs in heat they were, and the only thing that would calm those heifers down was a hard tap on the nose with some newspaper."*

At that point, Curtis doubled over with laughter and almost fell out of his chair. He said, "Mr. Tommy is crazy."

"Yeah," Maurice added, "Mr. Tommy knows he is on some different stuff. Who knew that ho'in' had gotten so organized and high-tech?"

"I hear you, man," Curtis added. "I just wish Kordell and Castilleo were as serious and organized about their jobs as they are about planning those ho junkets they are always running off to."

"Question," Yvonne said. "Why did Castilleo's mama and daddy name him that? It is way too fancy for a lil' broke negro running around Durham County thinking he's a bona fide pimp. Y'all feeling me on that one?"

"Yeah, we are definitely feeling you on that one, Cuz," Maurice said. "Because I can't imagine why anybody would want to name their child *Castilleo.*"

"You're right on that one, baby," Trina seconded. "Because even Metro Mitchell and Dayeesha Hamilton's children don't have names like that."

"They sure don't," Yvonne said.

"They may not have names like that," Maurice began, "but still, I'm kinda scared to find out what their names are. We are talking about Metro and Dayeesha, right?"

"Their names are Joseph, Jeremiah, and Jeneene," Yvonne told them evenly.

"We really are in the last days," Curtis said. "'Cause those names are relatively normal."

"They have middle names, too," Yvonne replied with a big grin on her face.

"And I can surmise that you know what those names are," Curtis said, now curious about the middle names and how Yvonne came across this information. She was good and that scared him a bit. Made Curtis wonder what she knew about him—even though he wasn't so sure he really wanted to ask her that question.

"Yep."

"And they are?"

"Joseph Crayshawn, Jeremiah Crentwan, and Jeneene Crystawn."

"Whew," Curtis said, as if in sheer relief. "Just when I thought that the predictability of everyday life was in jeopardy, I discover that all is well after all. Crayshawn, Crentwan, and Crystawn. I can sho' sleep good tonight."

"Yes, Lawd," Maurice stated. "Dayeesha had me scared there for a moment with those first names. I was on my way to Kroger to take the baby to the hospital to get her ghetto-fabulous genes checked out until I heard the middle names."

"I love Dayeesha Hamilton," Trina said with a hearty laugh. "That baby is definitely cut from the same cloth as her daddy."

"Who is Dayeesha's daddy?"

Trina, Maurice, and Curtis all looked at Yvonne like she had just told them she wanted to be Kordell Bivens's new boo.

"What? Why y'all looking at me like that?"

"I cannot believe that your retarded butt don't know who Dayeesha's daddy is. She looks just like him. Don't look a thing like her mama. The mama is a little underweight, brown-skinned woman.

And Dayeesha is kind of red and thick just like her daddy," Trina said, shaking her head. Sometimes she didn't know where Yvonne's head was. Probably stuck down in a bucket of paint, trying to make sure it was the perfect shade of lemon yellow, avocado, or pumpkin.

"Okay, Dayeesha's daddy is short, thick, and red. Does he also have three-inch nails with tiny silk-screened pictures of his grand-babies on each thumbnail?" Yvonne asked.

"Pictures on the thumbnail? Who has pictures on their thumb-nails?" Curtis inquired. "And where would a woman find someone who knew how to do that?"

"Now see, Coach Curtis Parker, that is why the two of you be-long together," Trina said, not even cognizant of what she'd just said. "First off, Yvonne, Dayeesha Hamilton's daddy is Big Dotsy Ham-ilton, the cohost of *Apostle Grady Grey's Half an Hour of Holy Ghost Power* on the cable access TV station. And secondly, Curtis, they do some kind of special silk-screen process for nails over at Yeah Yeah Hip-Hop Store, and you can have your children's pictures put on your nails. They are the only store in the Triangle that can do this on nails."

"Is there anything they can't do over at Yeah Yeah?" Maurice asked his wife.

"Yeah," Curtis told him, "there really is something that they don't do at Yeah Yeah. They don't do church hats, they don't take per-sonal checks, and they definitely don't print up church fans with the funeral home name on one side and pictures of Dr. Martin Luther King Jr., Jesus, and JFK on the other."

Yvonne laughed and hit Curtis on the shoulder. "Boy, you are so crazy."

Curtis drenched a fresh piece of fish with Texas Pete hot sauce before he said, "Yeah, I'm crazy all right, crazy about you, baby," and then gave her a fresh wink.

"You know what," Yvonne said, deliberately changing the subject at hand between her and Curtis, "how can Kordell Bivens, who is one broke-down negro, be such a player? It takes money and some dap to be a real player—like, take Charles Robinson. Now, Charles qualifies as a bona fide player."

Curtis was a bit put out with Yvonne over that statement. Didn't she know that a bona fide player was sitting right next to her?

"That negro ain't broke," Curtis snorted out, suddenly feeling better when it occurred to him that Yvonne was not into players. "But he is always walking around campus acting like he is so down on his luck, and playing on the sympathies of the unsuspecting women who are stupid enough to feel sorry for him."

"You are so right, Curtis," Maurice added. "Those women are always bringing Kordell lunch and packaged-up dinners to take home when he gets off work. And one fool was outside the Athletic Department washing his car."

"Why?" was all Yvonne could say to that craziness. There was nothing about Kordell Bivens that would make her want to do anything but walk the other way when she saw him coming. And in fact, there were a few times she'd seen him on campus and done just that.

"I guess they are aching for a taste of the Dentist," Maurice said, rolling his eyes.

"I think it's *the Physician*," Curtis corrected.

"No, it's *Herr Doktor*," Trina told them. "Kordell calls himself *Herr Doktor*."

Yvonne rolled her eyes and stuck her finger in her mouth like she wanted to puke.

"You can roll your eyes all you want to, Cuz," Maurice said. "But there are some women on that campus who consider it a privilege to be able to say *they've had an appointment with Herr Doktor*."

"Maurice is right, baby," Curtis said, adding *baby* on purpose just to get under Yvonne's skin. "Prudence Baylor loves to be able to call him by that name."

"We're talking about the same Prudence who is now all hugged up with your very married athletic director, right?" Trina asked. She couldn't help but wonder how that was going to affect Gilead Jackson and Kordell Bivens's relationship. But then, maybe it just didn't matter. People like that did those kinds of things to each other. The world was something to deal with if you were entrenched in it.

"Yep—one and the same. Prudence was with Kordell first, and

dropped him for Gilead when she learned that Kordell couldn't override my decision to keep her son off of my team."

"But, Curtis," Yvonne said, "why do those women call Kordell Herr Doktor? He's big and thick. His legs are thick, without a defined muscle in his calves, and they are actually kinda girly-looking, if you ask me. Plus, he has too much hair all over him, except on his head—that hair be foaming all over his shirt like an afro. And then, when he grins, he looks just like the Grinch in Dr. Seuss. Maybe it's me, but Kordell is 180 degrees from being cute."

Curtis was hollering with laughter. He'd heard women say a whole lot of stuff about Kordell Bivens. But he'd never heard one call him ugly, or say that he reminded her of the Grinch. Yvonne was right. Old boy did look just like the Grinch when he grinned. Curtis had always thought he was the only person in Durham who saw the striking resemblance. It was good to know that somebody else saw it, too.

The kitchen was quiet. It was a shame that there were people out there doing so much dirt, and into so much lying and deception at the expense of other people. Curtis felt a powerful revelation tug on his heart. He knew in that moment that the team would not progress and be blessed with victory as long as Kordell and Castilleo worked for him. He realized that what he knew about these two men was merely the tip of the iceberg, and God couldn't honor anything harboring this kind of sin, greed, and debauchery.

"You know something," Maurice said solemnly, "if those men don't stop what they are doing and repent, they are going to have to answer for all that they have done in the worst way. God will not be mocked. And as much as I know y'all don't want to hear this, we need to pray for those men and their families."

Trina sucked on a side tooth, rolled her eyes, and said, "Before or after I stick my pistol up Kordell, Castilleo, and Rico Sneed's nose?"

"Girl, you don't even own a pistol," Curtis told her.

Trina snapped her head back, raised a finger in the air, got up out of her chair, and then did a 180-degree twist before she went to the study and came back with a red lacquered box with TRINA written on it in bold, gold cursive letters. She put the box on the counter, snatched her purse off the chair it always sat on, took out her keys, and proceeded to open the box. She then whipped out the thirty-eight and held it at the gangster angle—tilted to the side rather than pointed straight toward an intended target.

"Whoa," Curtis said and made to move out of his seat.

"Now," Trina said with a whole lot of attitude, "what were you saying about me and my pistol?"

"Baby, *put* that away," Maurice admonished. He didn't know what possessed him to let that girl buy that pistol the last time they were at the gun show. He knew he shouldn't have let Trina, Yvonne, and Rochelle go with him. They were running around the gun show like some little kids, scaring a few of those hard-core gun enthusiasts in American flag fitted caps. One of those men had eased over to Maurice and said in the most polite Eastern North Carolina–laced accent, "Man, you got somethin' on yo' hands with those three. I'd hate to think what them there lil' ladies would be like running around all excited with some steel in their hands."

Trina waved the gun around with her hand on her hip and said, "You need to recognize, Curtis Lee Parker. I'm tired of people doing raunchy stuff to decent folks and then getting away with it."

"Baby, we are sick of it, too," Maurice said calmly. "But this is something only God can handle. This is His battle, not ours. So please put the gun away 'cause not a one of those negroes are here to do any target practice on."

Trina sighed heavily and said, "Oh, all right," and put the pistol back in the red box.

Yvonne was now laughing so hard tears were rolling down her cheeks. She said, "Y'all are killing me. If I knew there was this much drama going on over here in Garrett Farms, I woulda been camped out on the front porch a long time ago."

"Well," Trina said, "I kept telling you that you needed to get out more and come and chill with us. But you kept saying, *Nawwww, I got the girls, I got to work, I got to . . . blah, blah, blah . . .*"

"And now I'm here, so you can put a sock in it, Trina."

Trina raised an eyebrow, thinking, *Umph, Miss Lady is kind of testy. Most times I say some mess like that, she just shakes her head and tries her best to ignore my crazy self. But tonight is different and I know why.*

Trina locked the pistol box. She looked Yvonne dead in the eye and said, "Why you trying to get cute on a negro all of a sudden? You showing out because Curtis is here?"

When Yvonne's mouth dropped wide open, Trina smiled. Yvonne was so easy to mess with because she made it so much fun.

"Trina," Yvonne began, groping for a good comeback. "I . . . I . . . No, I ain't trying to be cute on account of him," she managed to say in a relatively calm voice, hoping that she was reppin' some decent amount of cool. Curtis Parker had enough women clamoring for his attention as it was. And he didn't need to add her to the list of wannabe boos.

Yvonne and Curtis had been crossing paths with each other for years—back in high school, during college, at concerts, and whenever he took a notion to come to church. And until very recently, whenever they encountered each other, Curtis was always cool, calm, collected, and apparently unmoved by her presence. There had been a few occasions when Yvonne had run into Curtis on campus and greeted him in the most respectful and friendly of manners. But she always felt it necessary to cut those brief encounters short. She had no desire to be bothered with one of his women, who could pop up from out of nowhere to run off any potential competition.

"Okay," Trina began, voice breaking right through Yvonne's thoughts, "so we need to pray for the team, the cheerleaders, and as much as I hate to say it, Kordell and dem."

"Yeah . . . I guess we do have to pray for *dem people*," Maurice said dryly. He sucked on his tooth, deep in thought over this matter. He said, "You know something, what I think I really need to pray for is this: I need to pray that the good Lord will stop me from going over to St. Joseph's AME Church, where all of those upscale, six-figure-earning-looking negroes are strapped, and borrowing a piece 'cause, baby, yours is too prissy. And then I'm gone pray that I don't get carried away enough to go over to Eva T. and bust a cap in Gilead Jackson's rusty behind, Sam Redmond's jive tail, Kordell

Bivens's lazy butt, Castilleo Palmer's triflin' tail, Rico Sneed's conniving, crusty butt, and some of those lil' negro children who call themselves members of our basketball team. I think that is what I need to be praying on."

"Oooo . . . ouch, dawg . . ." Curtis said, knowing that he was in full agreement with everything Maurice said. "Did you really have to go there with St. Joseph's like that? There are some good people at that church. And I know that our pastor, Reverend Quincey, and their pastor, Reverend Cousin, are boys."

"Oh," Yvonne interjected, "they are definitely some good people over at St. Joseph's. And Reverend and Mrs. Cousin are the best. But don't ever forget they are AMEs. And AMEs don't play—they ain't played since Richard Allen and *his boys* walked out of that white Methodist church back in the 1700s and started the AME church. They ain't never *skeered*, and they ain't never played. And they are strapped. From the top to oldest little old people on those rolling walker thingies—they are strapped. I'm telling you, I know those negroes with eighty-five college degrees apiece are strapped."

"Yes, Lawd," Trina said, patting her gun box and laughing. "They will pop you like some popcorn if you get crazy and mess with them and their pastor."

SIX

Curtis checked his speedometer. He didn't know he was going that fast—eighty-eight miles per hour. The speed limit was sixty-five. He was rolling down Highway 40. Good thing it was almost seven in the evening, or else he'd have been in trouble. Curtis checked the rearview mirror just to be on the safe side. No need to drive this fast and not have sense enough to look for the cops.

He was running late and trying his best to make the thirty-five-minute drive to North Raleigh in as close to fifteen minutes as he could. Curtis couldn't believe that Gilead had summoned him to an impromptu meeting in the president's office. He was even more put out when he walked into Sam Redmond's plush office overlooking the university's well-stocked lake and Jethro Winters, Eva T.'s newest trustee member, was sitting in a chair sipping on some Johnnie Walker Blue on the rocks like it was a glass of iced tea. Curtis knew that Sam Redmond loved Johnnie Walker Blue and always kept it on hand for special guests.

Curtis did not like the feel of this meeting. Nothing good could possibly come out of a meeting with Gilead Jackson, Sam Redmond, and the rich, white, and very greedy developer Jethro Winters. He thought about all the trouble Jethro had caused his friend Lamont Green, when Lamont would not back down and allow Jethro to roll over him and take the contract to rebuild Cashmere Estates.

The idea that these three snakes had taken time out of their busy day to slither up together long enough to meet with him was troubling enough. But Curtis was even more concerned when he remembered seeing Kordell and Castilleo leaving Sam's office two days ago. Neither one of those two men was in the ranks of faculty members who would have direct access to the university president. Maurice, who was much higher on the food chain than Kordell and Castilleo, had never met with Dr. Redmond in his office. In fact, Curtis hadn't met with Sam in his office more than four times since he became the head coach four years ago.

Even more disconcerting was that Kordell and Castilleo left Sam Redmond's office in a hurry, and then hopped into Rico Sneed's red Cadillac. Curtis had never taken Rico's affair with Tangie Bonner at face value like most other folk. He'd always suspected that the affair was a front to give him a reason to be on campus every day. Anyone who understood how affairs worked knew that a man involved in an affair would try to be with his other woman as much as possible. For Rico, it meant that he could come and go as he pleased, and no one would ever think to question his real reason for being at Eva T. all the time.

Curtis was astounded when Gilead told him that the meeting had been called to discuss pending cuts in his budget for uniforms, shoes, towels, and the water, cups, and Gatorade used during a game. That Gilead would want to buy second-rate shoes and uniforms, only to have to turn around and spend money again when they fell apart mid-season, was stupid.

In the past he would have been furious and ready to do battle in a heartbeat over something like that. And Curtis suspected that was exactly the kind of reaction Gilead and Sam Redmond were hoping for when they summoned him to the president's office to tell him this in front of Jethro Winters. Throughout that entire contrived conversation, Curtis had to remain prayerful to keep his cool. Gran Gran kept telling him to get stronger in the Word so that he'd have something to anchor him when faced with a trial like this one. How he wished he'd been obedient. A good Word from the Lord would have blessed him down to the bone, especially when Gilead handed him a spreadsheet itemizing the proposed areas targeted for the budget cuts. But Curtis didn't flinch or move a muscle. He took the spreadsheet, folded it up, and put it away in his briefcase before saying, "Is there anything else you need for me to know? I'm already late for an appointment."

Gilead and Sam Redmond, satisfied that their work was done even if they were disappointed that Curtis had kept his cool, nodded, indicating that the meeting was over. Curtis picked up his briefcase and was on his way out when Jethro Winters, who had never learned how to read black people, opened his big mouth and said, "I would guess that the mere thought of buying one of your players another pair of 200-dollar athletic shoes is pretty ominous about now, huh?"

Curtis tightened his grip on the briefcase, hoping that would help him keep his hands from colliding with that white boy's face. But God gave him the strength to keep himself in check. He remembered that Jethro loved to race-bait. The room was tense. Gilead and Sam Redmond had just closed their eyes praying that Jethro wouldn't say another word. Because if he said anything else about those athletic shoes, one of the two of them was going to put a 500-dollar shoe right up the crack in his behind.

Curtis opened the door, said, "Gentlemen," and walked out. At first he was real upset over what had transpired. And then, miraculously, God placed the words of Psalm 37, one of his favorite psalms, in his heart. Curtis was strengthened and encouraged when he remembered: *"Those who are evil spy on the godly, waiting for an excuse to kill them. But the Lord will not let the wicked succeed or let the godly be condemned when they are brought before the judge."*

He didn't have to worry about any of that, God would be right there working it all out on his behalf. Curtis glanced down at his watch and hurried out of the building to his car. He eased into the plush leather seat, turned on the ignition, slipped in a gospel jazz CD by Jonathan Butler, and pulled off. It didn't take him long to reach Highway 40.

Curtis started to relax and then tensed back up when he happened to look in the rearview mirror and saw blue lights flashing and headed in his direction. He moved out of the far left lane to let the cop pass him by, hoping for the best. His heart sank all the way down to the bottom of his feet when the car moved with him, as if on cue. Curtis drove for another couple of minutes and then pulled all the way over when it was clear that those blue lights were flashing for him and him alone.

Curtis opened the glove compartment to get his registration, and then raised up to get his driver's license out of his wallet in his back pocket. This had been some day, and it just kept getting worse. A part of him wanted to call Maurice and ask him to tell Reverend Denzelle Flowers that he was not going to be able to make the Friday-night service held every month at Denzelle's church, New Jerusalem Gospel United Church. He rolled the window down.

"License and . . . Coach? Dawg, that you driving like a bat out of Hell on my highway?"

Curtis rolled the window all the way down and stuck out his hand. He couldn't believe that it was Reverend Flowers's brother, Officer Yarborough Flowers. He said, "Man, I am trying my best to get over to your brother's church for the service, and it just ain't working for me this evening."

"That's right," Yarborough said, "Denzelle wanted you and Maurice there as special guests tonight. He called and asked if I could make it. But as you can see, I have to keep watch on a few negroes with some heavy feet."

Curtis laughed and handed Yarborough his license and registration card. Yarborough handed it back to him. He said, "Coach, I wasn't supposed to tell you this because it was to be a surprise. But God laid it on my brother's heart to get the church to raise money for you and the team. He said that God told him you would need it, and they have a check for 18,776 dollars waiting for you at New Jerusalem. So you go on and please slow down. I'll call Denzelle and let him know you've been delayed and will be there as soon as you can."

Curtis clasped Yarborough's hand and nodded in thanks. He was glad that Yarborough had to hurry off, because if he'd stood there a minute longer he would have seen the tears streaming down Curtis's cheeks. Gran Gran kept telling him that God was an amazing and wondrous God. And right now he was bearing witness to it. His budget was about to be cut by 13,000 dollars, and God had already taken care of the deficit, with surplus to boot.

"Thank you, God," Curtis whispered and pulled up a handful of napkins from McDonald's to wipe his face. He laughed. Maurice had once seen the stash of Mickey D's napkins trying to masquerade as tissues and said, "You are such a negro, Curtis man."

He relaxed and before he knew it was turning into the parking lot of New Jerusalem Gospel United Church. Maurice was pacing the parking lot, and waved him into the space they'd saved for him. Curtis jumped out of the car and followed Maurice into the church.

"Man, Denzelle wouldn't start the service without you. So the Praise and Worship Team has given a concert, and they were revving up for a finale when you drove into the parking lot. What took you so long?"

"Gilead called just as I was getting ready to head over here and said that he needed to see me in Sam Redmond's office. I'm looking at the phone wondering what this was about and if it could wait. Naturally, when I asked if I could come at another time, you know the answer was no. And get this, Maurice, when I get to Sam Redmond's office, Sam Redmond, Gilead, and Jethro Winters—"

"Jethro Winters," Maurice said. "Why was he there? He has been getting chummier and chummier with Sam Redmond and Gilead, and that does not sit well with me. He's on the board of trustees; there is no reason for him to be in a so-called budget-cutting meeting with you and the head of the Athletic Department. Something is real funky."

Curtis nodded. All of a sudden he felt tired and hoped he could make it through the service. As much as he loved his job, he wished he could do it without being bombarded with stuff that didn't have anything to do with basketball. University politics at an HBCU could get as messy and ominous as the politics at church. And he hated it when someone's personal agendas seeped over into an area of the university that was none of their business. But if it offered the means to the end they were working so hard to attain, then they would seep over to wherever they needed to be to get what they wanted.

Curtis and Maurice walked into the vestibule of the church.

Curtis had never been to Denzelle's church and was impressed. It wasn't as large as his church, Fayetteville Street, but it was a lovely and rather unusual pale pink stone structure. Reverend Denzelle Flowers hurried to greet Curtis and gave him a warm and welcoming handshake.

"Man, my brother called me and let me know you were running late. Come on, before the Praise and Worship Team starts doing the remixes of their songs."

Curtis smiled and took note of the suit Denzelle was wearing. He said, "You're kind of sharp there tonight, Preacher. If you don't mind me asking, where did you get that suit?"

Denzelle grinned and stroked his chin. "It is pretty sharp, isn't it," he answered, and pulled back the coat of the sea-foam-colored suit jacket with charcoal pinstripes to reveal a matching vest with shawl collar, sea-foam-colored shirt, and a charcoal tie with bits of sea foam and coral specks in it. The outfit spelled "preacher," down to Reverend Flowers's matching sea-foam slip-on gaiters.

"But where'd you get it, man?" Maurice asked, wanting to know where to find some suits like that himself. He also wondered about the cost but had too much home training to ask. But he'd be able to find out, if Denzelle was willing to tell them where those suits were sold.

"I got it wholesale from Mr. Booth," Denzelle said, and gave a smooth wink to a sister with a butt that could only be classified as a *bodunkadunk*. She smiled and then giggled before saying, "Reverend Flowers, you so crazy."

Curtis shook his head and said, "Man, you are too much. You know you are doing nothing but asking for trouble."

"Dawg, I'm single just like you. I don't even have a steady boo."

"But I'm a coach. You are a minister—a pastor, in fact. And man, I just don't think it's wise to be running around this church like that. You're not dating any of the women in this church, are you?"

Denzelle, who looked like a burnished copper version of the late Bernie Mack, got quiet and took a quick look around to make sure nobody was in earshot. He said, "Man, I've dated a few. Nothing serious. Just dinner, a jazz concert, good movie."

"Was it the same lady, or did you take one sister to dinner, another to a concert, and one more to a movie?" Curtis asked him, now concerned. He was a coach, and women liked to chase coaches just as they did preachers. He didn't know why—it took a very special, secure, and wise woman to be married to a head coach of any visible sport. And to be the first lady of a church was an even more difficult job. Because unlike the coach's wife, the pastor's wife had to minister to her husband and serve in some sort of ministering capacity at the church.

Denzelle grinned sheepishly. He knew he didn't need to date those women in his congregation. His brother had been telling him that all he was doing was asking for trouble.

"Uh . . . huh . . . thought so," Curtis said. "Man, you need to check that and start praying and asking God to send the right woman in your life. You a man, with a man's needs, and being up in here with all of these women willing to do any- and everything for the pastor is not a good thing for you, dawg."

"A disaster waiting to happen, is what it is," Maurice said. He'd been watching all of the women vying for Denzelle's attention, and none of them was someone he would have picked out for the good reverend. He wondered why the skoochies were so active when it came to trying to lock in on a brother. And he wondered why brothers always gave so much attention to those types of women, ignoring and neglecting the real jewels in their midst, and risking having to wake up next to a skoochie with a weave she wouldn't even let you put your hands on in the heat of the moment.

"Don't be so rough on a brother, Maurice," Denzelle said as he pulled out his wallet and gave the two of them business cards.

"Oh, I know who this is," Curtis said. "This is Miss Hattie Lee Booth's brother-in-law. You know, Miss Hattie Lee, who is the cook at Rumpshakers. Charles had been telling me about him—said the brother had some sharp suits for a good price."

It took Maurice a moment to place Miss Hattie Lee because he had been to Rumpshakers on only one occasion. But he did know who she was because the lady could cook. He turned the card over in his hands. It read DAPPER DRESSING MEN'S WEAR, LOWELL BOOTH, PROPRIETOR. "What are his prices like?"

"Like none you've ever seen. Mr. Booth has the best suits, ties, shoes, shirts, and the kind of hats we brothers like. His prices are so good because he doesn't have a store. You can go to his house, where he has a room just for the merchandise, or he'll bring it straight to you. Go on his website and check out his suits and the rest of his stuff. I think you'll like what you see."

Maurice raised an eyebrow. If Mr. Booth was Miss Hattie Lee's brother-in-law, he was in his seventies. And from the little bit he'd seen of Miss Hattie Lee, he just didn't get the impression that this family was Internet-friendly.

"He has a good website," Denzelle said, fully understanding the question on Maurice's face. He knew Mr. Booth, and he was definitely not the kind of old school brother who was interested in designing and running a savvy website. "Mr. Booth's great-nephew, Miss Hattie Lee's grandson Lil' Too Too does the website."

Denzelle heard the Praise and Worship Team stop singing and start giving what he knew would be lengthy testimonies. He opened the door to the sanctuary and said, "We need to hurry and get into the pulpit. If Sister Doreene in the purple suede suit starts talking, we'll never get out of here."

Maurice said, "I heard that," when he spotted Sister Doreene in the purple suede church suit with the matching suede hat with hot pink suede flowers covering the entire brim. Miss Thing looked like she could concoct a testimony that would make Jesus give serious thought to making a trial run of cracking the sky, just so He could tell that girl to take a chill pill, and then go on back to glory to wait to the appointed time to come and gather up His saints.

The three men walked down the side aisle and hurried up into the pulpit. Denzelle sat down in the pastor's chair, right in the middle of the pulpit podium. Maurice sat to his left, and Curtis, who was very uncomfortable with the overall seating arrangement, was on Denzelle's right. Curtis would have preferred to sit in one of the front pews with Trina and Yvonne, who he didn't know was going to be here. But then again, maybe this was the best place to be. He had a full view of Yvonne and her every move—and that was a mighty blessed thing as far as Curtis was concerned.

He took great pleasure in being able to look at Miss Lady in that pretty mint-green knit suit, with what Trina had once told him was a shawl collar, and a skirt that he just knew without seeing hugged every delectable curve on the baby girl's body. What had started out as an *upside of the rough side of the mountain* evening was practically looking straight up to glory. Curtis sat back in his chair and smiled at Yvonne, who lowered her eyes, reminding him of how sweet and delightful an authentic church girl was. And while there were a good helping of churchgoing women in the sanctuary this evening, not all of them qualified to wear the title of *church girl*. Sister Doreene, for one, was anything but authentic. Her need to be seen and heard to the *n*th degree was proof of that, as far as Curtis was concerned.

The church was packed for a Friday night. Maurice, Trina, and Yvonne had arrived early and were able to get good seats at the front of the sanctuary. The only drawback though was that they had to sit through the Praise and Worship Team too long. Sometimes the Praise and Worship Team leaders had trouble knowing when to bring a song to an end. This group sang one song for fifteen minutes straight, which really worked on Yvonne's nerves. She was on the Praise and Worship Team at their church, along with Miss Baby Doll Lacy and Marquita Robinson Sneed. They knew how to usher in the Holy Ghost during the pre-service. And they also knew when it was time for a song to end and, even better, when it was time for them to go and sit down.

And not only was this service packed, it was filled with a few very surprise guests. One of the most surprising was Charles Robinson, who Maurice later learned came for two very disparate reasons. One, Charles, who was a millionaire, and trying to find a way to the Lord without giving himself over fully to the Lord, wanted to help with Denzelle's efforts to support the basketball team. He had written a pretty generous check and had given it to Reverend Flowers to add to the amount raised by New Jerusalem for the Fighting Panthers.

And two, Charles wanted to be able to sit near Veronica Washington, whose divorce was scheduled to be issued any day. He could not understand why Veronica's pending ex-husband, Robert, actually believed that Tracey Parsons, the woman he had left her for, was the way to elevate himself out of the muck and mire of being a lowlife and a jerk.

Maurice was well aware, sitting in the pulpit watching Trina smile and wave at him, that Denzelle hadn't called them over to Raleigh for their health—Reverend Flowers planned on making a difference in their lives as it related to their needs for the basketball team. That was one thing Maurice really liked about Denzelle, in spite of his skirt-chasing—the man had heart that led him to help so many people, groups, programs, and organizations in need. Plenty of folks around the Triangle had powerful testimonies about how the Lord used Reverend Flowers to help them when they were in dire need.

Maurice and Yarborough were good friends, and they constantly lifted up Denzelle, asking the Lord to lead him to the right woman, and to give him peace with the time he was to spend with God alone while he waited on the Lord to point the girl out to him.

Denzelle got up and smiled at his guests and favorite parishioners. Unbeknownst to many churchgoing folk, the favored members were not the most prestigious ones, or the ones with the most generous tithe checks. Folks forgot that the most noteworthy tithe in the New Testament amounted to a few pennies because it had been given with such faith and love.

His favorite members were the ones who kept him lifted in prayer, forgave him when he fell short and had to struggle with his battle with the flesh, and always treated him with the love of Christ blazing out of their hearts. They were people like Veronica Washington, L. C. and Lynette Smith, Kevin and Kimberly Wade, Timothy and Sheila Reed, and Marsha Metcalf, who was the only woman at his church who pulled at his well-guarded heartstrings, and she didn't even know it. Charles Robinson was the only other brother in Durham who guarded his heart more fiercely than Denzelle did.

"Praise the Lord, everybody!" Denzelle said, his heart getting warmer by the second at just the mere thought of the glory of the Lord. Contrary to public opinion, Denzelle Flowers loved the Lord but had a serious battle with being obedient to the Word of God when it came to the area of romance and what he could and could not do. He knew that for him marriage was the answer. God had placed that on his heart years ago when he asked for help after a horrific and embarrassing breakup with a woman Denzelle *knew* he was not going to marry the first time he went over to her house for dinner. God had told him then, and God kept telling him now, but the boy was just hardheaded when it came to matters of the heart.

Denzelle glanced back at Coach Parker sitting in the pulpit looking like he hoped the Lord wouldn't *get him* for sitting in a place he didn't think he deserved to be. But as much as Curtis would have argued with Reverend Flowers over that decision, Denzelle knew that Coach had a right to be in that seat. Because Denzelle knew that Curtis had a deep hunger for the Lord, and that unlike Charles Robinson he wasn't trying to barter and purchase his way to salvation. The only reason Denzelle had accepted that check for ten thousand dollars from Charles was to get him in church for a reason other than trying to mack on the sisters he himself didn't have time for or any desire to be bothered with. This skirt-chasing was getting old, and Denzelle knew his days at his church, the church he had built up from nothing, were numbered if he didn't repent and get himself together. His brother was right. It would be a sin to let that happen as a result of some trifling booty-call foolishness.

The *Praise the Lord*s, were kind of feeble-sounding, so Denzelle came out of the pulpit and said, "Praise the Lord, everybody. What's wrong with y'all tonight? We had enough gas money to get here. We're in our right minds—"

"Some of us are, Pastor," Lynette Smith called from the back of the church, causing folks to laugh and relax and begin to let the Holy Ghost start to flow again through the church. She always wished that the pastor wouldn't let Sister Doreene be on the Praise and Worship Team because the girl always managed to throw a wet blanket on the fires of the Holy Ghost when she opened her mouth to testify. She knew that in this case Reverend Flowers was being kind and compassionate. But sometimes that wasn't all it was cracked up to be—especially in the case of Sister Doreene.

". . . Okay," Denzelle said, flashing the smile that got him in so much trouble, "some of us can praise the Lord because we are in our right minds. And the rest of us can praise Him for giving us enough money to buy our medications so that we can think we are in our right minds."

"Praise the Lord, everybody" came from one of the ushers sitting on a pew in the back of the church.

By now everybody was smiling and laughing and warming back up. Denzelle decided that he would change the service around a bit. One of the things that he really liked about his Friday-night services was that they could relax traditional service protocol and follow God's lead concerning what to do and when and how to do it. He said, "You know something, church, tonight we are going to get up and greet each other in a big hug of Christian love. Go find somebody you haven't seen all week and tell them *I love you, and there ain't nothing you can do about it.*"

Curtis came out of the pulpit and headed straight to Yvonne. He wrapped her up in a big, warm hug, kissed her cheek, took in the lovely fragrance of her Stella McCartney perfume, and said, "I love you and there ain't nothing you can do about it."

Yvonne stood there in Curtis's warm and secure embrace, trying to return this church greeting, but found that she couldn't say a word. So she hugged him back and mumbled out, "Ditto."

Curtis laughed and kissed her soft cheek again and then went back to his seat. Maurice and Trina just looked at each other. Everybody else was hugging everybody they could find. Curtis had hugged only Yvonne and then gone back to his seat to sit down.

Denzelle decided he needed to go back up in the pulpit when he saw the choir making its way to the choir loft, and two women, whose offers to bring dinner by his house he'd turned down, making a beeline in his direction. When one of the women saw him going back into the pulpit, she ran toward the pastor and almost fell flat on her butt, when Denzelle, who used to be a star basketball player for Eva T. back in the early eighties, leaped out of her way and back up to his podium.

Charles Robinson, who was sitting with his boy and Rumpshak-ers' manager, Pierre, started laughing. He leaned over and whispered, "Pierre, man, playah wasn't playin', was he?"

"Naw, boss," Pierre said, cracking up and reaching out his fist for some dap from Charles. "Baby girl was on a mission, and playah wasn't havin' it. You know I love coming to Denzelle's church."

"Me, too," Charles said as he took a quick peek at Veronica, who was looking all sweet and churchy in a pale pink St. John dress that wrapped around her body like it was some GLAD wrap trying to keep all of that fresh fineness in. He nudged at Pierre, who was looking toward the back of the church, nodded in Veronica's direction, and said, "Check it out."

Pierre turned back around and said, "No, you better check that out."

Charles frowned. There was Robert Washington standing in the back waiting for an usher to seat him and his woman in the crowded church. The head usher saw them, too. He stared up at the pastor, waiting for a sign as to what to do.

Veronica Washington was the usher's neighbor. He remembered the day Veronica called him and his wife in tears because Robert had a Triangle Company moving van sitting in her driveway and three movers standing at the door waiting for their orders. Without any warning, Robert had ordered movers to Veronica's house so he could live with that woman the usher had seen him sneaking around with in Cary because he was dumb enough to believe that he wasn't going to run into anybody from Durham or Raleigh in Cary, North Carolina—a suburban enclave located between both cities.

His wife had told Veronica to calm down and get herself together. The two of them prayed over the phone while the movers took a seat on the front steps, and the usher went and burned a complete CD of Beyoncé's *Irreplaceable*, to be played over and over and over again until the move was complete. It worked. The Lord blessed Veronica with courage and grace she didn't even know she had. That *You must not know 'bout me . . . you must not know 'bout me*, playing constantly, tickled the movers to no end, even though it had made Robert feel like he would go crazy every time it started up again.

The movers figured out exactly what was going on when Robert strolled up to the front door, determined to supervise and control a move at the house he no longer resided in, and found the head usher/neighbor, who was a locksmith by profession, busy changing every single lock in the house. The movers, who were now sitting in lawn chairs and sipping on fresh-brewed gourmet coffee, knew that Veronica was a classy lady. They favored her, ignored Robert, who had to wait in his car during the move, and made sure nothing left that house that needed to stay there.

Denzelle stared at that grinning, raunchy negro marring the back of his church and frowned. He couldn't help but think about Malachi 2:16: *"For I hate divorce!" says the Lord, the God of Israel. "It is as cruel as putting on a victim's bloodstained coat," says the Lord God Almighty. "So guard yourself; always remain loyal to your wife."* The first time he'd read that scripture, it had cut through him like the sharpest knife. It was ten years ago and his divorce papers had just arrived in the mail. Denzelle had read the papers, read that scripture, and then gone and sat on his back porch and cried like a baby. That Word hurt him down to the bone. But today he really understood what God was telling him, looking at Robert Washington flaunting around with his woman, Tracey Parsons. This kind of thing was a disgrace, and it was cruel.

Reverend Flowers made eye contact with the usher, who in turn gave the signal to the other ushers to go sit down and act like they didn't see Robert and the woman with the Stewie-in-*Family-Guy*-shaped head. Robert bristled, with his nose flaring and air puffing up in the front of his mouth, making him look like a pissed-off swamp monkey. His woman Stewie was hot, and walked right out of the church, with Robert hot on her tail.

The choir was now in place and the musicians started playing the instrumental part of one of the pastor's favorite songs, which was sure to have folks up on their feet dancing and praising the Lord. But Denzelle didn't want to stifle the flow of the Holy Ghost when things heated up and decided that he needed to make the presentation right now before the choir started singing.

He motioned for the musicians to calm down for a minute, and then signaled for Curtis and Maurice to join him at the pulpit podium. He said, "New Jerusalem is one of the fastest-growing Gospel United Churches in the Triangle. We've been so blessed. We celebrated our mortgage burning a year ago, we have money invested and our investments are earning money, we own property outside of this church, we have built and furnished more houses for Habitat for Humanity than any church, black or white, in Raleigh, and our monthly Friday-night services have been constantly gaining in popularity throughout the Triangle.

"Now, ever since we started our Friday-night services, one thing we decided to do was help someone out. Coach Curtis Parker and Coach Maurice Fountain have been called to lead our beloved Fighting Panthers to a mighty victory this season. I believe that they have a chance to make it into the SNAC play-offs, and at some point make a bid for an invitation to the NCAA dance."

There were a lot of Panthers in the congregation, and they started cheering, "Gooooooo Panthers!!!!"

"In the name of Jesus," Denzelle said, laughing, "we are going to the dance. But to get there takes faith, perseverance, and preparation. Our coaches need our help and we prayed as a congregation, and God led us to give you all this." Denzelle reached inside of his breast pocket and then put two checks in Curtis's hand. The first was for the expected $18,776. The second, from Charles Robinson, was for an additional ten grand. It was a miracle.

Hours ago, Curtis had walked out of the president's office facing deep slices into his budget. And now the Lord had made up for the deficit and given them far more than he ever expected to carry the team through. The Lord had truly supplied their every need according to His riches in glory by Christ Jesus. Curtis felt himself tear up, and prayed that he wouldn't punk out and cry. He glanced over at Maurice and saw that Maurice was fighting that exact same battle. They both laughed through the tears, thankful that the good Lord didn't let one fall.

At that moment, Trina was so happy she was a female and could cry shamelessly. Yvonne, who didn't cry as easily as most folks, felt her eyes watering. She stood up and said, "Praise the Lord," only to be followed by the rest of the congregation. She looked at Curtis struggling to man up and not cry, and her heart was touched. This was the kind of man she would love to have in her life.

A twinge of sadness swept across Yvonne's heart when it occurred to her that Regina Young was a part of Curtis Parker's life. She gave that sorrow over to the Lord and was encouraged with Holy Ghost–anointed joy when God reminded her that He was her true source of joy and contentment, and that she was not to worry because He had everything in control. All she had to do was trust Him and be patient because her blessings were on the way.

Denzelle gave both of the coaches that good old black boy hug, where they leaned toward one another, grasped hands, and parted with a firm pat on the back. He went and sat back down, now ready to hear the choir throw down on the Mississippi Mass Choir's "I'm Not Tired Yet": *I've been runnin' for Jesus a long time . . . and I'm not tired yet.*

Maurice liked this song, too. He loved that earthy, warrior-for-Jesus-sounding voice of the soloist on the CD. That lady sounded like she'd really been runnin' for Jesus since she put on her first pair of walking shoes. He turned around to see who the soloist was, and was a bit disappointed to discover that it was the woman with the bodunkadunk booty in the lobby. He couldn't help but wonder if a sister so bent on swinging that thing in full view of the pastor could really throw down on a song that required a good dose of the Holy Ghost to make the delivery just right.

The musicians gave a robust and hot run of the introduction of the song, getting folks up off their feet before anyone sang one note. Denzelle stood up and turned around, grinning, just ready to be blessed with this song. The musicians played the introduction one more time, wondering if the soloist had missed her cue. She didn't open her mouth, so they played the intro one extra time for good measure, silently lifting the girl up in prayer.

The choir director started clapping on that third cue, and glanced over to the musicians, indicating that they should give the song intro one more run to make it look as if they were doing this on purpose. She didn't know what was wrong with the soloist this evening. She'd picked this song because it was on the pastor's list of favorites, and the pastor was like her brother. She'd also picked this song because she knew the soloist, who loved to get attention, would show out for the company, or all of the visitors in the audience. She also knew Miss Lady had a crush on the pastor and would work extra hard to work that song.

But Bodunkadunk would not open her mouth. She put her hand on her hip and then curled up her lips when they started the song a fifth time. Miss Thing was mad, and she'd been mad ever since she saw her pastor dodging those two heifers during the meet-and-greet, making it clear they were trying to be his woman. She thought she'd made it clear to all of the pastor's wannabe boos that she was the Head Wannabe Boo In Charge at this church. Pastor Flowers needed to quit ducking and dodging heifers and make a choice. She knew she had the biggest booty of all the women chasing after the pastor. He was a black man, and what black man didn't like a big booty, especially when it was attached to a woman who could sing?

By now the choir director and the musicians were done with fooling around with this girl and her tantrum. She nodded for the musicians to change the song and gave a signal to one of the tenors to come up and sing another one of the pastor's favorites, Marvin Sapp's "Never Would Have Made It." But they couldn't get past the first chords before Bodunkadunk sucked on her teeth real loud into the microphone, breathed out like she was too through, and then leaned down and popped Reverend Flowers upside the head.

Charles and Pierre were in the back of the church all under the pews, they were laughing so hard. Charles said, "I saw it coming, man . . . I saw it coming. When Big Booty wouldn't sing after the second long intro to the song, I knew something was up. I don't know why Denzelle won't check these heifers in his church."

"He can't do that, boss—not unless he is clear that he is not going to try and hit on that. You know that is the only way a brother can brush off a sister with a bodunkadunk hanging off the back of her like that, who also knows the power of a big butt."

"You ain't never lied, playah," Charles said, and sat up straight to see what else was going to happen. Maybe he did need to join church if all of this was happening in here. He'd wait on the saved thing, though. Getting saved required a bit too much from a brother.

Denzelle was stunned. Yarborough had told him about flirting with that girl, said she was crazy and a mess waiting to happen. He massaged the back of his head and gave that girl a look that clearly said, "Hit me again and I'm gone forget I'm a preacher and a gentleman."

Miss Thang had been around before coming back to church. She didn't miss one word of that unspoken message and made to leave the sanctuary. But she wasn't the only one mad at Reverend Flowers for not paying attention to her. The two women he had jumped away from now got bold and walked down to the front of the church and stood there, feet apart, hands on hips, with "What you gone do now, Pastor?" expressions on their faces. As if that wasn't enough trouble, one of the woman ushers came off from the side, picked up a collection plate and tossed it, Frisbee-style, into the pulpit. All three men jumped up as if they were intercepting a pass to catch the plate. It slid past Denzelle's hand, and Curtis reached out and caught it.

"Thanks, Coach," Denzelle mumbled and went up to the podium, praying for God to help him out of this mess. He whispered, "I'm sorry, Jesus. You've been trying to tell me to straighten up and fly right. This is my deathly wages for my many sins. Lord, I confess this sin of lust and selfishness and fornication. I repent, Lord, in the name of Jesus. And I ask to be forgiven, delivered, and set free."

"Amen!" "Amen!" "Amen!" came from all around the church, which had heard this prayer clearly over their very high-tech and sophisticated sound system. "Hallelujah!" was shouted everywhere. Folks stood on their feet and began praising God. Despite all of his wayward ways, New Jerusalem loved their pastor. A whole lot of them had been praying for him, and they'd been praying for their church to be set free from that Jezebel spirit on those women who kept trying to run and ruin their beloved church.

The musicians took their cue from the congregation and started playing "Never Would Have Made It" until the soloist could get to the microphone. The choir director was crying. She had been praying so hard for her play brother, and was blessed beyond measure to see him repent and be set free. What a powerful testimony to the entire church to see their pastor freed from this yoke of sin.

Tears were streaming down Denzelle's cheeks. For the second time this evening, the Book of Malachi was on his heart. This time,

Malachi 2:5–8 sliced through him, convicting Denzelle Flowers down to the bone when he thought of what God had to say to him with this scripture, which read:

"*'The purpose of my covenant with the Levites was to bring life and peace, and this is what I gave them. This called for reverence from them, and they greatly revered me and stood in awe of my name. They passed on to the people all the truth they received from me. They did not lie or cheat; they walked with me, living good and righteous lives, and they turned many from lives of sin. The priests' lips should guard knowledge, and people should go to them for instruction, for the priests are the messengers of the Lord Almighty. But not you! You have left God's paths. Your "guidance" has caused many to stumble into sin. You have corrupted the covenant I made with the Levites,' says the Lord Almighty.*"

Denzelle's shoulders shook from the sorrow and sobs tearing through him. He always knew folks in his congregation loved him. But he never knew how hard they'd been praying for him until right now. He didn't understand and truthfully didn't want to understand how his sin had hurt and injured them so deeply. He didn't know that they had seen it all and they loved him in spite of himself. And he was in awe of God's mercy, grace, and forgiveness to a sinner like himself. He walked out of that pulpit and went down to the altar to rededicate his life to Christ.

Maurice went to stand next to him. Curtis remained in the pulpit, feet feeling like lead, as he resisted the urging of the Holy Ghost to go and join Denzelle at that altar. He wasn't ready. He hoped the Rapture wasn't on the horizon because today he wasn't ready.

Charles's heart was convicted, and he grabbed the back of the pew to stop himself from going down to that altar and getting saved. This was the first time in his life that he'd ever wanted to get saved. Watching Denzelle be transformed in front of his very eyes was a testimony to the power of the Lord he'd never forget. He took a step and then sat down when he remembered all the money he stood to lose if he went down to that altar.

Curtis had sat down and was gripping his chair, so convicted he thought he'd explode. But he'd have to deal with that conviction because he was hardheaded and wasn't going down to that altar—not today.

SEVEN

Curtis, Maurice, Trina, and Yvonne took their time walking to their cars. They were silent because nobody knew what to say about this evening's service. *Memorable* came to mind but even that word was just a tad bit too tame for what had transpired in the sanctuary of New Jerusalem Gospel United Church. The four of them had belonged to the Gospel United Church all their lives, and they had either seen or heard about some wild and crazy stuff happening behind the scenes in the denomination over the years. But they couldn't recollect witnessing a showdown with the pastor's wannabe boos that had brought the man to his knees with a truly repentant and contrite heart before the Lord. It was something to see.

Maurice grabbed Trina's hand in his. He needed to feel the comfort of her touch. What a blessing it was to have the privilege of touching Trina's hand. What a blessing it was to be so in love with his babies' mama. So many men had wonderful children who were being raised by good women. *But those women were not bone of their bones and flesh of their flesh.*

Now, Maurice wasn't blaming anybody for anything. He knew that things didn't always work out. He also knew that far too many folk entered into holy matrimony without ever giving a single thought to asking God, the one who created such a holy union, for His opinion on their choice of a spouse. If they did, the divorce rate would plummet. But when folks fancied themselves in love, they didn't want to hear from God; they wanted things to be the way they wanted them to be, and that was that.

Unfortunately, that was not that. Because good people like Veronica Washington were entering marriages that had not been sanctioned by God, only to wake up one day and discover that they had erred seriously in their judgment. He remembered Trina telling him that when she asked Veronica what happened, and how did she miss so many red flags in Robert, all Veronica said was, "I never asked God. If I had asked God, I would have known to wait for God to reveal to me all the reasons why I should have given Robert Washington his walking papers before there were any papers drawn up to give."

Maurice thought that Veronica was right. If she had gone to God, He would have blessed her with a peace that would have enabled her to be patient and wait for Him to reveal qualities about Robert that would have sent her running as fast and as far from him as possible. But folks didn't always know how to do that. Sometimes, it was only after going through that a righteous person got it and learned the true value and blessing of trusting and obeying the Lord.

To obey God was a privilege, and far too many Christians missed that point. They always acted as if obedience were an imposition to be endured, rather than a way for God to keep them safe and able to receive the many blessings He had set aside for them. They didn't understand that God's call for obedience was a tremendous act of love on His part.

Maurice glanced over at Curtis trying to act like he wasn't absolutely delighted to have Yvonne walking next to him on this beautiful fall night. The boy was just happy and content, and too dumb and stupid to figure that out. He wondered how much Curtis had been touched by what had transpired this evening. How much longer was Curtis going to be bound and determined to keep running from the Lord?

Curtis saw Maurice watching him intently in the soft lighting of the church's parking lot. He knew from the solemn expression on his friend's face that he was thinking about him and why he'd remained in that pulpit rather than join Denzelle at the altar. It certainly would have been easier to stand next to a brother whose business had been put all in the streets, rather than to be down there by yourself, having folks thinking long and hard about why you were so distraught coming back home to the Lord. That could be embarrassing.

Curtis smiled and chuckled softly to himself. He could just hear Maurice's response to what he would have considered jibble-jabble about being embarrassed to come home to Jesus. He knew as well as he knew his name that Maurice would have said something like, "Well, don't you think it would be more embarrassing to be standing there when Jesus returns, and you're one of the few among your friends and family who were unable to get up off the ground? I say that would be a cause for embarrassment."

Yvonne looked up at Curtis, curious as to what made him laugh like that to himself. When Curtis saw her watching him with a raised eyebrow, he pulled the checks out of his breast pocket and then thumped them hard before saying, "Now this is something to praise the Lord about."

"You know it," Maurice added, so thankful that his prayers had been answered about their budgetary needs. He had not known how they were going to make it if Gilead cut their funding any more than he already had. He had told the Lord that He was their Source, and they needed their Source to bless them with some resources. God had come through big time and made sure that Maurice knew the money was from Him. Only God could have led Denzelle Flowers to raise that money for them, and move Charles Robinson to give like that at a church service. In fact, it was only the Lord who could have moved both Charles and his boy, Pierre, to come to church on a Friday night. Everybody knew that Friday night was a top moneymaker for a business like Rumpshakers Hip-Hop Gentlemen's Club.

"We also need to be praising God about Reverend Flowers rededicating his life to Jesus like that," Trina added. "I had been worried about him and his reputation with the women. Denzelle is a good preacher. I couldn't bear to watch him flounder over some triflin' tail like those skoochies I saw prancing and flouncing in his face this evening. I hope that after tonight, old boy will figure out that he needs a helpmeet to help him in the ministry God has placed in him."

Trina shook her head. "What is so terrifying about falling in love with a decent woman? That is crazy to me."

"It's not crazy, Trina," Curtis told her. "It's about being selfish, self-centered, dumb, and arrogant enough to believe that you can have your cake and eat it, too. A brother like Denzelle wants a good woman at his side. But he knows that with a good woman, you have to submit to God's direction concerning her, you have to commit to her, you have to do right by her, and you have to let her inside of your heart. That's a lot for a brother dealing with fear of love and commitment, and a selfish desire to do everything his way, while at the same time having all of his needs met."

Everybody stopped walking and just stared at Curtis.

"Negro," Maurice said, "I think that is about the most profound thing your commitment-phobic behind has said in a long time. Maybe something in tonight's service did touch you."

Curtis bristled and then calmed down. It was beginning to unnerve him that every time the Lord spoke to his heart, he with his dumb self blurted it out, letting the whole world know that he was listening to God, and capable of heeding the direction of the Lord for his life. He snapped at the checks to draw attention away from him.

"You bet not put that in your coach account, Curtis," Yvonne said.

"Why not?"

"Gilead will know it's there and then he'll cut your budget down even further and you all will be right back where you started."

Everybody was quiet again. Trina stared at Yvonne and said, "Girl, who are you? That kind of insight could have only come from the Holy Ghost."

Yvonne started laughing. Whenever Trina said "Who are you?" it meant that you had said something that really needed to be said.

"You talking good now, baby," Curtis said. "But where should I put the money? Can't put it in my personal account—will make it look like I'm earning money I don't have. And that might not sit too well with the IRS around tax time."

"Talk to L. C. Smith, here at New Jerusalem. He does all of the life insurance and investments and stuff like that for both New Jerusalem and Fayetteville Street. He'll know how to help you set up that account and keep Gilead out of your business."

Curtis smiled at Yvonne and tweaked her ear. He said, "I need to keep you around, baby girl. You have been a big help to me and my team."

Yvonne blushed and said, "Awww, Curtis, it wasn't nothing."

Curtis laughed. Yvonne was so goofy at times. But that was all right. He secretly liked goofy. All goofy said to him was that a person was genuine enough to let you see the real deal, even if the real deal was sorely lacking in cool points when you saw it. He got closer to her to smell her cologne.

"Stella?"

"Huh?"

"Stella McCartney cologne, right?"

"How did you know what kind of cologne I was wearing?"

"Baby, I just know. I know what smells good on a woman. And you, Miss Yvonne, smell scrumptious in Stella."

Maurice and Trina nudged each other. Maurice sniffed up under his arms and said, "I wonder what I smell like."

"Like bodunkadunk," Trina said, knowing she was being so wrong.

"Girl, I took a shower before I left for church, and I know I don't smell like booty."

Yvonne and Curtis were cracking up. Maurice and Trina were a trip.

"Naw . . . I have to take that back because that bodunkadunk back at church was gigantic," Trina said.

"I know," Yvonne added. "She had the biggest booty I have ever seen in my entire life."

"Amen," Curtis said, thinking that was too much booty, even for a brother who liked big booties.

"Hey," Maurice said, not wanting to end this interesting yet delightful evening. "Why don't we go and get something to eat? I'm hungry."

"Me, too," Trina said.

"Me three," Yvonne said.

"Don't the three of y'all have some little chirrens to get to?" Curtis asked, hoping they did because he was tired. He was hungry, he was enjoying this evening, but he was so tired he could barely see straight.

"Those chirrens are all at Yvonne's house with Rochelle," Maurice said. "They didn't want to go to church on a Friday night. They are over there playing that new Wii that Darrell sent Yvonne's girls. They are not trying to have us come home early."

Curtis yawned. "I want to go but I'm tired, man. I mean it, I'm really tired."

"You need to eat, too, Curtis," Trina told him. "That might be why you are so tired. Come on, we can find someplace fun to eat and we'll get you home. Both you and Yvonne need some downtime."

Curtis thought about it and then said, "All right. Let's go."

Yvonne went to her car, trying hard not to skip. She was so glad she had agreed to come to church with Trina and Maurice when Trina called and said, "You need to come with us tonight. You need to get out, and you'll be blessed."

Curtis was about to pull off right behind Maurice and Trina but waited and gave Yvonne enough space to pull in between his and Maurice's car. She waved at him, smiling so sweetly it pulled right at his heartstrings. Curtis's mother smiled like that whenever anybody talked about him or his dad, who had died six years ago. He missed his father. Lee Parker was a good guy, and had treated his mother as a woman deserved to be treated. Sometimes he felt guilty that he was not married and treating a woman as his father had raised him to treat a woman.

His father always told Curtis that if he would just drop to his knees and recognize from Whom all his blessings flowed, all would be well and things in his life would work out. He also told Curtis that he would never find his true bride, the woman the Lord had picked out for him from the beginning of time, without prayer, obedience to the Word of God, faith, and God's help. Lee Parker had given his only child, Curtis Lee Parker, this Word from the Lord five hours before he left to go home to be with the Lord. Curtis had forgotten those words until Yvonne had flashed that incredible smile at him.

Curtis didn't understand it, but he could not resist this girl. He had been with Regina for almost a year. He'd been sleeping with Regina and tapping that very high-end tail for eleven months, three weeks, and six days. And he had never felt anything remotely close to what he was feeling for this woman in all of that time. He thought back to when his boy Lamont Green kept trying to act as if he wasn't falling in love with his frat's sister Theresa Hopson. Lawd, if that thing didn't drag out ad nauseam between those two. Lamont was determined not to get caught. And Theresa was determined to make sure he knew that if he didn't want her, she didn't care.

Maurice, Trina, and the boys had missed all of that excitement because they had been in Trinidad almost the entire time the courtship had been going on. Maurice had been granted a special leave of absence to work with Eva T.'s sister institution in Trinidad, coaching their newly established basketball team. They had so much fun over there, folks barely heard from them until they arrived back in Durham and needed somebody to come and pick them up at the airport.

Driving behind Yvonne, Curtis thought about Maurice and Lamont telling him how and when they figured out that their wives were *the one*. It occurred to him that what he was feeling for Yvonne was very much like what he'd been told you felt when you found the one. That was a terrifying revelation. The woman in the sea-blue Infiniti was the one he wanted to spend the rest of his life with. Curtis started sweating. He rolled down all the windows when he felt as if he were getting ready to start hyperventilating.

The main reason Curtis was with Regina Young was that he knew that she was not the one. Second, he could drop her in a heartbeat when he got tired of her. Anybody with half a brain would understand when he and Regina stopped seeing each other.

But while his folks would welcome them breaking up, Regina wouldn't be so amenable to this idea. It wasn't because she was so in love with Curtis. Rather, it would be her ego plain and simple. Regina had an overrated opinion of herself. She would never understand a man wanting to leave her to be with someone else—especially an uncomplicated, feet-flat-on-the-ground type of woman like Yvonne Fountain. Regina hardly even spoke to women who didn't wear designer shoes. So Curtis knew what she'd do when faced with a rival like Yvonne.

EIGHT

Curtis, Yvonne, Maurice, and Trina had a good time staying out late, laughing and talking to one another until the folks at the restaurant gave them each a complimentary bottle of champagne and told them it was time to go home so they could close up and get off work. Curtis had been wide awake and had not wanted to go home. If he went home, he couldn't be with Yvonne.

But that was then, and this was now. Because this morning Curtis was so tired and sleepy he could barely get out of bed to go to the bathroom and pee. He stood in front of the toilet, sleepy, wishing his body would hurry up and cooperate so that he could crawl back in bed and get at least thirty more minutes of sleep. His head was throbbing so badly he felt like he had when he used to go out drinking with his boys back in the day—talking about a real-life love hangover.

Curtis finished his business, shook out the most essential thing, flushed the toilet, washed his hands, yawned, stretched, and got in bed, only to find out that he was unable to go back to sleep. He grabbed the clock off the nightstand—eight-thirty a.m. and two hours past the time he was usually up, out, and heading to Idea's Coffee House out on Highway 55 before making his way to his office at the university.

But he had not been able to pull those hours this morning because he was exhausted. He hadn't gotten any rest last night. He tossed and turned, ground and gritted his teeth, heaved and sighed, and just about drove himself crazy—not to mention Regina Young, who was asleep in his bed when he got home.

Now this was a fine mess to be in. Curtis had driven up to his house with joy flooding his heart for the first time in a long time. Up until these past couple of weeks, he had not even comprehended that his heart was so heavy. He smiled and then frowned when he saw Regina's car in the garage. Here he was feeling on top of the world because of Yvonne Fountain, and now his heart dropped down to the soles of his feet at the mere thought of having to see Regina lying in his bed. How was he going to fix this, this time?

Curtis sat still in the car with the garage door up, his heart and spirit down for the count. He flipped the radio to the gospel radio station. The words *He will . . . work it out, I tell you that He will . . . work it out . . .* came on. Curtis gripped the steering wheel and then let it go. He made himself get out of the car and went inside his house, encouraged by the song and the Lord's firm touch on his heart with these words: *Love the Lord with all your mind, with all your heart, and with all your might, and I will make it work out.*

That peace was short-lived, though. All night Curtis tossed and turned, thinking about Yvonne. Fortunately, he always woke up before calling her name out loud. Unfortunately, the tossing and turning woke up Regina, too. Several times throughout the night he woke up to find himself staring right into Regina's hard eyes. Curtis didn't know what he was on the night he gave that mean and stuck-up girl the key and alarm code to his house. That had to be the dumbest thing he'd done in a very long time. Well actually, going out with Regina in the first place was the dumbest thing he'd done. Giving this heifer the key was sheer insanity.

Curtis was having a hard time accepting the revelation that there really was a *the one*. It was simply unbelievable. And right now about the best thing he could do would be to keep this revelation to himself. Nobody else needed to know about this. It could remain a well-kept secret that only he and Jesus knew about. And this plan would work, too, if only Jesus would allow him to keep this business to himself. Past experiences had taught him that Jesus would put a brother's business in the street if that business didn't need to remain unknown.

Curtis had lost count of the times when there was something

he wanted to remain hidden in the shadows. And then *BAM*—the Holy Ghost would go snitch on him, putting all of his dirt out there for all to see. That *"what you do in the dark will be revealed in the light"* stuff was no joke. It could get a negro in some serious trouble if he wasn't careful.

He didn't know why people didn't fear the Lord like they should, or even more than they did. The Bible held countless examples of what the Lord would do to people who were stupid enough not to fear Him. Who but an imbecile like Pharaoh would be impudent enough to follow some people in the sea who were under the protection of such a mighty God that He wiped out your entire kingdom without ever sending one super assassin, poisoned drink, chariot, knife, spear, sword, projectile rock, fire missile, javelin, or whatever they were packing back then to your house? Now that was asking—no, begging—for something to jump off.

Folks didn't have sense enough to revere and fear the Lord God Almighty back then, and they sho' didn't act like they had that kind of sense now. And Curtis didn't know why folks were so obtuse on this matter. God didn't bite His tongue in the Bible.

People always try to make it seem like God wasn't clear, or didn't really mean what He said in His Word. But that wasn't so. God didn't mince words and He didn't play—He's always been pretty clear about where He stands because He was the same yesterday, today, and tomorrow. He was the same God who played Pharaoh and all of Egypt when they tried to get cute. And He hadn't changed. He said it quite clearly in Isaiah 61:8 that He loved justice and hated wrongdoing. He also said in verse two that *"He has sent me to tell those who mourn that the time of the Lord's favor has come, and with it, the day of God's anger against their enemies."*

God could not be more simple and direct than that. Yet folks always found a way to convolute the obvious, so that they had a reason to justify their willful disobedience to the Word of God.

Curtis closed his eyes tight to stop his train of thought. He was one of those justifiers, and he didn't even know that he had that much remembered Word in him. He rubbed the spot right above the bridge of his nose. His head was throbbing, he was tired, Yvonne's face was permanently etched on his brain's memory card, Regina's eyes had turned into deadly lasers, and all his crazy self could think about was the Word and why people rebelled against the Lord.

Curtis was turning into Gran Gran. Why not his mom, who was more mellow about these matters? But Gran Gran? And on today of all days. Could it get any worse?

He thought about that for a moment. Yeah, it could definitely get worse. Regina could figure out what was going on with him. That definitely qualified as a get-worse type of scenario. But this morning was not the morning. One of the two most important games of the season was getting closer and closer. Plus, his department was hosting the quarterly SNAC Basketball Coaches Meeting, to begin at eleven-thirty this morning.

Curtis could not believe that he was experiencing such a dramatic shift in his heart and spirit in so short a time. And he didn't have time for this—not today. There was entirely too much going on between the SNAC meeting and prepping for the big game with Bouclair College. Curtis had to deal with Bouclair's head coach, Sonny Todd Kilpatrick, at the meeting. And the last thing he needed to be doing was pondering over some scriptures.

What he needed to do today was figure out how he was going to get his star players back in the game. He didn't care what Maurice said, what Trina said, or what Gran Gran said. Praying and supplication and finding the right sections of the Word to apply to your situation was a luxury—a luxury he would not be able to indulge in until after the problem was solved.

Curtis reached over to grab his playbook, which was lying underneath a large Bible on his nightstand. He was too lazy to sit up and move the Bible, and snatched at the edge of the playbook. But the Bible was very heavy and the playbook wouldn't budge. So he pushed the Bible onto the floor, grabbed his playbook, and dropped it on top of the comforter.

Regina, who was lying on her side with her back to him, had not moved. She was so still, Curtis wanted to poke at her to make sure she had done him a solid and passed away in her sleep. It wasn't like her to remain so still and quiet with all the noise he was making.

The Bible was lying facedown on the floor. He wanted to lean over and pick it up but didn't feel like going to all of that trouble for that big heavy book. Curtis pressed his head back against the headrest and got comfortable. He'd put the Bible back when he finally got up.

Curtis opened the playbook and then leaned over the side of the bed to stare at the Bible. What was wrong with him? He needed to be studying this playbook and figuring out how they were going to kick Bouclair College's butt. But all he wanted to do right now, was read his Bible. He had to be going through some kind of midlife crisis. Only it wasn't about chasing other women to feel young and alive—it was about opening up to Jesus to find out what life was really all about.

He opened the playbook and closed it. He opened it again and closed it. Again, Curtis opened that playbook, this time making an attempt to flip through the laminated pages, only to find himself closing it again, and then leaning over to stare at his Bible.

He leaned over to reach for the Bible, and then stopped when Regina started moving around. She stopped moving and Curtis leaned over again, only to stop when Regina turned over on her back, then on her other side to face him with her eyes wide open.

"What are you doing?" she snapped in the middle of a heavy yawn.

Curtis blinked hard. Regina's breath was hot and stanky. What did she eat last night—that fancy goat cheese she loved so much? He hated goat cheese—couldn't stand the smell of it, and abhorred the taste. It had to be the nastiest cheese on earth.

"What's wrong with you, Curtis?"

"Wrong? Girl, what you talkin' 'bout?"

Regina sat up. The strap on her gold silk nightgown fell low on her shoulder. It was a very pretty nightgown and it illuminated her pale, cappuccino-tinted skin.

"You are sitting there blinking like something is wrong with you and there are tears in your eyes?"

Curtis wiped at his eyes. *Dang it*, he thought, *baby girl's breath is kickin'.*

"I'm just tired and my eyes bothering me, baby," he lied, hoping she'd turn over on her other side and take her stankin'-breath self back to sleep. 'Cause if she kept talking all up in his face, he was going to have to hurt her feelings to stop that goat-cheese breath from burning his eyebrows off his face.

"I have not been able to get a decent night's rest because you tossed and turned and moaned and groaned all night, keeping me up."

"Then why didn't you go and sleep in the guest room?"

Regina punched her pillow. She wished it were Curtis's big head. He made her so sick sometimes. But then again, she didn't want to rock the boat with Curtis. Even though she was not in love with him, and couldn't begin to imagine herself with him past this academic year, she liked being Coach's woman. There were so many women on campus who wanted this man and she had him. And even though Regina really didn't want Curtis, what she did want was for somebody else to want what she had. She'd been that way most of her life—wasn't happy unless she was able to make somebody else unhappy.

Regina's response to Curtis's request was to act as if he had not said a thing. She snatched at the covers and rolled back over and pretended to go back to sleep.

Curtis didn't move and he didn't say anything, either. If he had, he would have pushed that presumptuous, stuck-up heifer out of his bed and right onto the floor. If he had opened his mouth, he would have given that girl a few choice words that a man who was raised right didn't say to a woman—not even a woman who deserved it. Then he would have told her to get out. He was sick of being expected to act like she was the cat's meow when there were times she was more akin to something the cat dragged in.

He waited for Regina's breathing to take on a regular rhythm before opening up the playbook. What he needed was not in this book. As good a coach as he was, he had not written any plays of miracle proportion. And he definitely didn't have anything tucked away in this book worth using against a team as formidable as Bouclair College.

It was going to take a miracle to win that game. Bouclair College, as much as they loved to fight and cuss and act crazy while on court, was the strongest team in the Southeastern Negro Athletic Conference. They were hard to beat and even harder to whip. The last time the Panthers played Bouclair, they scored sixteen points against Bouclair's eighty-eight. Then Bouclair mopped up the court with the Panthers after two of Curtis's players, DeMarcus Brown and June Bug Washington, threw the first punches over one of those trifling, whorish cheerleaders.

What self-respecting young man threw punches during a crucial game over some piece of tail that half of the state had gotten a taste of? DeMarcus and Sonny were supposed to be two of the most eligible brothers on campus. They could have any woman they wanted—especially if she was a jacked-up and glorified skank-hoochie, or skoochie.

But why was he even thinking along these lines? Any self-respecting playah knew better than to go sniffing around another dog's territory. That was a guaranteed fight. He'd never seen it go down any other way. And the two starters on Bouclair's team had messed with those little heifers just to get his players kicked out of that game and benched for enough games to roll right up to this one.

Curtis could not stand the cheerleaders who made up the school's varsity squad. They were the most selfish, self-serving, backstabbing, covetous, and whorish young women on campus. What team had cheerleaders who slept with members of the opposing team to help them win the game?

Now, he'd heard of cases where the super-hos on the squad were asked to mess with the opposing team to make them lose. But to help the opposing team triumph over one's own school was something that even the skankiest and most self-serving little cheerleader would scoff at. Unfortunately, the little girls who made up this season's squad were so bad, they had run the best cheerleaders back to Junior Varsity. It seemed that these young women would rather be on the second-string squad if it guaranteed peace of mind and freedom from all the drama that practically exuded from the pores of the so-called elite squad members. Curtis had seen the best and sweetest cheerleaders sitting on the sidelines during a game, watching what they referred to as the "Skank Squad" with disgust all over their faces.

It was a shame the way the team's advisor had let a handful of scheming, conniving, and nasty-acting little girls, without an ounce of home training, make a mockery of what could have been the best cheerleading squad in the state. And the leader of the pack, Shaye-Shaye Boswell, along with her sidekick, Larqueesha Watts, was running the team into the ground.

Although he couldn't prove it, Curtis knew that those two were right in the thick of the mess where the bad blood between DeMarcus and June Bug and the players on Bouclair College's team were concerned. And for some reason, he had a terrible feeling that Castilleo Palmer had set that whole thing up, right down to paying those girls off. He didn't know why he felt that way, but he did. For some reason, Castilleo was getting some perks whenever they lost to Bouclair.

Gran Gran always told him that the Devil was busy. And she kept telling him to get prayed up and anointed before trying to go out and coach that team. But that just seemed so churchy and over-the-top to Curtis. This was basketball business and not church business. He could understand if it had something to do with Fayetteville Street Church, or if he were a pastor instead of a head basketball coach. But he wasn't any of that. He was a head coach at a state university, and he needed to keep church business at church so that it would not interfere with the business of what had to be done up at the college.

NINE

The game with Bouclair College was way too soon for comfort. In fact, Curtis felt as if he were walking around campus with a giant ax positioned over his head. He wasn't ready. And the team? They were about as ready to fight off those angry Hornets as he was ready to be America's Next Top Model. DeMarcus and June Bug were still benched, and the better players had yet to be cleared to start. If he couldn't get around this mess, they didn't have a prayer.

After watching countless tapes and plays from previous games with Bouclair, the one thing Curtis had figured out was that you had to get in and kick butt when the game jumped off. If not, it was a losing battle, and the best a coach could hope to do was help his team avoid what amounted to a scoring massacre. The last thing any team needed was to be so outscored it gave the appearance that they weren't even in the game. That could work on the team's psyche and set them up for further losses during the season.

Plus, if it was the last thing Coach Curtis Parker did, he wanted to beat the draws off of Bouclair's head coach, Sonny Todd Kilpatrick. Curtis and Maurice could not stand that sawed-off white boy from one of those small Mecklenburg County communities not too far from Charlotte. Sonny Todd always bragged when they ran across him at their sections of the NCAA coaches' meetings that his father, the head supervisor at one of the smaller textile mills in the area, had taught him everything he knew about handling "your boys."

He said in a voice that twanged like a cheap dulcimer, "My daddy taught me when I was just a little bitty thing how to handle my boys. He said, 'Son, when your boys don't wanna work and start getting all fancy on you, picking at those big Afro-American hairstyles, and talking junk about their rights, shut them down with either doing more work or getting so few hours they can forget having enough money to pay their bills and buy some Afro Sheen. Do that and see who will be talking about who ain't treating them right.'

"You know, I've applied that philosophy to my basketball players for the past ten years, and I win. I win and I win and I win. And those boys know better than to complain about a thing. In fact, they betta not if they know what is good for them."

When Sonny Todd spewed that mess at their bi-annual meeting for coaches working at historically black colleges and universities, Maurice had to drag Curtis out of the conference room to keep him off of that little white man with the wrap-around hair—a big, bald lightbulb-shaped head with the bottom half wrapped around with hair. Here they were at a meeting to talk about grades, SAT scores, retention rates, and getting these players out of undergraduate school before they reached their sixth year of college, and this clown was talking like he was having flashbacks to another time and place when he was a paddy-roller.

There were times when Curtis simply could not stand to look at Sonny Todd's grinning, Chester Cheetah teethy face. And whenever they encountered each other, he wanted to snatch that white boy and beat him down like he stole something. He hated the way he treated the players on Bouclair's basketball team.

But even worse, he detested Sonny Todd's recruitment strategies. Every year he took along some Uncle Tom flunky who desperately wanted a job as an assistant coach, and combed the streets of some of the roughest sections of predominantly black neighborhoods looking for raw talent on the playgrounds, schoolyards, and parking lots with hoops. And he always found brothers who could ball like nobody's business.

But as good as these players were, there was a problem with those young men. Many of them didn't have good foundations at home. A lot of them didn't even have a good amount of home training under their belt. And while Bouclair potentially offered the chance of a lifetime for these players, Sonny Todd did absolutely nothing to provide them with the leadership and guidance they needed to acquire some social skills and polish, and leave Bouclair College with what they allegedly came there for—a college degree.

Sonny Todd had his finger on some young men who had the ability to become movers and shakers in the black community. But he didn't care about those children, and tossed them aside like two-dollar crack hos when they had run their course and he had no more use for them. Sonny Todd once confided to the only other white head coach at a SNAC school, Coach Dave Whitmore at Tyler University down near Beauford, North Carolina, his true feelings about the players at Bouclair. Sonny Todd said, "Dave, I've had enough of all of this criticism and scrutiny from these black guys who think they have the final say on what these boys need. I didn't go and find those blacks to help them get a good education. I chose my team because I know they can get out there and get that trophy. Every time they give me some lip, I remember that the only thing those wannabe rap stars can do for me is bring that trophy home and put some extra cash in my and the school's bank account."

Fortunately for the eight black coaches in the conference, this white boy was right and had a conscience. Dave Whitmore was so put out with Sonny Todd's callous attitude toward a group of young men trying to get a shot at life using the best skills they had to offer, he made it a point of sharing that encounter with his SNAC colleagues. He liked the other coaches, had played ball with a few during his college years, and respected the healthy competition that existed between them. He said in his warm, no-nonsense western North Carolina voice, "That is one white boy who makes me wanna snatch his 'white card' out of his wallet and stuff it down his throat."

Coach Whitmore was one of the coaches in the conference who was liked and respected by all. It was ironic that the only white coaches in SNAC were polar opposites. Most of Coach Kilpatrick's players rolled in and out of Bouclair College at the end of their second season and without a degree. Coach Whitmore, on the other hand, had such good retention and graduation rates that many coaches in SNAC and other small conferences wanted to know his secret. And every time they asked him to share how he did it, all Dave Whitmore said was, "I trust God, I stay on my knees, and I keep a blood covering over the team, and then over every single player. I also make sure that my players pray. You all just don't understand the power of being right with the Lord, even on the court."

As much as Curtis liked Dave Whitmore, he didn't want to hear his mini-sermons on prayer and basketball. If Curtis hadn't known better, he would have sworn that Dave was sneaking over to Gran Gran's house to meet with her prayer group. And he became particularly suspicious when Dave said, "What y'all don't understand is that I answer to a higher authority than you brothers, the university I work for, SNAC, SNAC students, parents, alumni, and the NCAA. There is no way I want to be standing in front of the Lord trying to come up with an explanation as to why I did one of God's little babies wrong. You all are not my motivation, Jesus is."

Nobody messed with Dave Whitmore, on or off court. Because as Maurice once put it, "Who in their right mind would have the nerve to mess with a white boy running around talkin' 'bout he got the Holy Ghost—not the Holy Spirit but the Holy Ghost. Y'all, that's a dangerous white boy. 'Cause the Devil can't bamboozle him with some craziness about the merits of being able to claim that your people came over here from Europe on some ships wearing brocade, velvet, leather, suede, and wool in ninety-degree weather."

But just as the SNAC coaches understood and respected the decision to put Dave Whitmore in one of those coveted Southeastern Negro Athletic Conference head coaching spots, not a one could figure out why Sonny Todd was at Bouclair College. Rumor had it that Sonny Todd had something on Bouclair's president. The gossip mill alleged that the president had been caught drunk, with a skank in his lap going through his pockets at one of those "boob and booty shacks" off Interstate 95 South going toward the South Carolina border by none other than Sonny Todd Kilpatrick.

If the story was true—and something in Curtis told him that it was—Sonny Todd stopped the attempted robbery, threw the president (who was a small and slender man) over his shoulder, took him back to his hotel, and figured out a good lie to tell the man's wife. After that, there wasn't anything Bouclair's president couldn't do for Sonny Todd, including hiring him as the new head coach for the basketball team.

There were several glaring problems accompanying this decision, however. First, Bouclair's Athletic Department had just come up with a short list of three very good candidates for the job. Second, Sonny Todd had been fired without any warning from two previous coaching positions. One of those positions was at a tiny, conservative, all-white college that had never recruited more than six black players in its thirty-year history of having a basketball team.

Those white folk at that school could not stand Sonny Todd Kilpatrick—which was irony at its best, since Sonny Todd shared all the political, social, and cultural likes and dislikes of his colleagues on that campus. As the athletic director wrote in what was supposed to have been a letter of recommendation:

> I have never come across an individual who for all practical purposes should have been a perfect fit at our esteemed institution of higher education. A problem that we have experienced on a consistent basis is the ability to recruit and retain faculty willing to live in our town, which is far from everything, except of course the local Wal-Mart. Furthermore, it has been a nightmare trying to find employees we believe would find themselves quite happy here.
>
> Coach Kilpatrick did not experience any of these problems. We, however, were ridden with the problem of hiring a man that no one could stand to lay eyes on. In fact, our oldest staff member, seventy-six-year-old part-time secretary, Mary Elizabeth Tremonte, once confessed that she wished for the days when she still had cataracts so that she did not have to have a clear view of "that man." Nobody liked this man. He was a mean, hateful, controlling, dishonest, lying, cheating scumbag.
>
> I regret that I have had to put my professionalism on the shelf while writing this letter. But honestly, there isn't any-

thing other than what you are reading that I can say about this chap. Oh, yes, there is something else I can say—don't hire him. I mean it. Do not hire this man. Because if you do hire him, you are a weak and spineless ninny who deserves everything he will do to you, your faculty and staff, and your players.

Unfortunately for Sonny Todd, Curtis knew that this letter was not a rumor or an urban myth concocted for the purposes of creating a chain e-mail to distribute among the man's many enemies. Neither was this letter fabricated by a vicious and bitter ex-colleague. Curtis had received a copy of the letter from one of his old girlfriends and read it for himself shortly after its introduction to the search committee. He knew the athletic director of that school. While the man was on the tight side, he had integrity and wouldn't have ever written such a thing unless he had had a horrible experience with Sonny Todd and didn't want another athletic program to bear the burden of working with this man.

Everybody knew that you didn't write bad things about people like Sonny Todd. Because he belonged to that group of folk who were mean and vindictive and loved to keep up some mess. But write the letter this gentleman did. And he got away with it, too. Sonny Todd never blinked an eye when confronted by Bouclair's search committee over the content of the "recommendation." He did, however, request a private meeting with the president in the presence of every member of that committee. The athletic director for Bouclair College described the committee meeting this way.

"I knew it was the beginning of the end for the basketball team. That trailer-park scum practically commanded the president to meet with him. And what did the president do? That negro upped and followed him like he was a crack ho going to get a hit."

A few members of the search committee had tried to reason with the president when he came back from his meeting with Sonny Todd, dusted off an ancient bylaw that should have long since been stricken from the books, and announced that they were hiring the man as head coach of the basketball team. The folks in that meeting got hot, somebody jumped up and threatened to kick the president's narrow behind, and a few threatened to resign. What began as a business meeting deteriorated into a hot ghetto mess with some trailer-park intrigue thrown in for good measure. But nothing mattered. Sonny Todd got the job and that was that.

When interviewed at a televised press conference about this unprecedented and controversial decision, all the president would say was that he wanted to win the conference title and get a shot at a place at the dance during the NCAA tournament. When asked if money was a factor, the president looked at his watch and announced that he was late for another meeting.

And now, thanks to an ill-advised administrative decision, SNAC had a white head coach who openly claimed that minimum wage was too high, accusations of racial profiling had been fabricated by blacks in gangs who were stopped by the police in the midst of committing a crime, the NBA needed to start checking SAT scores before signing on new players, Kobe and Shaq made too much money, and he was sick and tired of the jersey number 23.

Curtis pushed the playbook and the Bible aside. He needed to quit wasting his time, get up, get dressed, and head on over to the campus. If he got in early enough, he might be able to find enough of a peaceful moment to think on a strategy for beating Sonny Todd at his own game.

Regina rolled back over to face him. It was clear that she was now fully rested and game for anything he wanted to put on her. She sat up, making sure that both straps had fallen down around her shoulders.

Curtis paused for a moment and then changed his mind. He didn't need that this morning—not from this woman. What he needed was to quit wasting his time, get up, get dressed, and go to work.

Regina smiled at him and then gave into a big, wide-mouth yawn. Curtis blinked back the tears from his now-watering eyes. It had been over a month since the girl had extended him an "invite." But that yawn was as good a wake-up call as ever. He got up, hopped in the shower, dressed, and backed out of his garage without so much as a nod in Regina's direction.

TEN

Curtis was glad he had gotten up and made it to his office before folks started arriving for the meeting. If he had not taken advantage of those few moments of peace and quiet, his day would have been shot. Because as soon as Curtis emerged from his office and walked down the hall to the Athletic Center's conference room, it was on.

Some of his colleagues acted just like the bratty players who had been the doo-doo on their high school teams, and who had to be checked and put in their place for the good of the whole team when they got to college. And a few of the brothers who had done a stint in the NBA, warming those pro benches and watching all the action from the sidelines, were the worst. This cohort forgot that as good as they had been in college they were not Iverson, Kobe, Shaq, Magic, Dr. J, Kareem, Jordan, Rodman, Latrell, Ben, the Mailman, and the baby boy LeBron James. Sometimes, the most arrogant ones acted like they had been solely responsible for schooling Michael Jordan on how to be like Mike.

And if that Sonny Todd Kilpatrick wasn't a pain in the butt, Curtis didn't know who was. Sonny Todd was bold, brazen, and derisive toward his colleagues until Maurice whispered, "Does he have some kind of brain malfunction going on here and doesn't realize that this is 2009 and not 1809? He's like, say, two centuries off."

Several other coaches shared this sentiment, and were still in disbelief that a man like this had a head coaching position at a SNAC school. But these coaches didn't need to spend any time trying to figure out why Sonny Todd Kilpatrick was at the helm of one of those prized and uncommon black head coaching spots. All they had to do was think green—not environmental green, money green.

Money was the sole reason for hiring Sonny Todd. Money the president of Bouclair College didn't want to pay for the jams he stayed in. Money the president didn't want to pay his wife if she got angry enough to bail out and jump ship from what had to have been a bad marriage due to his trips to scuzzy places located off the nearest exit on I-95 South. Money—lots of money—to be earned by Sonny Todd's highly questionable coaching strategies for the school. Money, money, money, money—*money*. This was about money, pure and simple.

Sonny Todd had just finished giving a brief status report on his program. The other coaches were glad he was done, and hoped he would hurry up and shut up and sit down. But if Sonny Todd was anything, he was shrewd, crazy, and bold beyond belief. That fool knew his colleagues were sick of him, and he didn't care that they were. Instead of sitting down, he decided to talk some more and started speaking about what he considered to be his best qualities.

He said, "I know how to win a game. I know how to pick and coach my players to a win. And I know where every single stripper shack is, up and down every North *and* South Carolina highway there is to know. And I know that if I catch you in one, and you know you're not supposed to be there, you'll wake up wishing I didn't know. Because know this—I go to them all."

Then he frowned and scratched at his head a moment.

"No, I take that back. I don't go to them all. I don't make it a habit of going to Rumpshakers Gentlemen's Club here in Durham. Because I don't know what you brothers find so appealing about that club."

Almost every coach in that room shook his head. What in the world were they going to do with this white boy? With the exception of a handful of the coaches, they had been looking forward to going to Rumpshakers as soon as this meeting was over. In fact, most of the coaches at this meeting had come for the sole purpose of having an excuse to go to that club. Rumpshakers was the best strip club in the entire Triangle, and maybe the best in the state.

"And they charge an arm and a leg for admission," Sonny Todd was saying, as his voice broke through the reverie of the men seated at that conference table.

"The drinks cost too much, they serve too much Hennessy and Crown and not enough Budweiser; I can count the long and leggy blondes with one finger and they are not even white; and the dancers they do hire have behinds that have too much volume, wiggle, and bounce for my personal taste. Plus, those are some of the snootiest strippers I've ever come across. One actually turned up her nose at me and gave me my money back the last time I was there. Now how is that for service?"

Curtis stood up abruptly and said, "I think we've covered everything. Anybody have something they need to share before we dismiss?"

"Naw," several coaches said, and got up, with the rest of their colleagues following suit.

Curtis tried not to sigh with relief but couldn't help it. One more moment of listening to Sonny Todd and he would have hauled off and pimp-slapped that joker in front of all of the other SNAC coaches.

Maurice and Dave Whitmore went and shook hands with the rest of the visiting coaches, acting as if they didn't see Sonny Todd, and left to join Reverend Quincey and Reverend Flowers for lunch at the Chop House Restaurant in Cary. The last thing they wanted was to be around a bunch of loud-talking, drunk and tipsy athletes at a boob-and-booty bar.

Maurice and Dave made eye contact—they were going to lift Curtis up in prayer on the way to lunch. He didn't have any business going to Rumpshakers. Some places, no matter how enticing and popular, were not places folk needed to go to. It reeked of the world. And as much as someone would want Rumpshakers to be good, clean fun with just a taste of naughty thrown in—it was anything but that.

The other coaches followed Curtis out to the parking lot.

Curtis found it curious, when he peeled out of the parking lot in his prized silver Escalade EXT truck, that Sonny Todd was hot on his heels. He checked the rearview mirror and saw Sonny Todd hopping into his white Lexus sedan, starting that car up, and burning some very expensive tire rubber as he broke the campus speed limit to make sure he didn't get separated from the rest of the coaches.

Curtis turned on the radio and hiked up the volume when an old school joint, "Low," blasted out on 97.5. His favorite hip-hop station DJ, Brian Dawson, was on the air. When in a mellow, old school mood, Curtis favored Cy Young of Foxy 107. And when in need of some good gospel on The Light, who could resist the big voice of Melissa Wade, or her colleague Michael Reese, who made sure that every listener in the Triangle heard "I love you" at least once a day?

That "Apple bottom jeans, boots with the fur" was sounding good as Curtis steered his car through the traffic on Highway 55, heading east. Rumpshakers, and the over-thirty black nightclub, The Place to Be, were both off 55. Whereas you could see The Place to Be from the street, Rumpshakers was nestled in an inconspicuous and very woodsy spot down in the cut, off of a side street that intersected with another street off 55. Rumpshakers was near to impossible to find if you did not have specific directions. Map-Quest couldn't help you find this place, either. Folks often joked and said that the only way a negro could roll up on Rumpshakers was with *Blackquest*.

Curtis turned onto the narrow gravel road, and drove a fifth of a mile to reach the Rumpshakers building. He hated having to drive on gravel for that length of time but understood why Charles Robinson left this section of the road unpaved. It was a deterrent to folks who didn't need to be there. Black folk in Durham (or most folk period, for that matter) were not prone to wandering down a dirt and gravel road out in what appeared to be the middle of nowhere. A lot of folk never made it to Rumpshakers because they got tired of looking for it. And for a few, they found the road but just couldn't believe that a black establishment was situated in this location.

One brother, who found the club out of sheer stubborn determination, said, "Man, the first time I rolled up on Rumpshakers, I got to wondering if I'd taken the wrong turn to the *Deliverance* movie people's house. I kept hearing that banjo music playing 'do-do-do-

dooo-do-do-do, do-do-do-do-dooooo-do' in my head. Then I kept looking around making sure that a bro wasn't about to get axed or shot, or shot or axed."

The one group the dirt and gravel road and obscure location held absolutely no deterring factors for was the wives, fiancées, and girlfriends of some of the patrons. An angry sister, whose man had been lying to and mistreating her, was more dangerous to a brother than CSI could ever be to a criminal. They could find information that an unsuspecting brother just knew was hidden and protected.

Charles didn't know how they did it, but those women would find out that the man was lying and cheating, and then go and find that man at Rumpshakers. About the only thing they hadn't found to date was how to get past the ultra-tight security system. And those praying sisters were the most dangerous because they had some serious backup from above. Charles always told folk that he didn't mess with those women. When they showed up, he went and got their man, escorted him out to the parking lot, and left him to her, her mama, her auntie, her sisters, her missionary group, her choir members, and on occasion her first lady and pastor.

Rumpshakers was always a surprise for first-time patrons. The SNAC coaches filing out of those fancy, university-leased cars were no exception. Most first-timers held the expectation that the club would be housed in some kind of 1920s-styled Southern mansion with roses, azalea bushes, and dogwood trees abounding everywhere. Or they thought it would be a restored warehouse with steel beams in the ceilings, old-fashioned plank-style wooden floors, and a few large industrial windows that had been allowed to accumulate dust and soot for privacy and effect.

It was quite natural for folks to presume that a business like Rumpshakers would be housed in a dwelling of that nature. Just about every TV and book brothel and strip club worth its salt was set in such an environment. But Charles wasn't having any of that nostalgic nonsense creating the ambience for his club. Rumpshakers catered to a sophisticated twenty-first-century clientele. Charles Robinson was way too cosmopolitan and crunked to try and run a hip-hop gentlemen's club in a setting that was so outdated and cliché.

Rumpshakers was a three-million-dollar, expansive pale yellow brick ranch that was set in the middle of nine acres of scenic, woodsy land. There was not one rose in sight—especially in the midst of the beautiful sunflowers and colorful daisies and foliage. This was the kind of playah's house that could easily qualify for a spot on an episode of *MTV Cribs*.

It was late afternoon when they arrived, affording all the newest clients a full view of the house, the pond off to the left, and the landscaping that would have surely been in *House and Garden* magazine had the house not been in reality a strip joint. Curtis noticed Sonny Todd standing in front of the magnificent house with his mouth hanging open, almost drooling, before one of his assistant coaches poked him and told him to quit holding everyone up and go on inside.

Less than an hour ago, Sonny Todd had complained about his time at Rumpshakers. But judging from his reaction, Curtis suspected that he had lied. There is no way that boy could have been to Rumpshakers on another occasion and carry on like that.

The other SNAC coaches discerned what Curtis had figured out. It was clear to all of them that this joker had never seen a business of this type that was so classy and beautiful. He didn't even look like the type of man—black or white—who would have ever come to a place like this. Plus, he kept taking pictures with his phone and saying, "I wouldn't have expected this," clearly not remembering what he had told them earlier.

They walked into the gigantic foyer of that fabulous, sprawling ranch and waited, while standing on the cream, ruby, and black marble floor with gold veins running through it. Pierre Smith, Charles's manager, and the one responsible for making all of the arrangements for large parties, came into the foyer followed by five fine waitresses holding an assortment of trays weighed down with shrimp cocktail, caviar, homemade gourmet crackers, and Long Island iced teas.

The men couldn't take their eyes off the waitresses, who were toned and beautiful enough to be dancers. And their uniforms could rival anything anybody had ever seen on any TV show, movie, or documentary about Hugh Hefner's Playboy Club.

Sonny Todd clutched his hand to his heart and inhaled and exhaled over and over again while viewing the delectable scenery. His wife kept telling him that refined white sugar was bad for his health. Maybe she was right. Because this display of brown sugar was making him feel like a dose of that stuff would do wonders for his constitution.

The waitresses wore black silk stockings with red roses embroidered in them, black silk thongs, black silk bustiers with red silk ribbon woven through the rich material, and red lace garters on their left legs. Each woman had a perky ponytail held up by a red-and-black silk ribbon. Their makeup was refined and tasteful, and they walked with so much grace and class the worst ho in the SNAC group had to put some restraints on and try and act like a gentleman.

All of the women were at least five-nine, full-busted, with long legs and generous curves. They were toned and of a healthy weight. And they ranged in color from the palest shade of gold to the deepest hue of ebony brown. It was like being in a candy store, and a few of the men felt as if they were about to get a sugar rush.

Pierre made quick eye contact with one of the waitresses, who in turn gave a signal for the women to start serving the men. Charles had given him a rundown on the twenty-six coaches who were on the guest list. It didn't take him long to find Kordell Bivens and Castilleo Palmer.

Pierre had not made his final selection of the girls who would dance for this group. But after seeing the coaches, he knew just whom to pick. He'd pull from the A list for the group dance, and would go to the D list for that white boy taking pictures with his cell phone as if he'd never been around black people before. He'd also have to pull from the C list for the private dances ordered by Kordell Bivens and that negro standing next to him with the fancy, overdone name. And as for the rest of the coaches, the B list would serve just fine.

The B list dancers were very pretty and good. They just weren't as interested in striving to become professional dancers as the A-listers. The A-listers had dancing coursing through their veins. They trained and worked hard to be the best dancers possible. And when they left Rumpshakers, they usually went on to some kind of professional dance job—the dancers for concerts, the theater, music videos, movies, and the like.

The B-listers were most often students, or looking for a better job. So this was just a job. It paid the bills. And Pierre knew that most of his B-listers would be up and out of there as soon as they either finished school or could find a decent-paying job.

As for the C, D, and the E list dancers, they didn't want to do anything else, they liked the money, they liked the benefits, but most of all they liked stripping. Pierre had a soft spot for the A and B list dancers, and always lent them a helping hand. He kept an eye on the C-listers because some of them were actually A- and B-listers who had gotten lost in the shuffle of women coming in and out of the establishment. And as to the D- and E-listers, he just made sure they were treated fairly, took care of themselves, and were discreet with the behind-the-scenes arrangements they made with some of the customers. He also made sure that they didn't get hooked up with some of the dangerous men who came to the club from time to time. Those women may have been some bona fide skeezers and hooch-ies, and some of them were a bit on the ugly side, but they deserved protection and to be treated right.

Pierre could tell that a few of these men were on the cheap side and would not want to give up a decent tip. Two in particu-lar—Kordell Bivens and that negro with the fancy name—were real cheap. He knew just by looking at them that they still drank cheap liquor because they were too stingy to spend money on something decent. Rumpshakers served only the best liquor. But Pierre sure did wish he had enough time to run down to the nearest ABC store and get something befitting the two of them. Rosie O'Grady, Mad Dog 20/20, and that scotch mess in a plastic bottle his wife bought to make her barbecue sauce with would have been perfect.

He had to remember that this group was made up solely of bas-ketball coaches. They were all former basketball players. A few had done a short stint in the NBA, and most of them felt that they were owed favors and goodies whenever they stepped in an establishment like Rumpshakers. He didn't know why, though.

Rumpshakers entertained some serious high rollers (some of them pro athletes), who felt it a privilege just to come in here and spend their money. It was extremely rare that one of the high rollers didn't drop down some good tip money for good service. It was the broke negroes trying to be more than they were who were cheap with the dancers. And they always wanted somebody who was on the A list or high on the B list.

Pierre led the group down the marbled hallway. He could tell the first-timers. All first-timers lagged behind the rest of their party to take a few minutes to check out the digs. But he understood because he did the exact same thing the first time he set foot in Rumpshakers. It was a beautiful place and Pierre had walked around for half an hour admiring the scenery—he didn't even remember seeing one woman, just the beautiful decor of the establishment.

Rumpshakers had been built with the highest-quality materials. There were marble floors in the entry area, top-of-the-line and ebony wood floors in the main dance rooms, handmade area rugs Charles had found and shipped from Morocco and oil paintings that had been purchased at fancy art auctions around the world were placed throughout the house.

The entire house was done in crimson and cream with black and gold accents to highlight the main color scheme. The interior was painted a muted creamy yellow, with ivory trim on the molding. There were high ceilings and picture windows in the main areas. The dance hall and private rooms had smaller windows and allowed for the kind of privacy needed for their patrons to have a good time.

Black velvet, black suede, and black leather chairs, love seats, stools, and sofas were all over the house. The chrome-and-glass tables were the perfect choice to help keep a masculine edge on the decorating style for the interior. It was a fabulous setup that made most of the patrons feel so welcome they were inspired to dig deep into their pockets for the dancers.

The coaches finished their first round of drinks, put their glasses on a tray and followed Pierre to the main dance room. The area was decorated in the same colors as the rest of the house, had a large conference-type table that was perfect for the customary table dance, and eight chrome and black leather chairs placed around it.

Some of the most comfortable chairs Curtis had ever sat in were posted all over this room. Those chairs were so comfortable that the last time he was here, he fell asleep right in the middle of what he was told had been the best part of the dance. He avoided that big black suede chair and went and sat by the door in one of the less inviting velvet Queen Anne chairs.

The waitresses went around the room and pulled at the clusters of coaches to find a seat. Sonny Todd didn't want to be in the mix with the other coaches. So he went to the far side of the room and tried to make himself comfortable in one of the window seats. He wanted to ask if there were any white or at least Latina dancers. He nixed that notion when the music came over the sound system, and one of the songs his players used to listen to started playing. He didn't know what was so fabulous about the song "Walk It Out." But it obviously held appeal to the majority of folks affiliated with SNAC.

What Sonny Todd didn't know (and really didn't care to know) was that before Rumpshakers, there had been nothing like this for the brothers in Durham. Oh, there were several strip clubs catering to a predominantly black clientele. But there had never been anything on this order. Rumpshakers was elegant, comfortable, tasteful (at least as far as the decor was concerned), and had the finest women working in this industry in the Triangle on the payroll.

Any man who had paid a visit to Rumpshakers could tell you that the women employed by the club were fine. And those fine women loved working for Charles Robinson, who they all said was as fine and sexy as any brother could be. A bona fide light-skinned man, Charles Robinson didn't have a problem finding all of those good-looking sisters.

There were women in Durham County who couldn't dance a lick but wished they had the kind of skills that qualified them to swing around a pole for him. That long, slender, and muscular body, wavy brown hair with a sprinkling of silver running through it, and hazel eyes, made women drool over the brother and slip their panties in his breast pocket. Charles Robinson was fine, single, rich, smart, educated, and sexy. He was the kind of brother every gold-diggin' and stuck-up skoochie would do anything to make her man.

The only group of women not chasing Charles Robinson was what he referred to as the "Kingdom Women"—sisters who were genuine, humble, sweet, fine, smart, saved, Word-filled, and obedient to the Lord. This group, even the ones who found him attractive, could care less about chasing a man like Charles Robinson. As Veronica Washington had once put it, "Why would I want a man who was so comfortable with the world? What could I possibly say or do that would be of interest to him?"

When Denzelle Flowers told Charles what that fine Veronica had said about him, all he did was laugh. What he wanted to tell Miss Veronica was that even though there wasn't anything she could say to his worldly self, he'd be more than happy to tell her what all she could do for him.

And as worldly as Charles knew he was, the one thing he wouldn't have done was leave a brand-new custom-built, 3,800-square-foot home in Durham's Carillon Forest for a 976.5-square-foot "bachelor's pad" with the brand new linoleum in the kitchen at Bismarck Ridge, as Veronica's ex-husband Robert had done. Who in his right mind would want to leave a fine woman like that, move out of a beautiful neighborhood like Carillon Forest, and go and live in Bismarck Ridge of all places? Bismarck Ridge was a decent neighborhood. And it was a good choice for many folk. But for a negro with an ego bigger than the Triangle? That was tantamount to trading in your Lexus to go and buy a Ford Focus because you were desperate to beef up your image as mack daddy.

He knew that the man's leaving a woman like that wasn't about anything but some tail. And it couldn't have been tail worth anything. Because Charles had learned about that a long time ago, the hard way, when he let go of a good woman he could have spent the rest of his life with over some cheap and worthless tail. He'd been just like Robert Washington, and he knew that when you throw away a beautiful treasure, the Lord may not ever let you have another one.

Charles had more women than he knew what to do with but he didn't have any that were remotely close to being a treasure—not the kind of treasure the Bible talked about, or like the one he let get away. Charles shook off that thought by remembering what one of the movers, who also did his landscaping, had told him about Robert moving out of Veronica's house.

He'd said, "Boss, that lady packed that man right up. She put his suits and shirts in wardrobe boxes, and then"—the man started laughing—"and then she went and stuffed all of old boy's funky draws down in that box with all of his good clothes."

"Mookie, how did you know his draws were in the wardrobe boxes?"

Mookie just looked at Charles like he was crazy, and then said, "Dawg, dawg. You know what your draws smell like when you take 'em off and drop 'em in the hamper, right?"

Charles didn't say anything. It wasn't exactly something that you had a whole lot to say about, even if that crazy boy was right. The longer Charles remained silent, the more certain Mookie became that his boss knew exactly what his draws smelled like when they were real funky and lying in the clothes hamper just drawing in even more funk.

"Uh-huh. You know, don't you, Mr. Robinson? It's the kind of funk that comes when you wear your draws way too long and they practically walk to the hamper on their own accord."

Charles couldn't do anything but laugh. That is the very reason he kept a decent supply of clean draws in his office. He hated that feeling—funky draws he'd been wearing way too long.

"Well, that box was 'wearing your draws too long' funky. I was glad I was helping with the other stuff because I didn't want to handle that particular box. Know what I'm sayin', playah?"

"Yeah, I know exactly what you are sayin', Mookie, man," Charles told him.

"But it gets better, Mr. Robinson. While old boy was out in the driveway, sitting in his car looking stupid, Miss Thang started playing Beyoncé's *you must not know 'bout me* song over and over again. Every time that negro thought the song had ended, Beyoncé started singing, 'To the left, to the left . . . everything you own is in a box to the left,' all over again. I know it liked to drove that man crazy—especially whenever he came up to the front door, trying to get in the house, and his wife started dancing and singing, 'You must not know 'bout me, you must not know 'bout me.'"

Charles loved that story about what had to be the stupidest negro in all of Durham County, North Carolina. He was a true player, and would have never been ignorant enough to let Veronica go free. That's how he knew how to hook up Rumpshakers—he was a playah and a very good one at that.

He had designed the club to be the black man's boob-and-booty paradise. Only thing, Charles, unlike many of his patrons, didn't even need his own paradise to get what he wanted. Brothers on the prowl in the Triangle complained about Charles Robinson and all of the women who had taken it upon themselves to pledge their loyalty to him. They maintained that he had all of the free booty on lockdown, and was rather selfish and unwilling to share the goods.

Charles Robinson could have cared less about what the brothers in Durham County thought he should do. Maybe those negroes just needed to bone up on their skills and leave him the heck alone. That was one of the main reasons he was so reluctant to get saved and make Jesus Lord of his life—having too much fun with the fleeting pleasures of sin, and obviously oblivious to the fact that the *wages of sin was death.*

He reasoned that God had blessed him with his first cousin, Marquita, and her mother, his Aunt Margarita, who were super-saved as far as he was concerned. And between the two there had to be enough Holy Ghost going around to cover a multitude of his transgressions through intercessory prayer.

But as smooth and worldly as Charles Robinson was, he was honest about who he was and what a woman could expect from him. Charles didn't cheat on anybody because he didn't believe in cheating. He didn't believe in monogamy, either. But he didn't cheat. He was honest, straightforward, and fair. While his women grumbled about his candid, stubborn honesty, his employees adored him for it. Charles Robinson was straightforward. It was this virtue that helped to keep him in bondage to sin. On the one hand, Charles could pride himself on treating the folks who worked for him right. Then on the other hand, he was extending an invitation to employees and patrons alike to travel down the wide and easy highway that carried his folks right up to the gates of Hell.

ELEVEN

The coaches started filling out the order forms for their private dances and getting cash off their debit cards. Sonny Todd pulled out a money clip holding a wad of twenties in place and ordered a beer. His assistant coaches acted as if they didn't see him and went and sat with the other brothers.

Curtis kept his seat. He'd been happy to follow his colleagues out here for some R & R. But right now he was regretting the decision to come. Maybe he should have just led them out here and then gone back to the office. Or better yet, maybe he should have just gone home and gotten some much-needed rest. Or, even better than that, maybe he should have opted to spend some quality time with Maurice, Dave Whitmore, Reverend Quincey, and Reverend Flowers.

Charles, who had known Curtis for a long time, didn't like it that he was here at the strip club. When it was time for the dancing to begin, Charles made a decision to pull him out of all of this. Rumpshakers' prized dancer, Sweet Red, sashayed all the way over to where Curtis was sitting and turned around so that he could see how well her black thong complimented her black-and-red tattoo that read SPANK ME DADDY across her right cheek.

Charles didn't want her messing with Coach. He went over to Sweet Red, slipped a C-note right inside the thong, and twisted it into a neat bow. He then gave her instructions to go over to the table of coaches where Kordell Bivens and Castilleo Palmer were busy chowing down on huge tiger shrimp, stuffed grilled portobello mushrooms, spicy wings, potato skins, and the house specialty—

deep-fried, red-pepper-coated string beans. He also made sure there were plenty of complimentary pitchers of Rumpshakers' famous homemade Mojitos, created with the finest imported Jamaican rum, fresh-ground sugar cane, and mint leaves that Charles grew himself in his private garden out back.

Sweet Red left Curtis alone and turned her attention to the two men the boss had schooled her on an hour before the SNAC coaches made their way down that dirt-and-gravel road. She bounced her fat but exceptionally toned booty around a few times. As soon as Castilleo saw the tattoo he stood up, pulled off his suit coat, dug in his breast pocket, and pulled out a wad of bills. He couldn't wait to throw money her way because he was dying to discover all that Sweet Red knew how to do. And he secretly hoped he could play "daddy" to Sweet Red and spank that thang.

Charles made quick eye contact with Sweet Red to take all of Castilleo's money and keep the house's part as a bonus for handling her business right. He had every intention of sending that negro home flat broke because he didn't like the way he'd tried to run some raggedy game on his frat's niece—a sweet and beautiful assistant principal at the gifted elementary school who deserved far better than that FNN (fancy-name negro) with barely a pot to piss in.

Sweet Red pulled a cherry Dum Dum lollipop out of her low-cut bra, which was red with black lace running through it, took the candy out of the wrapper and began sucking on it with those sparkling ruby-red lips. She licked her lips and held a hand out toward Castilleo, who promptly put ten dollars in it. Sweet Red frowned and started to walk away. Castilleo pulled off nine more of those tens. She slowed her roll, smiled, slurped on that Dum Dum, turned around, put her behind right in Castilleo's face, clapped her booty a few times, and stood still until he put another set of ten tens in her hand.

Happy, Sweet Red dropped down and didn't come back up until "to the window . . . to the wall" was blasting out of the sound system. She bent over and jingled a single cheek. Castilleo started hyperventilating. Kordell handed him one of the paper bags that were on all the tables. They looked like the barf bags on airplanes.

Castilleo took a few slow, deep breaths, sat back in his chair, took another swig of his Mojito, and put another hundred dollars in Sweet Red's outstretched hand. She looked back at Castilleo, crunched the Dum Dum, and jiggled the other cheek.

Both Castilleo and Kordell broke out in a cold sweat. Kordell grabbed a red linen napkin and mopped the top of his bald head. He always bragged to his posse that the ladies called him Herr Doktor because he had the cure for what ailed them. But sitting here watching Sweet Red work that thang like that gave Kordell cause to pause a moment, and contemplate if he was the one who needed to see the doctor.

Kordell winked at Sweet Red, who pretended that she was moved by this football-player-looking basketball coach with the gleaming pomegranate-shaped head. She knew that he fancied himself a ladies' man and believed his own hype that he had some serious game. Sweet Red had taken one look at Kordell Bivens in that JCPenney special and quickly discerned that he was cheap. It was clear that this Kordell planned to bamboozle the younger coach into spending all of his money on the dance Kordell was dying to see.

But that was just fine with Sweet Red. She knew that the boss was settling a score with the younger coach and had decided to hit him where it hurt—his pockets. On the other hand, the big pomegranate-head negro just needed to be played. She could look in his eyes and tell that he thought he had special powers where the ladies were concerned. Sweet Red knew men who sincerely had it going on with the sisters—her boss, Pierre Smith, and Coach Parker just to name a few. This joker, however, didn't have anything close to the class and down-home dap that those three men possessed.

Sweet Red knew that this negro was hoarding his money for a private dance. She was going to give him a private dance he'd never forget. And just when he thought he had her right in the palm of his hand, Sweet Red was going to collect all of her money and then give him her gangsta cousin Lil' Too Too's cell phone number when he asked the inevitable question, "When can I see you again?"

Sweet Red and Lil' Too Too had an understanding—she paid him one hundred dollars a month just to threaten and cuss out everybody calling his number looking for "that fine thang from the strip club." Lil' Too Too stayed in trouble at school and relished the opportunity to act bad for the right reason. Plus, Sweet Red didn't even sleep around. Her man was in the Navy, and she was dancing to pay the bills and help them save money to buy a house when he came back from his tour of duty.

Sweet Red winked at Kordell, and then clapped her booty real close to Castilleo's face. When he picked that barf bag back up, she dropped down and then went into a split and came back up with such grace even Charles wanted to see her do that move again. Castilleo was still breathing in the bag and Sweet Red was now popping her booty to the remainder of the song, and kept popping right into the new song, "Big Things Poppin'" by TI.

She clapped her booty one more time, and held that clap until she saw Castilleo pull out a hundred dollars. This time she frowned and made as if to walk off. Castilleo reached back into his wallet and put what was left on the table. Sweet Red smiled and plopped her butt on that table and picked up the money with her behind.

The coaches were beating on the tables and giving wolf calls. Sonny Todd had moved from his spot over in the cut on the window seat to a chair with a much better view. And Kordell was now on the lookout for another mark to pay the sweet red thang enough money to keep the floor show going. This girl was good—she was doing all that dancing and there wasn't a pole in sight.

Charles, smooth as can be, clapped Curtis on the shoulder. He had gotten up and stood next to Charles so he could get an eyeful of this incredible floor show.

"Coach," Charles said. "I need to speak to you for a minute."

He made sure the other coaches were so deep into Sweet Red that they had absolutely no interest in anything Curtis was doing. Curtis glanced backward at Sweet Red for a hot second and followed Charles. He was relieved that he didn't have to stay in the room with the other coaches. Not that Sweet Red wasn't entertaining—the girl was putting a hurting on that dance floor. Good or not, though, Curtis found that he wasn't in the mood to be up here today. He was glad to go and hang out with Charles. As good as Sweet Red was, the last thing he wanted to look at was some woman popping her butt around—especially a woman he did not know.

Charles knew Curtis didn't have any business in Rumpshakers. If Eva T. had not been the host school for this meeting, he would have told his boy to go home, go see his grandmother, go and try to talk to that fine Yvonne Fountain over in the Department of Design at Eva T. Go and break off that foolishness with Regina Young. Go and do anything but hang around up here.

Plus, Charles knew Regina because he had tapped that tail on several occasions before she got hooked up with Curtis. That's how he knew, firsthand, that Regina wasn't worth the thread used to tie in the hair on that fancy weave.

She couldn't even be classified. The girl wasn't a gold digger—she had plenty of money of her own. She had just enough class to get past being a skank. She was a skeezer of sorts, but again had too much class to remain in that classification for too long. And she was too stiff and boring to qualify as a hoochie.

That made the girl dangerous. A brother could get an angle on a woman with one of the above classifications. But a woman like Regina could get you twisted up in a foul game that was hard to end because you couldn't dig into a little bag of tricks and pull up a simple formula for handling gold diggers, skanks, skeezers, and hoochies.

These groups of women may have had high drama indexes but they could be handled. Furthermore, they could handle what you dished out. They knew they fit a high-drama index classification, and were well schooled concerning what could happen between them and their man at any given time.

Regina, who thought she was above all of that, demanded everything she didn't deserve from a brother. She expected to be treated with a level of respect she wasn't in any way inclined to give back. And she insisted on a brother being loyal and honest at a level she wasn't even capable of thinking about giving back to him. That was why the girl could be all up under Curtis, block his ability to find the right kind of woman, and then go off and sleep with his boss, Gilead Jackson, when she felt the need for some variety in her life.

Sometimes Regina Young reminded Charles of his cousin

Marquita's trifling husband, Rico. His sister, his mama, and his Aunt Margarita could not stand Rico, or any of his people. Aunt Margarita always said that those Sneeds thought they were so much better than everybody else, even when they were still living in the old Cashmere Estates, using food stamps and eating government cheese just like everybody else.

Charles didn't like any of those Sneeds, either. They were the meanest, nastiest, and coldest people he'd ever met. Charles's folks were hustlers and hood rats. But the Sneeds were hateful, and they talked to folks any kind of way—just saying anything, no matter how nasty, spiteful, and hurtful it was. Aunt Margarita made it her business to stay away from those people. Said she'd never met such a bunch of plain and mediocre negroes who were always prancing around being mean and acting like they were the cat's meow.

Whenever Charles and his sister, Charmayne, talked about Rico and his mean family, they couldn't help but think about the need to be in church and getting right with God. If there was ever a reminder of what people acted like when they didn't know the Lord, it was the Sneed family. Even though the two of them were out in the world, they knew about church and living for the Lord. They had been visiting Fayetteville Street Gospel United Church for so long, folks didn't even know that they were not members.

Charmayne had once told him that there were times when she thought about getting saved and making Jesus Lord of her life while she was still ahead. That day Charmayne had put her arms around her baby brother, whom she loved so much, kissed him on the cheek, and then popped him on the back of his head like she had when they were kids and he was getting on her nerves.

"I feel like we are running out of time, Charles. We can't keep running from God and think that things will continue to work for us."

"You really think we are running out of time?" Charles had asked his sister, looking at her with the same expression in his eyes that he had had when they were home alone and he'd asked her when their mama was coming back home.

She hugged him tight with tears in her eyes. Truth was their time to be in the world was almost up. But she didn't have a clue as to how they could let go of all that they were gaining in the world to live for God. She didn't ever want to be broke again, and neither did he.

Charles steered Curtis down a few corridors far away from the music, conversations, and coarse jokes going on in the main section of the club. As far as Charles was concerned, Curtis needed to be as far away from Kordell Bivens and Castilleo Palmer as possible— especially when all of that gyrating and booty-popping was going on.

Charles didn't like Kordell and Castilleo, and he didn't trust them, either. Actually there were very few people Charles Robinson liked, and even fewer that he trusted. Curtis Parker was one, and the others were Maurice Fountain, Obadiah Quincey, and Yarborough and Denzelle Flowers. They weren't his boys, even though he liked and respected them all. But Charles knew that they had integrity and could be trusted.

On the other hand, Charles knew that not one of the men he had left salivating over Sweet Red could be trusted. And out of that group, Kordell Bivens and Castilleo Palmer were the least trustworthy—especially where Curtis was concerned. Charles had good instincts and he always trusted what his gut told him.

He knew, just by watching both Kordell and Castilleo, that they wanted the head coach position at Eva T. so bad they would do anything to get it—including trying to use one of *his* girls to help them get some bogus dirt on Curtis Parker. He didn't know what made those two second-rate coaches believe they were capable of doing Curtis's job. But that is exactly what they thought.

Charles had figured out that Gilead Jackson wanted Kordell and Castilleo to make it hard for Curtis to succeed. And he wanted to know why Gilead didn't want the basketball team to prosper and grow when he stood to gain so much with a winning team—especially one that took a conference title. And it didn't make any sense that Sam Redmond was sitting back and allowing this to happen.

Charles's cell buzzed a text from Pierre that read "Check this out, Boss." Charles turned back to Curtis and said, "Wait here a minute." He opened the door to a private dance room and nodded toward a comfy sofa. "I'll only be a second, man."

"No problem," Curtis answered and sat down, wondering what happened in this room. It didn't necessarily look like the kind of place where the only thing that a brother received was a lap dance. There wasn't even a chair in the room, and he knew that the best lap dances were done with sturdy chairs. At least the best lap dances he'd ever been a party to were done with a sturdy chair.

This room had gold-painted walls, a plush red-and-gold shag carpet, a cushy gold leather sofa, a dark cream Ultrasuede fainting or reclining couch that resembled a daybed, a red silk throw on the reclining couch, a small, high window, and several novelty items in a big red wooden basket with cream silk moire ribbons all over it. Now, Curtis was a grown man who had gotten down and dirty on a few occasions with the kind of girl the late R&B singer Rick James used to sing about. But he'd never, ever been in a room like this, and it made him very uncomfortable. He thought about how Gran Gran always tried to get him to carry a small vial of anointing oil.

Gran Gran had once said, "Baby, you never know when you're gonna run up on or find yourself in a situation where the first thing you are going to want to do is call on the name of Jesus, and then anoint yourself in Jesus's name."

At the time Curtis had thought that Gran Gran was having one of those senior moments and being just a tad over the top. But right now, sitting in this room and looking at that basket with the mysterious stuff in it, made him wish he'd listened to his grandmother and taken that oil she'd purchased for him.

Curtis closed his eyes and touched his fingertips to his heart. He whispered, "Cover me with the blood of Jesus, Lord," and worked overtime to keep his eyes from straying over to that basket. But every time he looked away, it felt as if a string or something were pulling his eyes right back to the spot he kept trying not to see. Finally, Curtis closed his eyes and whispered, "Where is Gran Gran when you need her?"

Pierre buzzed Charles again.

"Where are you, Boss? You need to hurry up so you can see this going down."

"Where are you?" Charles asked as he'd headed toward Pierre's office and then found it locked.

"In the security control room with Bay. He's the one who texted me about this."

Charles turned all the way around and headed back in the direction of his office, where the tightest level of security was. Bay was the head of security, and if he said to come to the control room, where all the monitors for the club were, Charles knew to get there in a hurry.

Charles punched in the security code and hurried into the control room. Pierre and Bay were deep into what was happening on the monitors.

"Check this out, Mr. Robinson," Bay said and pointed to the monitor for the parking lot.

Charles stared at it for a moment and then frowned. He was not happy watching Kordell Bivens, Gilead Jackson, Sam Redmond, Jethro Winters, and Sonny Todd Kilpatrick huddled up together as if they were discussing the next play for a football game. How they had gotten out of the room with Sweet Red, and to that parking lot that fast concerned him. But what made Charles so mad he felt steam blowing out of his ears was the sight of Rico Sneed coming up on the group grinning and puffing on a cigar as if he were somebody worth the time of day.

"What the hell is that negro doing with that pack of wolves, and on *my* parking lot?" Charles demanded.

Pierre shrugged, and Bay said, "That's messed up, Mr. Robinson. Rico is married to your cousin and he should have told you he was coming here with a bunch of men he knows you don't like."

"Yeah, Boss," Pierre said, "that's messed up." He punched his big, meaty hand with his huge fist. "So when are we gonna mess that negro up? He is just getting more and more beside himself—and more and more out of control."

"True that, Mr. Robinson," Bay said, frowning at Rico's image on the monitor. "I know he's married to your cousin and all but there are times when he comes up in here that I want to cuss him clean out. I know Miss Marquita. She is good people. She deserves better than that trash standing out there doing who knows what with God knows whom."

Charles studied Rico for a minute. He could not believe the negro was at his club with those men and dressed to the nines in a suit he'd bought from Charles's suit man, Mr. Booth, who was Sweet Red's uncle and his cook Miss Hattie Lee's brother-in-law. Lowell Booth got his clothes at discounted wholesale rates and was able to sell them at some seriously good prices. Charles bought practically all of his suits from Mr. Booth, and he was one of the best-dressed brothers in Durham.

Rico had never been able to afford suits like the one he was wearing until Charles had turned him on to Mr. Booth. He should have known better. Because now Rico was in Charles's parking lot, wearing a sharp chocolate silk-and-wool suit with mint-colored chalk stripes, full-cut pleated pants, mint shirt, and a chocolate, powder blue, and mint green diamond-print silk tie, making deals with the Devil and betraying his entire family.

"Look, Boss, Rico is ushering them towards the door and they are . . ."

" . . . Coming right in . . . every last one of them," Bay said.

Charles's hazel eyes narrowed into slits.

"Can you get some audio on them, Bay?"

"I can do better than that," Bay answered and started typing in commands on the computer in front of him. "I can go back to when they first pulled up and get the audio on all that."

Bay typed in a few more commands.

The voices came on loud and clear, with Kordell speaking first, confirming Charles's suspicions about him.

"I don't know how you think you are going to pull this off. Both Curtis and Maurice are very good coaches, and they stand a good chance at winning the next game with Bouclair College in spite of any concerns about being ready and which players they can play."

"How did you come to that conclusion?" Sonny Todd snapped. "We have a perfect record and will get that title and all of that money again at the next tournament."

Kordell turned to face Sonny Todd. He said, "The team wants

to beat you bad, and they've been working hard to get ready for this game. But you already know that because I've sent you the DVDs of all of our practice sessions over the last month."

Sonny Todd was quiet for a moment before he said, "So, how are you going to get the 'Mighty Five' out at the beginning of the game? LeDarius Johnson, Earl Paxton Jr., Sherron Grey, Mario Lincoln, and Kaylo Bailey are some top-notch ballers. They will put a hurting on my team if they start at that game."

"I'm working on finding out if they have some problems with grades. So far, the only class we might be able to use against them is that newfangled mess over in the art department," Gilead Jackson said.

He snapped his fingers a couple of times, trying to remember the name of that class.

"Help me, somebody. What is the name of that class? It's worth six hours and taught by Yvonne Copeland."

"Fountain now," Kordell corrected.

"Whatever," Gilead said. "All I know is that a good grade in that course will boost their grade point averages past the red zone if they have some problems in any other classes."

"And take them out if they get a bad grade," Jethro Winters said, grinning. He loved mess. And he was in heaven being able to be all up in the mix at this black school. So much to see and learn. And the women? He felt as if he were going to get the sugar diabetes every time he was on that campus and ran up on some brown sugar.

Sam Redmond frowned and said, "They are at Eva T. to earn an education, not to be taken out, Winters."

Jethro turned a deep shade of red. It was clear that he'd gone too far.

Sonny Todd sighed heavily before he said, "Sam, you are the one who wants to hire me as head coach. And the last time we talked, you were not all that concerned with those boys getting educated."

Sam Redmond squared his shoulders and advanced on Sonny Todd. He said, "What could you possibly know about educating a black man?"

Jethro Winters started looking nervous. He and Sonny Todd

were outnumbered by some big and tense-looking black men. He placed a firm hand on Sonny Todd's shoulder and said, "You need to remember where you are."

Sonny Todd gave Sam Redmond a conciliatory nod.

"I don't want to sound pushy," Jethro Winters began carefully, "but I'm confused as to the significance of this game and Coach Parker keeping his job."

"It's tied to his contract," Gilead Jackson said. "He has to win so many games by a certain time in this season. Or he has to defeat one of Eva T.'s fiercest opponents. Curtis has been on a losing streak for many reasons—real and created."

Gilead made eye contact with Kordell, who sucked on a tooth and gave a sly smile.

Charles slammed his fist on Bay's desk.

"I knew that negro was up to something—I just knew it."

"Shhh . . . shhh . . . shhh," Bay said, waving his hand at Charles. "You are going to miss something. Check this out."

"I'm confused," Jethro Winters said, scratching the back of his head. "How can you fire a man for losing if he's not at the end of his contract? I want Sonny Todd in Coach Parker's spot as badly as the rest of you. But this plan is anything but airtight."

Kordell Bivens, Sam Redmond, and Gilead Jackson all started cracking up. "That is some funny mess," Gilead Jackson said, and then started laughing again. He slapped Jethro on the back. "You a funny white boy. You know that, dawg?"

Once more, Jethro Winters had that uncomfortable look on his face—as if he were hoping some extra white folk would show up in a hurry.

They started laughing again, and this time Sonny Todd joined in with them. He'd been working with a bunch of black men at a black college for a while, and he knew exactly what was so hilarious about Jethro's concerns.

Rico, who was talking on the phone, standing a ways off from the group, came to join them.

"I miss something," he said.

"Not now, dawg," Kordell said.

Rico said, "Okay," and then spoke into the phone, "I'll tell 'Quita I'm going to see Glenda to get my hair cut. And we'll be able to catch a quickie, baby." He paused and pressed at the earpiece before saying, "Naw, baby. That won't be a problem. I'll just tell her that Glenda didn't cut my hair low enough. 'Quita so love-struck over me, she'll believe anything I say."

"One of these days I'm gonna mess that negro up real good," Charles said.

"Will you quit fussin' about that clown and hush," Pierre told him. He felt the same as Charles, and when the time was right, he would tell him all that he and Bay had found out on Rico Sneed. Marquita was his girl, and he'd had enough of watching Rico dog her out behind her back.

"Sam, you have not given me an answer I can work with," Jethro said in a tight voice.

The laughter stopped.

"Jethro," Sam Redmond said, "I'm a black college president. About the only head of anything with more power than me in any organization in the black community is a black preacher."

"Bishop, Sam," Gilead corrected. "The bishops have a whole lot of power."

"I don't know," Sam pressed. "I think it's changing a bit with some of the preachers of these really big churches. They ain't scared of the bishops, and will get them told. So we are back to preachers."

"Bishops, preachers, black college presidents. Will you just tell Jethro what the deal is," Sonny Todd snapped.

"Dang," Bay said in a low voice, "they are really working that white boy's nerves."

"They are working mine, too," Charles said.

"Jethro," Sonny Todd continued, "just joined the board of trustees, he's loaded, and ready to drop some serious cash on the Athletic Department if he understands how this works."

Jethro nodded.

"A clause, a very fine-print clause is available for use at the discretion of the president of Eva T. It says exactly what we've been telling you, Jethro. In any given season, I have the right to override the signed contract if I'm not happy with the coach's performance due to losing too many games or if he loses to one of the top teams in our conference more than once."

"That has to be the dumbest, stupidest mess I've ever heard, anywhere for any reason, created by anyone—black, brown, red, white, and blue," was all Jethro said.

Pierre was cracking up. He said, "Now that is some funny mess. That white boy is right."

"Dumb or not," Sam Redmond said, voice tight, "it is what it is. And I am using the clause. So, if you want to have some allies affiliated with this school when you bid on the contract to build luxury housing for our exclusive and elite faculty, you can rely on Gilead and Sonny Todd to drum up some support from those boosters."

"Your boosters? How can they help?"

"They have money, many of them have clout, and not too few have the kind of influence that will make a difference when you come up against the opposition that will support Lamont Green, who is the number-one draft pick for that contract by half of the trustees."

"Lamont Green," Jethro said incredulously. "I can't believe this mess. I'm going up against Lamont Green? Again? In the black community? Sam, why didn't you tell me any of this before now?"

Sam Redmond rolled his eyes and sighed. "Are you retarded, man? Eva T. is a black college," he said and waved a light brown hand in front of Jethro's face. "We have to have a brother, or a sister, making a bid. So take a chill pill and go somewhere and calm down. I got this."

Jethro opened his mouth to check Sam Redmond when Sonny Todd shook his head, as if to say, "I wouldn't if I were you."

"Okay, Sam," Jethro said, "handle your business. Get Curtis out and Sonny Todd in. Win the money you need for the school. And use your newfound victories to get me in good with some of the same black people who wanted to pimp-slap me when I went after the contract to rebuild Cashmere Estates."

"Yep," Rico Sneed said, coming up from behind, finger adjusting the Bluetooth in his ear, "there were definitely a lot of black folks who had their hands poised for a good pimp-slapping."

Jethro tilted his head to the side and then pointed in Rico's direction. "Who the hell are you?"

Rico opened his mouth but stopped when Kordell shook his head. He adjusted his Bluetooth one more time and walked off to answer another call.

"Who is that negro talking to?" Charles asked, irritated to the point of wanting to go through one of those security monitors to beat the crap out of Rico Sneed.

"A woman," Bay said matter-of-factly.

"Coworker?" Charles asked, knowing that wasn't who it was but hoping for the best anyway. As much as he could not stand Rico, he loved his cousin and couldn't bear the thought of having to watch her mend from a broken heart. Marquita really loved Rico. Charles didn't know why she loved him because he couldn't stand him. Being Rico Sneed's wife definitely qualified Marquita for a nomination to sainthood—*or* a padded room at the nuthouse.

"Okay, if that is what you are now calling the other woman these days," Bay said.

"Huh?" Charles said.

"Coworker, Boss," Pierre said. "You asked if Rico was talking to a coworker."

"Yeah, coworker," was all Charles said.

"I can help you with this Rico thing, Boss," Bay said. "But first, let me help you with this mess brewing around Coach. Nothing about it is right. But let me tell you something, it is gone get right if I have anything to do with it. "

Bay was good with security systems and investigating folks who were not right. He was working on his bachelor's degree at Eva T. in its Crime Scene Investigation Program. Bay could find out anything about anybody, hack into any computer system, and put together anything about anybody who wasn't right.

"Rico ain't right, Mr. Robinson. He plays a good game but he ain't about nothing."

"I hear you, man," Charles said, heart heavy. It wasn't fair that good folk had to suffer at the hands of people like Kordell Bivens and Rico Sneed. Curtis Parker was one of the best coaches Eva T. had had in close to ten years, and Sam Redmond and Gilead Jackson were ready to sell him up the river for thirty pieces of silver. And Rico. That was working up to something very ugly.

TWELVE

They're getting antsy in the reception room, and ready to get down to business," Pierre said, watching Rico on the monitor covering that area. Rico was wolfing down stuffed baby portobello mushrooms and sipping on Crown Royal. Pierre heard him say, "Pierre is slipping on his job. I'm going to have to talk to Charles about that. Don't know why he lets an employee get away with slacking up on the job like that."

Pierre frowned and said, "As if that clown qualifies for employee of the month. I mean, where does *he* work?"

"Chapel Hill," Bay answered. "Rico works for a consultant firm that designs computer programs for the administrative offices at UNC. I doubt seriously if they know he's taken the afternoon off to spank that thang on Sweet Red."

"Point well taken" was all Pierre said. He stared at the monitor a few more seconds and then asked, "So what do you want me to do to him?"

"Send Fatima in to dance for Rico."

Bay started laughing. "You are so wrong, Mr. Robinson."

Pierre was laughing so hard he had tears in his eyes. Miss Hattie Lee Booth, Rumpshakers' resident gourmet cook, aka Fatima, was on the secret list of dancers hired to run folks away. She used to be one of the top exotic dancers in Durham County—that is, in the late 1960s and early 1970s. Just about every brother in the state made a beeline to the old Lucky Lady Club in the Bottom to watch Fatima dance in one of those old school cages. According to lore, Fatima would turn it out to the point where the bouncers had to stop the patrons from climbing up into one of those cages with her.

But now, Hattie Lee Booth was the proud mother of thirteen children, with twenty-two grandchildren and six great-grands. She was still a voluptuous size ten, and gave new meaning to the term "senior" when she put on her Fatima outfit and started dancing.

Miss Hattie Lee didn't dance like an old lady, either. She knew all of the new dances and could drop it like it's hot with the best of them. Bay and Pierre figured that she had to have been the baddest thing around in stiletto heels when she was young—'cause old girl could dance.

Miss Hattie Lee was what folks in the hood referred to as a *red bone*. She was very pretty, limber, and toned due to decades of dancing. As good as Sweet Red was, she really couldn't hold a candle to what folks said her grandmother was like back in the day. But while Fatima danced when she was needed, Miss Hattie Lee's love was cooking. And her real position at Rumpshakers was as the head cook.

One of the best-kept secrets in Durham County was the quality of the food served at Charles Robinson's establishment. A lot of men, once they sampled the fare and had the pleasure of enjoying Miss Hattie Lee Booth's charming company, couldn't wait to get to that elaborately designed kitchen to eat. Oh, they threw some Benjamins at a few of their favorite dancers, and paid for some good liquor. But then they found their way to that kitchen, pulled out a deck of cards, started a good bid whist game, and made sure they got platefuls of Miss Hattie Lee's exquisite cooking.

Charles and Miss Hattie Lee had an agreement about the dancing. Fatima had two sets of clients. The first were men in their seventies and eighties who came to the club *only* to see Fatima. These men didn't like watching what one man described as "them lil' gals who need to eat a Happy Meal and get some meat on their bones."

The second set were the men Charles didn't want at his establishment and knew that assigning Fatima would be sure to keep them away. These were the ones who couldn't be discouraged with the D and E list dancers because there was always a chance for some undercover activity with one of them. So being given a sixty-nine-year-old great-grandmother to drop it like it's hot was just too much to digest for the men who were out in the parking lot scheming, conniving, and plotting harm to decent folk.

Charles had never seen Miss Hattie Lee dance, out of respect for her. But he had been told that Fatima could work it. One of the older patrons told him that he, Pierre, and Bay didn't know what they were missing. He said, "Boy, Fatima does what me and my partners call the *floor jam*."

Charles closed his eyes, hoping that the old man would not elaborate on this dance. The last image he wanted in his head before he fell asleep was Miss Hattie Lee doing something this old dawg was calling the floor jam. But that hope was in vain. That old man couldn't wait to tell Charles about the floor jam. And neither could his boy, who was next to him, sitting in one of those motor scooters with an oxygen tank and mask attached to the back of it.

"Looka heah," the old man began, "Fatima started doing this twisty move."

He pantomimed what Charles surmised was a gyrating hip roll, only it looked as if he were trying to get some very painful kinks out of his back. His boy in the scooter hit the steering handles and said, "Tell him, tell him, tell him about the part when Fatima dropped down on the floor and started doing this scooching-her-butt-on-the-floor thingy to the music."

"Oh . . . oh . . . he's right, son. That's the move."

"The move," Charles said evenly, hoping they would stop. But they only got more excited and more determined to tell him what Miss Hattie Lee had done to get them so riled up.

"She was all down on the floor dancing and twangling her hips . . ."

"Twangling?" Charles asked. "What in the world is twangling?"

"He young, man. He don't know nothing 'bout no twangling," said the man in the scooter. "But if he did, he sho' wouldn't be standing there with his eyebrows raised and his mouth hanging open like that. 'Cause, whew . . . eee . . . whew! When Fatima got to twangling, I just about . . ."

"Calm down, man," the friend said as he whipped out the mask and flipped on the oxygen machine. "Here, breathe in this."

The friend took the mask and wrapped the elastic part around his head. He took in several deep breaths and then calmed down enough to let the oxygen get him straightened out.

When the friend's breathing stabilized, the man signaled for them to leave. He clasped Charles on the shoulder and said, "I guess you just too young to really appreciate what we trying to tell you."

"Yeah," the friend mumbled through the oxygen mask, "he still got formula on his breath. You give him something hot and spicy like twangling, it ain't gone do nothing but go right through him."

Charles loved himself some Miss Hattie Lee Booth. And it was clear from testimonials such as these that Miss Hattie Lee's services were sorely needed for the pimp-daddy seniors who rolled up to the club's front door riding a medical scooter. As much as Charles loved Miss Hattie Lee, however, he wished that those old men had not shared all of the information about her routine. He was glad they loved her dancing as much as they did. But the mere thought of "twangling" was sure to give poor Charles nightmares.

Charles went back to Curtis and led him to his plush office. He closed the door, and then poured some Patrón into two heavy crystal shot glasses. Curtis, who was relieved to be rescued from that other room, sank down into a luxurious crimson suede chair. He took the glass of liquor out of Charles's hand and leaned back in the chair.

Charles put on a Kem CD and went and sat behind his massive ebony wood desk. He leaned back in an expensive black leather orthopedic chair and sipped on his drink. The view outside of the picture window behind his desk was awesome—a rose garden that was hidden from view of those driving up to the main section of the club, a vegetable garden, and that pond with deer drinking out of it.

Curtis sat up and took a big sip of his own drink.

"Man," he said as he surveyed the rest of the office, with its ebony-colored plank floors, crimson suede chairs, crimson leather love seat, crimson, cream, and charcoal area rug, cream textured walls, and crimson-framed artwork. There were plants everywhere, and a huge crystal vase filled with red roses sitting on the sleek, custom-designed glass table resting on stainless steel legs. "This is sweet."

Curtis sipped some more Patrón and then smiled. "But don't you think you were a bit heavy-handed with all of this crimson and cream?"

"Negro, please," Charles told him. "I'd bet some good money that your office has more than its fair share of purple and gold."

Curtis laughed. He had a huge purple leather chair behind a gold-tinted, pecan wood desk. The walls were a dark cream and the area rug was purple, lavender, cream, gold, and cocoa brown. Every time James Green, and Theresa Hopson's brother, Bug or Calvin Hopson, came by his office, they looked around and started barking and cutting the fool.

"Crimson and cream or not, this is a sweet setup, Charles."

Charles put the drink down and lit up a cigar. He puffed on it a few times and then flashed his famous smile. Rumor had it that Charles had gotten more than his fair share of thongs and string bikinis with that smile.

"Well, you know how it is, Curtis, man," Charles said and went and pinned a pair of sheer gold lace thongs that were lying on his desk on the bulletin board.

It's true, Curtis thought. At first he was impressed. Then his grandmother's teaching took over.

"They're clean, man," Charles said, laughing. "I like getting the panties but a honey has to send a new, clean pair to qualify for the famous Panty Board."

Curtis laughed and asked, "Has anybody ever sent a pair that didn't meet the requirements?"

"Hell yeah, man. I run a strip club. You know somebody has gone there thinking that it'll get them some points. I'm far from being a saint, Curtis, but there are things that just don't cut the mustard with me. And that kind of triflin' mess is one of those things.

"And you know something, man. You would be surprised at the ones who send the dirty draws. Just as stuck-up as they come. Walk around barely speaking to folks they think aren't as good as they are, and *voilà* they ain't nothing but some skanks in some six-hundred-dollar designer shoes and seventy-five-dollar un-washed draws."

Curtis lit up a cigar. He said, "Maybe you need to turn over a new leaf."

"And do what?"

"Go to church?"

Charles started laughing.

"Come on, dawg. You are starting to sound like Aunt Margar-ita and Marquita. Every other day they are asking, 'You been to church, Charles? Are you going to church? You know you need to go to church.'"

"Well, you do need to go to church," Curtis said matter-of-factly.

"I know and I do. You saw me at New Jerusalem."

Curtis raised an eyebrow and said, "And you and Pierre got more entertainment at New Jerusalem that night than anybody ever got right here at Rumpshakers."

Charles tilted his head to the side and grinned. He said, "So what you are telling me is that you were bored stupid up in that pulpit watching the headliner floor show."

Curtis chuckled. "So I was entertained. Who wouldn't be watching *Chutch Gurls Gone Wild*? But that still doesn't change the fact that you need to go to church, and not for the entertainment, either."

"No, it doesn't," Charles told him. "But you, Coach, need to be in church more than I do. You got a mess on your hands over at Eva T. Plus, you were fidgeting and squirming more than I was when Denzelle ran down to the altar. Don't think I wasn't watching you, Curtis. I had to focus on something to keep from going down there myself. Nothing more emotional than watching a hardcore and ef-fective playah turning in his card to Jesus—especially when it's one of your frat brothers."

"I guess Heaven needs to be filled to the brim with the men of Kappa Alpha Psi fraternity, huh?" Curtis asked drily.

"You want it full of Omegas?"

"Why not?" Curtis asked him with a crooked grin spreading across his face. "'Cause, I mean, we all know that the streets are definitely paved with gold."

"Negro, please," Charles said. "But, uh . . . on a more positive note, *dawg*, you might want to rethink that Kappas-in-Heaven thang. 'Cause you know Yvonne's daddy will bleed crimson and cream if you cut him."

"Oooo," Curtis said and gulped down some more of his liquor. He'd forgotten that Marvin Fountain was one of those fifty-some-odd-year Kappas. He drained his glass and looked around for something to set it on.

Charles handed him a crimson leather coaster with Kappa Alpha Psi stamped on it in very pale gold. He said, "Thought you could use this."

"Negro, shut up" was all Curtis said.

"But I'll tell you this much, Curtis, there are some fine women sitting up in Denzelle's church. I kinda felt sorry for the brother after he went down to that altar, 'cause . . . whew . . . he was giving up a lot! That is definitely a church I need to spend more time at."

"I hear ya', dawg," Curtis told him, thinking that Charles wasn't fooling anybody. That negro knew he was going over to Denzelle's church because that was where Veronica Washington was. Curtis had watched Charles checking Veronica out on several occasions, and the boy had it bad for that girl. Only problem was that Miss Thing was super-saved, and the only way he was going to roll up on that sister was via the Lord.

The room was quiet for a moment before Charles said, "Curtis, man, you need to get up out of here. Rumpshakers ain't a place for a brother like yourself. There're some sweet girls here. They work hard and they are straight up. But I have yet to encounter one who knew about the Lord or was contemplating trying to make His acquaintance."

Curtis couldn't say a word. He was convicted down to the bone.

Maurice had been getting on him about coming to Rumpshakers for some time now. But Curtis *knew* he was wrong to come here when the owner told him that his butt didn't need to be in his establishment.

Charles's cell buzzed. He flicked it open.

"Yeah. He's still here. Okay, man. Come on down."

Curtis raised an eyebrow.

Charles flipped the cell closed and said, "It's all good."

"Why don't you have a Bluetooth?"

"Awww, man," Charles said. "I know I should but I can't stand that thing in my ear."

There was a heavy-fisted knock on the door.

"Come on in, Bay," Charles said. Bay was the only person who worked for him with such a distinctive sound to his knock. Charles couldn't even describe what distinguished Bay's knock. But he always knew when Bay was knocking on the door.

"Coach, you need to check this out," Bay said and handed Charles and Curtis some information he'd just pulled off the Internet.

Curtis scanned the first page and frowned.

"Is this my contract?"

"Yeah. But it's the part that you've never seen," Bay told him.

Curtis read all three pages quickly.

"Is this saying what I think it is saying?"

"Ummm . . . hmmm," Bay said. "It is saying exactly what you think it is saying. In any given season, Sam Redmond can terminate you at will if you don't win a certain amount of games."

"Is there a number of games to be won?"

"Nope, not really. The number is at Dr. Redmond's discretion. And he is planning on using one of his discretionary numbers at your expense in a couple of weeks."

Curtis sat back and ran his hands across his head. He knew that his job—and Maurice's for that matter—was on the line. He knew that it wasn't due to anything that he'd done or hadn't done. But he also thought that he had time to fix it.

"Uh, Bay, how did you get this? Why are you showing it to me?"

Bay smiled and pulled up a seat. It was at times like these that he loved his work and being able to make a difference in someone's life. He'd recently turned his life over to the Lord, and knew that he'd have to leave this job at some point. But while he was here, he'd used his gifts and talents to help as many people as he could. Bay felt blessed that he had stayed at Rumpshakers long enough to help two people he thought very highly of—Coach Curtis Parker and Marquita Robinson Sneed.

"Coach, I got it after I discovered the plot that is on this DVD to snatch your job right out from under you for all of the wrong reasons." Bay put a copy of the DVD chronicling what he and Pierre and Mr. Robinson had recently witnessed in Curtis's hand. "This is a copy of a meeting between Sam Redmond, Kordell Bivens, Sonny Todd Kilpatrick, Jethro Winters, Gilead Jackson, and Rico Sneed."

"Rico Sneed," Curtis asked, trying to figure out what in the world Rico Sneed was doing all up in the mix with anything that had to do with the basketball program. Come to think of it, he wanted to know why Jethro Winters was there, too.

"Sam Redmond wants to fire you and give Sonny Todd your job. Gilead Jackson and Kordell Bivens have been working overtime to make it hard for you. And I'd bet some money that some of your losses were not by accident. Some were setups. Jethro Winters wants the contract to build the luxury housing development the university wants for its elite faculty members. You know about that project, don't you?"

Curtis nodded. "But," he said, "what I don't understand is how the rest of all of this fits with that. Jethro Winters is always trying to find a way to make a big buck off of black folk."

"They believe that if they hire Sonny Todd, he'll win the conference title, the school will get a lot of money, folks will be happy, and they will be able to use this newfound clout to garner support for Jethro being awarded the contract. And don't forget that if Jethro gets that contract, then Sam Redmond and Gilead Jackson will get more money to line their pockets."

"And Kordell Bivens. What does he get?" Curtis asked.

"Honestly, Coach, I think he'll get to continue doing what he is already doing, just with more money."

"But he doesn't do anything," Curtis said.

"Well, he can keep doing nothing. He'll just make more money doing it."

"So what am I to do with all of this?"

"Put your foot all the way up their behinds and twist it around a few minutes before you pull it back out."

Curtis raised an eyebrow.

"You didn't read all of the information I gave you."

Curtis flipped through the rest of the pages and grinned. He said, "Sam Redmond gets to select the number of games I have to win so he can fire me. He gets to select the team I have to replay so he can fire me. But I get to control when and where the game is played. Is that right?"

Bay nodded, grinning. Most folk wouldn't see that last part as a reason to get glad in the midst of a storm brewing. But he knew that Curtis Parker would see this as the opportunity of a lifetime. Coach loved a good fight—especially a fight that gave the appearance of a no-win situation. And if winning was on the side of right—Coach Parker was good to go.

"Bay is the man," Charles said. "So what are you going to do now?"

"I am going to follow procedure, request a rematch with Sonny Todd's team—"

"I thought you all already had that in about two weeks," Charles said.

"He has six weeks," Bay said, grinning from ear to ear as he gave Curtis some dap.

"I like the way you think, Bay," Curtis said.

"Could somebody clue me in?" Charles asked. There was nothing about this that made sense to him.

"You keep up with Coach's stats, right?"

Charles nodded.

"But do you keep up with Coach Kilpatrick's stats?"

"No."

"You ought to," Bay told him. "See, Sonny Todd is strongest at the front end of the season. Coach here gets stronger and stronger as the season progresses. Sonny Todd's players are reckless and aggressive. So the best ones get hurt or kicked out of the game by season's end. And Coach's best players get better and stronger as the season progresses."

"So how does that work for Curtis? And why is it that Sonny Todd wins most times?"

"The president of Bouclair College lets him do his own schedule and he knows exactly who to play and when. Plus, Sonny Todd is the conference champ and gets first dibs on the schedule. And the coaches who get pissed and protest the schedule—"

"Coaches like Curtis?" Charles queried.

"Yeah, the coaches in SNAC like Curtis—the ones who know that Sonny Todd should not have that kind of carte blanche in the conference—those are the coaches who are either bought off, up for new contracts, or have athletic directors like Gilead Jackson, who are on the take and run roughshod over the coaches demanding to have the schedule modified to their specifications."

"That is triflin'," Charles said. "Curtis, you and I both know some serious criminals from back in the day who would never do something as low and raunchy as that."

Curtis nodded. Charles was right. They had grown up with some thugs who had matured into some of the biggest and most dangerous underworld figures in the area. And not one of those men, as scary as they were, would stoop to do something that low. They had standards—that's why they were so good at doing wrong.

"Coach," Bay said, "I've pulled up this info on Sonny Todd."

He put a folder in Curtis's hands.

"You need to play him after Thanksgiving break, right when you get ready to go into finals. You'll see after reading that information that this is when Sonny Todd is at his weakest. So ask for these dates—November thirtieth or December third."

"Done," Curtis said and stood up. "I better get going. There is a lot to be done and I need to get up with Maurice."

"And you need to get up with the Lord," Bay said in a serious voice. "You've been blessed, Coach. God is letting you know that

He has your back. So what are you going to do about your relation-ship with the Lord?"

Curtis didn't say anything. He didn't know what to say. Here he was at the hottest strip club in Durham, and everything coming out of the mouths of the folks who worked here was about the Lord. If that wasn't a trip. But Gran Gran always told him that the Lord worked in mysterious ways. Couldn't get much more mysterious than this.

Bay sighed heavily, not caring if they saw him look up and then heard him say, "Jesus, give me strength." He said, "Coach, the Lord just dropped this in my spirit. Look, you can beat this thing. I'm telling you, as bad as it looks, this is a win-win, pimp-slap-Goliath-and-his-mama-too situation. But the only way you are go-ing to triumph is to get right with God and let Him direct your path. Please, Coach, go to church this weekend, fall on the mercy seat, rededicate your life to the Lord, and let God get the glory.

"Because guess what? This really ain't about you or that team or your job or winning against Sonny Todd Kilpatrick. This is about you letting folks see God working in your life and letting folks see the difference between being a Kingdom man, a carnal man, and a man of the world. As crazy as this must sound, this game is all about God."

Curtis nodded. He knew that was a true Word from the Lord. Gran Gran had pretty much told him the exact same thing about a week ago.

"I'm outta here. It's been real."

"See you in church on Sunday, man," Charles said.

"You'll be there?" Curtis asked. "I thought you were headed over to Raleigh to help out a frat brother in distress."

"Heck yeah, I'll be at Fayetteville this Sunday. Do you honestly think that I am going to miss seeing you falling prostrate on the altar of the Lord? Man, that will be almost as good as what hap-pened at New Jerusalem."

"Whew!" Bay said, eyes lighting up. "That thang was something. I found the whole episode on YouTube. And that soloist? Baby had a booty hanging off of her that made getting pimp-slapped by her worth it. She could slap me any day, if she just let me bounce the palm of my hand off of *that* thang."

Bay slapped his palm in the air to emphasize his point.

"Bay, I thought you were now among the redeemed," Charles told him. "You can't go around harping on the booty like that."

Bay grinned and said, "I was having a moment in the flesh." He then waved at them and went back to his office to keep tabs on all the lowlives doing business at Rumpshakers today.

THIRTEEN

Yvonne eased into one of the many parking spaces surrounding the Athletic Center, trying not to fuss about the injustice of this parking lot situation. It got on her nerves so bad that the Athletic Department was so selfish about this. She kept threatening to park in Gilead Jackson's spot. But she always changed her mind when she thought about her baby languishing in that Chapel Hill towing parking lot, surrounded by all of those mean dogs.

Yvonne was ten minutes early for her nine-thirty meeting with members of the basketball team's coaching staff and the athletic director about five of the players who were taking her class. She didn't have a clue what this meeting was about, and hoped Maurice would be there. Yvonne did not like Gilead Jackson, Kordell Bivens, or Castilleo Palmer, and didn't want to be in a meeting with those men minus somebody who she knew had her back.

She finished listening to one of her favorite songs, "Jericho" by Senior Pastor Jason Nelson of Greater Bethlehem Temple Apostolic Church in Randalstown, Maryland, right outside of Baltimore. His twin brother, Jonathan, had lit up the gospel music charts with his song "My Name Is Victory," and was about to do it again with his newest song, "Right Now Praise." Those twins were some singing fools, and their older brother, James, could preach your shoes off your feet and put them back on, laces tied to perfection. "Jericho" was an upbeat song filled to the brim with Holy Ghost power for being victorious on the battlefield of spiritual warfare. And Yvonne knew she did not need to waltz herself in that meeting without getting girded up just like the Word instructed her to do at the end of Ephesians 6.

Something wasn't right about this meeting. Yvonne didn't know what it was. But she knew in her heart that something was up. She dug around in her purse and pulled out a tiny vial of anointing oil, put a few drops in her hand, and anointed her head.

"Lord, keep a blood covering over me in Jesus's name. Father, give me wisdom and the courage to do Your will in this situation. In Jesus's name I pray, amen."

Yvonne got out of the car and made her way to the conference room, which Maurice had told her was on the first floor. This was an impressive building and it was clear that the school had dropped a whole lot of money in it. But she thought her building was much nicer—even if it didn't have enough parking spaces. There were some definite advantages to being in the Department of Design. They could make sure that their building represented what was going on inside.

Yvonne loved her job. It was the first time in a long while that she'd had a job where she got to do what she loved to do—interior and exterior design, painting, furniture design, and teaching. She worked with some of the kindest and sweetest people on campus, and had great hours for a single mom.

The only problem was that a lot of folk in her department, Yvonne included, did not have permanent, tenure-track appointments. They were contracted annually as consultants, and without benefits. She was paid well—69,000 dollars a year with bonuses for off-campus contracting. But she knew that she needed to be given a permanent, tenure-track position with benefits.

Still, she couldn't complain because this job had been a blessing. And as her mother told her, God would step in and fix it all in due season. All she had to do was continue to work hard and stay strong in her faith in the Lord. Her main job was to trust Him and He would do the rest. A simple requirement that at times was one of the hardest things a child of the King had to learn to do.

Over the past two years, Yvonne had been able to become debt-free and buy a new car, and could afford a lovely three-bedroom cottage in Cashmere Estates. Right now money, unlike two years ago, wasn't a problem. But she needed and wanted and deserved more job security. Yvonne was learning, up close and personal, what it really meant to walk by faith.

There were times when it was scary. She'd walk through her house at night, when it was peaceful and the girls were in their rooms happy and content. Then the temporariness of her job situation would send a wave of fear through her entire being. The first time that happened, Yvonne thought she'd lose it. She went and sat on the side of her bed and cried like a baby.

She had come so far and life was so good. Yvonne and the girls loved their home, they had great neighbors, and she was enjoying life for the first time in many years. The mere thought of having to go back to where she had been when Darrell put her out was unbearable. In that scariest moment, Yvonne picked up her Bible and searched for a Word concerning her situation. The only words that she kept hearing spoken softly and gently to her heart were, "Trust Me." She then turned to Hebrews 11:1, where she was reminded that faith was "*the confident assurance that what we hope for is going to happen. It is the evidence of things we cannot yet see.*"

God blessed Yvonne in that moment and reminded her to remain confidently assured that her hope for a permanent position was going to happen. He also let her know, just as He did Joshua, that He would never leave her or forsake her. Right now, while looking for the conference room, Yvonne was reminded that no matter how things appeared, God was right there by her side.

Yvonne walked down the hall of the Athletic Center. Judging from the austere black carpet and gray walls with red stripes painted in the middle, it was clear that nobody in this department had taken it upon themselves to call her people for some much-needed help and advice.

If Yvonne had been on the design team, she would have laid down black Berber tile carpet, painted the walls a deep smoky gray, and used a brick red on the molding and trim. She would have had the uniforms of past star players on the wall in steel-gray frames. And instead of the plain industrial track lighting, she would have opted for stainless steel lamps that hung low from the ceiling all the way down the wide entry hall.

She found the plain gray door leading to the conference room. It was a lot better than the rest of the area she'd seen, but it had a long way to go before it would measure up to her department's standards. She could not believe that somebody had ordered that long wooden table in a generic brown that did nothing for the rest of the room. All that was needed was a heavy glass conference table with stainless steel trim and legs, surrounded by black mesh high-back chairs with the same stainless steel trim.

Yvonne was the first one there and had her pick of where to sit. The only problem with this plan, though, was that she didn't have a clue as to where the head of the table was. There was no telling where the person running the meeting was going to sit.

Curtis walked into the room and lit up in a bright smile when he saw Yvonne sitting at the conference table. He had not seen her since they all had dinner in Raleigh, and he had forgotten how good he felt when he was around that girl.

"Hey, lady, how you be?"

"Good morning, Coach," Yvonne said in a very polite and formal voice. She had figured that Curtis would be at the meeting and thought it would be easier to see him in a business setting. She and Curtis had had so much fun together in Raleigh, and it was hard for her to believe he could have that much fun with her and then go off and never even think about getting in contact with her. Maybe it was a guy thing, and she wouldn't understand.

Curtis was caught off guard by Yvonne's cold response to him. The last time they saw each other had been wonderful. Yvonne had been so sweet and warm until he couldn't even sleep for thinking about her. Now she was acting as if he'd done something wrong . . .

Shoot, he thought. Curtis remembered that he'd asked Yvonne if she'd like to have lunch with him on campus. She told him yes, and made it clear that she looked forward to spending more time in his company. Curtis had been around scheming and conniving skeezer types for so long, he'd forgotten what a woman with a genuine reaction to you was like.

He'd also forgotten that genuine and honest women would think that you were jive and playing games if you never followed up on suggestions that you made without their prompting to get together. So of course the girl would be cold and distant. He had given the distinct impression that he liked her and wanted to see her again, and then hadn't had the decency to make good on his own promise. Curtis smiled again. Yvonne liked him and that was a good thing.

"Let's try this again," he said.

Yvonne just looked at him and then put her chin in her hands, elbows on the table.

"I . . . I . . ." he began, not really knowing how to say this in a cool way, and feeling as if he were suddenly thirteen years old again.

"Let me see if I can help you out, Coach," she said. "You made it clear that we should get together for lunch, and then just went about your merry way when it occurred to you that *you're just not that into me*."

Yvonne had been on her own with her girls for two years. In that time, not one man worth a nanosecond of her time had expressed any interest in her. In fact, they acted as if she were invisible. And right now she just didn't have the patience to pacify a man who enjoyed her company on a short-term basis but was just too much of an idiot to see what a jewel she was. The good thing is that Yvonne knew she was a jewel. It just hurt sometimes that there wasn't a man around with sense enough to see that she was and act like it.

Curtis opened his mouth to dispute that foolish claim. He was very into Yvonne and regretted how he'd handled her. She was kind, honest, and forthright. And she wasn't trying to play games and not act as if she didn't want to be around him. It felt good for a woman to react to him like that.

The door to the conference room opened and Gilead Jackson, Kordell Bivens, and Regina Young walked in. Regina took one look at Yvonne, turned up her nose, and promptly went over to Curtis to make sure that Polly Pocket–looking heifer knew to back off and stay away from her man. Plus, she didn't like the way Curtis was acting around that woman. He was just too comfortable, content, and slaphappy to be with her. In fact, if her eyes served her right,

Curtis was acting just as Maurice Fountain carried on when Trina was around.

Gilead was not happy that Regina had her butt all hunched up on her shoulders over Curtis Parker's reaction to Yvonne Copeland, Fountain, or whatever her name was. He'd left home at five a.m., under the guise of going to work out, just so he could spend a few hours in Regina's bed. They had been some good, freaky hours, too. Gilead wondered if Curtis knew that his woman was the kind of freak "you don't take home to Mother."

Maybe not, he surmised. Regina complained endlessly about having to be around Miss Doreatha Parker and Curtis's mother, Miss Daphine. She wasn't into mothers—especially the mothers of men like Curtis Parker and Maurice Fountain. They were the kind of mamas who always saw past the smoke screen of a woman who didn't mean right by their boys.

Regina has some nerve, Gilead thought, watching her slip her hand through Curtis Parker's arm and press into him. *And she really believes the world revolves around her.*

Curtis had been trying to catch up with Regina for two days but to no avail. She'd been avoiding him and he didn't know why. But what he did know was that he didn't appreciate this mess, and especially in front of Yvonne. It was clear that Regina was blocking. And judging from the expression on Yvonne's face, she was doing a bang-up job at it, too.

He pulled away from Regina, and went and took a seat next to Yvonne, who got up and moved. She did not want to be bothered with anybody in this room. She didn't want to be at this meeting because she suspected that it was about some mess. And right now she did not want to sit next to Curtis, who apparently did not want to sit with Regina, who definitely didn't want this man anywhere near her.

"Coach Jackson, you called my department and demanded that I be at a meeting concerning some of Coach Parker's players. My time is short and precious. I'd like to know why I need to be here like this."

Kordell Bivens tried to hide his surprise. He'd never pegged

Yvonne Fountain as somebody with enough guts to speak up. She always struck him as a woman who was concerned with making sure she did and said the right thing. Kordell couldn't recall ever hearing Yvonne raise her voice to anybody.

Yvonne glanced over at Kordell and suppressed an urge to cut her eyes at him. She didn't like him for the sole reason that he was best friends with Rico Sneed, and was always helping Rico get away with his dirt at Marquita's expense. If that negro wasn't so big and mean-looking, she would have gotten up, gone to his side of the table, and slapped the ugly off of him. But on second thought, she could hurt herself trying to slap all the ugly off of that man.

Gilead wasn't used to small-fry faculty talking to him like that. Because it was rare that an untenured, non-tenure-track member of the faculty like Yvonne had the gumption to face off with Gilead. A lot of people at the university were afraid of Gilead. He had a lot of pull with the president and could execute a hit on an employee's job in a heartbeat.

"Are you tenure track, Ms. Copeland?"

"Fountain. My last name is Fountain, Gilead," Yvonne responded, knowing that she was pushing the envelope calling him by his first name. But she didn't care right now. It was turning out to be a very bad morning and she just wasn't up to being nice.

"Well then, *Yvonne*," Gilead stated with a sly grin on his face. "Did you know that Sam Redmond is intent on hiring Dr. Darrell Copeland, who I believe is your ex-husband?"

Yvonne stood up and picked up her things. She didn't know where this man was going with this mess but she wasn't going to take it from him. Regina stared at Yvonne, surprised. She had no idea that Darrell Copeland was her babies' daddy. Wonders never ceased.

"And his wife, Dr. Bettina Copeland, needs a job. We are looking for funding to pay her. Your job is eating up money that could be used as salary for a *real* faculty member—not some jacked-up janitress."

Yvonne picked up her bag and backed away from the table. She'd heard that Gilead Jackson was mean and nasty and a piece of work. But no one had ever told her that this man was just plain evil. She looked up quickly, hoping that she'd successfully pushed back her tears.

Regina wrote a note and passed it over to Kordell. It said, "Let's see 'Polly Pocket' get out of this one. You think Jesus gone swoop down and save the day?"

Kordell started laughing. He wondered why folks were always depending on Jesus. Because it was during moments just like these that people needed Jesus to lend them a helping hand. And here was Yvonne Fountain, who was as churchy as Rico's annoying wife, standing there trying not to cry because Jesus had left her out on a ledge—high and dry.

Yvonne fought back those tears and put her hand to her heart. She thought, *Lord, I need You. These people don't fear You and they definitely don't think You are capable of helping me when faced with them. Let them know that this is not the case.*

"Why is Yvonne here, wasting time with the likes of you, Gilead?" Curtis demanded, glad that Maurice, who had been running late, had finally shown up.

"Sorry I'm late. Junior got sick at school and I had to go get him," Maurice said breathlessly. It suddenly occurred to him that there was a whole lot of tension in this room, and that his cousin was standing there looking pissed and trying not to cry.

"I miss something?" he asked, now ready to jump in the fray. He didn't sit back and let people mess over his kinfolk.

"Don't worry, frat, 'cause I got this," Curtis told him. He knew Kordell hated that they were Omegas because he and Rico had never gotten past having their applications to pledge the graduate chapter tossed right in the trash as soon as they were taken out of the mailbox.

"Like I said—why is Yvonne here? And why are you trying to beat her down, Gilead? What is it that you want to bully her into doing?"

It was clear that Gilead did not like being called out like that. He said, "She hasn't turned in grades for three of the players you want to start at the game with Bouclair College. Remember the game you postponed after you whipped out a hidden clause on the president? *Those* players, *dawg.*"

"LeDarius Johnson, Kaylo Bailey, and Sherron Grey have to finish up an exterior painting project for the university's day care center. It's been raining a lot and we had to postpone it, so I sent in incompletes during the midterm grading period."

"So, what you are saying is that without that grade, they are failing, right?" Gilead sneered.

Yvonne had enough of these people. She remembered the scripture *"In this world you will have trials and tribulations. But cheer up, for I have overcome them all,"* and felt a beautiful peace in her spirit. She also knew that just as with Joshua, God was right in this room with her. Her mother was right when she always told her and Rochelle to stay in the scriptures because you never knew when you'd need one at a moment's notice.

"No. Those boys are excellent students and a joy to teach. But this assignment is thirty percent of their grade and I want them to get the A-pluses they have been working so hard for all year. That's why I sent in the incompletes. I wanted them to get the A-plus instead of an A-minus or B-plus."

"Well, what about Sonny Washington III and DeMarcus Brown? I noticed that they have incompletes as well. Are you saying that they are on the verge of an A-plus, too?"

Yvonne started laughing. She could now see where this was going. Trina, as well as Rochelle, who served as legal counsel for the university, had schooled her on what was going on in the Athletic Department. Gilead was trying to bully her so that Curtis Parker couldn't play the players most capable of kicking Bouclair College's butt when they faced off in two weeks. He knew, she knew, everybody on campus knew that Sonny III, or June Bug Washington, and DeMarcus Brown didn't have what it took to take on those thugs from Bouclair College.

The Panthers needed some players who had skills and just enough gangsta in them to know when and how to get down and dirty when they went up against those criminals masquerading as basketball players from Bouclair College. They also needed to start the players who would do what their coach told them to do to win. They needed some players who listened, behaved, could play the game, and had some sense.

"They have incompletes because I'm trying my best not to fail them," Yvonne said as she put her bag back on the table and pulled out a very pretty pink leather Dell laptop.

Yvonne opened the computer and turned it on.

"This will only take a minute. I just got this and it's fast."

Gilead looked at Kordell, who shrugged as if to say, "The heck if I know what this crazy girl is doing."

Yvonne tap, tap, tapped on the laptop keys for about twenty seconds. Regina rapped her fancy red ink pen on the side of the table, hoping that Yvonne would get the message and hurry up with whatever HGTV activity she was taking up their time to do.

"Done," Yvonne said, smiling brightly and looking as if she held the winning ticket for the North Carolina Lottery.

Curtis thought she looked adorable with her face all lit up like that. He made a quick mental comparison between the two women and Yvonne won hands down. Regina was definitely the better dressed of the two women—if you focused solely on the obvious expense of their clothing.

Regina was wearing a forest green two-piece St. John's suit with black suede boots and a black suede shoulder bag. Her immaculate light brown weave with reddish blonde streaks running through it was straight and hanging down around her shoulders. Regina was tall and striking, and she didn't do a thing for Curtis right now. The girl didn't have an ounce of personality. And Curtis was not happy with the way she was suddenly so chummy with Gilead Jackson.

Yvonne didn't have on anything close to what Regina was wearing and she looked ten times better. First, her work attire didn't always call for a business suit. But it was clear that Miss Lady was suited up for work and looking fit and good, too.

Curtis thought her black overalls with the tiny red bows all over them, long-sleeved white tee, red oversize oxford shirt, and red-and-black LeBron James athletic shoes were perfect. Her dark brown curly ponytail was pulled through a black hat with red bows that matched the overalls. Curtis knew that ponytail was real and didn't have an ounce of weave in it. He had to refrain from the urge to tug at it.

Those overalls fit Yvonne's body so well that Curtis could only surmise she'd bought the outfit at Miss Thang's Holy Ghost Corner and Church Woman Boutique. It was the only place he could think of that would have those overalls and the matching hat.

"Do you think you can quit tap-tapping on that laptop before Jesus returns," Regina snapped.

Yvonne cut her eyes at Regina Young and said, "What could you possibly know about Jesus, with all of your rotten fruit clinging to you like mold?"

Gilead and Kordell wanted to say "Ouch" because that little janitor had just sliced Regina down to the bone.

Normally, Regina would have torn somebody talking to her like that to shreds. But she opted to back down this time. The glint in Polly Pocket's eyes let her know that she would do well to leave Yvonne alone.

Plus, she was eager to get on with the business of the day. And after getting exactly what she wanted earlier this morning, Regina knew that Gilead was expecting her to make good on the promises she had vowed to keep during a pivotal moment in their earlier meeting—mainly finding an airtight way to keep Kaylo Bailey, LeDarius Johnson, and Sherron Grey on the bench during the Bouclair College game.

Right now Gilead Jackson was frustrated, exhausted, and mean as a snake. In addition to all of that action with Regina, there was Prudence Baylor, and of course his wife—couldn't forget her. Folks just didn't understand. Life could get real stressful and complicated for a brother like him.

"Done what?" Gilead asked, wondering what all of that tippy-tippy tapping-tapping on that prissy-looking computer had to do with him and this meeting. Yvonne Copeland had been summoned here to sign papers certifying that the three players in question were failing her class. And she was also expected to sign another set of papers that indicated that June Bug Washington and DeMarcus Brown were in good standing and could play in the Bouclair College game.

"I've calculated and sent in the grades for the five players, so that your department can put the three with passing grades in the game, and give June Bug and DeMarcus a helping hand to the bench, where they belong."

"But you can't do that with incompletes," Kordell said, jumping up in Yvonne's face. He could not believe that this goofy little heifer was messing up everything with a click of the mouse on that pink laptop. Who did important business on a *pink* laptop?

Yvonne backed away from Kordell Bivens, reached down in her overall side pocket, and pulled out a pair of red-handled pliers that she kept on hand when working with those athletes. Some of those little negroes could get crazy if grade time clashed with a big game.

Maurice jumped up but wasn't as fast as Curtis, who practically leaped over that table to get at Kordell, who was about to cuss his own self out for acting so impulsively. He was always getting on Rico about acting without thinking things through, and here he was needing to take his own advice.

Kordell backed away from Yvonne fast. But not fast enough to escape Curtis's fist making contact with his face. He fell backward against the wall, and was getting ready to throw his own punch when Maurice body-slammed him against the wall and Yvonne, with her little self, advanced on him with those dainty red pliers.

"Don't you ever, *ever* blink at this girl wrong, Kordell," Curtis hissed. "Or I swear I'll mess you up. I'll mess you up, man—MESS YOU UP."

Regina was now at the door, with all of her fancy, bogusly drawn papers still in her briefcase, while Gilead made a feeble effort to break up the fray between his coaches. He was careful, though. He knew this heifer was Maurice's cousin, and that those Fountains loved a good fight. But he had not expected such a reaction from Curtis Parker—never thought a Goody Two-Shoes like Yvonne Copeland, or whatever her name was, held any appeal for a player like his head basketball coach.

Kordell collected himself and left. As mean and hateful as he was, Kordell Bivens was still smart. He knew that he could not win this fight. In fact, if he stayed a moment longer he was going to get his tail whipped, not to mention lose his prowess as Herr Doktor if Yvonne got a hold of him with those pliers. He'd forgotten how gangsta the Fountains and Parkers were. They had all grown up in Cashmere Estates when it was still the projects. He, on the other hand, had grown up in the middle-class Hillside Park.

"So," Gilead Jackson said, "three players are back in the game, and June Bug and DeMarcus are benched for the rest of the season."

"I didn't know that Kaylo, LeDarius, and Sherron had ever been out, Gilead," Maurice said.

Gilead chose to ignore that comment and said, "So which one of you is going to call the Athletic Department's biggest supporters and tell them that their grandson and son are not eligible to play?"

"You are the only one with Bishop Sonny Washington's and Reverend Marcel Brown's phone numbers, Gilead. So I guess it'll have to be you," Curtis told him and made a gesture toward Yvonne to get her things.

"The Washington and Brown families always express their feelings through their bank accounts," Gilead said. "When they are happy, they give generously to the school and to our department. And when they are pissed, well, I don't want to think about how they'll act when somebody like Yvonne here pisses them off. Humph, they may even let Sam know that he doesn't need people like her here."

Gilead was about to jab his finger in Yvonne's direction but thought better of it when he saw the deadly expression in Curtis Parker's eyes.

Parker's nose is wide open over Polly Pocket. Makes me wonder how that "I love to go to the library" Zeta flew low enough under his radar to get that close to the brother's emotions, Gilead thought.

"Come on, Cuz, let's get out of here," Maurice said, thinking that Gilead Jackson was full of Hell and didn't have any business running the Athletic Department. Sometimes it was so hard to wait on God to work things out. But he knew that this was something that only God could work out. Putting his finger in this pie would be the precursor to creating a great big mess.

Yvonne gathered up her things and hoped that she could keep her tears from falling while she was still in this building. Curtis noticed that she was getting close to losing it. He grabbed her hand and led her out of the conference room.

It was taking everything in him not to wrap the baby up in his arms and make it all better for her. Curtis couldn't remember the last time he had felt like this about a woman. He stood at her car waiting for her to open the door and get in. He liked this car—chic, artsy, and classy, just like Yvonne. Maurice came and stood next to Curtis to make sure his cousin was okay. He hated to see those tears streaming down her cheeks. The girl had already been to Hell and back and didn't need this.

"Baby, don't cry," Curtis said, heedless of the expression on Maurice's face. "Nothing is going to happen to you, your job, and those baby girls. You hear me, Yvonne. Baby, you are going to be all right."

Yvonne nodded and tried to stop the tears. It felt as if the weight of the past two years were pressing down on her like a ton of bricks. Part of her hurt like heck, and the other part felt that she was being washed clean with some kind of sparkling elixir from Heaven. It was a most incredulous, yet confusing feeling.

Curtis took her hand off the steering wheel and kissed it. "You okay now?"

Yvonne nodded and smiled through her tears.

"Where you headed?"

"The hairdresser."

"Will I see you tonight?"

Yvonne sniffed up the last of her tears and said, "Tonight? What's going on tonight?"

"I saw your name on the list of folks with invitations to the Athletic Department's Annual Fall Semester Reception at the Sheraton Imperial."

"You mean 'The Negro Imperial,'" Yvonne told him with a smile. In the middle of all that was going on, she'd almost forgotten about tonight—the main reason for getting her hair done and the makeover her sister had been pestering her to get for months on end.

"That's what I'm talking about," Curtis said. "There is my baby's winning smile."

He conveniently ignored Maurice's poking at him and whispering, "Can you school a bro on what's happening."

"You know that just about everything that's hip, hot, and happening in black Durham goes down at the Sheraton Imperial Hotel."

"True dat," Curtis said. Black folks in Durham loved themselves
some Sheraton Imperial, and were always holding some kind of ma-
jor event there.

"So, Curtis," Yvonne said, smiling, "I'll see you there tonight."

"Why don't you pick her up at the house, dawg? She lives in
Cashmere Estates, less than a mile from your town house."

"Oh, really," Curtis said, grinning. This was getting better and
better. He said, "Well, since we are neighbors, I'll just have to pick
you up fo sho'. What time?"

"Six," Maurice told both of them. "The reception starts at seven,
so pick up Cuz at six."

"Six it is," Curtis said and closed Yvonne's car door. He stood on
the parking lot watching her car until it was no longer in sight.

"You got it bad, you know that don't you, dawg?" Maurice said.

"Forget you, man," Curtis said. But all Maurice did was laugh.
He was enjoying this. Never thought he'd see his best friend fall for
a woman worth falling for.

FOURTEEN

Yvonne was running way behind for her hair appointment. Now that she had her first date in two, no almost twenty years, if she counted the time she was married, the girl definitely wanted to get her hair done. Rochelle had set up four appointments trying to get her in to see Elaine for a new do and makeover. But every time Yvonne had come up with a reason to cancel.

She couldn't explain why she kept canceling. But it had taken this much time for Yvonne to let go of what Rochelle called "The Excessive Intellectual's Wife Do." Rochelle had told her, "Okay, so now that you have been liberated from postmodern I'm-so-smart-I'm-crazy, do you think you'll get the hookup like the regular sistah that you are? Or do you want to walk around looking like Bettina?"

As soon as those words left Rochelle's mouth, Yvonne ran to her bathroom mirror and studied her hair.

"Ooh, yikes. It really is time for a new do."

"Uh-huh," Rochelle said, coming up behind her.

"Yeah, Mommy," D'Relle said, standing next to her sister behind their aunt. "You need some crunk in your system real bad."

Yvonne reached up and touched her bouncing afro puff sitting on top of her head.

"But I don't look as bad as Bettina, do I?"

"Naw. Don't nobody look that bad. You know she got that thang under lock and key," Rochelle said, laughing. "But the point is this—you can look so good. And it's time for you to get out of the rut you've been in, so you can really enjoy moving forward with your life."

"And the bad thing about Bettina," Danesha said, putting in her customary unsolicited two cents, "is that she thinks she looks good. But she don't. And I don't know why Daddy doesn't tell that lady to pull those sundresses she is always wearing out of her booty. It don't look right. And I bet those crease parts that go in Bettina's booty smell like booty."

Yvonne and Rochelle were cracking up. Danesha was the only person they knew who always voiced what everybody else was thinking.

"Yeah," D'Relle said, laughing. "Bettina looks like this in those ugly dresses. Don't know why Daddy won't make her wear some different kinds of clothes."

D'Relle stuck her pants way up in the crack of her butt, sucked in her behind and started walking around. She looked just like Bettina when she was walking around thinking she was all that and a bag of chips with some dip.

Yvonne was making good time until she came up on two red lights that seemed to last forever. When they finally turned green she shot off, only to come upon another set of lights about to turn red. She zipped through those intersections when she knew good and well that those yellow lights were practically orange, they were so close to red. Yvonne was still racing the car as fast as her heartbeat when she came to the third yellow light and decided that it would be a good idea to stop when she reached the intersection.

The car jerked and lunged forward, spilling the contents of her purse on the floor. House keys, lipstick, mirror, gum, change, mints, comb, eyeliner, pen, coupons, tampons, and cleaners' tickets were all over the place.

"Daggone it!" Yvonne exclaimed as she tried to reach down and get her stuff before the light turned green, and then gave up after the car behind her honked for the fourth time.

She slowed down and took a deep breath. It had been a long and emotional morning. First, dealing with Gilead Jackson. And then Kordell Bivens jumping all up in her face, like he was actually going to make her do what they wanted her to do. What was up with that? And who could forget Regina Young, who called herself *going with*

Curtis, and all the time had been sleeping with that nasty Gilead Jackson.

Rochelle kept telling her to take a chill pill where Curtis Parker was concerned because that mess he was doing with Regina had been doomed the day it began.

She said, "Girl, Regina is knocking boots with Gilead Jackson. She's only with Curtis to make Gilead jealous because he keeps her in the cut—something Regina cannot stand. That hussy loves to be in the spotlight when she is kicking it with a man. Plus, if the truth be told, Regina is in love with Charles Robinson. She'd do anything to get Charles to hook up with her again."

"How do you know all of this, Rochelle?"

"Her office is down the hall from mine. Regina is stupid and talks too loud. Plus, she's a Delta—although most of my sorors are not too fond of Soror Young."

"Y'all the ones who let her pledge grad chapter, Rochelle. I told you to tell your girls not to let that skank into the ranks. But y'all wouldn't listen to me."

"No, some of the other sorors wouldn't listen. A handful of them were momentarily bedazzled by her credentials because the girl looks pretty good on paper. But most of us wished they would have turned her down. Honestly, Yvonne, there are times when that girl makes me want to snatch her Delta card out of her hand and cut her with it."

"Well, we wouldn't have had her," Yvonne said.

"You are a Zeta, Yvonne, and you know that Regina was not trying to go for the blue and white. Regina always wants to be part of what she has determined to be the coolest group with the most clout of anything."

"She ain't a Zeta because the finer women of Zeta Phi Beta Sorority Incorporated would not have had her."

Rochelle shook her head. Her sister was all Zeta—earnest, studious, and just as happy to be a Zeta. Yvonne could have pledged any of the other three sororities when she was an undergrad. Both the Deltas and the AKAs came to her and asked her to pledge on their next lines. The only reason she didn't get an invite from Sigma

Gamma Rho was that they didn't have a chapter nearby at the time Yvonne decided to go on line. But for whatever reason, Yvonne appreciated the more low-key and quieter style of her sorors. And despite the jests and teasing, Rochelle believed that being a Zeta suited her sister just fine. Yvonne was a walking, breathing testament to what loyalty and "Finer Womanhood" truly were.

"Why did Charles Robinson quit going with Regina?" Yvonne asked.

"Why does Charles break off with any woman, especially skanks like that ho-hussy-heifer who think that they are more than they are? He gets tired of them, and they get on his nerves. Plus, Charles has a serious crush on Veronica Washington."

"Robert Washington's ex-wife?"

"Ummm, hmmm. Charles would love to hook up with Veronica. He is crazy about that girl."

"But I know for a fact," Yvonne told her sister, "that Veronica is not trying to hook up with another man who doesn't know the Lord—not after what Robert put her through when he left her for that thang up in Baltimore."

"The woman with the head shaped like Stewie's on *Family Guy*?"

"Yeah," Yvonne said, laughing. "Tracey Parsons's head definitely qualifies her as a double for Stewie Griffin."

"When did you see Robert and that woman, Yvonne?"

"At Southpoint Mall."

"So what she look like?" Rochelle asked.

"Okay, Rochelle," Yvonne said real slowly. "Tra-cey looks like Stew-ie with a bunch of blonde braids on his head. Okay?"

"Well then, what did she have on?"

"Blue-jean capris, matching blue-jean slip-on sneakers, and a green-and-blue print T-shirt."

"Oh . . . oh . . . heck-ee naw. Heck to the naw . . ." Rochelle said. "I *know* Robert was not at the mall flaunting *boo-boo kitty head supreme*, and this heifer was wearing blue-jean capris? Girl, do you know how many times *that* negro told Veronica that he hated capris and that she better not wear them out to the mall with him?"

"We have to pray for Robert, Rochelle. He can't help it. Remember, this negro is retarded enough to believe that he is a real player. Veronica told me that Tracey sent Robert an e-mail note to their joint e-mail by accident. Said Stewie was going on and on about how much she *luuuuuvvvveeddd* that negro, and then went on to write some crazy mess like, *You make me feel so . . . so . . . free, so much like a woman, a vixen, a sex kitten, the ultimate hottie.*"

Rochelle was dying with laughter. She said, "That skank is crazy. The only real *hottie* that I know of is Hottie from the first season of *Flavor of Love.*"

Yvonne started to cheer up thinking about her crazy sister. She turned on the radio to hear Cy Young cutting up, and then being on point, when he played "What's My Name" by Brian McKnight.

She bobbed her head around and got in the groove of Mr. McKnight's ultra-smooth and sexy voice as he put a hurting on singing, "what's my name, say it, say it, say it, what's my name."

Her cell buzzed. She picked it up off the seat and realized that there were four missed calls—all from Rochelle. She flipped the phone open right before it clicked off.

"If you'd get a Bluetooth, you'd be able to answer that daggone phone," Rochelle fussed.

"Hello to you, too," Yvonne said, and put the cell on speakerphone.

"Where are you? Are you all right? I just got off the phone with Trina. She said that y'all negroes were getting ready to throw down up in the Athletic Center. And did Kordell Bivens really have the nerve to get all up in your face, Yvonne?"

"Kordell Bivens did what?" Yvonne heard Elaine saying in the background. "I hope they kicked his How-the-Grinch-Stole-Christmas-looking-lips-self behind. I can't stand that man, with those old thick cornhusker-looking legs."

"Yes," Yvonne said, "Kordell tried to get cute with me but Maurice and Curtis nipped it in the bud."

"Oh. Coach was there?"

"Rochelle, the meeting was about basketball players, why wouldn't he be there?"

"Oh, yeah . . . good point. So, what did Coach do?"

"He jumped up in Kordell's face and told him he'd mess him up bad if he ever did anything like that to me again."

"Coach did that for you, Yvonne?" Elaine hollered out.

"Tell her yeah," Yvonne said.

"She heard you because we have you on speakerphone, too."

"How far are you from the shop, Yvonne?"

"Twenty minutes or less, Elaine. Will that cause a problem for you?"

"No. Miss Hattie Lee Booth is on her way. I'll get her going while we are waiting on you. Right now, it's just Rochelle and me in the shop, waiting on you."

"Is that the same Miss Hattie Lee who cooks all of that good food at Rumpshakers?"

"One and the same."

"Elaine," Yvonne began tentatively. She had wanted to ask somebody who could hold their counsel this question for a long time.

"Yeah, sweetie, what you need?"

"Did Miss Hattie Lee ever do any kind of . . . you know . . . dancing? And I don't mean just going to a dance and dancing."

"She used to be a stripper back in the day at the Lucky Lady Club down in the Bottom. Folks say that she was the baddest thing on two legs."

"But has she turned in her pole?"

"Yvonne, you are a nut," Elaine said laughing. "But to answer your question, the answer is no. Miss Hattie is still on the pole. And from what I've heard, she be working it over there at Rumpshakers, too. Put some of those young dancers to shame. And I shouldn't be surprised since she is Sweet Red's and Lil' Too Too's grandmother."

"Who told you that? Somebody you know has seen her dance?"

"Mr. Tommy at you all's church."

Yvonne could hear Rochelle hollering with laughter in the background.

"Y'all know that Mr. Tommy don't miss a thing," Elaine went on. "If something is going down, Mr. Tommy is going to be there, looking over those glasses and making sure he is getting the skinny on everything and everybody."

"What he say, Elaine," Rochelle said. "You know I'd love to be a fly on the wall when Mr. Tommy is watching Miss Hattie Lee do all of that dancing."

"I don't know if I want to see all of that, Rochelle," Yvonne said.

"Mr. Tommy said that Miss Hattie Lee dropped it like it was hot for him one time, and it liked to run his pressure straight through the roof. He said that she made him feel like he was in his prime again," Elaine told them. "He said that he loved how after she got through dancing like that for him, she pulled out pictures of her grandbabies and great-grandbabies. Said looking at those pictures and talking about the grandbabies while Miss Hattie Lee was still in that outfit was almost as good as the dance itself."

"Mr. Tommy knows he needs to stop," Yvonne said. She slowed down. "Elaine, will it be okay if it's more than twenty minutes? I just ran into some roadwork."

"Take your time. I only have two customers coming in this morning—you and Miss Hattie Lee."

FIFTEEN

Your sister will not be here for about thirty minutes," Elaine said.

"You think she is going to back out again?" Rochelle asked.

"Nope. But she is scared to death about going through with this makeover. She wants it and knows she needs it. You know this will be the complete end of who she thought she used to be."

"You're right," Rochelle said and went and pulled out one of Elaine's DVDs. "I didn't know you watched *Apostle Grady Grey's Half an Hour of Holy Ghost Power.*"

"Girl, I love that show—try to catch it whenever it's on."

"Lawd knows I love me some *Grady Grey's Half an Hour of Holy Ghost Power*, too," Rochelle said.

The door opened and Miss Hattie Lee Booth walked in smiling and carrying a plastic container of huge homemade coconut, chocolate chip, raisin, and pecan cookies. Rochelle followed the delicious smell of those baked goods, hoping Miss Hattie Lee had brought them for the people at the shop.

"Here, baby," she said to Elaine, just grinning. "I made these for you and your customers. Get one and taste it."

"Let me wash this stuff off of my hands. You gone have me big as a house with these cookies, Miss Hattie Lee," Elaine said.

"You want one, baby?" Miss Hattie Lee asked as she turned toward Rochelle and held the container of cookies out toward her.

"Yes, ma'am," Rochelle said and took one of those big fat cookies. She bit into it and closed her eyes. It was chewy and so good.

"Are you getting your color touched up, Miss Hattie Lee?"

"Yeah, Elaine. The gray is beginning to show and I need to have it looking better now that I have a new man."

Rochelle gave Miss Hattie Lee a sly once-over. She was really pretty with that blonde hair, pale reddish-brown skin, shapely figure, and a smile that could light up an entire room.

No wonder Mr. Tommy loves going to see her dance, Rochelle thought. *I'd bet some good money that girlfriend can put it on a brother.*

"Yeah, I heard about you and this new man," Elaine told her as she took a cookie and bit into it. "Oooh, this cookie is so good."

"Well, baby, it's about time I got myself a new man. You know it's been four years since Booth passed. Girl, I loved that man. Had thirteen babies by him. And Lawd, if Booth didn't have some good loving. That man put it on me almost until the day he died. Sweet man, too."

Rochelle started blushing and Miss Hattie Lee just laughed and then said, "You know something, Elaine. I didn't think that I would ever want to be all cozy with another man after Booth passed. But then I got to know Tommy and it's like I've been given a new lease on life. And Tommy sweet, just like Booth—neither one of them got issues with my dancing."

Whew, Rochelle thought. *Old people know they be getting busy. Stripping and getting a blonde touch-up 'cause you have a new man. And Mr. Tommy at church*? She knew Mr. Tommy, who was a widower, still had a playah's card tucked away somewhere in his usher suit. But now it appeared as if he'd closed down shop on account of Miss Hattie Lee Booth—one of the hottest old ladies in Durham County.

"Come on, Miss Hattie Lee. Rochelle's sister is stuck in some traffic and running late. I'll have you colored up by the time she gets here."

Miss Hattie Lee sat down in the first comfortable chair she saw.

"Not there, Miss Hattie Lee. Come on over to the bowl."

Elaine washed and rinsed out Miss Hattie Lee's short and very stylishly cut hair. She dried her hair and mixed up some color—dark gold with just a touch of reddish brown in it.

"This is some pretty color, Miss Hattie Lee," Elaine told her. "Mr.

Tommy is going to love how this looks. And knowing that booger, he might snatch you up and try to run off to the nearest hotel with you."

"Well, if I'm at work, won't be no need for all of that. There are plenty of hanky-panky rooms at Rumpshakers if you really need one," she answered with a wink.

"What kind of rooms?" Rochelle asked.

"Hanky-panky."

"What goes on in a hanky-panky room, Miss Hattie Lee?"

"Why, hanky-panky, baby. That's what goes on in a hanky-panky room. I thought that you would know that."

"But isn't that illegal?" Rochelle asked her carefully, wondering how Charles managed to do such a bang-up job getting around the law like that.

"No money changes hands. It's just hanky-panky. It ain't right, baby, but that is what goes on. Only a handful of high rollers with special membership perks have those privileges. Charles is something else. But that boy ain't never been stupid about anything that he does. And he sho' ain't trying to get in trouble with the law.

"There some men who would love to get up in a hanky-panky room and cut up. But they ain't going there. Charles barely letting them through the front door of Rumpshakers as it is."

"I bet Rico Sneed is one," Rochelle said.

Miss Hattie Lee's lips curled up at the mere thought of Julia Sneed's son Rico. She had been sent to dance for him and his boys simply to get rid of them. But Rico had been cheap, and he talked ugly to her and the rest of the girls in that harsh and mean voice of his.

She said, "Yeah, Rico is one of the men who'll never find out the location of one of those hanky-panky rooms. That boy walks around like he thinks he's God's gift to women. But he ain't worth a dried-up piece of dog doo-doo."

"You have a point" was all Rochelle said, nodding her head.

"Rochelle," Elaine said as she brushed the color into Miss Hattie Lee's hair. "Get that DVD case off the shelf and look for a recent airing of Grady Grey's program. We need something refreshing to think about after all of that talk about Julia Sneed's son."

Rochelle reached down to the bottom shelf of the TV stand and pulled out a stack of DVDs in a clear case with GRADY GREY marked on it in a red permanent marker.

"You know," Rochelle said, "Grady Grey was in school with Yvonne at Hillside. But that was before he became an apostle. Remember when he used to run that hot office supply store out of the shed in his grandmother's backyard?"

"Girl, yeah," Elaine said with a chuckle. "Don't you know that a whole bunch of black folk in Durham shopped in that shed? 'Cause Grady Grey had the hookup. His stuff was better than what you could get at the regular office supply store—and a whole lot cheaper, too."

"And did you know that you could put your stuff on layaway? That boy would just charge you a small rental fee for storing your merchandise until it was paid off. Because you know Grady Grey didn't take checks or credit cards, and a lot of the people shopping in that shed didn't have enough money to pay their bill in full and up front."

"How do you know about this, Miss Hattie Lee?" Elaine asked as she rinsed the excess color out of her hair.

"How do you think I know that?" Miss Hattie Lee answered her. "I used to be a dancer at the Lucky Lady Club. I still do a little bit of dancing, and I'm almost seventy years old. Do you really think I had problems putting anything on layaway in Grady Grey's Office Max shed?"

Elaine smiled, dried off the excess water in Miss Hattie Lee's head, and put a plastic cap on her head.

"I see your point. Come on. Let me get you under the dryer for a few minutes to bake this pretty color into your hair."

"But I wanted to watch the DVD with you babies."

"Okay," Elaine said, took the plastic cap off, picked up a bottle of water, spritzed Miss Hattie Lee's head, and put the cap back on. "I don't want your hair to get too dry before you get up under that dryer. Mr. Tommy's not coming over to my shop getting on me about you and this hair."

"What made Grady Grey stop his business and get into preaching?" Rochelle asked as she looked through the DVDs, trying to find the best, most recent episode.

"His baby mama, Linda, got mad at Grady when she found out that he was sleeping around with a *very young* Prudence Baylor when Linda was pregnant with Sherron—the one playing ball for Coach Parker up at the college," Miss Hattie Lee told her. "That Linda saw the two of them going into the motel that used to be behind the Lucky Lady Club."

"What? The Good Sleep Inn?" Elaine asked.

"Thhhhaaattt's the one," Miss Hattie Lee said, and then started laughing. "I bet a quarter of Durham's black population born before 1990, when the motel and the strip club finally closed down, can thank the Good Sleep Inn for helping them get into the world."

"Yes, Lawd," echoed Elaine. "There was some stuff going on up in that motel but I can't really say it was about sleep."

"You all are crazy," Rochelle told them. She remembered the Good Sleep Inn when she was at Hillside. She and her friends used to go to the confectionery across the street from the hotel after school and watch who went in and out of that building.

"Well, I can tell you that Linda Grey followed Grady to the Good Sleep Inn. She sat in that parking lot for a good twenty minutes, and then she walked herself right into that little dinky lobby, asked to use the phone, and reported every single thing Grady Grey was doing to the police. They shut Grady down, and then put him in jail when he couldn't 'rightly 'member' who any of his suppliers were."

"You know," Elaine added, "I remember running into Linda while Grady was in jail, and her telling me that he had gotten saved and turned his life around. With the exception of his Jheri curl, Grady came out of jail a changed man who was determined to marry his baby mama and live right. Linda's mama said that as wild and crazy as Grady can be, he has been a model husband since the day they said 'I do.'"

"Well you know they started out at Jubilee Temple Holiness Church in North Durham," Miss Hattie Lee told them. "And they would have stayed there if the pastor had not asked Grady to start Jubilee Temple Holiness Church II over near Hoover Road."

"You mean that church over near that hotel with who knows what going on in it is Grady Grey's church?" Elaine said.

"Yep. The first Jubilee Temple has some members who used to hang out at that hotel before they got saved. They begged the pastor to put a church over there. Said there were a lot of lost souls who needed to find Jesus. And a whole lot of those people were not going to come all the way to North Durham—many of them didn't even have decent transportation."

"So where is the TV show taped?" Rochelle asked.

"At Grady's church," Miss Hattie Lee answered.

"How do you know so much about that church, Miss Hattie Lee?"

"I go there when I go to church because Grady Grey and his staff is real understanding about the struggles of people like me," she told Rochelle. "He's been getting on me about joining and turning my life over to the Lord but I've got cold feet. I know I'll have to stop the dancing and stop wearing my costumes. And that's just about impossible for me to do right now."

Rochelle thought about a Bible-study series her first lady, Lena Quincey, had taught the Women's Ministry on spiritual strongholds. Miss Hattie Lee was encased in a spiritual stronghold that had come from doing striptease dancing for all of those years. Sometimes, her heart ached when she thought about all of the seemingly innocuous ways the enemy used to get strongholds erected around people. And stripping was an open doorway for the Devil to come into your life—she didn't care what folks said to the contrary.

"Miss Hattie Lee," Rochelle said, "nothing is impossible with God—not even blessing you with the ability to stop the dancing and wanting to wear those costumes."

Elaine could feel the warring tension going through Miss Hattie Lee. Rochelle was right. But Miss Hattie Lee was stubborn and didn't want to give in to what the Lord had been calling her to do for many years. Elaine diffused some of the tension when she said, "Then that explains the interesting set. 'Cause I swear they must be taping that thang out of Mr. Mobley's old cleaners. You know the one that was off of Miami Boulevard."

"That is exactly where the show is taped," Miss Hattie Lee said, her heart feeling the sting of the double-edged sword of God's Word. She hoped she sounded more light and carefree than she felt.

"Grady bought the cleaners from Mr. Mobley and has started building a brand-new church on the old parking lot and land out back."

"Rochelle, have you picked out a show yet?"

"Naw, Elaine. The titles all look so good until I'm not sure which one to choose."

"Get the one where Grady Grey's old cellmate, Huge Hotsy, was a guest."

"Big Dotsy, Miss Hattie Lee," Elaine said as she checked the color and moisture in her hair underneath that plastic cap. She raised it up and spritzed a few times.

"Have you seen that one, Rochelle?"

"Uh-huh. But I want to see it again. Girl, that thang was so good until I had to sign up as a yearlong partner with Apostle Grady Grey Ministries."

"Me, too," Elaine said. "I heard that after the airing of this particular segment, Grady Grey's ratings went up, and his show is now the hottest underground TV program in the Triangle."

"But have you seen the commercials before and after the show?" Rochelle asked, laughing.

"Girl," Elaine said as she slipped the DVD in and turned on the television, "sometimes I watch the broadcast just for the commercials. I have learned about some of the most ghetto-fabulous establishments in all of Durham County watching Grady Grey. But folks tell me those ads have paid off. And right now, I'm wrestling with taking out one myself."

Rochelle cracked up.

"Girl, I can just see you now, with a three-foot lacquered burgundy-and-blue-dyed do to emphasize that you have skills."

"I don't even think I have any blue hair color in the shop," Elaine said.

"So, what you're telling me is that you do have burgundy. 'Cause you know sisters love that burgundy hair color."

"I am ignoring you, Rochelle Fountain," Elaine said as Yvonne rushed into the shop, all ready to get her hair done.

Elaine, Rochelle, and Miss Hattie Lee all waved and pointed to an empty chair.

Yvonne plopped down in the chair and looked at the three of them with a big question all over her face. She touched her head. "But my hair. You are still doing my hair, aren't you, Elaine?"

"Ummm, hmmm. Right after we watch this DVD."

SIXTEEN

Yvonne moved to a more comfortable chair and got settled just as a pulsating high praise song came on while still photos of Grady Grey, along with his wife, First Lady Prophetess Linda Grey, and their four children flashed across the screen. The choir, which had roughly eighteen members on the set, sounded like a powerful seventy-five-voice mass choir.

Their attire was simple, neat, and on the conservative end of ghetto-fabulous. The women were dressed in black oxford cotton shirts, white knee-length A-line skirts, black stockings, and white flats with black patent-leather bows on the toe. The men wore the same style of shirt, baggy khaki pants worn low on the hips, and black Timberlands.

Yvonne, who had never paid any attention to the *Half an Hour of Holy Ghost Power* when her kids were watching it, said, "Do they have on white skirts and black stockings?"

"Shhh!" was the only answer she got.

Those black stockings under those white skirts definitely got Yvonne's attention. She scooted her chair up closer to the TV screen to get a better look at the pastor and first lady, who were dressed in a vivid display of urban fashion wear that could only be purchased at the stores you didn't even know existed until you passed them on the way to your cousin Naye Naye, Boo Boo, June Bug, and 'nem's house.

First off, they only adorned themselves in matching his-and-her "Saint Suits" in turquoise, red, powder blue, hot pink, lemon yellow, peach, and purple. On this particular show Linda Grey was wearing a lime-green brocade satin suit with matching lime-green hat, shoes, and stockings. The hat had a very flat crown with a wide brim that had been fashioned from yards of pleated lime-green satin that was further accentuated with the rhinestones that were sprinkled across the entire hat. And her husband, Apostle Grady Grey, had on a lime-green clerical robe with a silver collar that had been made from the same bolt of fabric used to make his wife's suit. His shoulder-length Jheri curl was freshly done and styled so that the silver in his hair picked up on the silver on his robe.

"Elaine, people still give curls?"

Elaine sighed and nodded in resignation—seemed as if the Jheri curl would never, ever go away. No matter how hard she prayed for black men who used to be slick 1980s players to be delivered of this affliction, the good Lord just had not answered her prayer and taken this thorn away.

The song faded and Grady Grey stood before the cameras with such a warm and sincere smile spreading across his face, it almost made you want to forget that he was standing on TV dressed like the *Starsky and Hutch* character Huggy Bear's second cousin on his mama's side.

"Durham, North Carolina, I greet you in the matchless name of our Lord and Savior Jesus Christ. I don't know what the weather is like for those of you watching this show. But all I can say is that God is so good because He has blessed me with a beautiful day. I mean it, viewers. Today is gorgeous.

"And let me tell you a lil' somethin'-somethin'—if you've ever been in a place where you can't see the sky, you'll never ever fall short of praising God for a beautiful day again. We have the sick and shut in, and people in jails and prisons around this great state who would give anything to walk outside and feel the warm rays of the sun bathing their face."

"He is so flamboyant," Rochelle said. "But it is the strangest thing. The man is for real when it comes to the Lord, and just as humble and sweet when you run up on him in Durham."

"Yeah," Elaine agreed. "Everybody who meets Grady in person says that he is the sweetest and kindest man they have ever met."

"Well, that is nothing but the truth," Miss Hattie Lee chimed in. "I remember Grady being sweet when he was working out of that shed. He always gave his older customers an extra senior discount, he personally delivered their stuff to their houses, set up any equipment that required assembly, and would come back and make sure everything was okay from time to time."

Grady moved to a new part of his set where the chairs were set up talk-show style. He sat down opposite a short, stocky man, whose arms were so thick and muscular they looked as if they were about to rip the arms of the suit he was wearing in two.

"What does that man have on?" Yvonne asked.

Rochelle, the girls, and her parents kept telling her to watch this show. But she had been too busy, or absorbed in something important, to come and watch it with them. Now she wished that she'd listened because this thing was getting good.

"A silver lamé three-piece suit with a black satin shirt and tie," Rochelle answered, mesmerized by the shiny suit and how the set lights kept bouncing prisms of color off of it.

"Dang, if that sucker don't look hot," Elaine said, fanning herself.

"That's Huge Hotsy, right?" Miss Hattie Lee said.

"Big Dotsy. Dotsy Hamilton," Rochelle and Elaine said in unison.

"Well how come my baby Grady Grey knows somebody dressed like they 'bout to go to the club in outer space?"

"He was Grady's cellmate back in prison," Elaine said. "Dotsy ended up going back to jail and then doing some prison time. But Grady always kept up with him and didn't let up on ministering to him until he got saved."

"Shhh," Rochelle said. "Big Dotsy is getting ready to give his testimony."

Elaine turned up the TV.

Big Dotsy, now Elder Dotsy Hamilton, grinned at the camera, pulled out a silver lamé handkerchief, and wiped the glistening sweat off his bald head before saying, "Now, any of you out there in the viewing audience who has ever been to Jubilee Temple Holiness

Church II has already heard this testimony. So bear with me because the Lord told me this morning that I had to say this one more time. And I don't go against what the Lord tells me to do, no matter how small or simple that request might seem to me. See, I spent a lifetime of cutting the fool and ignoring the Lord, and I am not trying to go back to that craziness.

"People, God has been good to me. I have been delivered and set free of the hold the Devil had on me. I know you can tell just by looking at me that I used to like reefers, cheap wine, and women who'd let me *hit that* after giving them some Cold Duck and a few good drags off of a joint.

"But worse than that was my need to beat up people and shoot at them. Whew, that thang was some fun. I never took drugs stronger than reefers 'cause nothing gave me a thrill like starting up my car and running a nig—oops—a man down the street while I shot at him out of my car window."

Big Dotsy stopped talking and sat back in the chair and closed his eyes in remembrance of those times. When it appeared as if he wasn't going to come back from that memory, Apostle Grady Grey shouted, "GONE ARE THE THINGS OF THE PAST."

Big Dotsy snapped his eyes opened and continued.

"Now, I want you good people to know that I never ever had a desire to kill anybody. I've shot more than my fair share of folks. But I can stand here today and tell you that not a one of them died or was seriously injured. And by that, I mean none of my people are in wheelchairs or experiencing a loss of their most important faculties."

At that point, Linda Grey eased over to Dotsy and slipped him a crumpled piece of paper. He grinned into the camera and said, "Hol' up," and read the note.

"Durham, it looks as if God wants to keep me honest. And I have to confess an oversight. I never killed anybody or put somebody in a wheelchair. But I did interfere with one brother's faculties. I was trying to pistol-whip him and he wouldn't stop hollering or keep still, and I had to shoot him right near the corner of his mouth."

Dotsy pointed to the area on his own mouth where the top and bottom lips were connected to the jaw.

"His mouth ain't never set quite right since that unfortunate incident. And he drools just a tiny bit when he drinks too much, sees a fine sister with a big booty, or gets excited about something, like winning fifty dollars on a scratch-off lottery ticket. But he don't have to worry about money again. 'Cause I went to prison on account of that, when I pleaded guilty so he could win his insurance case 'cause the hospital didn't treat him in a timely manner because he was a known thug."

He started crying, trying to wipe his face dry with that ineffective piece of shiny silver cloth. Finally one of the choir members ran over and gave him a black facecloth. Dotsy wiped his face and head and fell to his knees.

"Durham, I am a sinner saved by grace. I've been the henchman for people who didn't want to get their hands dirty but needed some help with folks who were being irreverent towards them. Now, I know you saints out there are wondering why criminals would be insulted by irreverence. But that ain't the point. The people they sent me after got hooked up with those people on their own. And we all know that when you make deals with the Devil, you will have to pay your debt one way or another."

All of sudden Dotsy got still and quiet like a very important fact had just occurred to him. He stood back up and got right up on the camera.

"Durham, I just want you to know that even though I am telling you the stuff I used to do in a testimony, there is a whole lot I don't recollect anymore. I asked God to cleanse my memory of all details of my former life and my former business associates, and He answered my prayer. And if you don't believe me, you can come over to Jubilee Temple II any day and give me a lie-detector test."

Apostle Grady Grey ran up to the camera and said, "That ain't nothing but the truth. We have given Elder Dotsy five of these tests by three different top-rate companies, and he don't remember a thing. God has completely healed his mind of the past."

Dotsy looked relieved at Grady's revelation, and he said, "I know that I don't look or act like a regular saved man. But I want to tell you people that God brought me here to be a testimony to all of the brothers in jail, and brothers out there acting like they are trying to go to jail. So for you saints who've always been blessed with the good sense to act right, what I'm about to say and do next ain't for you. Y'all will have to wait until the next broadcast when somebody who fit the bill for you is on the show."

Elder Dotsy looked back at the musicians, who started playing a real hot and funky hip-hop beat.

"Girl," Elaine said, "I've heard that tune on the hip-hop station. Or am I just imagining that?"

"Nahh, Elaine," Rochelle said, while bobbing her head to the beat. "That tune is to one of the rapper Yung Joc's old songs."

"You mean the one where he telling the people to meet him at the mall?"

"How do you know about that song, Miss Hattie Lee?" Elaine asked.

"My grandbabies. Shawanda likes to practice her dance routine on that song, and Lil' Too Too plays and sings it when he comes by after school to help me with some housework."

"Lil' Too Too back in school?" Elaine asked.

"Yeah, he went back when he got off of house arrest for trying to steal those cases of microwave pancakes from Harris Teeter. You know that baby always did love himself some pancakes. But he is still at Hillside. I know he is not the best student. But it seems to me like the baby would have been able to get out of high school by now."

"Well, Miss Hattie Lee," Rochelle said, "if he doesn't hurry up, they are going to make him leave anyway. And he's been in trouble with the law. Hillside will try and work with you—but not if you too old and acting a fool on top of that. Lil' Too Too is what? Nineteen?"

"Twenty," Miss Hattie Lee answered, a bit embarrassed. She didn't know what was wrong with Lil' Too Too. All of his cousins were doing fine—good grades, working, and a few were in college.

"He better get it together soon," Elaine said, "because they will make him leave at twenty-one. And Lil' Too Too doesn't want to leave without that diploma. You better talk to him, Miss Hattie Lee."

By now Elder Dotsy was getting down, doing a smooth combination of a shout and the "lean with it, pop with it" hip-hop dance. And when it got real good to him, he said, "I wrote this rap for those of you out there who are always getting in some kind of trouble, and haven't figured out why you need the Lord and need to get saved. Jesus is coming back, sisters and brothers, and I want all of y'all out there to be ready to go and meet Him in the sky. So this is for y'all." He launched into his own gospel rap version of Yung Joc's song.

"When you hear the trumpet sound, it's goin' down . . . When Jesus cracks the sky, it's goin' down . . . When you rise up off the ground, it's goin' down . . . When you meet Him in the air, it's goin' down . . ."

The song was getting good to Elder Dotsy, and he really started getting down. The choir, who up until now had been sitting quietly on the set, hopped up and started dancing and singing, adding some harmony to the song. It looked as if they were having the time of their lives. Anybody watching the show who didn't think that Jesus was somebody they could relate to would be forced to rethink this assumption.

Apostle Grady Grey and the First Lady came on the camera.

"We are rapidly running out of time," Grady Grey said. "If any of you want to get saved, you need to invite the Lord Jesus into your life right now. Today's broadcast was for our viewers who have trouble with legal matters. And we want you to know that we have an anointed post-prison ministry, with many success stories. 'Cause I'm here to tell you future saints that you cannot come out of prison, start over, and make it without Jesus. It won't happen. God wants you to have life more abundantly. Give your life over to Jesus right now."

Three sets of numbers flashed across the screen.

"Our phone counselors are standing by to minister to those of you who want to get saved right now. They are available to pray with you. And they will work with you to get you to our church, or make a reference to a church that is best suited for your needs.

"See, we want you saved and Heaven-bound. So, while we'd love to have you at Jubilee Temple Holiness Church II, our greatest desire is for you to have a church home. Don't worry about hurting our feelings if our church is not the church for you. God has blessed us with tremendous increase and we are growing by leaps and bounds. So we don't care where you go, as long as it's somewhere."

"That's right," Linda Grey said. "Hallelujah! God led us to let Elder Hamilton do the broadcast this morning to reach people a lot of us saints can't reach. And the Lord has laid it on my heart that there are viewers out there who have just been released from jail and prison, you don't know where to turn, or what to do, and how to do it the right way.

"Well, you can let all of that go because God cares for you. And He has placed us here this morning to share His Word and let Him use us to get you on your way, which is His way, the Way. Call. Call. Call us in the name of Jesus and watch your life transform right before your eyes."

"That's right, call," Big Dotsy said. "If God had a miracle for me, I know He has one for you. Call us, please."

The choir came and stood behind the Greys and Elder Hamilton, as the music came on to signal that the show was about to end. The Greys started waving to the camera. Big Dotsy waved and then said, "I want to send a few shout-outs to my three baby mamas, the child support enforcement social worker at Durham County Department of Social Services who taught me about being responsible for my kids, my parole officer, Reverend Jerome King, and my seven kids— Dotsy Jr., Dayeesha, Sheldon, the twins (Tawantaye and Tawanaye), Kylone, and the baby girl, Dotsheema."

SEVENTEEN

Yvonne was laughing so hard tears were streaming down her cheeks. That had to be the funniest, most real church show she'd seen in a long time. No wonder *Grady Grey's Half an Hour of Holy Ghost Power* was becoming a big underground hit in Durham County. And unlike the other reality shows, this one was anointed with the Holy Ghost, and it made a difference in people's lives—even if it did make you laugh until your sides hurt.

"I told you it was a good show," Rochelle said to her sister.

"Yep. You won't have to worry about me missing another one after seeing that. And that was Dayeesha's daddy, huh?"

"Yeah," Elaine said, "that girl looks just like her daddy."

"She acts like him, too," Miss Hattie Lee said to them. "Got a temper like him, and will fight in a heartbeat if you ain't acting right with her. But she sweet as can be—just like her daddy."

Elaine wrapped a pink-and-white-striped cape around Miss Hattie Lee's neck. "Come on. It's way past time for you to get up under that dryer. Yvonne, you take this chair right here."

Elaine patted a sparkly pink vinyl chair and put another pink-and-white cape around Yvonne's neck. She took off Yvonne's hat and slipped the scrunchie off the puffy ponytail.

"Lawd, Yvonne, what have you been doing to your hair? It feels like a booger bear has been chewing on the back of it."

"But . . ." Yvonne began in protest, touching the back of her head, embarrassed because it did feel like a "booger bear" had been chewing on it. She hoped her hair wasn't looking as bad as it felt.

"Your hair looks fine" was Elaine's answer to her unspoken question. "But it's not as healthy as it should be. You have a beautiful head of hair, girl. Barely needs a perm. But it's a long way off from where it ought to be."

"Yeah, big sis," Rochelle added. "Your hair needs a makeover almost as much as your life."

Hot tears filled Yvonne's eyes. She couldn't believe Rochelle would front her like that. It had been a hard two years. And there had been a few times when she had questioned her ability to make it through this storm in one piece.

That divorce had been twelve times harder than anything she could have imagined. It seemed as if Darrell's decision to leave, or more exactly his decision to make Yvonne leave, had done little to appease his extreme unhappiness about being married to her. The harder Yvonne worked to move on with her life, the harder Darrell labored to create just one more difficult and uncalled-for hurdle to cross. Did every encounter with the boy have to be a quagmire of unnecessary mess simply because Yvonne refused to agree with him that he was right, when he was wrong?

Elaine broke into Yvonne's thoughts and put a style book and a board full of colored hair samples ranging from black to brown and red to blonde with a few yellows, purples, a green, and some blues thrown in, on her lap. She said, "Find a style that suits you, and select a color for highlights, while I go and get Miss Hattie Lee straight."

"Okay," Yvonne said. As much as she hated to admit it, Rochelle was right. Her life really needed a makeover. And this time in the shop was her first step in the direction of a brand-new and completely restored life. People believed that opening your heart to receive restoration from the Lord required something huge. Sometimes all it took was a baby step, like a new hairstyle, to let God know you were ready to make that move.

She waited until Elaine had finished with Miss Hattie Lee, and announced, "You know I have a date to tonight's reception."

"Aww sookie sookie now," Elaine said, smiling. "I know I'm gonna hook you up, now. Who is it?"

Yvonne started laughing and blushing. She couldn't believe it herself. "Coach Parker."

"Get out of town," Rochelle said with a huge grin spreading across her face. "Curtis Parker asked you to go with him? When? How? Why?"

"Why?" Yvonne exclaimed. "Why not?"

"That's right, baby," Miss Hattie chimed in. "You tell them. I know Curtis. He's a good guy and he needs to hook up with a good woman like you. You know the Bible tells us that a man who finds a wife finds a treasure and gains favor with the Lord. So, Curtis needs to find a wife and get some favor, so he can get that mess up at the college straightened out. And he sho' ain't gone find nothing worth having messing around with Regina Young. Now I know y'all know that Charles used to tap that tail on a regular basis until he got tired of Regina. That's when she started going out with Curtis."

"I thought Regina was knocking boots with Charles Robinson on the sly," Elaine said.

"That Regina wears some expensive clothes that look like they should be on somebody from *Sex and the City*," Miss Hattie Lee continued. "But she ain't nothing but a piece of Kmart trying to perpetrate as Nordstrom's. Now, don't get me wrong—I don't have anything against Kmart. But it's not Nordstrom's, and there is nothing that will change that fact."

"Miss Hattie Lee," Elaine said, as she sprayed her hair with setting lotion and wrapped it, "you know your dancing self is just as crazy."

Miss Hattie Lee chuckled and said, "You know I ain't telling nothing but truth."

"Nothing but the truth," the other three said.

"I'm going to put you back under the dryer, and then get to work on Yvonne's head."

Elaine made sure that the dryer was warm and Miss Hattie Lee had all that she needed before returning to roll up her sleeves to get Yvonne whipped into shape. She put a perm mask over her face, put on some gloves, and went and got the perm jar.

"You are going to like this perm, Yvonne. It's brand-new, no lye, and was created by a brother. It is so pretty on, and makes your hair silky soft."

As Elaine was spreading the perm into Yvonne's hair, Rochelle said, "You still haven't told me how all of this came about. I didn't even know that Curtis had finally kicked Regina to the curb. Did he find out that she is knocking boots with Gilead Jackson on the low-low?"

"You know what," Yvonne said, frowning. "Knocking boots with Gilead Jackson is as bad as somebody telling Kordell Bivens that they want to give him some."

"Ewwww, Yvonne," Rochelle said. "You are going to make me throw up."

"Me, too," Elaine chimed in, and wrinkled up her whole face at just the thought of that conversation. "Come on and let me wash this out so that I can do the color. You find something you like?"

"Yeah, I did. I thought it would be nice to warm it up with a brown that brings out some of the reddish highlights."

"I agree," Elaine said as she washed and rinsed Yvonne's hair.

"So, big sis, how did Curtis ask you out?"

"He asked me when he walked me to the car after that crazy meeting. I was about to cry and he comforted me and next thing I knew, Maurice was there and telling Curtis what time to pick me up."

Rochelle closed her eyes and just shook her head. Yvonne was the only person she knew who would get asked out by a fine brother like Curtis Parker by somebody else, after fussing and fighting, and then breaking down and crying in the parking lot. She could picture it all, including their cousin Maurice putting his two cents in and getting the time straight for the date.

Elaine finished drying off Yvonne's hair with a towel, mixed up her color of a dark golden brown with some red in it, and applied it to her hair. She put a plastic cap over her head and led her to the dryer, taking a moment to get Miss Hattie Lee so that she could finish styling and curling her hair.

Once Yvonne's hair color had baked in, it didn't take long for Elaine to wash, rinse, and condition her before she cut it wet. That perm was looking good—wet and unstyled. So Elaine knew what the girl's hair was going to look like when she finished. She picked up a pair of shears and began snipping off dead hair and giving Yvonne's hair shape and definition.

"You're not going to cut it too short, are you?" Yvonne asked, eyes glued to those scissors.

Elaine didn't open her mouth, just kept snipping away because she knew that this cut was going to make Yvonne's new look sizzle. She said, "This is nice."

"Yeah, Yvonne," Rochelle said, "that cut is off the chain."

Elaine pulled out the blow-dryer.

"Normally, I would put you under the big dryer. But I want to get you out of here so you can relax before it's time to get ready for your date with Coach."

"I agree," Miss Hattie Lee said. "That boy is so good-looking. Sexy, too. He looks like he *knows* what to do with a woman behind closed doors."

"I heard that," Elaine said, laughing. "You get all hugged up with Curtis Parker and you in trouble." She blew Yvonne's hair dry and pulled out the flat iron. "Girl, this color is out of sight. It has your complexion glowing."

Yvonne's hair was silky and the cut fell in place with the slightest move of her head. It didn't take but a hot minute for Elaine to flat-iron and style it.

"Umph," Elaine exclaimed. "That head is looking good. No one will say your hair looks like a booger bear got a hold of it today."

"Baby," Miss Hattie Lee said, "your hair looks like something in a magazine. I always knew you were cute. But now you look like a million dollars."

"Yeah, big sis. Your hair is gorgeous."

"Here," Elaine said as she handed Yvonne a mirror. "Check it out your own self."

Yvonne took the mirror and stared at the back of her hair. She then swirled around in the chair and gazed at the front. Her hair was silky soft and bouncy. Elaine had given her a chin-length bob that was cut thick and full, and moved and caught the light every time Yvonne moved her head.

"I love the color, Elaine."

"Now, your makeup," Elaine said as she handed Yvonne a pink-and-white bag full of face products. "This is your 'I'm glad the other negro left, so I could meet the new and improved negro' gift."

Yvonne opened the bag. It had face cleanser, toner, moisturizer, a mask, sparkling gold and golden-brown eyeshadow, ebony eyeliner, a shimmering blush, and that new mineral powder foundation Yvonne had been waiting to pick up at Sephora.

"Thank you, Elaine. You know you are my girl."

"Just take some pictures. I would have gone to the reception but it's been a long week and I need to get some rest. You know I'm flying down to Key West with my new man next week."

"Oooh," Rochelle said, "you so fast, Elaine."

"Nothing like that happening, even though it's gone be hard to keep my hands off of Ronald Newson. That's a whole lot of caramel to be gazing on over the length of seventy-two hours."

"I heard that," Miss Hattie Lee said. "Ronald Newson is a good-looking man. Good guy."

"Miss Hattie Lee," Rochelle said as she went to retrieve a bag from Elaine's closet, "how is it that you know all of these men and something about them?"

"Okay, baby, I work at Rumpshakers Hip-Hop Gentlemen's Club, and when I dance, I wear a long black wig, a red costume, and call myself Fatima. Doesn't it stand to reason that I'd be one of the best people to come to about some man in Durham County? Don't you think that most of them have graced the threshold of Rumpshakers at least once?"

"I guess you have a point," Rochelle conceded, and then got nosy. "So, who *hasn't* gone to Rumpshakers?"

"Your cousin Maurice has never been to the dance part. The one time he was there, he spent the entire time down in the kitchen with me. Reverend Quincey has never even set foot on the property. And Reverend Cousin won't even drive by the street. Oh, Apostle Grady Grey and Dotsy Hamilton have only come in to get some of their new members. But they didn't even stay to eat. So I packed them up some plates to take home."

"Who has come that don't want nobody to know they've been there?" Yvonne asked.

"Jethro Winters. And the only reason he didn't want anybody to know he was there because he keeps his taste for brown sugar on the down-low. He tried to get a membership pass but Charles turned him down.

"Sam Redmond, and that boy on the Durham Urban Development Committee that gave Lamont Green such a fit. You know that one black man on the committee whose name nobody can ever remember."

They all nodded. Nobody could remember that Uncle Tom's name to save their lives. And they needed to know his name because he did a lot of damage to black folks in Durham—especially poor black folks and the ones who ran into trouble with the law.

"And what ticks me off so much with that man," Miss Hattie Lee continued, "is that he is always running around Durham acting like he is so good and upstanding. That is so wrong and dishonest. I may do some things, but I am honest about who I am and what I do."

EIGHTEEN

Rochelle picked up the lavender satin garment bag with MISS THANG'S HOLY GHOST CORNER AND CHURCH WOMAN BOUTIQUE embroidered on it with black silk thread, unzipped it, and pulled out a baby-blue velvet suit with a pale blue, cocoa, and silver silk jersey halter top. It was one of the sharpest and sexiest outfits Yvonne had seen in a long time.

Yvonne took a peek at the price tag and almost started hyperventilating. This outfit clearly came from that new designer's corner in her friend Theresa Hopson Green's store.

Rochelle ignored Yvonne's theatrics and dug down in the bag for the shoes and handbag.

"Check this out," she said, grinning just like the baby sister that she was, and held up the baby-blue suede three-inch-heeled pumps trimmed in the same colors as the halter top. She put the matching clutch bag in Yvonne's hands.

"Don't this feel good?"

Yvonne ran her hands across the soft suede. It did feel awfully good. She handed it to Elaine, who said, "Rochelle, you know this thang ain't nothing but the truth," as she put the purse in Miss Hattie Lee's hands. "Feel this thang."

Miss Hattie Lee ran her hands across the beautiful handbag and then eyed Yvonne, who was sitting in the chair looking about as excited as somebody waiting to get a root canal.

"Baby, don't you like this outfit? It's got your name written all over it."

"That's what Theresa and I thought when we picked it out," Rochelle said.

"I love it," Yvonne said, wondering if any of them had taken the time to find out how much all of this "nothin' but the truth" merchandise cost.

Rochelle frowned. Yvonne was getting ready to get on her high horse about the sacrifices that had to be made when "one is a single parent." She wanted to shake her sister—Yvonne could be such an ol' stick-in-the-mud when she wanted to. Rochelle didn't care how much this outfit cost, Yvonne needed to get out of this rut she'd buried herself in. Plus, she needed to look especially good now that Coach was taking her to the reception. Yvonne was wearing that outfit if Rochelle had to beat her down and stuff her in it.

"Yvonne likes this suit," Rochelle began. "No . . . she loves this suit. She just doesn't have sense enough to let go and let herself enjoy liking something that looks this good."

Yvonne wanted to roll her eyes at Rochelle and say something asinine like "Forget you, Rochelle," the way she had when they were kids and she wanted to make her sister leave her alone. But she couldn't and didn't because Rochelle was right. Rochelle had been right since the very first time she shared this observation, and Yvonne got mad and hung up the phone midstream during their conversation.

"I see," Miss Hattie Lee said. "Other than the price tag on this outfit, what's stopping you from enjoying it, Miss Yvonne?"

"Yvonne," Rochelle jumped in before her sister, who was struggling for what she probably thought was the right and proper answer, "don't you think I know what your budget is like? This suit is a gift from your girl Theresa. She needs somebody to start wearing her high-end merchandise and wanted to hook you up, too."

"Rochelle, I can't take this outfit like that."

"Yes, you can. Yes, you will," Elaine said. "God put it on Theresa's heart to bless you with this gift. You mean to tell me that you, the one who's always praying for God to bless you with increase, are going to tell God, 'Thank you but no thank you'? Take the gift—it's a blessing."

"Yeah, baby. Take this gift. It's your first step to letting the Lord know your heart is open to receive the gifts He has in store for you. Otherwise, you are telling God that you ain't ready for a blessing to overtake you."

"But Miss Hattie Lee, we are talking about clothes. I've been praying for my job to become permanent and with benefits. I've been praying for God to send someone into my life. I've been . . ."

"Yvonne," Elaine asked, "don't you think that if God laid it on Theresa's heart to give you this outfit, He has other pieces to this plan? Do you think it is okay for the Lord to bless you with something you have secretly wanted, like a beautiful outfit, to show off the new you? I don't know why we black women do that to ourselves."

"Do what?" Yvonne asked. How was she supposed to be all pumped up over a suit when the other areas in her life were so dry and boring and in such lack? Because what in the tarnation was a fancy blue suit going to do to make her life better? Had somebody pinned the winning lottery ticket on the inside of the skirt?

"Read our situation with our natural eyes instead of trusting the good Lord to take care of everything, including the smallest and seemingly most insignificant of details, like a fancy new suit," Elaine told her. "God knows what He is doing, Yvonne."

"Elaine is right, baby," Miss Hattie Lee said as she swung her hair around. It had taken Elaine all of fifteen minutes to style and flat-iron her new do.

Mary J.'s old school "Reminisce" came on Foxy 107. Miss Hattie Lee swung her hair around one more time and then moved her shoulders and hips in a rhythm that was in sync to Mary J.'s funky beat.

"Whew . . ." she said, got a sip of water, and sat down. "I still got it."

"Yes, you do, Miss Hattie Lee," Rochelle said as she watched this so-called senior work it. Miss Hattie Lee was just as agile and smooth as could be.

"Are you going to the reception tonight, Miss Hattie Lee?" Yvonne asked her.

"Baby, I'll be there. But I'll be working. Marquita is catering the event. So I'll be working alongside her, Huge Hotsy's baby Dayee-sha, and Deena Carmichael."

"Well, we know we'll be eating good tonight," Rochelle said. Because all of those sisters could throw down in the kitchen.

"Yes, you will," Miss Hattie Lee replied. "But you know some-thing—Marquita has been trying to get Deena, Dayeesha, and me to incorporate as a company with her. She doesn't have a name yet, but we all believe we'd make a killing."

"Then why don't you go in on the deal with her? Marquita is a good businesswoman and already making money hand over fist," Rochelle said.

"Well, I just don't think that I will be able to be bothered with Rico. He gets on my nerves, and I know I'll end up going off on him one day if he talks to me wrong—which is inevitable with that boy."

"You are going to have to pray on that, Miss Hattie Lee. Go-ing in with Marquita is too big of a deal to let Rico get in the way," Yvonne told her.

She definitely understood Miss Hattie Lee's not wanting to deal with Rico, though. But Rico wasn't important enough to stand in the way of something like this.

The bell tinkled and the door swung open. A well-dressed older man walked in holding a dark gray fedora by the brim, old school style. Miss Hattie Lee rushed over to him and twirled around a few times.

Mr. Tommy smiled broadly and said in one of those sexy, raspy old-man voices, "You sure are looking good, girl. Making me feel like I'm sixty all over again."

The three younger women thought they had seen it all when Miss Hattie Lee told them what her dance costume looked like, and then busted a smooth move to Mary J. But this had to win the award. There were times when they each thought about what it would feel like to be seventy, eighty, or ninety years old. Judging from the twin-kling eyes of those two, it appeared that it might feel pretty good.

Miss Hattie Lee let her man help her into her coat, slipped her arm through his, blew a kiss at the younger women, and practically skipped out of the shop.

"What do you think they do on their dates?" Rochelle asked.

"Same thing you do on yours, probably," Elaine answered her.

"But I like to snuggle up to my boyfriend and get some of those sweet kisses of his."

"Okay, Rochelle," Elaine began, "first off, you never told anybody that you had a new man. So why don't we start there before we go any further into Miss Hattie Lee's business? Who is this man and when and how did this happen?"

"His name is Terrence Lockwood, he is an attorney and works with the Carolina Panthers Corporation, and he is a mighty man of God."

Yvonne smiled broadly. She said, "I know about Terrence Lockwood. He is supposed to be a wonderful and anointed man. What he look like?"

Rochelle grinned and whipped out her phone. She pulled up a picture of a light-brown-skinned man. He looked to be about five foot ten, was trim and well built, and had a mustache and some of the kindest eyes Yvonne had ever seen. And if he wasn't the sharpest thing on two legs in that silver-blue suit, dove-gray shirt, silver, light blue, and chocolate-colored tie, she didn't know who was.

Elaine checked out the picture. "Nice, very nice, Rochelle. And he knows the Lord. Even better."

"Yeah," Rochelle said softly and did something she rarely did— blush. "And he has some good kisses, too."

"Sooo, if you and Terrence can get all snuggled up, and you get some of his good kisses, then don't you think that Miss Hattie Lee and her new man are capable of doing the exact same thing?"

"But, Elaine, they are . . ."

"Old, Rochelle? But they aren't dead . . . just older. And I think it is a beautiful thing to know that I'll still want to be snuggled up and kissing on my man when I am their ages."

"I agree," Yvonne added. "But do you think they kiss like we do? I mean all warm and sexy like—French kissing. You think they do that?"

Elaine and Rochelle had to think hard on that observation. Neither remembered ever witnessing people that age kissing and making out.

"Girl, you have a point," Elaine said. "How *do* they make out?"

Rochelle started laughing and said, "We are talking just as crazy as Yvonne's kids. That sounds like something that little Danesha would ask, don't it, Yvonne?"

"Umm . . . hmm. It sounds just like Danesha. But I still wonder how they make out."

"Me, too," Elaine said.

"Well, you know how secretive that age group can be," Rochelle told them. "So we are just going to have to get old to find out. Remember, we didn't think people who were forty, and especially somebody who was fifty, would be making out and all over each other. But they do. And I think they are worse than any little college student trying to get all up on somebody."

"You ain't talking nothing but the truth," Elaine said, cracking up. She had crossed the fifty-mark some years ago, and loved being all hugged up with her new man.

Rochelle's cell phone rang out the late great Gerald Levert's "In My Songs." She flipped it open, grinning. "So, you finally got out of that meeting and decided to give a black girl a call."

Elaine and Yvonne strained their ears to pick up on a man's voice.

"You will be able to make it? Perfect. Can you stay over? You have time to meet with Curtis? Good."

Rochelle paused a few seconds before saying, "The Sheraton Imperial isn't too far from my house." She laughed and then said, "Boy, you so crazy," before she hung up.

"So where is 'Boy, you so crazy' spending the night? And why is he meeting with Curtis?" Yvonne asked.

"He has a room at the Sheraton Imperial but wanted to be able to come and hang out with me for a while. And Terrence is going to give Curtis some counsel on how to handle his department over your decision to send in those grades, and effectively bench DeMarcus Brown and June Bug Washington."

"Oooh, I didn't mean to cause that kind of trouble," Yvonne said, now a bit worried.

"Girl, please. Curtis is so glad you sent those grades in, he doesn't know what to do. He just wants to make sure he handles his business, so that Gilead can't get around him on this one. What you did was an answer to that boy's prayers. And I bet that he respects you immensely for standing up for what you knew was right."

"When and where did you meet Terrence, Rochelle?" Elaine asked.

"In Charlotte. I was at a meeting for attorneys who work with sports programs. Terrence was one of the workshop presenters. We hit it off, and we've been talking for months. And plus, Maurice had the skinny on the brother."

"Sounds good to me," Elaine said.

"Me, too," Yvonne seconded, picked up her things, and then put them down to give Elaine a check.

"This is on me, sweetie. But here is your card for your next appointment. I can't wait to hear how all of this goes."

"Thank you, Elaine," Yvonne said, suddenly tearful. She was so blessed to be surrounded by such wonderful and loving people.

NINETEEN

Yvonne walked into the kitchen, dropped the fancy garment bag on the counter, and then knocked it onto the floor and tripped over it trying to get to the alarm keypad before the alarm went off. She had forgotten to remind herself that she had finally remembered to set the alarm when she left the house this morning. Yvonne was good about setting the alarm at night but had to practically beat herself over the head to remember to do the exact same thing during the day. She was so relieved to reach that alarm in time. After a day like this one, she wouldn't have known what kind of password to give to the alarm people when they called.

Yvonne picked up the garment bag and headed down the hall to her bedroom. When they first moved into Cashmere Estates, Yvonne was sullen and droopy, refusing to let go of her hurt over having to leave 6,000 square feet in Richmond for a three-bedroom, 2,100-square-foot home. Back then Yvonne was so focused on her past, her losses, and mourning the life she thought she had, she could not appreciate the beautiful blessing God had dropped into her lap.

Like Lot's wife, Yvonne made the erroneous assumption that what she had been forced to vacate was worth a hardening of her heart and stubborn refusal to embrace change and start a new life. But God was prepared for Yvonne and her foolishness. As soon as she crossed the threshold of this lovely house, she sat down and cried at the thought of how much God loved her. God had blessed Yvonne with the perfect house in spite of her foolishness and ungrateful ways.

For the Lord had made a way out of no way for her and the girls to move into this house. Lamont Green, who owned Cashmere Estates, had leased this house out to Yvonne with an option to buy for a very affordable price. The only thing Lamont wanted from Yvonne was for her to decorate this house so beautifully, potential buyers would be sold on the remaining properties as soon as they completed a virtual tour of her home.

The one-story cerulean-blue Caribbean-style stucco with brick-colored shutters was nestled in trees, azalea bushes, and a blend of flowers that bloomed until late fall. There was a brick walkway leading to the front porch, which covered the expanse of the front of the house, a brick-colored door, two rockers in indigo and a rich creamy yellow, and a double rocker in the same brick red as the front door.

As soon as the door opened, there were café au lait hardwood floors Yvonne had installed with the help of the girls, and a large tree plant in a blue pot with tiny flowers painted all over it in colors matching the porch furniture. The walls were a rich creamy color with delicate hints of cocoa in it. The living room was small and cozy with a baby-blue velvet love seat, mint velvet oversize chair with pink and lavender silk pillows, and a hand-painted baby-blue trunk with Yvonne's, D'Relle's, and Danesha's names painted all over it in pink, mint green, lavender, and indigo. There were two small indigo end tables that held mint lamps and bright silk flower arrangements in pale yellow vases. And there were photos of Yvonne and the girls on the walls in a mixture of modern, antique, and hand-painted frames.

The dining room was more sedate with a walnut table and hutch with crisp clean lines, and matching Shaker-style chairs. This room was elegant and simply decorated with natural plants and original paintings of Durham's Black Wall Street section, or Hayti, which was a thriving area back in the first half of the twentieth century. The cocoa-colored family room and pale almond kitchen were spacious and comfortable adjoining rooms that afforded Yvonne and the girls a great place to play, work, and enjoy one another's company in the evenings.

Everyone loved the cozy dark gray Ultrasuede family room furniture, with the pale blue, mint, and dove-gray area rug covering most of the floor. The kitchen had toasted-almond-toned cabinets, and pale almond and chocolate stone countertops that were a perfect complement to the stainless steel and chocolate appliances.

Each bedroom had its own walk-in closet and bath, with the master suite being graced with a closet that was almost as big as a tiny bedroom, along with a wonderful Jacuzzi tub and double sinks. D'Relle's room was pale green with cocoa accents. It was simple, tasteful, and low-maintenance with lots of high-tech amenities. Danesha's room, on the other hand, was a soft pink and pale yellow. Whereas D'Relle had opted for natural-colored wooden blinds, Danesha's windows had pale pink mini-blinds softened with even paler pink sheers with tiny yellow butterflies all over them. There was a fluffy yellow rug in the middle of the floor, and pastel-colored satin pillows on the pink satin comforter and baby-blue chair.

When you walked into D'Relle's room you wanted to examine all of her cool stuff and read the books in her extensive library. But when you visited Danesha you longed to grab a cup of tea in a fancy porcelain cup, turn on some good music, and enjoy all of her original artwork, which was tastefully displayed around the room.

But if the girls' rooms were a delight to the senses, Yvonne's room was nothing less than a visual treat. Her walls were the palest of pale cocoa color, with lavender on all the trim and moldings. She had a lavender, cream, and cocoa area rug, and a dark walnut dresser, chest of drawers, and king-size sleigh bed. The bed always made everybody who came into Yvonne's room want to grab one of those plush pillows and take a long nap on the pale cocoa comforter with tiny cream and lavender hearts on it.

Yvonne's bedroom had lavender mini-blinds and pale lavender sheers on the windows. She had a hand-painted lavender desk and chair, and a cocoa velvet seat at the foot of the bed that matched her oversize cocoa velvet chair and the ottoman facing a walnut hutch with the TV, DVD, and stereo system in it. Like D'Relle, Yvonne had two bookcases loaded down with all kinds of wonderful things to read. And like her baby girl, Danesha, she had her own original art pieces displayed on the walls.

Yvonne took the suit out of the garment bag to inspect it more carefully. It really was an incredible outfit. She slipped out of her clothes and tried on the halter and skirt. Her first concern was that the skirt would not fit right, and then she wasn't so sure about the halter. She was a D-cup and knew that those "girls" needed support. She always wondered why folks went on so about big boobs—they were very high-maintenance. And contrary to public opinion, it seemed to Yvonne that most clothes were really designed for women with much smaller cup sizes. So she didn't know what there was to get so excited about when your cup overflowed.

This was a top-of-the-line outfit. The halter fit and had built-in support that fit. In fact, it felt wonderful on her breasts—not too tight, not too loose, with the proper coverage on the sides. The skirt was shorter than she normally wore her skirts, but it felt good on her body.

Surprised and satisfied, Yvonne took the clothes off and went to run her bathwater. She put in some bath salt and then added some midnight pomegranate bubble bath. She finished undressing, waited until the tub filled up, and then eased into the water. Yvonne leaned her newly done head on the tub pillow and sighed—the water felt so good on her lush, chocolate body.

She lifted a soapy leg up and examined it. Her leg was firm and shapely. She ran her hands over her stomach—it was flat and firm. She raised her soapy arms up—they had biceps and definition. She looked at her full breasts with the deep dark chocolate nipples that looked sweet to the taste. She examined the texture of her skin—so soft and smooth.

Yvonne sank back into the tub. The warm water came up above her shoulders, making her relax even more. She felt the water swirling around every part of her. It felt good and reminded her just how much of a sensual and loving woman she was. But who would ever discover this about her? Who would ever want to know who she really was? Was there a single man in her age group out there with sense enough to see her and want her, and do what he had to do to get to her?

A hot tear trickled down Yvonne's cheek and she whispered,

"God, why would you bring me to such a state as this? I'm a beautiful, wonderful woman. I'm not perfect, and I definitely have some areas where I need to grow and change. But I am worth a man wanting me and seeing all that You've given me and desiring that. It's not fair, God. It's just not fair."

More tears spilled over and before she knew it, Yvonne was sobbing so hard her chest ached. It wasn't fair that she had to be so alone with no end in sight. It wasn't fair that her ex-husband could break her heart, dump her, put her out of her own house, and then go off to find his happiness. She didn't care that he didn't want her anymore. But it simply was not fair that he got to have a life and she had to stay stuck. It wasn't fair and God needed to step in and do something about this.

Yvonne cried some more and then tried to will herself to stop. It only made matters worse. She felt bad because she was mad at the Lord, who she knew could change her situation in the blink of an eye, for letting her be here like this, and for so long. It wasn't fair.

"Whoever said I was fair as you all define fair, Yvonne," a soft voice whispered to her heart. "I'M JUST. I have not left you, nor have I or will I ever forsake you. So fear not for I have overcome the world."

The tears stopped, the hurt ceased, the peace came, and hope was alive and well in Yvonne's heart in a way that it had not existed in years. She relaxed. Rest, true rest, rest-in-the-Lord rest, finding that resting place promised in the Book of Hebrews, was what Yvonne felt. She realized as she submitted her will and weary soul to this rest that she hadn't known what rest was until this moment. She laid her weary head on the tub pillow, whispered "Thank You," and fell asleep until the water became tepid.

Yvonne finally got out of the tub, dried off, wrapped herself in a huge towel, and washed her face. She felt so much better. It had been a long day, full of twists and turns. And the one twist she'd completely forgotten when she threw that pity party was that she had a date with a fine brother.

After washing her face, brushing her teeth, and putting on deodorant, Yvonne went to her perfume shelf and selected her newest addition, Daisy by Marc Jacobs. She indulged herself in the wonderful body cream and then layered that with the cologne. Smelling good, she went into the bedroom in search of the perfect underwear for this suit—baby-blue lace string bikinis and a pair of silky, chocolate-flesh-toned pantyhose with light blue roses down the side of the leg. Yvonne had fallen in love with those stockings when she saw them but had never found anything to wear that did them justice until now.

She put on some light moisturizer, and then dusted her face with the new mineral foundation and shimmering pinkish blush Elaine had given her. She applied the sparkling brown shadow across her lid and added a navy metallic in the crease, finishing off her eyes with the ebony liner and a few brushes of mascara. The only thing missing was the shimmering dark rose lipstick that made Yvonne's wide and full mouth so lush, it looked like it was begging to be kissed.

She ran the comb through her silky hair, shook it, and watched it fall right back in place. A thick wisp of hair fell over her eye, giving Yvonne that "I just left my man" expression the makeup artists spent so much time perfecting on celebrity pictures in the magazines. And here she was, uncool Yvonne reppin' what women paid good money to get.

"Perfect," she whispered with a smile.

She sat down on the side of her bed and slipped those blue suede shoes on her feet. "Ooooooh," Yvonne purred in pure delight, "these things feel good."

Yvonne packed up the new purse with way too much stuff. She emptied and refilled it three times before she was able to fit the right amount of everything she needed into it, before looking for jewelry that would do this outfit right. She could not, in good conscience, wear something of this caliber and not put on the right earrings and necklace. Unfortunately, the only jewelry that met this standard was the pieces Darrell had bought her years ago.

She pulled at the "Darrell Drawer" on the jewelry box and selected a pair of thick platinum hoops with diamonds and blue and brown topaz stones sprinkled on them, two-carat diamond studs for her second holes, and the two-carat, heart-shaped diamond pendant hanging from a delicate and barely visible platinum chain.

Yvonne had not been able to stomach that jewelry touching her skin for the past two years. As pretty as those two pairs of earrings were, Yvonne practically threw up the last time she tried to put them in her ears. But that was then, and this was now—this jewelry looked good and she was wearing it.

But the necklace was an entirely different story. She had picked this chain out when Darrell, who was deep in his affair with Bettina, was trying not to spend extra money on Yvonne. She had figured correctly that Bettina's birthday had to be somewhere in the vicinity of her own, and that Dr. Darrell could not afford two expensive pieces of jewelry at one time. So he had opted to get rid of the Yvonne expense factor by offhandedly telling her to buy her own gift, thinking she'd get mad and refuse to do so—and therefore save him a lot of money.

Darrell was horrified when he discovered that his scheme had backfired, and his coveted Bettina cash had been spent on Yvonne, and by his own hand. The day the necklace was delivered to the house, Yvonne was forced to watch, horrified, as Darrell confiscated her necklace from the jewelry store's courier.

When she mustered up enough courage to protest, that boy actually formed his mouth to say, "See, that's what I keep telling you about yourself, Yvonne."

"Telling me what?" she asked gingerly, wondering what her necklace had to do with something this joker was always telling her about herself.

"You lack confidence. And this piece of jewelry has to be worn by someone with true confidence. It wouldn't even look right on you. So I'm going to keep it as an incentive to inspire you to display the kind of confidence that I endorse. You see, it's this kind of thing that makes me not like you, Yvonne."

As Yvonne allowed those harsh words to pierce through her heart, she did what she always did when Darrell was mean to her—she fought back the tears. She was in the process of holding her head back to stop the tears from falling when she heard a soft voice whisper, "Pull yourself together and pay attention."

Yvonne opened her eyes just in time to see Darrell going upstairs with the courier package in his hand. She was about to run up the stairs behind him when she felt a firm but gentle pressure on her chest, keeping her from moving forward for a good twenty seconds. As soon as she felt the release, Yvonne found herself yielding to the pull of the Holy Spirit on her heart—something she had not been in tune to in several years.

She walked up the stairs quietly and went to their bedroom door, pausing when she felt that pressure on her chest one more time. The door was open just enough to afford her the privilege of watching Darrell without being seen. Yvonne heard him whisper into his cell phone, "Bettina, baby, I have something for you," and hang up.

Darrell glanced over his shoulder and then surveyed the room for the perfect hiding place. As soon as he found that spot, he smiled, dropped the package into a drawer, and went into the bathroom.

Yvonne eased back down the stairs and went into her office near the kitchen and closed the door before she fell on the floor laughing so hard, tears were streaming down her cheeks.

"What an idiot," she whispered after another bout of laughter. "And to think that I once thought this man was smarter than me."

"Are you praying out loud again, begging and pleading with *God* to . . ." Darrell frowned and snapped his fingers, searching for the words he always overheard Yvonne use when he made her so distraught her only recourse was to run like a snitch and tell on him. Only thing, this silly girl didn't run to a person, she ran to something as intangible as *God*.

His long, lanky frame cast a shadow over Yvonne, who had stretched out on her back on the floor to ease the laugh cramps in her side.

"Oh, I know what it is you're always bugging *God* to do," Darrell said. "Deal with me. Is that why you're on the floor in tears? You're running and tattling to *God* to *deal with me*."

Yvonne sat up and wiped the tears of laughter off her cheeks in the same manner as when she was crying. She hoped that she was affecting despair well enough to make Darrell so disgusted with her that he left before she lost her cool and started laughing all over again. She was simply amazed at how fast and how well the good Lord worked.

In Darrell's haste to hide the necklace, he'd made the mistake of dropping the packet into a drawer on Yvonne's side of their dresser. God led Yvonne to get that necklace as soon as Darrell left the house to go see Bettina. She then ran to the post office and mailed it to her parents in North Carolina.

Until this evening Yvonne, who had long since retrieved the necklace from her parents, had not known what to do with it. She had always assumed that God had led her to keep her necklace because she might have to sell it when she needed some extra money. But for some reason, the Lord meant for her to wear this fabulous jewelry. For some reason, He wanted her to wear it this evening—and that is exactly what she was going to do. Yvonne had learned (and many times the hard way) not to question God, but to obey Him without thought or question when He led her to do something that did not make sense to her finite, "her thoughts were not His thoughts" mind.

Yvonne's walk with the Lord had been weak back when she was married to Darrell. Even though she was born again and believed the Word to be the absolute truth, Yvonne read the Bible when it suited her purposes and rarely prayed for the sheer joy of communing with the Lord. Rather, it was her preference to throw herself prostrate on the floor at the first sign of trouble with Darrell, in an effort to make the Lord "do something with him."

That had been Yvonne's walk with God back then. But she had been growing by leaps and bounds in the Lord ever since she moved back home to North Carolina. The blessings of her relationship with God were so great until Yvonne wondered how she had ever allowed herself to become so sluggish spiritually that she ran from the Lord and the joy of knowing His presence in her life. This new walk had brought her so much closer to God that more and more she was able to hear and discern that "still small voice" at a moment's notice.

TWENTY

The alarm beeped, and the front door opened and closed. Yvonne closed her bedroom door and strutted into the family room, where the girls and her dad were gathered on the floor getting ready to play their Wii game. Her mother was in the kitchen rearranging the countertops, the table, and even parts of Yvonne's refrigerator.

"Mama, stop. There is nothing wrong with my counters," Yvonne admonished. "I don't understand why you always feel a need to come over here and fix what ain't broken. Right, Daddy?"

"Goongad's name is Wes and he ain't in that mess," Danesha said from across the room. She got up off the floor and turned around to finally see her mother.

"Your hair, Mommy," Danesha said.

"What about my hair?"

Yvonne's mother stopped rearranging her daughter's kitchen and gave the girl a second once-over. That was what was so different about her—the hair.

D'Relle stopped fussing with her grandfather over the Wii control and came into the kitchen to get a better look at her mother.

"Oh . . . snap," D'Relle said, dipping down her shoulder with her fist held to her mouth like the rappers did on the videos. "Mommy, you almost look cool."

"Uh . . . thank you, D'Relle . . . I think," Yvonne stated, not sure what to make of that comment.

"I mean, you don't look so *mommyish*," D'Relle told her.

Danesha sighed loudly. "Mommy, what D is trying to tell you is that you look real good and not like the regular Mommy. I mean, not that the regular Mommy isn't pretty. But this Mommy looks like somebody who has a boyfriend."

At that point Yvonne's dad stopped playing with the Wii and decided he needed to take a good look at his oldest baby girl himself. Yvonne was so breathtaking that Marvin felt tears well up in him. He had not seen the baby looking this beautiful in years. There was a glow and beauty about her that made him think of the scripture in chapter three of First Peter, where wives were encouraged to be known for *the beauty that comes from within, the unfading beauty of a gentle and quiet spirit,* which Marvin knew from watching his wife, Jeanette, all of these years, *is so precious to God.*

"Aww . . . sookie sookie now," he said with a big grin and grabbed Yvonne in his arms for a big hug and kiss.

"Daddy, you are going to mess up my makeup."

"Okay," Marvin said and let her go.

"What time do you and Mama want me back?"

"Whenever you get back" was all Jeanette said as she started setting the table for dinner, and then stopped to answer the doorbell.

"Y'all expecting anybody?"

"It might be Tiffany, MaMa," D'Relle said. "Remember you and Goongad said that she could come over and eat and hang out with us."

Danesha got excited. Tiffany Birkshaw was one of her favorites of D'Relle's friends. She got up and ran to answer the door but stopped and hollered out, "It's a great big black man standing at the door. He's dressed up. And . . . oh, it's Coach Parker from church—I mean when he comes to church."

"Coach Parker is at the door," Jeanette said, raising an eyebrow when she noticed that her child was suddenly all fidgety and rearranging her purse. She didn't know why Yvonne liked to pack her purses up with so much stuff.

"Coach Parker, Coach Parker?" Yvonne's dad asked and got up to answer the door. He knew that if a man was coming to the house to see Yvonne, he was getting in this Kool-Aid, and he didn't care if he didn't know the flavah.

"You know about this boy coming over here, Yvonne?" he asked his daughter in the tone of voice he used when she was a teenager and about to go to a dance at Hillside.

"Yes, Daddy. He's my date for the evening. We're going to the reception together."

"Oh . . . well, it's good I'm here—so that negro will know that we Fountains don't play no mess with nobody."

"I think he already knows that, Daddy. He is one of Maurice's best friends."

"Oh, well, okay" was all that Marvin said as he went and opened the door for Curtis, who had heard everything that played out in the house while standing outside on the porch. He thought he'd holler with laughter over what the youngest had said about the big black man.

"How are you doing, sir?" Curtis said and extended his hand to Mr. Fountain, whom he liked and respected. Marvin Fountain was a good man just like his nephew Maurice. The Fountains were just good people, period. Made him wonder why he had never tried to get to know Yvonne in the past. But then, he knew why—he wasn't ready for the kind of commitment that was required to be with a woman like Yvonne. You didn't roll up on a sister like that unless you were serious and bent on acting right.

"Doing fine, son," Marvin said, putting emphasis on the word "son" to make sure that Curtis knew his place. He grabbed his hand and gave it a firm shake, squeezing it harder than necessary to let this boy know that he wasn't playing with him. His baby had been through enough, and he would hurt a negro bad who came in here trying to mess over her and his grandbabies.

Curtis read that handshake and the hard glint in Marvin Fountain's eyes. He knew that this man did not play, and would shoot him and drag him in this house as if he were a would-be burglar before he let him mess with his babies—especially that big one standing next to her mama looking all fine and delectable in that baby-blue velvet suit.

Umph, umph, umph, he thought, *I don't know how I'm gone keep my hands off of all of that. Lawd, ha' mercy.*

"You taking our mama out," D'Relle said, hands on her hips.

"Yeah, you the big black man who gone take our mama out," Danesha said, now standing by her big sister trying to look tough.

"Well," Curtis said, "would it be okay with you two ladies if I took her to the basketball reception this evening?"

"As long as you act right," D'Relle said with a whole lot of attitude. And she wasn't trying to look tough, she did look tough. "Our little mommy is *our mommy* and we don't like it when somebody tries to be mean to her. You know she has a gun and likes to go to target practice to shoot with my granddaddy."

"And she'll shoot you if you don't act right, Mr. Coach Parker," Danesha said.

Curtis glanced over at Yvonne, who was staring at her children as if to say, *Have y'all little heifers lost y'all's minds.*

"Girl, you didn't tell me about you and this gun thing. I knew about the wire pliers but not the gun. What kind of gun do you own?"

"One like this," Marvin said as he ran off and came right back with the gun in his hand. Curtis hoped that the safety was on and secured.

"It's a beauty, ain't it? I got it for baby girl as a divorce present."

What is it with this family and guns? Curtis thought, remembering Trina and her gun.

Curtis took the gun out of Marvin's hand and examined it. Marvin wasn't lying—this was a beautiful gun. Gray metal with a pink mother-of-pearl handle. It was heavy and Curtis couldn't help but wonder how Yvonne managed that thing with those dainty hands of hers.

He bounced the gun up and down in his hand a few times.

"It's heavy, ain't it," D'Relle said. "But our mommy is good at handling it. She can walk around our house with the gun in her hands like she's a detective on *CSI: Miami*—which is one of her favorite TV shows. Can't you, Mommy?"

"Yes, baby. Mommy can do just what you said," Yvonne replied.

It always tickled her to know how proud the girls were that their mother could handle firearms.

"I bet you could shoot a negro right between the eyes fifty feet away from him," Curtis said, and gave Marvin the gun.

"Well." Yvonne shrugged, grinning, hunching up her shoulders, and rubbing her chin like J. J. Walker in the 1970s sitcom *Good Times*. "What can I say?"

"Girl, take your silly self on out of this house so Curtis can get to his own reception on time," Jeanette said.

"Yeah, we better get going," he said and started for the door, then stopped and said, "Good to see all of you."

"Does that include me and Danesha?"

"Most definitely, Miss D'Relle."

The doorbell rang again and Danesha ran to answer it. She came back with Tiffany, who ran over to D'Relle and said in her customary high-pitched and fast-paced Tiffany voice, "D, ain't that Coach Parker? And what he doing with yo' mama, walking out the house with her like that?" Before D'Relle could shush and then try to answer Tiffany's questions, she said, "Oooh, D. Yo' mama look good. That suit is crunked."

"Bye, Mommy," the girls said and waved, and then ran to the window and tried to be inconspicuous, staring out to see what kind of car Coach Parker was driving.

"That's hot," D'Relle said, admiring the Cadillac truck. "He just needs some better rims, though."

"I like the rims, D," Tiffany told her.

"You would, T. They are the same kind of rims your daddy just put on his Explorer."

"Like I said, D, I like the rims."

Yvonne stared back at the house, hoping they read her face and got their nosy little butts out of the window.

"Whewwww. Girl, you got your hands full with those two."

"I know. They are something else. But they are some very sweet girls."

"I know they are sweet. They can't help but to be sweet, as sweet as their good-looking mama is."

Yvonne smiled and blushed and then said, "Boy, you are so crazy. And you ain't shortchanging nobody your own self. That's a nice suit. Where'd you buy it? From Mr. Booth?"

"How did you know I bought this suit from Mr. Booth?"

"Mr. Booth is the only person I know who has suits of this quality at affordable prices," Yvonne told him, and rubbed the fabric on the sleeve of the suit between her fingers.

"Cashmere and silk. Nice. I love this red chalk stripe on the black. And the black silk vest with red stripes running through it and matching tie and handkerchief is tight . . . oh, crunked."

"Why thank you, Miss Fountain." Curtis smiled, face really lighting up next to that fancy white diamond-print jacquard dress shirt.

Whew, Yvonne thought. *I didn't know a Mounds Bar was as appetizing as it is right now. Glad I ate a snack before I left the house.*

Curtis liked that she was checking him out on the low and liking what she saw. He slipped in a CD. The Ohio Players' "Honey" was playing. Curtis snapped his fingers and said, "That takes you waaaayyyy back, don't it, girl?"

Yvonne, who had thought that she was going to be so nervous she wouldn't know what to say to Curtis when they were all alone in the car, started cracking up.

"You are a fool, Curtis Lee Parker."

"A fool for you, baby," he answered, surprised at those words that popped out of his mouth seemingly of their own accord.

"Curtis," Yvonne said and tapped his arm playfully, as she would have done back in the day when they were at Hillside High School.

"That's my name, don't wear it out."

TWENTY-ONE

Curtis turned his car in to the Sheraton Imperial and drove around searching for a parking space that wasn't what amounted to several blocks away from the hotel's entrance. Yvonne liked this Escalade truck. She'd always seen them on the street and thought they looked good but she didn't realize how good a ride the car was. But then again, truck or not, it was a Cadillac. She'd never been in a Cadillac that wasn't a smooth ride.

"I like this car, Curtis."

"I love it. And when I get a chance, I'm going to take that D'Relle for a spin because I know that this is right up her alley."

Yvonne gave Curtis the sweetest smile and said, "How did you know?"

"How could I not know with all of that big, bad talk about guns and *our mommy*? But it's all good. You are blessed to have such beautiful, funny, sassy, and smart children."

"Thank you, Curtis. You know there are men who don't appreciate funny, mouthy, sassy, and confident girls like D'Relle and Danesha."

"Then those men are fools. Because they don't know what they are missing getting to know little girls like that. They are so much fun and will grow up to be sweet, kind, and wonderful women just like you and your sister and your friends."

"There's your space," Yvonne said, pointing to a sweet parking space with a cone and one of Eva T.'s security guards holding a neon red sign with COACH PARKER written on it in huge black letters.

"Girl, you have some good eyes. I need to have you riding shot-gun with me more often," Curtis said and eased into his parking spot in a space right near the hotel's lobby entrance.

The Gap Band's "Early in the Morning" started playing in the car, even though Prince's "Purple Rain" was playing on the CD.

Yvonne dug her phone out of her purse and flipped it open.

"Where are you?" Rochelle asked.

"We just parked the car. I'll see you in a few minutes."

"Was that Maurice?" Curtis asked.

"No, Rochelle. She always gets the best table at any event and is holding our seats."

Curtis hopped out and came around to help Yvonne out of the truck. She gave him her hand and swung one leg out of the door.

"Ooooh, baby, where did you get those stockings?"

Yvonne didn't say a word. Just smiled and got out of the truck. Some-times a comment wasn't necessary when a simple smile would do.

Curtis clicked the alarm and grabbed Yvonne's hand. Yvonne's first response was to pull her hand from his, but he held on to it.

"I don't have cooties, you know."

"I know," Yvonne said softly.

"Then why do you have so much trouble letting me hold your hand?"

"Uh . . . well, I'm not used to the feeling," Yvonne said before she could stop herself.

"What feeling?" Curtis asked, smiling down into her eyes.

"Your hand around mine."

"And you have to get used to that because?"

Yvonne searched for a better answer than the real one, which was, *because I can feel the touch of the palm of your hand in the center of my heart.*

Rather than come up with a goofy lie to try and save face, she decided not to give Curtis an answer. Instead she squeezed his large hand with her own, looked up into his eyes, and smiled. This time it was Curtis who was at a loss for words. He felt that smile traveling from his chest to the pit of his stomach, and on down to the tips of his toes.

"Come on, girl. Let's find Rochelle's table. And then I want to make sure that none of Bay Bay's Kids are here tonight. I gave the team specific instructions to stay home and get some rest."

"Bay . . . who?"

"The team. You teach those children, Yvonne. You know they are Bay Bay's Kids."

"Oh . . . you mean 'Bébé's Kids,' as in 'We don't die . . .'"

" . . . We multiply," Curtis finished with her, laughing, and then he looked down at his date and asked, "say Bay Bay again."

"Bébé."

"Spell it."

"B-e-b-e."

"But why not b-a-y-b-a-y?"

"Because that's how it's spelled in the Robin Harris joke and in the movie *Bébé's Kids*," Yvonne told him. "You said it kinda slow-like. But it's faster than the way you pronounced it, Curtis."

"I hear ya, baby" was all Curtis said. This had to be the silliest, most unnecessary, and yet most heartwarming conversation he'd had with a woman in a long time. His father had once told him that the right woman was the one you could have a meaningful conversation with over something that was trivial at best.

Rochelle, followed by Maurice, met them at the door. They nudged each other and smiled. Yvonne and Curtis looked like they were going together. Rochelle couldn't wait for Darrell and Sundress, who were here tonight lobbying for those fancy faculty positions they were licking their chops over, to see her sister. That Bettina was wearing the ugliest black Ultrasuede A-line sundress with spaghetti straps and a white silk shirt underneath. Her ensemble couldn't hold a melted-down candle to Yvonne's outfit. Rochelle was just thankful that Bettina had the good sense not to wear white opaque stockings with her black suede flats.

"Cuz, Cuz," Maurice hollered across the room as if he were calling her from across the parking lot.

Yvonne smiled. Their family was notorious for hollering at folks, heedless of how loud they sounded to others.

"What up, Cuz," Maurice said, and then stepped back to get a better look at Yvonne. "Dang, Cuz. You tryin' to catch you a man at this reception?"

Curtis cleared his throat and pulled back his suit jacket to reveal that sharp vest he was wearing. He said, "The suit works 'cause Cuz just caught the big catch of the day."

Yvonne looked up at Curtis and said, "Oh no, baby boy. You are the one who was bestowed the honor of escorting this rare treasure to the reception tonight."

Rochelle and Maurice looked at each other as if to say, *Awww, so it's like that.*

Curtis got close to Yvonne, leaned down, and whispered in her ear, "You dang skippy I got the treasure tonight, baby." He slipped his arm around her waist and continued, "And you know something, sweet thang? I can't wait to explore the entire package, slowly and with great pleasure one day."

Yvonne was about to do her customary schoolgirl blush. But she sucked that blush back up to where it came from and got close to Curtis, inhaling a second because he smelled so good.

"You know you are too grown for your own good. But I got something for you, Coach Parker."

"Oh . . . you got something for me, Miss Yvonne," he said, grinning and sucking on his tooth. "You think you can handle all of this?"

He opened his arms and stood with his feet apart.

"Brang it" was all Yvonne said and headed over to the food table, knowing that Curtis was watching as she gave him an eyeful of her sashaying that big, round booty across the room.

Curtis started after her, eyes glued to that booty. Rochelle tapped his arm and pointed to their table.

"We are over there at the fun table with Obadiah, Lena, Denzelle, Trina, Lamont, Theresa, James, and Vanessa and dem. The only problem is that we are just a few tables too close to those jokers over there."

Rochelle nodded in the direction of the president's table, where Darrell and Bettina were sitting with Sam and Grace Redmond, Gilead and his wife, Delores, and Regina Young, along with Jethro Winters and his wife, Bailey Catherine.

Darrell saw Rochelle pointing at their table like she was telling folks they were sitting in the quarantined section. He was really trying not to stare over there, but couldn't help it. He wanted to make sure that his eyes were not playing tricks on him when he saw Yvonne looking like a million dollars, *and* that she was with a man. And his ex-wife was not with just any old man—she was with the head coach of the school's basketball team—a high-profile man, one high on the food chain as far as the sisters were concerned.

Try as he might, Darrell had a hard time keeping his eyes from darting back and forth from his ex-wife's chic and sexy suit to his current wife's black-and-white uniform with those ugly shoes. He didn't know why she thought that a flat was the shoe of choice for her big, wide, and flat feet.

Dr. Darrell Copeland was not the only one at his table eyeballing Yvonne. Jethro Winters thought he was going to lose it if he didn't find a moment away from Bailey's eagle eyes to ask Sam Redmond the age-old player's question, *"Who* is that?"

Under normal circumstances, Yvonne looked good enough to Gilead Jackson to make him want to hit on her. But his dislike for that little chocolate version of Polly Pocket was so intense that Gilead wouldn't have laid a finger on Yvonne if she had jumped him naked in the hotel's cloakroom. And that was saying a whole lot because Gilead was an old pro when it came to ho'in' around.

Regina Young saw Polly Pocket walk in with Curtis, looking fabulous—which set her teeth on edge and put her in a horrible mood. And if that wasn't bad enough, she was sitting at this couple's table without a man on her arm. Even worse, she had to sit next to that boring-tailed Delores Jackson. Regina could not stand Gilead's wife, and wished she could just haul off and slap that woman before going upstairs and getting in bed with her man. Now, that would make this torturous evening worthwhile.

She reached under the table, bent on rubbing her hand on Gilead's knee while his wife sat there running her mouth about what kind of grass seeds she was considering putting on their lawn. Plus, it gave her something to do to keep from falling asleep. Gilead's wife took a deep breath and then launched into part two of her monologue—this time on aerating the lawn and getting it ready for the seeds.

Regina yawned as her right hand connected with what she thought was Gilead's knee. But it didn't feel like Gilead's knee. Gilead had very big bones and joints. This knee was thicker and meatier, and the material on the pants leg was luxurious to the touch. Regina glanced to her right and almost swore out loud when it dawned on her that Gilead was next to her left hand.

All of a sudden a strong and well-manicured hand covered Regina's under the table. She blushed and tried not to squirm when that hand began to misbehave something terrible. Gilead glanced over at her in the middle of his wife's describing in excruciating detail how exhilarating it was to plow through hard and fallow ground, preparing the soil for the new seed, and gave her the "what's wrong with you?" look.

Regina shrugged, as if to say, "Nothing," while Jethro Winters turned up the heat on her and began to play footsie with her fingers. Jethro knew that Regina had been reaching for Gilead's knee, and it did his reprobate mind and heart some good to intercept that pass. Regina Young was a fine-looking sister, with all of the physical attributes he appreciated in a woman. She was tall like Bailey, and had long, thick hair, a full mouth, sexy eyes, and a mind like a steel trap. She was the first woman he'd run into in a long time, since Charmayne Robinson, who set his blood to boiling. And the girl had better be glad that his wife was at this table, or else he would have given her a reason to slide right under it.

Regina tried to pull her hand from under that table and found it held in a vise that was not going to yield anytime soon. So she opted to relax and enjoy this game of cat and mouse between her and Jethro Winters. Maybe it was time to get a change of scenery and hook up with a new man. While she definitely preferred chocolate, she was always down for a little vanilla extract in her life when the need arose. And there was no better way to pimp-slap a black man than to hang on the arm of a white one—especially when the white man was one of the richest and most sought-after players on the market.

What did it matter to her that Jethro was married? Regina wasn't trying to up and marry anybody anytime soon. She only wanted a good-looking and wealthy man who would make it worthwhile to be with him. And Jethro Winters definitely fit the bill. If Regina couldn't have the man she really wanted, then hooking up with the best man she could get was a smart move.

Once Jethro was satisfied that Regina was his for the taking, he relaxed his grip on her hand and paid some attention to Bailey. He had to stifle the grin that came when he had been smooth and slick. Last thing he needed was for Bailey to get an inkling that a new other woman was about to be interviewed for the job. He'd been monogamous for the past eight months. And while it had been real, as the brothers would put it, he needed something to jump-start his engine.

Jethro's doctor had suggested that he quit running around with so many women for a while, and then proceeded to write him out a prescription for Cialis to help with some of the problems he'd been experiencing lately. Jethro had just known he was dying of some advanced form of prostate cancer when he drooped worse than somebody with the dropsy disease in the middle of an illicit, late-night, for-old-times'-sake tryst with Patty Harmon.

But thankfully he was just run down and a lifetime of whoring around was finally catching up with him. Some rest and a steady diet of two fine women would do the job. Bailey always kept his fire going. And this Regina would ignite that pilot light for him. He could tell from just looking at the girl that she was a high-quality freak, and better medicine than any Cialis pill could possibly be.

Plus, nothing got him going more than playing games with folks, especially black men he didn't like. And knocking boots with Gilead Jackson's backdoor woman—a woman with all kinds of knowledge about the workings of this university—could keep Jethro going without the need for Cialis for months on end. Jethro eyed Bailey carefully. When he was satisfied that she was content with one of her favorite activities—people watching—he reached down and sneaked one more squeeze of Regina's hand. He was glad that the cold weather was rolling in with these two women to keep him warm.

Bettina had been thoroughly pissed when Yvonne walked in with that good-looking man. And even worse, the girl looked so doggone good herself. That was the worst feeling—when the ex-wife, whose marriage you plotted and schemed to destroy, stepped up somewhere looking ten times better than you, *and* with a new man.

Bettina had spent many a sleepless night plotting and scheming to get Darrell to leave Yvonne. And on one or two occasions she'd actually felt sorry for Yvonne because Darrell chose her over his own wife. Now she wondered if Yvonne was the one to be envied. The girl looked so good and happy it made Bettina wonder if she'd actually done Yvonne a solid.

Bettina had not had any fun since Darrell whisked her off to southeast Asia to be married in an ancient temple by a monk who gave her an eerie feeling that he had killed quite a few Americans during the Vietnam War. What Bettina didn't know while she was lying awake scheming and plotting Yvonne's demise was that Darrell was pretty boring, and didn't like to do a lot of stuff black folks their age enjoyed doing.

The boy wasn't heavily into sports. And in fact, the only reason he was at this reception tonight was to hobnob with the powers that be to get the job, salary, and perks he wanted. He didn't go to dances. And he acted as if he hated old school music. If Bettina had to listen to one more folk performer from the region of never-never land, she was going to bust a cap in somebody.

Darrell used to complain to Bettina that one of the reasons he could no longer stand his wife was that Yvonne had simple tastes and did not appreciate music that was noncommercial and true art. He was incensed that the girl hated the music of the Brahmin Folk Shamans. But he would have had a hissy fit if he discovered that not only did Bettina hate the Brahmin Folk Shamans, with that lead singer who sounded like Chewbacca from *Star Wars*, she detested Darrell's other favorite group, the Cambodian Monks Chorale.

Why couldn't an African-American just listen to something worthy of being played on Durham's Foxy 107? Why did she have to listen to the Cambodian Monks Chorale sing a song in a language she did not know, and with melodies that brought new meaning to the term avant-garde? All a black girl from Shreveport, Louisiana, wanted to do was hear herself some Al Green, Luther, Chaka, the Queen, James Brown, Prince, and the late great Gerald Levert. Could a sister just hear some Charlie Wilson at the end of the day?

TWENTY-TWO

Trina and Theresa stood up and waved when they saw Yvonne and Curtis wandering around with their plates loaded down with Marquita Sneed's good food and looking for their table. Curtis saw them first, popped a big, juicy shrimp in his mouth, and nodded in the direction of the table. Normally he and Maurice sat at the table next to the president's. But tonight they opted to sit with friends.

As soon as Yvonne approached the table, Trina, Lena, Theresa, and Vanessa all gave Yvonne a thorough once-over. Trina said, "I'm scared of you. Girl, what did you do to your hair?"

"You like it?" Yvonne asked softly, hoping that she hadn't gone too far with this new do.

"Naw," Trina said. "I don't like it. Just wanted to talk about it."

Yvonne tossed her hair and said, "Look good, don't it?"

"I'll say," the extremely well-dressed white man, whom Yvonne knew to be Jethro Winters, said in one of the sexist voices she'd ever heard coming out of a white man's mouth.

Everybody at the table got quiet. They didn't know how this white boy had appeared out of thin air. Just a few minutes ago Trina had seen him sitting at the president's table trying to act like he wasn't hitting on Regina Young. And now he was over here trying to find out who Yvonne was.

Trina had never thought she'd come to this conclusion about a white boy but Jethro Winters was an old pro ho in the tradition of Reverend Marcel Brown out of Detroit, Reverend Brown's now-deceased daddy, Reverend Ernest Brown, Bishop Sonny Washington in Fuqua Varina, North Carolina, Parvell Sykes, Gilead Jackson, and Kordell Bivens. She couldn't include Rico Sneed in that list of Hall of Famers. Even though he was a bona fide ho, Rico didn't have the kind of game that qualified him as an old pro. People often didn't understand that there were degrees, levels, and ranks to being a ho.

Yvonne knew all about Jethro Winters. She doubted he remembered that she had been the one playing the piano and singing church songs while Lamont Green was beating him out of that coveted contract to rebuild Cashmere Estates. Jethro had been so mad that day that he had turned beet red and stayed that way for a good hour or so.

As far as Yvonne was concerned, Jethro Winters got exactly what he deserved that day. Because he didn't have a right, or any business coming up in their church with a camera crew to announce that he was getting the DUDC contract to develop Cashmere Estates. Only heathens did some craziness like that. And judging from the way he was trying to roll up on her right now, it was clear that Jethro Winters was a heathen. It didn't matter that the boy was rich, educated, and one of the movers and shakers in their community—he was a heathen.

Yvonne surmised that the odds of her running into Jethro Winters in a setting where he'd be able to flirt with her were slimmer than her chances of being shot with a blowgun by a warlord from a South American rain forest. Yvonne didn't know if she should ignore this white man or just smile politely and sit down. But Jethro Winters was not one to let a beautiful woman ignore him or give him the brush off with a polite smile and ladylike sit-down.

"Little darling," he said in that low drawl that attracted every high-end, gold-digging skank in Durham County to him, "don't you think a thank-you or something is in order?"

"Uh . . . thank you . . . uh . . . I think," Yvonne said and put her plate on the table. She noticed that Curtis, who had been trailing behind her, was now at that table, taking off his coat.

Jethro, oblivious to the impending beatdown, smiled and adjusted one of his suspender straps. As much as he wanted that Regina, it had been a long time since a woman had captured his attention like this piece of rich milk chocolate. He loved chocolate, especially when it was all wrapped up in delicate baby blue. He'd bet some money that this woman was wearing baby-blue lace lingerie.

Jethro Winters's wife, Bailey Catherine, started to get up, go over to that table, and snatch a patch of his moussed-up hair right out of his head. But she opted to keep her seat when the woman's man came to stand by her side and started preparing for an altercation. If that big black fine representative of African-American manhood put his foot up Jethro's behind, it would be the best entertainment she'd had in a long time.

Bailey absolutely did not appreciate her husband acting as if he was ready to take that exquisitely beautiful woman, dressed in that baby-blue suit to die for, upstairs to the hotel suite he didn't know she knew he had. She didn't know why he had persisted in the chase with this one. It wasn't as if the woman acted like that hussy sitting at their table. This woman was clearly one of those goody-goody black church women. She did not like or want this kind of attention from her philandering husband, or any whorish man treating her with disrespect for that matter.

This girl was what her two black employees, Charmayne Robinson and Chablis Jackson, called "old school." And she knew enough about traditional "old school" to know that this woman only wanted to hook up with a black man who was single and more importantly interested in serving God. Her husband wasn't black, he wasn't single, and he was about as interested in God as he was in doing his business honestly and above board.

Bailey didn't know why she continued to put up with Jethro's blatant infidelity. But then again, she did know—love. Bailey Catherine Fairfax Winters, a beautiful and wealthy woman in her own right, had fallen hopelessly in love with this old reprobate the very first time she laid eyes on him at Duke University. She'd been standing in the midst of several athletes laughing and flirting, when Jethro, who was on the football team, broke through the circle of basketball players to capture her heart with his smooth "What's your name, darlin'?"

Jethro sighed longingly and smiled at just the thought of what he could do with all of that chocolate, especially if he got his hands on some whipped cream. Bailey studied him a few seconds, got furious, lost her cool, hopped up, and made a beeline for Yvonne's table. Just as Curtis was getting ready to dust the floor with her husband, Bailey Catherine pulled out her checkbook and laid it on the table right in front of Jethro. He almost choked when Bailey picked up the checkbook and removed the cap of her platinum pen with tiny topaz chips sprinkled all over it.

The last check Bailey had written to get back at him for his cheating had been for over two million dollars. And if that had not been bad enough, she had given that money to his rival, Lamont Green, which was one of the two deciding factors enabling Green to win the contract from the Durham Urban Development Committee to rebuild what had once been the Cashmere Estates Public Housing Community—a place he would not have set foot in if his life depended on it when it was a flourishing neighborhood for low- and moderate-income families.

For years Jethro had sat back, practically rubbing his hands together in pure glee, every time something happened in the Cashmere that would push the political and economic powers in Durham to close it down. It didn't matter to him that innocent families were suffering while the community deteriorated right before the city's eyes. He didn't care that mothers and fathers couldn't even let their children play outside for fear of a gun battle between opposing drug cartels. Jethro certainly didn't lose any sleep when the families left in the blighted development made desperate and heart-wrenching appeals to the public because they didn't have anywhere affordable to go.

One day Jethro's patience (along with a few under-the-table financial incentives to some well-placed folk) paid off and his dream of the community being dismantled finally came true. The Cashmere was closed down in the early 1990s and was allowed to further deteriorate until Green Pastures won the contract and started rebuilding in 2006.

He always blamed that series of unfortunate events on his wife's money being improperly placed. But that wasn't the only reason Jethro lost that contract. The second incentive to give that contract to Lamont Green's company came as a result of the beatdown Bailey Catherine gave Jethro's trailer-park hoochie, Patricia "Patty" Harmon, at what was supposed to have been a private work session between the Winters Corporation and the DUDC.

Bailey threw a right hook that was so deadly she knocked Patty Harmon out cold. The members of the DUDC knew they couldn't give Jethro that contract as soon as Patty's unconscious body hit the floor with a loud thud. And Patty, who was also a member of the DUDC, knew she wasn't giving her soon-to-be ex-man that vote if her big, swollen-up eye and head depended on it.

"What is wrong with this crazy white boy?" Yvonne asked out loud, not caring who heard her.

"Girl, your guess is as good as mine," Trina replied, not giving a hoot that these two rich white folks could hear every single thing that was being said. Jethro should have kept his trifling butt where he belonged—over at Sam Redmond's table with all of those other unsaved, itching-to-hop-on-the-bullet-train-to-Hell heathens.

"The only thing I've ever been able to figure out is that he is a straight-up ho with Thirty-one-flavor Baskin-Robbins taste," Rochelle said flatly.

Bailey started laughing. She'd seen Charmayne and Chablis play that game with folks they were pissed off with—blatantly and openly dissing them while they were standing in earshot of the conversation being held at their expense. She leaned over and started making a notation in her checkbook for 1,500,000 dollars. Jethro looked at that check and started choking. The money was coming out of the petty cash account he shared with Bailey. He turned red and hurried away from the table when Bailey tore the check out of her checkbook.

She said in a rich and sultry contralto voice that sounded like a smooth chord on the alto saxophone, "One of my most valued employees' mom, Miss Shirley Jackson, once told me that there were times when the good Lord gave you 'double for your trouble' when somebody's done you wrong. It took me a moment to place you, Ms. Fountain. But now I know you as the woman in charge of remodeling the day care center and the new hospitality building for the university's alumni, booster club, and trustees. I liked your work and did a background check on you. Ms. Fountain, you are a classy woman, and you deserve a permanent position at Evangeline T. Marshall University."

Bailey put the check in Yvonne's hands.

"What's this?"

"The seed money for the endowment fund for your new distinguished professorship—The Bailey Catherine Fairfax Winters Professorship in Interior and Exterior Design. I think that should give you peace of mind. And I believe there's enough there to cover health insurance."

Bailey reached out and hugged Yvonne. She had a whole lot of respect for a woman who had to go it alone after the breakup of her marriage, and yet refused to succumb to the okey-doke when men like Bailey's own husband tried to hit on her.

Yvonne grasped the check in her hand in complete shock. She didn't know how to respond until she heard Lena Quincey say, "When God gives you a blessing you thank Him."

Yvonne glanced at the check and then embraced Bailey. She was in tears—more at the miraculous, behind-the-scenes works of the Lord than anything else.

"Thank you, Mrs. Winters," Yvonne whispered. "Thank you from the bottom of my heart."

"No," Bailey told her as she stepped back and collected her things off the table. "Thank you for letting me witness what a true woman of God looks like. Don't change, Miss Fountain. God will bless you for being patient and faithful."

Bailey walked off before the tears flooding her eyes started streaming down her cheeks. She didn't know how much longer she was going to be able to stay with Jethro. Time was passing and life was too precious to waste it on foolishness. She picked up her scarlet cashmere wrap off the back of her chair at the president's table and left. For the first time in months, Bailey felt peace in her heart. She now knew that the only reason she'd been sent to this university was to be a blessing to someone else.

Jethro reached out and grabbed her hand but she pulled it away.

"I have to go home" was all Bailey told him.

Everyone at the table had the question "why" plastered across their faces. But no one, not even her husband, dared to ask. That was the nice thing about being in the minority. Bailey could always make a move that was chalked up to her being rich, privileged, and white when she didn't want to be asked or have to answer to anyone about her motives or behavior.

Jethro followed his wife but she hurried out of the banquet hall and hid in a corner so he couldn't see her. When Bailey was confident that Jethro had gone back to his table, she went to their car and peeled off, not caring how Jethro was going to get home, that she was burning rubber on the expensive tires on his fancy brown Mercedes, or that she scraped the side of Gilead Jackson's wife's red Infiniti sedan.

"Serves that boring, Chatty Cathy hussy right," Bailey whispered. "I never did like a dumb woman who talked too much—and about grass of all things. Not gardening—grass."

Back in the banquet hall the DJ had finally finished setting up, and some smooth R&B sounds came through over the buzz of voices, silverware on china, the clinking of fine crystal glasses filled to the brim with champagne, and the rustling about of all of those finely dressed black folk. There was nothing like a gathering of dressed-up black people. The Ebony Fashion Fair paled in comparison to the real thing.

"Let's see that check, Miss Yvonne," Lena Quincey said as she pulled out a bottle of anointing oil and got up to anoint and bless that check.

Yvonne put the seven-figure check in Lena's hand and waited for her response.

Lena smiled and said, "Praise God. We need to make sure that your pastor is here for this," she told Yvonne as she pulled out her cell phone. She waited a couple of seconds and then said, "Baby, get over here. And bring Lamont, Maurice, James, and Terrence with you.

Curtis is already with us . . . I can't explain it on the phone. Put that food down and come on across the room to where we are . . . Yes, I see you."

Curtis had not seen the check and wasn't sure if it was right for him to ask to see it. Then he remembered Yvonne crying in her car earlier today and how he'd comforted her that things would be all right. He knew that it was okay to ask to share in this blessing.

"Baby, let me see the check."

Yvonne opened it for Curtis and then passed it on to her sister, who had not seen the amount either. Both of them were in shock—a good shock but in shock nonetheless. Rochelle held her head back to steady those tears. She had been praying for God to do a mighty work in her sister's life. Witnessing this was like catching a handful of manna from Heaven.

"Lena, what is so important that you had to separate me from Marquita's shrimp?" Obadiah asked as he approached the table with Maurice, Lamont, James, and Rochelle's friend Terrence Lockwood in tow.

"This," Yvonne told him and put the check in his hand.

Obadiah did what he always did when one of his members, and moreover a friend, was the recipient of a miracle. He let his eyes flip up under his lids for a second, shook his head, and touched his heart. Then he tilted his head to the side, took Yvonne's outstretched hands in his and said, "You are evidence that God takes care of His own, Yvonne. Now you know for yourself what a mighty God we serve and that He will not let the righteous be forsaken or begging bread."

By now the whole table had gathered around Yvonne and Curtis, who didn't realize that he was about to be blessed as well. Lena passed out two bottles of anointing oil and waited for everyone to put some oil on their hands, including Curtis and Yvonne. Obadiah laid a hand on both of their shoulders and began to pray.

"Lord, everyone standing here has read in Your Word how much You desire to bless Your righteous ones. We've read the words of our Lord and Savior, Jesus Christ, that if we but have faith the size of a tiny mustard seed, we can cast a mountain into the sea. We know, because Jesus told us, that in this world we would have trials and tribulations. But despite that truth, He also instructed us to cheer up because He had overcome the world.

"We know that You answer prayers and we know that You want us to have life more abundantly, and to prosper even as our souls prosper. Well, Lord, we have watched this daughter of Yours come through the storm. And in spite of all of the high waves and fierce winds, she held on to Your hand and trusted You. And tonight, we see the fruits of her labors, the evidence of things that have been hoped for, for years. Bless Yvonne Maxine Fountain, Lord, in the name of Jesus."

"In the name of Jesus," Lena echoed.

"Bless her job, the check, and bless the establishment of her professorship right now, in Jesus's name. We bind up, in the name of Jesus . . ."

"In the name of sweet Jesus of Nazareth," Trina said.

" . . . The enemy. Stop him dead in his tracks and do not allow him to do anything to cause any kind of problems with getting this all worked out. Dispatch Your angels, Lord, to go forth before Yvonne and work it all out right now, in the name of Jesus.

"Lord, thank you for answering our prayers concerning this situation. And thank You, Lord, for letting us see and experience the answer to these prayers in the land of the living, as You have promised us in Your Word.

"And last of all, Lord, we ask that You touch Coach Parker, anoint him with the Holy Ghost, and cover him with the blood of the Lamb of God. Touch and anoint every starting player on the team with the ability and wisdom to play that game with Bouclair College like they've never played before.

"Lord, let them play this game for Your glory, so that folks will know that You are ever-present and that just 'cause folks are on the court, doesn't mean that You are not there. Bless Curtis and Maurice with this win. Clean house in their department and get rid of those other two assistant coaches who don't need to be there. Get rid of those bad players. And bless them with favor and victory. Lord, we thank You, we praise You, we bless You, and we claim the victory in the name of Jesus, amen."

Everybody lifted up their hands and said "Amen" loud enough to be heard and observed by folks at the tables close to them. But they didn't care. They had just witnessed a miracle of biblical proportions, and the only thing left to do was to praise God and acknowledge Him as the Author of their fates.

"One-point-five million dollars to start your own professorship doing what you love," Trina exclaimed. "Can it get much better than that?"

"I don't know," Yvonne said with a big grin spreading across her face, "but I'd sure like to see if it will!"

"Now that we've prayed and blessed and come back to earth, I want to know how all of this came about. I didn't even know that you knew Bailey Winters, let alone well enough for her to want to sponsor something of this magnitude."

"Well, Obadiah," Yvonne began, "Mrs. Winters came and wrote that check because her husband wasn't acting right."

"Yvonne is not telling you the entire story, Obadiah," Trina interjected. "Jethro saw Yvonne and came over here to hit on her. I mean, it was a kamikaze hit."

"Yeah," Curtis said drily, "it was a pretty hard attempt to hit on Yvonne." He retrieved his suit coat from the back of the chair and put it on.

"Man, that's a sharp suit," Obadiah said, admiring the black silk vest with the red stripes in it. "Mr. Booth?"

"Who else," Curtis answered, mood finally lightening up. He was not happy with the way Jethro had rolled up on this table. This was the Dirty South, not the Ol' South. And maybe somebody needed to school old boy on that fact before he got a foot up his behind.

"Jethro was all up in Yvonne's face," Rochelle continued for Trina. "And Bailey just got pissed and rolled up on him and did what she does best—mess with his money. She whipped that checkbook out and put the check right in Yvonne's hand. And then she hugged her and thanked her for being a decent woman and left."

"And Jethro Winters?" Obadiah asked. He did not like that man and was sick of him and his antics. He remembered the last real encounter he had had with that white boy at his church. His members had to hold him off of Jethro. But if the man messed with one more person from Fayetteville Street Gospel United Church, Obadiah was going to forget he was a preacher and act like the street negro he used to be before he gave his life over to the Lord and was called into the ministry.

"There the negro is, over there all up in Regina Young's face," Lena said and pointed boldly at the president's table.

"He's white, Lena," Maurice said.

Lena laughed and said, "Well, to be honest, I wasn't actually, really, and truthfully calling Jethro a *negro*. I hate to tell y'all this but I had a lapse in decorum, and I momentarily resurrected the *N* word but tried to be nice and called him a negro. Pray for me."

"But he is still white."

"But he was acting 'niggardly,' which is a word used in *Webster's New Collegiate Dictionary* to describe a *meanly covetous and stingy person*," Obadiah, who made it his business to know the meaning and history of words, said. "And if we were to take liberties and stretch and doctor up Mr. Webster's meaning a bit, as we black people are prone to do, I would say that 'niggardly' could also include acting like a lowlife or a louse."

"Obadiah Quincey," Trina said, "you are the only *negro* in Durham, North Carolina, who could work that thing like that. And . . . oh . . . just for the record, I use the term 'negro' in the nicest way, as in, 'Obadiah, you *my negro*.'"

"Maurice," Obadiah said, "take your wife over to Marquita's food table and get her some of that delicious shrimp, and add a few extra pieces for me."

Yvonne looked down at her spot to munch on another piece of shrimp. But her plate was gone. She hadn't even noticed the waiters coming to get her food. If they had *wanted* somebody to scoop up a dirty plate, they would have had to chase one of them down.

"I'm coming with you. I'm still hungry."

"No, Yvonne," Trina said, "you are famished. What you just went through will make you sleepy or make you hungry. That's a lot of emotional roller-coasting to be on in less than an hour's time."

"Baby, get an extra plate for me," Curtis said. "I need to run a few things by Obadiah."

"Okay, Curtis," Yvonne said sweetly, and then wondered what in the world was happening today. In less than twenty-four hours her entire life had changed, and it felt odd. She was used to the drastic changes for the worse. But this drastic change for the better was so new. Yvonne understood what those folks must have felt when they came to Jesus with horrible problems and infirmities, and then walked away completely whole, blessed, and with double-for-your-trouble restoration in their lives. This was an amazing day that was full of the goodness of the Lord.

TWENTY-THREE

The music was sounding good. Yvonne wanted to get out there and dance to the Gap Band so badly. She loved it when they started singing, "You cain't keep runnin' in and out of my life." Right now, instead of dancing, these reception folk seemed bent on cutting deals, checking out the scenery, and scheming. Black college life was almost as complex, wonderful, and intriguing as life in the black church—nothing like it. And for all of the ups and downs a person could experience in these institutions, Yvonne loved them both with all of her heart.

Marquita's catering company had outdone itself tonight. The entire hall was decorated in the school's colors of black and red. The banquet tables were covered with black linen cloths with red napkins held securely with black napkin rings resting on black china trimmed in metallic red and silver. Dark red roses in translucent black crystal vases sat in the middle of each table, with rose petals sprinkled around the area of the vases. And each chair was covered with black muslin, and had a stiff red muslin bow attached to the back.

Around the room were six-foot-high black metal frames that resembled floor-length mirrors with huge photographs of the school, the president and his wife, the basketball team, and the coaches. And the food tables made you hungry just looking at them. There was so much to choose from, Yvonne didn't know where to start.

But the best part of a reception like this were the people themselves. There had to be every kind of African-American in the city of

Durham represented at this event. This crowd ranged from ghetto-fabulous folk, like Dayeesha Hamilton, to the hardworking staff members from the university, who worked quietly and diligently to aid in the education of folks' children, to the professors who worked hard to make sure that not one black child would be left behind when they left with a degree in hand, to the hinctified adminis-trators and high-profile faculty who held the erroneous belief that the university actually revolved around them, to the coaches, band directors, cafeteria workers, janitorial staff, and of course the stu-dents, alumni, and parents. It was a beautiful thing to behold.

Another Gap Band song, "Early in the Morning," came on, and this time Yvonne couldn't help herself. She did a smooth step all the way over to that food table where her friend Marquita Rob-inson Sneed was busy making sure that all was well with all of that delectable food. She was about to select some crackers and a delicious-looking lobster spread when she heard a friendly voice call out her name.

She turned around grinning at her girl, who was first cousin to Charmayne and the infamous and very fine Charles Robinson. Sometimes Charles reminded Yvonne of a bigger, buffer, sexier, and older version of the actor Terrence Howard. And that was saying something because Mr. Terrence gave new meaning to the term "redbone."

The Robinsons had always fascinated Yvonne with how very different they were. They loved one another to death. But the fami-lies of the two sisters—Charmayne and Charles's mother, Miss Ida Belle, and Marquita's mother, Miss Margarita—were as different as night and day. First off, Ida Belle was just downright gangsta. She loved the hood, and she was the consummate "hood entrepreneur."

Miss Ida Belle's sister, Margarita, on the other hand, was saved and filled with the Holy Ghost. She was an ordained minister and assistant pastor at Ram in the Bush Holiness Church of Prophesy and Deliverance—the hottest and fastest-growing holiness church in Durham County outside of the church pastored by Apostle Grady Grey and his wife, Linda. She worked tirelessly to get as many folk saved and living what she described as "the Kingdom life" as the

Lord would allow, and stayed in intercessory prayer on behalf of her unsaved relatives.

Miss Margarita also supplied Miss Thang's Holy Ghost Corner and Church Woman Boutique with all of that saved lingerie that folks were always going gaga over when they were in Theresa's store. Her best-selling items were the sheer PJs in pastel colors and matching lacy bra and thongs with PASTOR'S SHORTY, BISHOP'S BOO, DEACON'S DARLING, STEWARD'S SWEETIE, and FIRST LADIES SIZZLE, embroidered on the PJ top. Miss Margarita's favorite first ladies were Lena Quincey and Angela Cousin over at St. Joseph's AME Church. She personally designed and made their PJs and robes and an assortment of fancy, pretty, girly things.

Despite the obvious differences between the two sisters, there were also some similarities. Both sisters had children when they were not married back in the day when that was hard on folks.

Yvonne remembered her mother telling her that both sisters' baby daddies proposed but the weddings didn't go through. Charmayne and Charles's father was an undercover cop who was shot down by friendly fire when he was trying to infiltrate a ring of black bank robbers and they were busted by the police. Marquita's father was shot down, too. He was in the army, assigned to intelligence, and located in an unknown spot in southeast Asia. And the only reason they knew it was southeast Asia was that the Vietnam War was up and running, and most black folk from the hood were sent south and east when they were dispatched to serve overseas.

So the three little cousins grew up as Robinsons and without the men who loved their mothers and would have given anything to have held those sweet green-eyed, hazel-eyed, and gray-eyed babies in their arms. And the mothers struggled to rebuild their lives while raising the cherished offspring of the now-deceased loves of their lives.

Ida Belle threw herself into the cares of the world in a feeble effort to lift the burden of despair that blanketed her heart. She got so mad at God for taking Charles Kirby away from her until she'd forgotten what folks did when they needed the Lord in their lives—fall on their knees in prayer and supplication for help in a very present time of trouble.

Margarita ran straight into the arms of God, while holding tightly to her precious baby girl. She knew that the only way she was going to survive the death of her beloved Stanley Bishop was by the grace of God. She got saved, received the Holy Ghost, and gave her life completely over to Jesus.

And because God is so good to those who make Him the desire of their hearts, He healed Margarita of her grief and blessed her with the joyful task of raising her baby girl to be a mighty woman of God. And then he brought a husband, father, and man of God into their lives in the form of Thomas Robinson, who would have been childless had not the Lord saw fit to bless him with Margarita and baby Marquita.

Yvonne stood staring at all of those delectable dishes, wondering where to begin with her selections, and just how much food she could pile on a plate without appearing greedy and uncouth.

"Yvonne!" Marquita said with a huge grin spreading across her sweet pale copper face, dark gray eyes sparkling like brand-new diamonds. Her shimmering golden brown hair fell in her eyes and softly on her shoulders when she moved her head. Yvonne had always thought that Marquita had the most beautiful hair—long, thick, coarse, and naturally colored a shade that women, black and white, spent a whole lot of money trying to duplicate.

"I haven't seen you in weeks. Where has your little chocolate behind been and what have you been doing? Because I've missed you, Yvonne."

Yvonne walked around the banquet table and gave Marquita a big hug.

"I've missed you, too. But it has been crazy with work and all."

"Tell me about it. Girl, my business is going through the roof. But between taking care of the grandbabies and working, I'm running to catch up to meet with my own self."

"You still have the grans."

"Umm, hmm," Marquita said, shaking her head in disgust.

Sometimes it was nothing but the Lord that kept her from putting her foot straight up her daughter, Markayla's behind.

"You know something, Yvonne, I thought that by having Markayla in my early twenties I'd at least be able to be footloose and fancy-free in my forties. But here I am with four grandbabies, ranging from thirteen down to eight."

"But Marquita, you have to admit, they are some of the sweetest babies I've ever met. And they have brought so much joy to your life."

Marquita nodded. It was true. "And they are no problem, really. They are very self-sufficient."

"They have to be," Yvonne said. "I don't understand Markayla. She's not on drugs, she a fool but she ain't crazy, and she had you and Miss Margarita and Mr. Thomas, but she just—"

"Wants to stay out in the streets, partying and drinking and hooking up with all of the rappers and rap producers who come to the Triangle. I don't understand it. The girl has a good job working for Metro over at Yeah Yeah.

"Wait 'til you see what the cheerleaders are wearing to the game with Bouclair College. Markayla is the stylist for the squad. And she is picking up more and more clients, a few out in Hollywood, every time I look around. So I do not know what her problem is. And her house is nice—she lives down the street from me in Cashmere Estates. But the babies absolutely refuse to live with their mama.

"That youngest, June, said, 'Nana, Mommy has too many hip-hop people in our house. And I don't like them all in our bathrooms, either. They ain't mean but they ain't got no business at my house. So we are coming to live with you until Mommy gets saved and starts acting right, like you and Big Mama.'"

Yvonne didn't want to laugh but couldn't help it. That little June was something else. She said, "Where is their daddy?"

"Jail."

"Again? I thought he was trying to get himself together."

"He is. But this was about one of those old arrest warrants Jamal had dodged around back in the day when he was still gangbanging. I took him to see Grady Grey and Dayeesha's daddy, Big Dotsy, when this first came up. They both told him to go ahead and pay his dues.

"Dotsy said that he'd bet some money that this little arrest was nothing compared to what he suspected Jamal had done in the cut and nobody knew about it. He told Jamal that this way he'd be completely free when he came out because the system had what they wanted, and wouldn't go looking for any hidden dirt if he let this go and did his time like a man.

"Dotsy and Grady worked to get the time served down to eighteen months. And then they went behind the scenes and activated some protection and decent treatment while Jamal is doing his time. And surprisingly, it hasn't been as bad as we first thought it would be.

"Jamal gave his life over to Christ before he put on that orange suit, he has received the Holy Ghost, and has started an in-house prison ministry for his dorm-mates. The Lord has a blood covering over that boy, and He is doing a mighty work in Jamal—I hardly recognize that boy, the anointing is so strong on him. And I know that he is going to take care of his babies when he gets out. I just keep praying that Markayla will have it together when their daddy is finally free."

Yvonne felt like crying for joy for the second time that night. She remembered asking the Lord to bless her with the ability to experience one miracle in her life today. And the Lord, who always does exceedingly more than what she could think of or ask for, had given her two.

She said, "Marquita, just think, Jamal has been delivered and set free of the demonic stronghold that once ruled his life. He is saved. He is working to get others saved and set free. And soon he'll be physically free and able to finally enjoy life and take care of his children. That has to be one of the best things I've heard all day."

"Well . . ." Marquita began, "I don't think that's exactly the best thing you've heard all day. Seems to me like you have heard two other good things."

Yvonne frowned a moment as she tried to think of that third miracle and then remembered Curtis.

"Umm, hmm," Marquita went on. "You got that check securing your job situation, you're here with that big ol' sweet Mounds chocolate bar, Curtis, and I've given you a testimony about Jamal. You have a whole lot to be thankful for this evening, Miss Yvonne Fountain."

"Yeah, I guess I do," Yvonne told her as she broke out into a huge smile when she saw Darrell and Bettina trying to act as if they didn't see her when they came over to the table to get some more food. One look at that outfit that even Miss Baby Doll Lacy wouldn't wear let Yvonne know that Bettina had been put in her place tonight. It felt good, too. And what felt even better was that the Lord had fixed it so nothing about her job was tied to anything that had a thing to do with Darrell and his wife.

Yvonne smiled and then frowned and then tried to smile again when she remembered that she was standing with Marquita. But she wasn't fast enough.

"What's wrong with yo' butt?"

"Him," Yvonne told her as she watched Kordell make his way around the room, scoping out a woman to hit on.

Surprisingly, Marquita frowned, too. Lately, she found herself liking Kordell Bivens less and less. And she didn't like the way Rico always had to hop up and run out of town with that ugly man, simply because Kordell started whining about needing some time away from Durham to get his head straight. If he'd quit ho-hoppin' and lyin' to women, maybe he'd be able to keep his big fat head straight.

Tangie Bonner walked up to where Kordell was standing and planted a kiss on his cheek. He gave her a dry smile, along with a patronizing pat on the behind. Tangie smiled and walked off to join her friends.

"Sometimes I don't get Tangie Bonner," Marquita said. She didn't like Tangie but couldn't exactly explain why she felt this way. Tangie had never done anything to her—that is, not anything she could put her finger on. But there was something wrong with where Tangie was coming from as far as Marquita was concerned.

"What do you mean?" Yvonne asked, wondering just how much

Marquita could see in that girl. She didn't mess with people like Marquita. As sweet as they were, somebody like that could see through you once she took a mind to do so. But that was the operative concept—*take a mind to do so*. And right now, Marquita was not ready to go to that place.

"She's sneaky but I don't know why, when all of her business with men is always in the street," Marquita said.

Yvonne was quiet, but not too quiet as to tip Marquita off. She said, "I feel the same way. She has dirt out there for all to see but she is still a snake in the grass."

Marquita nodded in agreement. It was clear that she was working through some things where Tangie Bonner was concerned.

"So," Yvonne said, hoping to draw Marquita's attention away from Tangie, "why are you behind this table and not out there hobnobbing with the rest of the high-cotton folk? I saw your cousin Charmayne over there with some high rollers looking good in that black St. John with the crisscross design down the back of the jacket and the skirt. And Charles is over there huddled up in a serious conversation with the provost. Girl, you know it's a shame that that boy is so fine and so good at being bad."

"I know," Marquita said. "And look at that suit he's wearing."

"Girl, that thing is tight. And Charles is the only brother in this room who can wear that suit," Yvonne answered as she tried to get a better take on that crimson three-piece suit with black chalk stripes, black shirt and tie, and black gaiters trimmed in red.

"Look at the women trying to roll up on him, Yvonne."

"What you two little negroes over here talkin' 'bout?" Charles asked them as he walked up and then took Yvonne by the hand and gave her a twirl.

"You look good, baby! And look . . . look . . . look," he said and pointed at Bettina. "Ole' Sundress is pissed that you are looking so good and that you are so happy."

"You are crazy, Charles Robinson," Yvonne said. "And you are mighty clean your own self."

"Hey, baby. That's how I roll. You know a player gots to always be ready and up for anything."

"Boy, stop," Yvonne told him. "See, that's why you're always getting hooked up with the 'ready for anything.'"

"I hear ya', play cuz," he said as he glanced over to where Veronica Washington was standing with her friends, looking good in a black knit pantsuit with stovepipe-legged pants and a belted jacket with silver buttons down the front and the sleeves. He liked those black patent-leather boots with the silver spiked heels that Veronica was wearing.

Charles loved the way that woman smiled and cracked jokes and made others smile, even when he knew she was going through a rough time. Charles didn't know Robert Washington well, but what he did know was that Robert was a piece of work, and that one day he was going to get his.

Veronica was standing there with her friends laughing and having a good time, when, as could be expected, Robert came in with Tracey Parsons on his arm, acting like she was the catch of the day.

Charles took a good look at Tracey Parsons's head and said, "You know something, every time I see that woman, I keep expecting to see Brian the dog, Peter, Lois, Meg, and Chris come up right behind her."

"Now, you have just lost what little bit was left of a good mind—with your cray-zee self," Marquita said.

"I haven't lost all of it," Charles said, now suddenly serious, as he watched Robert walk over to where Veronica was with Tracey. "I'll be right back."

He hurried back across the room and walked up to Veronica and placed his arm around her shoulder. "I thought I saw your fine self standing over here holding court like the queen that you are, girl."

Veronica looked up into Charles's eyes with a silent "thank you" radiating from her own. Then she regrouped and said, "Boy, you need to quit," in a playful voice that didn't give a hint of how she really felt at the insult her ex-husband and his woman had just paid her when they invaded her space to be mean.

"Naw, I am not going to quit," Charles said, turning up the heat when he saw Robert's eyes narrow. "I'm gone mess with you some more, Miss Veronica." He kissed her cheek. "Umph, girl, what you got that got me going—and that was just your cheek."

"Charles Robinson, you know you are so wrong."

"Well," Charles said, "if loving you is wrong, baby, I don't wanna be right." He held out his hand toward Robert. "I know you know exactly what I'm talking about, don't you, playah?"

Robert bristled and blew air out of his cheeks. He said, "No, I don't know what the hell you are talking about."

"Oh, yes you do. 'Cause you are standing here flaunting this ho in Veronica's face, as wrong as can be, and actin' like you are right."

Robert took off his dark purple suit coat and put it in Tracey's hands. He rolled up the sleeves of his gold shirt and said, "You don't talk to me or my baby like that," and then took an empty swing at Charles, who started laughing and pimp-slapped Robert so fast he almost didn't know what happened.

Veronica's girl Lynette Smith started cracking up, and then whipped out her cell phone to call her husband, L. C. As soon as he said, "Hello," over the speaker, she said, "Have you parked the car?"

"Yeah, baby. I'm on my way into the banquet hall right now. What's up?"

"Charles just pimp-slapped the mess out of Robert Washington and called Stewie a ho. Only when he said 'ho,' it was like a real pimp would say it—you know, 'hoah.'"

"Dang," L. C. said on the phone as he made his way over to the group. "I hope he saves a piece for me. 'Cause I did not like how Robert did Veronica. Wasn't nothing right about that."

"I hope there is some left, L. C. But I will make sure to get some good pictures for you," Lynette said, and started photographing the altercation with her fancy cell phone.

Robert happened to turn around and see Lynette snapping pictures of him with her phone as if this were some kind of reality TV show. He walked up to Lynette and put his hand over the part of the phone capturing him on digital camera.

Lynette drew her head back and then snatched her phone out of

Robert's reach. She said, "Oh . . . *Oh* . . . *Oh*, no you did not just try and front me, Robert Herman Washington. I guess you must want this to be the ultimate throwdown."

"Hold on, baby," L. C. said as he pulled his fedora off his head by the front tip of the crown, put it in Lynette's hand, and pushed her back with his arm. "This ain't a fight for you as much as I know you want to be in it."

Lynette started jumping around saying, "*Yeah* . . . that's *my man* fighting for *my honor*. Get him, baby, get him."

Obadiah, who was talking with Curtis and Maurice about the pending game, looked across the banquet hall and said, "What is in the water up in here tonight?"

"What do you mean, Obadiah?" Maurice asked.

"Look." He pointed to the ruckus that was now taking place. "Over there. Charles Robinson and L. C. Smith are about to kick Robert Washington's butt."

"Shoot," Curtis said. "I'm not going to miss this. The only negro other than Rico Sneed that everybody in Durham County wants a piece of is that negro, Robert Washington."

The three of them practically sprinted across the hall, and made it just in time to see L. C. backhand Robert. At this point, two of Robert's boys showed up. But Charles's boys Pierre and Bay rolled up on them and quietly opened their suit coats, and Robert's boys got ghost.

Tracey could not believe how this had gone down. It had been her idea to come over here and rub the relationship in Robert's ex-wife's face. But she realized that this was not such a good idea after all. Her friends had warned her about coming down here from Baltimore and starting stuff with those crazy black folks in the Bull City.

Now, her man was getting his butt kicked like he was a little B on the corner. And that was definitely not sexy in her book. In fact, she'd been pondering on this relationship for a moment. Robert had lied and told her that they were going to live in that house he moved out of in Carillon Forest, only to have her move into that apartment in Bismarck Ridge.

Tracey would never forget how she felt when Robert picked her up at the airport and drove her to the new place he had been boasting about for months. And now, there was Veronica standing there eating a chicken wing, dressed to the nines, and watching Robert get a beatdown, as if she were watching one of those fights on a show like *I Love New York 2*.

"I guess I should try and do something like a good pastor and stop the fray, huh," Denzelle, who had just joined them, mumbled through a mouth stuffed full of shrimp, with about as much enthusiasm as somebody petitioning for an extra dose of the flu shot.

"Well, uh, I guess so, Pastor," Maurice said with great hesitation. "But you know—all in God's timing. Ecclesiastes clearly states that there is a season for everything."

"I see what you mean. We don't want to interfere with the workings of the Lord, now do we, church," Denzelle replied solemnly, and tried not to start laughing when he glanced over at his boy Obadiah.

Robert threw a hard punch in the air, hoping that the power of his swing would offset some of his reputation damage, and he wouldn't walk away looking like a total poot-butt. He stood up straight, squared off his shoulders, and walked up to Veronica, who was now working on the second chicken wing, which she personally thought tasted better than the shrimp everybody was gobbling down.

She stopped chewing and looked up at Robert, who was a big, thick brother, and obviously spent a lot of time in the gym.

He jabbed his finger at Veronica and said in that harsh, bellowing, and nasty voice he was so famous for, "This is your fault. That's why I'm with Tracey and not you. Couldn't teach you anything. All you want to do is read your Bible and pray. So what has God done for you, Veronica? Huh? *Tell me.*"

If Robert had said that to Veronica a year ago, those words would have cut through her like a knife. But God had done a lot for Veronica Washington in the time that Robert Herman had been out of her life. Perhaps it was time to give this man a testimony of just how much God could do.

"Robert Herman," Veronica began, knowing that Robert hated it when she called him by his first and middle name. "God answered my prayers and snatched you out of my house because you are crazy and don't need to be there.

"God provided for my mortgage so that I could live comfortably and enjoy my beautiful, custom-made home after you used our money to buy this ho-hussy-heifer a plane ticket down to Durham, when you stayed at the Four Points Hotel in Baltimore, ate at the Timbuktu Restaurant Lounge in Hanover, Maryland, etcetera, etcetera, etcetera, ad nauseam.

"God comforted me every time Stewie here called my house asking for you to pay her 280-dollar cell phone bill or take her shopping at Macy's in Columbia, Maryland, with money that was *stolen* from our household budget. God has restored everything about my money and I have more than enough. God took away all of the love I had for you and turned it into forgiveness and *agape* love so that I could live a blessed and prosperous life.

"*God,*" Veronica said, putting great emphasis on the word, "told me not to answer your phone calls, letters, or e-mails about coming to *my* house to get what you have erroneously assumed are your belongings. Because there is nothing, absolutely nothing in *my* house that belongs to the likes of *you*. And in fact, if you want to know where your little pitiful mess is, go on over to the Durham Rescue Mission and ask them if they'd like to sell it back to you.

"And my God gave me comfort and peace concerning all of your cheating and dirty dealing. Because all of the gym workouts and Viagara tablets in the whole wide world will not increase your stamina or add any extra inches to that short appendage you put such stock in. That's what God has done for me. And if you will excuse me, Robert Herman Washington, I have some chicken wings that I have to finish eating—and you and your big-head skoochie are interrupting the flow of my meal."

"You think you bad 'cause you got all of this backup. But they won't be with you all the time," Robert snarled.

"Oh, that is where you are wrong, dawg," Charles told him. And then turned to Veronica and said, "You better call me before you call 911"—he patted the holster under his arm—"because I got something that will definitely be the right answer to that call."

"I'm not through with you, Miss Veronica," Robert spat out, snatched Stewie by the arm, and turned to storm off. But he didn't get far before one of those chicken wings came sailing through the air and hit him upside his head.

"Dang," Lynette said to L. C. "I told you 'bout those little quiet ones. Robert Herman better get gone before he finds himself lying up under some dirt fertilizing Veronica's tomatoes. We go over there and will be asking her what she did to grow all of those pretty tomatoes."

At that moment, Dayeesha and Miss Deena, followed by Miss Hattie Lee, came from out back with more food and some new pastry dishes. They looked around the room and at the cluster of black folks bunched up in a corner looking pissed and whispering.

"Did we miss something, Miss M?" Dayeesha asked Marquita.

Yvonne nodded her head yes. This had been some day. She looked across the room for Curtis, hoping he was as ready to go as she was. And she didn't care if he was the head coach and one of the main reasons that everybody was here. This year it was different. They needed to go home and get some rest. And then they needed to show up at church on Sunday morning and pray. Curtis had to win the game with Bouclair College, and prayer—not this reception—was the only thing that was going to make that happen.

Curtis saw Yvonne looking at him and told Maurice and Obadiah.

"I need to get baby girl home. She is exhausted and so am I. Maurice, will you hold down the fort for me?"

"Bye" was all Maurice said and then he added, "What about the team? We're here because every single year, this school wants to celebrate its basketball team. And that team is nowhere in sight."

"And they aren't going to be anywhere in sight. I gave them the evening off after you left practice. You know that most of them would rather be anywhere but here. Plus, we have practice bright and early in the morning. Those boys need to be under the bed about now."

"What time?" Maurice asked.

"Seven-thirty sharp."

"I won't be too far behind you, dawg. I'll make the rounds and then head on out. You and the team are coming to the Family and Friends Day this Sunday?"

Curtis nodded. He'd told the team that if anybody missed service at Fayetteville Street Church, they'd be benched. And he knew that his best players would be there because they all went to church. The only ones he had to be concerned about were June Bug Washington and DeMarcus Brown. And since he wanted to keep those two on the bench, he hoped they stayed true to form and rebelled against anything he had to say—this time by not showing up for church.

He headed over toward Yvonne, who was already walking in his direction with her new purse on the old-lady spot high up on her arm—a clear sign that it was time to go.

"Ready?"

"Yeah . . . I'm tired, Curtis."

"I hear you, baby," he told her, marveling at how easy it was to be with Yvonne, and how comfortable he felt thinking of her as "baby."

"You wait here in the lobby while I go and get the car."

"Sounds like a good idea to me," Yvonne said. She'd gotten a good *whoosh* of that night air and it was a whole lot chillier than it had been when they first arrived.

"Enjoying your last semester at Eva T., Mrs. Copeland?"

Yvonne didn't even have to turn around to figure out whom that voice belonged to.

"She iggin' us, man," Yvonne heard Kordell Bivens say. Funny, she didn't remember seeing Castilleo Palmer tonight. He usually made it his business to be around when some dirt was going on.

"You short a troll tonight," Yvonne said, without even turning around.

"I beg your pardon, sweetheart," Gilead said and came to stand next to her.

"Beggin' my pardon for what? If you're short a troll, you're short a troll."

Yvonne couldn't believe how good and bold she was feeling

right now. Just this morning she was sitting in her car crying and wondering how she and her babies were going to make it. And now she had a check buried in her fancy new purse that guaranteed a sweet and very permanent position at Evangeline T. Marshall University. God was so good, and He had a great sense of humor.

"Let's go, Gilead. I'm bored with this gig, and want to head over to Rumpshakers for some much needed R & R," Kordell said.

"They're closed, man," Gilead told him. "Didn't you see all of the bosses here tonight?"

"Then where was Castilleo when he texted me and said for us to get over there ASAP? I had a taste for watching Sweet Red work that thang."

"Out at the strip club in the boonies not too far from Warren County."

"Ain't that kinda far?" Kordell asked.

"Yeah it is. But it's our only choice this evening," Gilead replied.

"Well, Warren County it is," Kordell answered, disappointed. "This club must be way out in the middle of nowhere. I've been to Warren County recruiting players and I've never seen anything remotely close to a club, except that hole in the wall that looks like it got lost in a time warp called Sock It to Me."

Gilead didn't open his mouth.

Kordell shook his head. He could not believe that was where they were going. Life was getting rougher by the minute. He pulled out his phone and texted his boy Rico: "Head on up to Sock It to Me in Warren County. Rumpshakers is closed tonight."

"You're kidding, right?" Rico texted back.

"Naw, dawg. That's where Castilleo is, holding down the fort, waiting for us."

"I'll be there as soon as I help Marquita load up."

"How are you going to get out?"

"Pick a fight and then tell her I need to get out and meet up with the fellas for a few beers. She'll buy it.

"Plus, she'll be happy to make it up to me when I act crazy about how she had the napkins and tablecloths folded and stacked up all wrong."

"You are so wrong, Rico."

"Maybe. But do you want me to come or not?"

"We'll see you in Warren County."

"Does this hole in the wall offer more than just some strippers?"

Kordell didn't know the answer to that question and he certainly wasn't about to discuss it with Marquita's girl standing there. He showed the text to Gilead, who grinned, took the cell, and sent the message he knew Rico wanted to hear.

"More than just strippers is an understatement . . . even Rump-shakers can't offer what you'll get at this place . . . It's a good thing it is a hole in the wall out in the middle of nowhere. Or else we'd be wearing some orange jumpsuits."

"My kind of place," Rico texted back and then sent a smiley face to emphasize his point.

Curtis pulled up in front of the hotel entrance, hopped out, and opened the passenger door for Yvonne, who couldn't get away from those men fast enough.

They drove off before any exchange could occur between Curtis and his so-called colleagues. This had to be the weirdest day he'd had in a long time—no, ever. He slipped a CD in but was stopped by Yvonne.

"Let's listen to the Quiet Storm on Foxy 107. It should be heating up quite nicely about now."

Curtis gave Yvonne a sexy wink and turned on the radio. "In My Songs," one of the last songs recorded by Gerald Levert, was playing.

"I love that song," Yvonne said. "Gerald Levert was one of my favorite singers."

"You and Theresa Green," Curtis said. "Lamont told me that Theresa cried all day when she found out that the Teddy Bear was gone."

"Me, too," Yvonne said. "I cried like a baby."

Curtis eased onto Highway 40. He reached over and grabbed Yvonne's hand in his.

"So, Miss Distinguished Chair. How does it feel to know that your job is safe? I told you not to worry. No matter what those folks at Eva T. tried to do, the good Lord was going to take care of you and those babies. The Lord doesn't play with people's lives like that. And He sure doesn't let others do it, either." Curtis laughed softly. "You know something, Yvonne. What I absolutely love about the Lord is that He doesn't look at the bottom line, and He doesn't get stopped in the 'here and now.' Because He has already determined the end right at the beginning of what is happening.

"That's why we have to keep the faith and believe that God will protect us and work it all out for the good of those that love the Lord, no matter how it may look 'in the natural.' We cannot let what folks who operate completely under the auspices of 'the flesh' affect what we know our God is capable of doing and working out on our behalf. And God sure did show up and show out on your behalf tonight, didn't He?"

Yvonne nodded, tears trickling down her cheeks.

Curtis lifted her hand to his lips and kissed her fingertips.

"I know your back was against the wall after the meeting this morning. But even in the midst of all that was happening, God kept speaking to my spirit. He let me know that you were not going anywhere and that you had a job."

"Thank you, Curtis," Yvonne whispered through her tears. She felt so bad. She'd been so scared this morning. And as much as she knew to trust the Lord, she couldn't help being afraid. It had been so hard to have her livelihood threatened like that, and especially after all that she'd been through. In that moment, Yvonne had gotten tired—tired of always getting surprise announcements of horrible news that threatened to rip her life to shreds.

"Baby," Curtis whispered. "Don't cry like that. God understands how you felt and He knows how scary it was. Just seek His forgiveness and give thanks for His goodness."

"Okay, Curtis," she whispered as the tears continued to flow.

"Oh, baby," Curtis said softly. "You've had a horrible time of it, haven't you? And every time you thought it was over, one more horrendous thing happened to make it feel like it would never end."

"Yes. I can't even begin to describe what this has felt like." She sniffled and wiped the tears that were now streaming down her cheeks. "Some folks don't know how good they have it. They've never had to worry about where their next paycheck is coming from, they get paid fairly and on time, and their livelihood is secure just because it's never been threatened. They have never known what it's like to not know how you are going to pay your mortgage and keep a roof over your babies' heads."

"And guess what," Curtis said, wondering what in the world was going on with him in this car. Every word that came out of his mouth qualified as something he would have expected Gran Gran, Maurice, Trina, or better yet Obadiah and Lena to come up with. He wouldn't have thought he was capable of issuing a "thus sayeth the Lord," and certainly not one of this magnitude.

"You are so blessed and highly favored, Yvonne. It's true. Folks like that probably don't know how good they have it. But did you realize that what you have is even better?"

"How so?" She couldn't figure out what was so much better about what she had been going through.

"Baby, you know. I mean *you really know* what the good Lord does when one of His saints' back is against the wall. You know better than most people that everything you have comes from God. You know that no matter how good you are, how successful, etcetera, you have to depend on the Lord for everything.

"Yvonne, do you realize that without these trials and tribulations Jesus promised you in His Word that He had overcome, you would not have been able to witness the scripture literally come to life on your behalf? You are living proof that 'eyes have not seen, nor hath ears heard' what the Lord has in store for those who love Him is absolutely true."

Curtis turned onto her street and pulled into the driveway. It was ablaze with lights. Yvonne hoped that nobody would be peeking through the blinds as soon as they heard a car motor sound as if it was close by. But that hope was in vain. D'Relle, Tiffany, and Danesha were all pulling at the blinds trying to get all up in "her grille." They hopped away from the window when they saw Yvonne watching them intently out of the car window.

Curtis turned off the car and lights and leaned toward Yvonne, and wiped the residue of tears off her cheeks.

"Can't send you back home looking like I did something to make you cry."

"Sorry about that. Didn't mean to break down like that. But what you said hit home so hard, I couldn't help it. You surprised me, Curtis. Didn't know you had it like that."

"Neither did I," he told her in all sincerity. "God has really been dealing with me lately. And I've been on my knees so much I have blisters on these old knees. But I know what I'm talking 'bout, baby. Remember, my back was against the wall, too, until you came into that meeting and fixed it so that my best players would play in the game with Bouclair College. I couldn't have done that on my own. That, and some very helpful information from Charles Robinson, came directly from the Lord."

Yvonne smiled at the mention of Charles Robinson. That boy was a trip and needed to give his life over to Christ. It was like he was running so hard from salvation he couldn't even see that he was catching up with his own secret desire to make Jesus Lord of his life.

"Baby, I have to tell you the truth. These last weeks have been just as rough and crazy. And I have not spent a minute during that time when I didn't think about you. Yvonne, I never thought I'd tell a woman this. But girl, I've got it bad for you. You know that?"

Yvonne wanted to say that she didn't know. But that would be a bold-faced lie. She had strongly suspected as much at Maurice and Trina's house. But if she hadn't known it then, she'd known it as soon as they met up at the meeting this morning. It seemed like an overnight thing but it wasn't. God's hand was all in this. And when the Lord made a move in your life, it could feel as if it were happening suddenly. But in reality the Lord had been putting that thing into existence before you had an inkling of the mere possibility.

"Yes, Curtis," she whispered so sweetly, all he could do was lift her chin with the tip of his finger and touch his lips to hers.

Another tear dropped down Yvonne's cheek. She hadn't been kissed at all in over two years. And she'd never been kissed like that in her entire life.

Curtis kissed the tear and then kissed her mouth again, only this time with more insistence and heated passion. He slid his hand to the nape of her neck and then slid his tongue into her mouth and moaned softly. He didn't know a kiss could work its way over his entire body, making him feel as if he were making love in this car.

"I'm falling in love with you, Yvonne."

"I'm falling for you, too, Curtis."

All of a sudden Yvonne felt as if she'd been hit with a splash of ice-cold water. She couldn't go forth with this, not with a man who had not made Jesus Lord of his life. She'd been there, done that, and it didn't work. It didn't work for her, it hadn't worked for Veronica Washington, and sadly, it wasn't working for her friend Marquita Sneed, either. That biblical edict about not being unequally yoked was no joke and shouldn't be tampered with.

Curtis pulled away.

"Did I do something wrong?"

She shook her head. How was Yvonne going to tell this wonderful man, whom she had it bad for, that they couldn't be together if he didn't want to turn his life completely over to the Lord? But she had to tell him. To do otherwise would be bold disobedience to the Lord. And after all that she'd had happen to her today that was the last thing Yvonne was going to do. Even if it meant she never had another man in her life, she was going to do what the Lord was leading her to do and let the chips fall where they might.

Yvonne took Curtis's hands in both of hers. She said, "I can't be with you if you don't want to make Jesus Lord of your life. I don't care how much we love each other, have in common, and want to be together, it won't work without Jesus in the middle of it all."

"What do I have to do?" Curtis asked.

He had planned on going straight to the altar this Sunday. So much had happened over the past weeks. And if Curtis had not been convinced then, he certainly was convinced now. He didn't know how he'd gone this far living like he did. He remembered reading Psalm 42 one night and understood what the Psalmist meant when he wrote that his thirst and longing for the Lord was so great, he could only compare it to a deer panting desperately for a drink in a cool, sparkling stream.

"This. This is all you have to do," Yvonne told him. "Curtis, do you believe that Jesus was crucified on the cross, and on the third day rose from the dead and is now sitting on the right hand of God?"

"Yes."

"Do you believe that Jesus is the Christ? That Jesus is the Holy Son of God?"

"Yes."

"Do you confess and repent of your sins here in the sight of God?"

"Yes."

"Do you believe in your heart and confess with your mouth that Jesus is Lord?"

"Yes, I believe it with all my heart that Jesus Christ is Lord."

"Do you want to receive the Holy Ghost?"

"Yes, baby, I want to have the Holy Ghost and the gift of speaking in tongues. And Lord, bless me with that gift in the name of Jesus of Nazareth."

"Curtis, do you want to totally rededicate your life to Christ and be quickened in your spirit as a new creature in Christ?"

"Yes," Curtis whispered in a broken voice full to the brim with his tears as he felt the light of God's love, forgiveness, deliverance, and redemption sweep through his soul.

By now tears were streaming down Yvonne's face. She dug into her purse for her anointing oil, poured some into her hands, and laid hands on Curtis as she prayed this prayer.

"Father, in the name of Jesus, I ask that you bless Curtis Lee Parker with salvation, deliverance, the anointing of the Holy Ghost, and the gift of speaking in tongues. Thank You for coming into his life and becoming the Lord of his life that he so longs for You to be. Set him free of all strongholds of the enemy. Forgive him his sins, and bless him with the desire to know Your Word, to seek You in prayer, and to be obedient to You."

By now, both Yvonne and Curtis were crying together. They held hands a moment and Yvonne finished the prayer.

"Lord, we thank You for this incredible moment in eternity and claim the victory in Jesus's name."

She grabbed his face between her tiny hands and kissed him on the lips. "I love you, Curtis. Lord knows I do."

He smiled, wiped his eyes, and said, "We need to get you inside. Plus, I don't think you need to face the tribunal without me at your side to help and explain how you left looking like a million dollars, came back with a million dollars, and now look broke off."

"Yeah, I guess you better do that, baby," Yvonne told him, enjoying watching Curtis blush when she called him "baby."

TWENTY-FOUR

Curtis stood in center court taking a mental count of all of the players who were on time and present for this practice. Everyone but June Bug Washington and DeMarcus Brown was here and ready to do what had to be done to get ready for Tuesday's game. It was clear just by his looking at the young men standing before him that they were going to put a hurting on Bouclair College and earn their rightful place in the play-offs at the SNAC Basketball Conference during March Madness. They had not forgotten the brutal beatdown they'd suffered at the hands of Bouclair when they played them earlier in the season. And now, after weeks of hard-core preparation, the Fighting Panthers of Evangeline T. Marshall University were ready to go out on that court and turn Bouclair College every which way but loose.

Both Curtis and Maurice were confident that the Lord was going to bless them with victory and that they were going to win this game. How it happened, how close or how wide the score would be, was something they couldn't and didn't care to know. But what they did know was that victory was imminent. It couldn't be any other way. As Trina had written in her e-mail to both him and Maurice this morning—how could God get the glory if they were defeated by Bouclair College?

They were on the side of the Lord and Sonny Todd was of the world. How could it possibly be any other way? No matter what it may have looked like to the natural eye and as a result of natural circumstances, it could not and would not be any other way. This was supported by the Word of God. And it wasn't any secret that God's Word did not return void. God was not going to let the enemy win and get up in Eva T. to run a reign of terror and ultimately destroy the basketball program Curtis and Maurice were working so hard to rebuild.

Coach Sonny Todd Kilpatrick may have won every game he played. But he destroyed every program he ran. His players rarely received their degrees. The incarceration rates for the teams he coached were way too high for college students. He did not put any significant amounts of money back into the programs he worked for. And in all of the years that Sonny Todd had coached, he had only two NBA draft picks under his belt—one of the two was dead as a result of a shootout in the player's old neighborhood with a rival gang member.

And as Charles Robinson and Bay Bowzer had recently discovered, many of Sonny Todd's wins were actually losses. Bay Bowzer had gone down in the back alleyways of black college basketball. He discovered that Sonny Todd had a very elaborate system of picking and buying off the referees for each game he was concerned about losing. Consequently, Bay and Charles managed to get a jump on old boy when they bought back the refs for Tuesday's game—paying them double to be honest over what Sonny Todd had paid them to cheat, and therefore tripling their take at this next game.

Charles and Bay had Pierre cracking up when they told him what they'd done. Then Charles said, "I cannot wait to see old boy's face go old-school-white-boy red when those referees get to making the right calls during the game. You know the red-face flush I'm talking about when a white boy like Sonny Todd gets caught with his hand in the cookie jar."

Pierre pulled out a C-note. "My bet is that he'll lose at the end of the third quarter."

"I'll raise you a hundred. Because it'll happen somewhere during the second quarter," Charles said and laid two hundred-dollar bills on his desk.

"You both are going to lose your money," Bay told them and laid five hundred dollars on the table. "He is going to bust a gasket towards the end of the first quarter. Y'all in or are you too punked out to go there with me?"

"Oh . . . Hell naw . . ." Charles said and laid another four hundred dollars on the table. "I ain't nevah skeered. What about you, Pierre? You want to teach this youngblood a lesson or two about doing business with us?"

"I'm in, Boss," Pierre said, and put down five hundred dollars.

"All I can say," Bay told them as he put down his extra hundred dollars, "is that I am going to have a very very merry merry Christmas on da house."

The team was hyped about this game and had done and was doing everything that Coach told them to do. There was too much to lose if they didn't win this game—and so much to gain from a win over Bouclair College. First, due to Bouclair's high ranking in the league, the team who beat them automatically won that spot in the Conference play-off games. And second, the team knew that such a win would raise their status in their league—which translated into attracting NBA scouts from across the country.

Because what a lot of folks didn't know about Curtis's best players was that they all had NBA potential. His top draft picks were Apostle Grady Grey's son, Sherron, who although only six feet six was the top center in the state. Then point guard Kaylo Bailey, at five foot ten, would bring back fond memories of the days when Spud Webb set the courts on fire.

Curtis and Maurice glanced up at the clock. It was eight-thirty, the team had just completed their warm-up routine, and Coach Bivens and Coach Palmer had yet to arrive. Maurice pulled out his cell phone but Curtis shook his head. He needed them to be more than an hour late to make his next move.

It was the oddest feeling to experience God moving in his life in such a powerful and provocative manner through a basketball game. Curtis would have thought that "a mighty move of God" such as the gospel artist Norman Hutchins sang about with such fervor would come about through something dealing with traditional church life. But as Gran Gran had to tell him, this was not about "church" but the Kingdom of God. And since the Kingdom could not be confined to a building, no matter how sacred the edifice, it shouldn't have surprised him that the Lord wanted to play this one out on center court.

The side door of the gymnasium opened. June Bug and DeMarcus strolled in, dressed to the nines in full-cut baggy designer jeans, their leather team jackets, and throw-back jerseys. Two of the cheerleaders that Maurice swore were the long-lost descendants of the biblical Jezebel were hanging on their arms. The squad captain, ShayeShaye Boswell, and her best friend, Larqueesha Watts, gave the other players a *y'all are so lame* sneer, and then went to sit on the benches even though this was a closed practice.

As Curtis made his way over to where they were sitting, he thought that those two had to be some serious skoochies. Because only overheated hoochie mamas could wear those tight lowrider jeans with identical black sweaters that came off the shoulder and stopped right under the curve of their breasts, revealing some buffed and cut abs and waistlines. As much as he couldn't stand those little heifers, he had to admit they did look hot and good—and it was cold outside.

"You and your skoochies are excused," Curtis told the four of them in an icy voice that made the brisk winds outside feel like a warm Caribbean breeze.

DeMarcus, who looked so much like his father, Reverend Marcel Brown, it was uncanny, stood up and stepped up to Curtis. "We have practice, Coach."

"No, you don't have practice, son. But we do," Curtis told him firmly as he got up in DeMarcus's face. He didn't know who this little boy, with milk still on his breath, thought he was. But he was getting ready to find out who he wasn't.

DeMarcus backed down and moved away from Curtis.

"My grandfather is not going to be happy," June Bug said, trying to pick up where he felt DeMarcus should not have left off.

When he stepped up, Curtis put the palm of his hand on June Bug's chest and shoved him back onto the bench with so little effort it scared the other players. They knew you didn't mess with Coach Parker. But they didn't know he had it like that.

Curtis pulled out his cell phone and flipped it open. He stared down at June Bug, who was trying desperately to collect himself and act as if that shove hadn't hurt.

"Now you really have something to tell the bishop." Curtis held the phone out toward June Bug. "Here, call him. It's on me, son."

June Bug didn't say a word, just glared at Curtis with pure venom in his face. He hated Coach Parker and would have done anything, including throwing that game, to get back at him. He got up and said, "Let's go. We don't need to practice for the game 'cause we got plenty of game."

"The only way any of you will be at that game is if you buy a ticket. You are no longer benched. You"—Curtis pointed to June Bug—"and you," he continued, and pointed at DeMarcus, "are permanently dismissed from my team. So take your little hoochies and get out of my gym."

Curtis walked off without so much as a thought to giving them a backward glance. The team had been glued to the middle of the gym, watching all of this play out. When Coach kicked them out, Sherron Grey said, "*For the Lord Most High is awesome. He is the great King of all the earth. He subdues the nations before us, putting our enemies beneath our feet.*"

"Amen," Maurice shouted out, to be followed by several more "Amens" from the team. He loved it that the team captain was so filled up with the Word that he could pull those verses from Psalm 47 at the most perfect time.

Curtis waited until the side door slammed shut and then blew his whistle to get the team ready for the real practice. Quiet as it was kept, he was glad those two little negroes had shown their butts like they did. He hadn't just wanted to bench them. He didn't want them anywhere near this practice session because he did not want June Bug and DeMarcus watching their moves and strategies. He knew they couldn't stand the ground he walked on, and they would sell out their entire team if it meant getting back at him.

He was about to do a practice run with half of the team pretending to be the most intimidating players on the Bouclair side, but was stopped dead in his tracks by Maurice. Kordell and Castilleo had just walked in through that same side door, and Curtis and Maurice didn't want those two to watch this practice, either.

Maurice leaned over to Curtis and whispered, "Is that particular door some kind of portal to the Devil's family room?"

Kordell walked over to Curtis and Maurice, adjusting his coach's whistle as if he were really getting ready to do something. He said, "Why are your grandmother and her girls walking around the grounds of the Athletic Center with huge bottles of oil in their hands, praying and speaking in tongues?"

"If you want to know the answer to that question, I suggest you get on your knees and take it up with the Lord," was all Curtis said.

"He can't do that, dawg. Because he don't know God's number," Maurice said.

"Oh, you got jokes, huh?" Kordell said.

Maurice didn't answer him. He didn't want this next level of business to take any more time than necessary.

Curtis started over to where Castilleo was still standing. He turned back and beckoned for Maurice and Kordell to follow him.

"We have some quick administration business to take care of before we get into the practice."

Castilleo sat down on the bench and stirred his coffee.

"So, what is so important that we can't get practice going in a timely manner?" Kordell said, as if he were the one running the show.

Curtis could not believe the presumption of this negro. He had planned to handle this matter in a professional manner but thought, *Bump that*, and said, "You and your boy here are fired."

"You can't fire us," Castilleo protested. "We have contracts."

"Not anymore" was all Curtis said.

Kordell's eyes narrowed. He was playing it cool but he was panicking inside. He knew that if Curtis fired them like this, he had done his homework and his decision was based on an airtight contingency clause. He just wanted to know what it was.

"Castilleo's right," Kordell said calmly. "You can't just up and fire a man with a contract without due cause. We can sue you and this entire university."

Curtis glanced over at Maurice, who retrieved two envelopes from his coach's playbook. He handed one envelope to Kordell and another one to Castilleo, and then waited for them to open them and study the photos.

"I see you went out to Sock It to Me last night."

"And what if we did," Castilleo spat out at him. He couldn't see what pictures of them getting lap dances had anything to do with their jobs.

"Well, what if I told you that those girls on your laps are only fifteen years old? And then, what if I told you that the next set of photos shows you, Kordell, and your boy Rico pouring liquor for these little teenyboppers? And what if I told you that a sting is going down right now as I speak, out at Sock It to Me?"

"And what if I told *you* that if we were in trouble, we'd be in handcuffs about now," Kordell shot back at Curtis, who just started laughing and then said:

"Okay, so what if I told you that the only reason you have on a black coach's warm-up suit instead of an orange jumpsuit is because Yarborough Flowers is running the sting and will leave you alone if you and your boy pack up your mess and get to stepping to wherever it is that chumps like y'all go to?"

"He can't do that without any real evidence."

"So you think a fifteen-year-old giving you a lap dance and drinking liquor out of your pimp glass isn't any real evidence in the eyes of the law?"

"Why don't we start with statutory rape," Maurice said.

"We didn't sleep with those hos," Kordell said smoothly.

"You didn't but he did," Curtis said, wondering why Castilleo couldn't tell that little girl was underage. Everything about her screamed jailbait.

Castilleo's eyes got real big and that fool blurted out, "But I paid her, man. I thought—"

Before Castilleo could finish, Kordell hopped up and knocked him to the floor. Hot coffee went everywhere.

"I told you," Kordell said in between a series of blows. "I told you not to pay that girl and to wait . . ."

By now the team had gathered around to watch this fight. They were athletes and a good coach-to-coach fight didn't upset them much. They'd seen a few good ones between Coach and one or two coaches Curtis didn't like. But a fight between coaches on the same team? And over some underage booty? That was a fight worth seeing.

As far as those young men were concerned, both Coach Bivens and Coach Palmer deserved to be fired and have a foot crammed up their butts. They were all under the age of twenty-three, and they knew better than to pay for anything other than admission, a dance, and for those twenty-one and over, something to drink at a strip club. And they also knew that underage girls slipped in, and they had learned to spot them out.

Plus, Sherron Grey's daddy had told him which clubs were breeding grounds for legal trouble. Sherron was saved and didn't go to the strip clubs but he made sure that his teammates knew where to go, and which clubs to stay clear of. And Sherron knew, just from talking to his daddy and godfather, Big Dotsy, that if there was one place no decent, self-respecting, and thinking brother should go to, it was Sock It to Me—*everybody on the club scene knew that*. It was a miracle that Coach Palmer wasn't lying up in the morgue with his throat slit after laying up with one of the women at that place.

When Castilleo's voice reached a feminine pitch, Curtis and Maurice pulled Kordell up off of him. Maurice helped Castilleo to his feet, and then smacked him upside the head.

"That was for the baby girl you should have kept your hands off of."

"She was a ho," Castilleo said.

"She was somebody's lost child," Curtis snapped. "And I guess you were dead intent on taking the baby straight to Hell. I feel sorry for you. Because you have a lot to answer for."

"I would, if I believed that hype about God and retribution. I've seen too many people do what they please and not have one thing happen to them."

"Keep living, son" was all Curtis said. "But in the meantime, you and your boy get out and don't come back."

Castilleo staggered out of the gym smelling like stale, dried-up coffee. Kordell made an attempt to walk out like all that had gone down wasn't about nothing he needed to be concerned about. But as soon as he got to his car, he put in a call to his boys—Rico, Paulo, and Larry. Those pictures Curtis and Maurice had were just the tip of the iceberg. He grabbed a tissue and wiped at the sweat that was dripping off his head.

As soon as the door closed, Curtis turned to the team in a feeble effort to try and get something accomplished at this practice. They had a game to play and win, and had not gone over one decent play. He took a deep breath and sighed, wondering how they were going to work this out in the time they had left.

The door opened on the opposite side of the gym and Gran Gran, Miss Queen Esther, Miss Baby Doll, and several other members of The Prayer Warriors came in carrying those big Sam's Club–size bottles of oil. It wasn't olive oil, either. They had real anointing oil that could only have been special-ordered from Theresa Green's store.

Doreatha Parker had been so busy interceding in prayer for her grandbaby that she hadn't seen the boy in weeks. And that was odd because they hated not seeing each other for too long. But the Lord had her sequestered in prayer, and didn't release her to see Curtis until this morning. Doreatha was a seasoned soldier of the Cross. And when the Lord gave her instructions, she obeyed. Years ago she would have asked the Lord some questions. But now, when God told her to do something, she did it—no questions asked.

"Gran Gran," Curtis said and went over to hug her. He wanted to run but that was so uncool. Right now she was definitely a sight for sore eyes. And she couldn't have come at a better time.

Doreatha, who was tall for a woman her age, and a feminine version of her grandson, wrapped him up in her arms. Her baby had been going through. But it had to be that way to get him to where he needed to be. And if he had to suffer, then so be it. If that was the only thing to get his attention, then that is what he had to go through. But standing here, looking the baby in his eyes, Doreatha realized that all of that had not been for naught. This Curtis was a new creature in Christ, and the anointing was all over him.

"Baby, the Lord touched Baby Doll's heart and led her to call us here to anoint the grounds around the Athletic Center, to anoint this gym, and to pray over you, Maurice, and the team."

"And," Miss Baby Doll added, "the Lord has a Word for you and this team. It's 'chill.'"

"Chill?" Curtis asked. "The Lord told us to chill? Chill?"

"Uh, yeah," Baby Doll said, looking perplexed. "If the Lord said 'Chill,' why you questioning that, boy?"

"It just don't sound like a Word that God would use."

"So God has sent you a Word list that He uses when giving a Word?"

Curtis sighed. He should have known better than to try and argue with Miss Baby Doll. She used to be homeless and knew how to handle herself. She also used to be crazy and was now healed, delivered, and completely in her right mind. You didn't mess with people like that.

"Look, I didn't question the Lord when He told me to tell you to chill. I just obeyed and brought you this Word. Now, do you want to know the rest, or are you going to have a debate with me on the validness of *chill*?"

Curtis didn't open his mouth.

"Umm, hmm, didn't think so. Boy, the Lord wants you and these children to go and get some breakfast, then go home and get some rest. Then, He wants y'all in church tomorrow, and after that to rest and stay in prayer and the Word. He wants y'all to just chill. Trust Him because He has already given you this win. Now go and chill out so you will have the mental and physical energy to really play that game. You all have been working hard for weeks. And now it's time to chill."

The Prayer Warriors gathered around Curtis, Maurice, and the team, and indicated that they were to get on their knees. They poured oil in their hands and anointed everybody. Then Gran Gran started praying.

"Lord, in the name of Jesus, we thank You for bringing us this far. My grandbaby is now saved, sanctified, and filled with the Holy Ghost."

"Hallelujah" came from The Prayer Warriors.

"And, Lord, these children kneeled before You, the ones who are now saved and the ones who are hesitating on getting saved, have hearts that keep turning, turning, turning, towards You."

"Praise You," Miss Queen Esther said.

"So, Lord, we thank You, we praise You, and we bless You in the name of Jesus. And, Lord, we praise and claim the victory over Tuesday's game. Give this team a sweet victory. Place Your angels all in the parking lot, at every door and window, and all over this building to protect this team and these coaches. Lord, anoint them with abilities from Heaven to play like they ain't never played before. Lord, keep them safe, and we bind up all injuries in Jesus's name."

"In Jesus's name, Lord," Sherron said.

"And Lord, let folks see Your glory at this game. Let folks know that the Kingdom is far greater than a church building. Your Kingdom is everywhere and extends to everything. For Your Word states that everything on the Earth belongs to You, and the Earth is Yours. Lord, this game and this win is Yours. We dedicate this game to You and give praises to Your name for the victory in Jesus's name, amen."

"Amen, amen, and amen," Sherron said, followed by a series of amens from the coaches and the team.

They all got up and Kaylo said, "So, what do we do now, Coach?"

"Go over to Cashmere Estates and eat breakfast at the Senior Center. They prepared a meal for you all as a treat," said Miss Baby Doll, who headed Janitorial Services and Grounds Maintenance Services at Cashmere Estates.

"And don't worry about transportation," said an older man with a white cane with a red tip, through one of the side doors. "We have the Senior Center vans outside for you young men."

"Oooh, Lacy," Miss Baby Doll said, grinning like she was a co-ed. "You so sweet, baby."

"Heh, heh, heh" was all Mr. Lacy said as he got the team loaded up in the vans.

"How long is that honeymoon gone last, Doreatha?" Miss Queen Esther asked her best friend.

"Probably until Jesus cracks the sky," was all Doreatha said, and then started laughing as they started blessing the gym and finished anointing it with oil.

TWENTY-FIVE

Curtis and Maurice were glad they had left their cars at the school and opted to ride the bus with the team. It was Family and Friends Day at Fayetteville Street Gospel United Church. This year's guest church was none other than Jubilee Temple Holiness Church II, pastored by Sherron's dad, Apostle Grady Grey. Everybody was excited about them coming. Everybody was here, and it appeared as if every single car in Durham County was in the church parking lot.

They hurried the team into the vestibule and signaled to Mr. Tommy, the head usher, that they were all in place and ready to be seated. It took a few seconds to get Mr. Tommy's attention—he was knee-deep in conversation with Miss Hattie Lee Booth. Curtis had heard the rumors about some fireworks between those two but hadn't given it much thought until now.

There was always some talk about Mr. Tommy, who was a widower, having a new girlfriend because Mr. Tommy loved women—and women loved him back. He was one of the few single seniors at the church who didn't have to worry about cooking because every able-bodied senior sister at Cashmere Estates Seniors Apartment Building made sure that he always had something good and healthy to eat.

But judging from the way Miss Hattie Lee was giggling and blushing and "swashing" at him with her fan, Curtis surmised that there was a whole lot of truth to that rumor.

"I think you better do more than signal to ol' boy, Curtis, man,"

Maurice whispered. "'Cause he's not about to leave all of that fine alone just to seat a bunch of basketball players."

Maurice scratched at his chin. "How does she stay so fine, man?"

Curtis shrugged, and made a mental note to ask Mr. Tommy that very same question when he caught him on one of his walks around Cashmere Estates.

Miss Hattie Lee saw them standing there. She poked at Mr. Tommy and pointed in their direction.

Mr. Tommy, who wasn't very tall, looked up at all of those long-legged young men and said, "Lawd, what y'all been feeding these children over at Eva T. You don't have a child in front of me who is under six feet in height."

"Five-ten, sir," Kaylo said, raising his hand so that he could be seen over his fellow teammates.

"Well, you come on up to me, so I can sit you up front so you can see what's going on over all of these trees."

The team followed Mr. Tommy to a special spot off to the side, where they could all sit together and the rest of the folks could see over their heads. Curtis looked around for Yvonne and her family, and then spotted his mother and grandmother sitting with them on the pew to the left of where the team was seated. As soon as the two families discovered that he and Yvonne were "going together," they bonded and started making plans for Curtis and Yvonne's future. And that included those two little missies, who had given him the thumbs-up when Reverend Quincey asked them what they thought about Coach Parker. That little Danesha told Obadiah, "We like him a lot. And now that he has made Jesus Lord of his life and shows that he has some decent fruit to back it up with, he can hang with us."

Then she looked around carefully and made sure no one was in earshot, and said, "You know, Reverend Quincey, that my little play sister, June, wishes you'd talk to her step-grandfather, Mr. Rico. She said that he is mean and is not fair, and that she is reporting him to Jesus, but just thought you'd like to know that she has taken this to a higher Person. You need to jump in that, Reverend Quincey, okay?"

Obadiah nodded solemnly. He would do just that. June was his little sweetie and most likely a genius. If she said something was wrong, something was wrong.

The folks at Fayetteville Street Church were very sociable. And on most Sunday mornings they were laughing and running their mouths so, the ushers had to practically drag them into the sanctuary so service could begin on time. But that was not the case this morning. This morning everybody was in their seat and waiting for the service to begin. Jubilee had one of the best choirs in the area. Plus, a lot of folks were only able to see and hear Apostle Grady Grey on TV, and considered it a rare treat to be able to hear what he had to say up close and personal. The ushers started closing the doors of the beautiful Caribbean blue and cocoa-colored sanctuary, but had to swing them back open when the entourage from St. Joseph's AME Church hurried in and made a desperate appeal to the ushers to seat them.

Curtis could not believe the ushers had packed all of these dressed-up, cologned, and perfumed folk in this sanctuary. He could not remember the last time he'd seen this many people at his church. But they were here—packed up tight and just as happy as can be. He stood up so that he could get a better view of what his baby was wearing this morning.

"Umph, umph, umph" was all Curtis could say. Yvonne was wearing a creamy yellow form-fitting knit dress with a matching coat, winter-white suede boots with gold stiletto heels, big gold hoops, and a yellow, peach, and gold heart-shaped pin on the lapel of her jacket.

He pulled out his phone to turn it off and thought to text Yvonne before things got to jumping.

"Baby, baby . . . u make me wanna hollah."

Yvonne stood up and gave Curtis a wave and then winked when she was sure he could see her face. He winked back and sat back down. D'Relle rolled her eyes and texted Tiffany, who was sitting right next to her.

"T, this old people luv is a trip."

"I know," Tiffany texted her back. "They haven't started playin' Luther songs, have they?"

"NO, whew," D'Relle texted back and then pretended she had stopped when she saw her grandmother giving her the eye.

"Your security guards r in your grille," Trina texted Yvonne.

"Umm-hmm," Yvonne texted her back.

"Curtis is sharp," Rochelle texted them both.

"Yep, yo' man sho is, homey," Trina texted and they all started laughing.

Because Curtis was definitely no joke in that black silk-and-wool three-piece suit with silver pinstripes running through it, and set off with a red shirt with thin black and silver stripes in it, and a black-and-silver striped tie and pocket kerchief with tiny red dots on it.

"Stop & behave," was the text message that Yvonne's father sent to all of them.

"*The Lord is in His holy Temple. Let all the earth keep silent before Him,*" Reverend Quincey called out from the back of the church. Looking around this church filled to the brim with all of these beautiful folk did his heart some good. And he couldn't have asked for a better group to help him usher in this morning's service than the men and women who stood behind him—Reverend Sharon Simmons-Harris, Reverend Denzelle Flowers, Prophetess Margarita Robinson, Reverend Philip R. Cousin Jr., who was the best pastor in the AME Church's Second Episcopal District, and on either side of him, the guest pastors, Apostle Grady Grey and his boy Elder Dotsy Hamilton. Everybody in this processional was a G—stone-cold gangstas for Jesus.

The ministers walked all the way down to the altar and then waited for the musicians from Jubilee Temple to start playing. They started off playing a smooth and jazzy version of "Near the Cross" to give the ministers time to get up into the pulpit and take their seats. When the last one was seated, the band, which consisted of a keyboardist, pianist, organist, saxophone player, guitarist, bass player, and percussionist, kicked the beat up a few notches, causing some of the folk in the audience to get up out of their seats and get into that hot and anointed music.

The mass choir, dressed in their customary black tops and white bottoms, moved into place down the aisle and across the back of the church. The choir director stood up in the choir loft and signaled to the musicians to get ready for the choir's processional. Just as they were preparing for the opening song, Mr. Tommy opened the sanctuary doors and let Marquita and Rico and their grandbabies hurry into the church and take the first available seats.

Obadiah thought about what Danesha had told him and made it his business to watch Rico with those children. He didn't like what he saw. Rico was frowning when they walked through the door, he snapped and scowled at the kids, and he scolded Marquita when she got the kids settled and took her seat next to his. About the only thing that made Rico stop scowling was when that Tracey Parsons woman walked her Stewie-shaped-head self past their seats and then stopped to take a second look at Rico. Obadiah definitely didn't like what he'd seen and made a mental note to run this by Lena.

The musicians switched over to the choir's processional song for the morning, and all the young people in that church hopped up and started getting excited. The mass choir, which had folks from the ages of five to sixty, and today had to number roughly sixty people, started moving from side to side to the beat of a gospelized version of "Crank That," or the "Superman Song" by the rapper Soulja Boy.

They started singing gospel lyrics that had to have been written by one of the teenagers in the group, and when they sang out, "Who's the real Superman . . . you know," the little kids raised their arms up, called out "Jesus," and waited for the older teens to pick them up and swing them up in the air like they were Superman.

By this time all of the teenagers, including D'Relle, Tiffany, and Danesha, were singing with the choir, smiling and dancing and having the time of their lives. But what put the icing on the cake of this processional was watching the older choir members sing and do the Superman dance. Every one of those older choir members knew every single move to Soulja Boy's Superman dance.

Trina leaned over and whispered to Yvonne, "They are throwing down and having a good time."

"They are not the only ones," Yvonne said and hopped up and started singing and doing the Superman with her kids. This song was so much fun. And even though she knew it was something totally different in its original form, she loved this adaptation. There were a lot of people here this morning being moved and touched by words set to the music of a song they recognized and loved. Sometimes you had to make folks understand just how crunked Jesus really was.

The choir took its place in the choir loft, waited for the last chords of the song to be played by the musicians, and sat down. Apostle Grady Grey stood up at the podium. He was in rare form this morning, dressed in a red silk clerical robe with a black brocade collar and cuffs, and a huge platinum chain with a large black diamond cross set in platinum. His curl was newly done and glistened under the overhead lights in the pulpit.

"Do you think that Linda does his hair?"

"She has to," Yvonne whispered back to Rochelle. "I don't think he could go to Elaine to get his hair done."

"Speaking of Elaine," Rochelle said, "did you remember to remind her about today?"

"Yeah, I did. But she is down in Atlanta at a hair show this weekend."

"Okay, 'cause you know that Elaine loves herself some Grady Grey."

"Umm . . . humm," Yvonne murmured.

"Hallelujah! Praise the Lord!" Grady Grey said with a smile lighting up his entire face. "I don't know what y'all came to do on Friends and Family Day," he said, "but I . . ." Grady Grey put a hand to his ear and leaned his head in the direction of the congregation, as if to say "I can't hear you." "I said I don't know what you came to do but . . ."

"I CAME TO PRAISE THE LORD!" the congregation yelled back at him.

"Now that's what I'm talking 'bout. Looka heah. You all are blessed and highly favored. Now look at your neighbor and say, 'I'm blessed and highly favored.'"

Folks turned toward one another and said, "I'm blessed and highly favored."

"I'm telling you people that you just don't know how blessed you are. Is there anybody who is blessed up in here? If there are, jump up and give the Lord some real praise."

Folks got up out of their seats and started cheering.

"Is that all you all got for Jesus after all that He's done for you? Come on, you can do better than that."

This time everybody got louder and they cheered and jumped up and down for a good fifteen seconds.

"That's what I'm talking about. You need to pump it up when you giving God the praise. Because whether you know it or not, God has really blessed you. Even when you don't feel you are being blessed, you are. Is there anybody out there who is having trouble with what I'm talking about?"

Two teenagers stood up and raised their hands.

"Anybody else?"

An older man and his wife stood up, along with three young men in their early twenties.

"Just one more, two more," Grady Grey said. "People, it's time to get saved. Is there anybody out there who is tired of the world? Anybody out there wondering how to have a better life? Annnyyyyyy . . . eeeee! Body out there," he went on in a high and melodic falsetto voice, "who wants to know what it really feels like to know the Lord?"

Twenty-three more people stood up ranging in age from five to seventy-five. Mr. Tommy looked over at Miss Hattie Lee and nudged her to get up with the rest of the folk. She shook her head.

He said, "Sugar, you sure you don't want to stand with the people? You know you need to do this and soon. 'Cause, baby, you are running low on decades."

Miss Hattie Lee shook her head again and Mr. Tommy left her alone. He would continue to pray for her. The baby needed to get saved.

Grady Grey surveyed the sanctuary one more time and had perfect peace that this was the final count for the morning. He looked back at Reverend Quincey to make sure it was okay to proceed.

All Obadiah did was nod. If Grady Grey could get all of these people down to the altar to get saved, and at the beginning of service, he could do backflips out of the pulpit for all Obadiah cared.

Sending as many people to Heaven as possible *was* the business at hand.

Grady Grey came out of the pulpit and stood at the base of the altar. He turned back toward Obadiah and said, "Can we get some anointed saints down here with some oil?"

Obadiah nodded and looked out at The Prayer Warriors. They all made their way down front, vials of oil in hand, and began to anoint the people at the altar.

Grady Grey said, "Do you all want to get saved?"

Everyone standing at the foot of the altar said yes loudly and with great enthusiasm. Grady Grey led them through the Sinner's Prayer and then laid hands on each one and anointed them with the Holy Ghost.

After that he said, "I want each one of you to find a permanent church home, if you don't already have one. This is the first, and an extremely important step. You all are babies and need the milk of the teachings of the Word to grow and flourish and be close to the Lord. It's a wonderful journey but you must be determined to take it and stay on it."

Then he went and took each person in his arms, wrapped them in a hug full of the love of Christ, and blessed them.

Yvonne sat there thinking that watching Grady Grey on his TV show could be very entertaining. But experiencing the apostle firsthand was a blessing beyond anything she could describe. And if that Jheri curl made it work better, then she was more than willing to tithe him a box of curl activator. Reverend Quincey had once told them how God loves to use the most unlikely folk to do His work. He was right.

Apostle Grady Grey ran back up to the pulpit and said, "Well, church, I know you all want to hear some more music after that. And I want to ask my Uncle John Lee Grey to come down with his ensemble, The Holy Vocalaires."

An old man in a light blue three-piece suit, white shirt, light blue bow tie, and matching light blue gaiters rode his scooter to the foot of the altar with his electric guitar resting in his lap. He was followed by four old ladies, who could have only been The Holy Vocalaires, because they were the only people in the church wearing light blue cotton knit culottes with elastic waistbands, white ruffled shirts worn tucked inside the calf-length culottes, white stockings, light blue pumps, and white turbans on their heads with light blue butterfly pins anchored in the middle of the turbans.

"How did we miss them coming in?" Maurice leaned over and whispered to Curtis. "I mean, I would have seen that. Wouldn't you have seen that, man?"

Curtis nodded. He couldn't believe he'd missed that, too.

Uncle John Lee Grey waited for one of The Holy Vocalaires to plug the guitar into the amplifier and set up the microphone for him. Then they took their places behind him. He tinkered with the guitar for a moment, stomped his foot on the floor of the scooter, and opened his mouth wide. He hit a few bluesy chords and then sang, "Chirrens," into the microphone.

As soon as D'Relle, Danesha, and Tiffany saw the gums in Uncle John Lee Grey's mouth, framed by two front teeth off to the side on the top and the bottom (four teeth total), they bent down under the pews, shaking with laughter. Yvonne absolutely refused to look at Rochelle and Trina, and then noticed that her parents were texting each other and laughing.

"I sayed, chirrens," he called out and plucked on the guitar some more. He reached down to the floor of the scooter, pulled up a jar with brown liquid in it, spat in the jar, and was about to put it back when Grady Grey frowned and ran out of the pulpit to where his uncle was.

He held out his hand and said, "Give me that." Then he hurried over to the side exit door, set that snuff jar outside, and hurried back to his seat next to Reverend Quincey.

The congregation was fighting hard not to lean over and ask the million-dollar question. How did that old man have that snuff jar and not spill any of it when he was driving that scooter and doing all of that stomping on it? Reverend Quincey was so tickled that he had tears in his eyes trying to keep from laughing out loud. And he absolutely refused to look at Lena. He knew that one look at that girl and it would have been over for him.

Uncle John Lee Grey massaged his gums with the inside of his lips for a few seconds, and then called out the key the song was in, started in on the melody, played a few riffs so that the other musicians could catch up with him, and it was on. That church got to jumping like they were at one of those old school Durham liquor houses folks used to sneak off to on Friday and Saturday nights and then tried to act as if they had not been to on Sunday morning.

The musicians lit into the vamp of Alvin Darling's "Nothing but the Lord," and got folks up on their feet. Uncle John Lee started singing the lyrics and it was getting good to him. He sang through those four teeth as if he had a mouth full of high-quality dentures. And he could sing, too.

But the best part of this song was when The Holy Vocalaires started singing the chorus, "Nobody, nobody, nobody but the Lord," in such tight and perfect harmony, the congregation had a new respect for those old ladies in the light blue culottes and white turbans.

And then they kicked it up another notch. Uncle John Lee Grey told the musicians to quiet down and carried the tune with his guitar. The Holy Vocalaires were on fire now, and they started dancing and singing like nobody's business.

Those old ladies could dance, too. They were lined up side by side like a 1960s R&B group, and every move was synchronized and precise. When they turned to the side and did a smooth dip-and-swing movement, the entire congregation hopped up and started dancing with them. Everybody, including Reverend Quincey, who was usually cool with his movements, was doing The Holy Vocalaires' dip-and-swing dance.

Uncle John Lee Grey brought all of those musicians back in and the music was so hot and jumping the folks were now coming out of those pews and were all over that church dancing and singing "Nobody, nobody, nobody but the Lord." This was definitely an old school gospel number and The Holy Vocalaires were working it until the church was on fire with praise for the Lord.

The song ended but the congregation wanted more. So Uncle John Lee started plucking out that universal and easily recognized Holy Ghost shouting song with his guitar. The musicians were on fire and added their part to this song, heating things up several more notches.

Folks were up and doing the Holy Dance all over the church. Reverend Quincey knew his church was hot for Jesus when two things happened. First, his boy Phil Cousin came out of his seat and cut a smooth step. And second, the man in the back of the church with his right leg four inches shorter than the left one started running around the church, and then lit into the Holy Dance. Obadiah marveled at how even the man's dance steps were—it was as if his legs were perfectly synchronized in length.

Never in a million years would anybody in the church, other than the folks from Jubilee Temple Holiness Church II, have believed that an old man in a motor scooter, a snuff jar, and four teeth to his name, along with four old women in some culottes, would turn this church out—and they still had a good hour of service left to go.

TWENTY-SIX

Tuesday came on them so fast that Curtis had a weak moment and asked himself if they were ready and could really do this thing. Then he remembered how Jesus had to check Peter when he jumped in the water with Jesus and then wavered in his faith when he started focusing in on what he saw happening around him instead of keeping his eyes on Jesus.

Curtis knew that fear was the opposite of faith. You couldn't be afraid and expect to find your way to a place of rest in faith in God. If you asked God to work it out, then your job was to please God by trusting Him to do just that, no matter what your circumstances looked like. As Gran Gran always said, "We see crisis, peril, and trouble, and God sees a miracle waiting to happen."

So Curtis had to choose. He could operate out of fear and lose this game. Or he could have the kind of faith that paid no heed to the circumstances, and let God use them to roll right over Bouclair College and put Sonny Todd Kilpatrick in his place.

He steered the truck into his parking space and headed into the Athletic Center en route to the locker room, where Maurice and the players were. But he decided to take a quick detour to his office, so that he could get on his knees and spend a moment alone with the Lord. Curtis pulled the bottle of anointing oil Yvonne had given him as a gift out of his inside breast pocket and poured a few drops in his hands. He touched the crown of his head and said, "In Jesus's name," and then started to pray.

"Father, cover me and this team with the blood of the Precious

Lamb of God. Anoint us with the Holy Ghost and let us play for You. Bless us by letting us play for Your glory. We need this win, Lord. Lot riding on this game tonight. Bless us with victory, Father. Thank You, in Jesus's name, amen."

Curtis got up off his knees and went down to the locker room. The game was scheduled to begin in forty-five minutes. His phone buzzed—Yvonne. Curtis smiled. That woman was a blessing sent to him straight from Heaven.

Why did he ever think that he could live without the companionship of a good woman? And things were so sweet and good between the two of them that they were just happy and content to know each other, to share sweet kisses, to spend time with each other and their families, to grow as friends, and to grow in the Lord. That was something he'd never had an opportunity to do—to grow in friendship and a relationship with the Lord with a woman he cared about. It was a beautiful experience, and Curtis Parker was a happy man.

He pressed his BlackBerry on and said, "What you know good, girl," in a low and very sexy voice.

Yvonne laughed softly and said, "You, boy," then told him, "We're all here, center court."

"Everybody?"

"Everybody. Well, Rico isn't sitting with us but Marquita, her parents, and the kids are. Rico told Marquita that he wasn't coming to the game to protest on behalf of Kordell." Yvonne paused a minute. "Umph, Rico has just strolled in with Kordell, Castilleo, Dr. Redmond, Jethro Winters, and Gilead Jackson. So I guess the protest must be tabled until further notice."

"Is Marquita okay?" Curtis asked.

"She okay, but she ain't happy with how Rico is behaving, and neither are her folks. Daddy T was about to go over there and go off on Rico but remembered why we are here. Oh, Paulo and Larry just walked in and joined them."

"Are there any bats left in Hell?" Curtis asked Yvonne. "'Cause it seems to me like they are all sitting in the president's box. But then, if they are all here like that, they are worried. And that's a good thing as far as I am concerned. Let me go. I'll see you after the game, baby."

"Okay, Curtis," Yvonne whispered so sweetly, he smiled at the phone.

"I'm gonna need some of that sweetness you sending through the phone after the game."

Curtis turned the phone off and walked into the locker room. It was clear that they were waiting on him patiently so that they could get the coach's word and get on with the business at hand.

LeDarius, who was usually quiet, said, "Dang, Coach, you are crunked tonight!"

"Yeah, dawg," Maurice said, "I'm scared of you."

"So, you like," Curtis answered and opened his coat. He knew he was sharp tonight. Mr. Booth had hooked him up with a sweet red suede casual suit. Baggy pants, oversize jacket, black silk mock turtleneck, and some black Timberlands with red laces and red trimming around the edge of the shoe.

He looked Maurice up and down and said, "But you know you are not shortchanging us, either, Coach."

"Well, what can a winning coach say," Maurice replied and gave his boss some dap.

"Mr. Booth?" Curtis asked.

"Nobody but."

Maurice was sharp in buttery soft black leather pants, black leather blazer, and a red shirt with thick black stripes running through it. He also had on some black Timberlands, only his were trimmed with black, gray, and red.

The team stood and joined hands. Curtis pulled out his oil but Maurice shook his head and said, "Your grandmother, Miss Queen Esther, Miss Baby Doll, and dem have already made their rounds anointing the team."

Curtis bowed his head and the team followed suit. He said, "Lord, thank You for bringing us to the point. And we thank You for letting us win this game, in Jesus's name, amen."

"Amen," they all echoed.

"Coach," LeDarius said, "that was an awfully short prayer."

"Did what I say touch your heart?"

"Yes, sir."

"Do you believe God is going to answer this prayer and bless us with winning this game?"

"Yes, sir."

"Then that's all that needs to be said. Let's go."

Curtis had told the coach of the cheerleading squad that he wanted the Junior Varsity cheerleaders to handle this game. The last thing he wanted to see tonight was ShayeShaye Boswell flipping and twisting and getting on his nerves. And mercifully, Christina Sprewell had done him a solid and honored his request. When they got to the entryway leading into the massive, state-of-the-art gymnasium, the lighting crew turned off the main lights and switched on red lights for the team.

The cheerleaders were looking good tonight. Marquita's daughter, Markayla, had outdone herself when she selected these outfits. They were adorable in low-cut and baggy red shorts that were rolled up several inches above the knee, black leggings, black tank tops with short red jackets that matched the pants, and red Chuck Taylor high-top sneakers. These were the best outfits any member of Eva T.'s cheerleading squads had worn for a game in a long time.

The captain of the Junior Varsity team, Brittany Taylor, did an air split, came down on the floor, hopped up, and did a high-flying flip. Each of the other six girls followed suit, and the crowd was up on their feet cheering and calling out, "Parker, Parker, Parker," with so much enthusiasm, Curtis, Maurice, and the team couldn't wait to get out there, warm up, and get this party started.

Brittany said, "Introducing the infallible, the infamous, the indescribable head coach of Evangeline T. Marshall University's mighty Fighting Panthers basketball team, Cooooaaacchhhhh Cuuuurrrrttttiiiissss Paaarrrrkkkkkeeeerrrrr!!!!"

Curtis jogged out into the red light and waved. He tried to find Yvonne but couldn't see well in the light.

"Oooooh snap, big sis," Rochelle said. "I've never seen red look like that on brown. *Dang*, Curtis!"

"You ain't never lied," Elaine, who had just taken her seat next to

Mr. Tommy and Miss Hattie Lee, said. "He should win the game just for wearing that red suit. Yvonne, how you gone keep your hands off of all of that? *DANG!*"

"Shhhh . . ." Trina said, "here comes Maurice."

Maurice did a smooth jog out onto the floor, gave a peace sign to the crowd, and then took his place next to Curtis.

"Is my man wearing that black leather or not? Shoot, we might get us another baby tonight."

"*MOM!*"

"Sorry, boys," Trina said, trying to pull herself together for the sake of her two teenage sons. *But*, she thought, *I'm still getting myself a taste of that later tonight . . . umph, umph, umph.*

"Coming from Hillside High School in Durham, North Carolina, is Number 12, Sherron Grey."

Sherron ran out and heard his entire church cheering and calling out, "God is good," as loudly as they could.

"All the way from St. Louis, Missouri's Beaumont High School is Number 21, Kaylo Bailey."

Kaylo ran out boxing at the air like he was getting ready to hop in the ring, and then gave Sherron some dap when he came to stand by him.

"From Atlanta, Georgia's Thurgood Marshall Lab School is Number 33, LeDarius Johnson."

LeDarius was shy. He jogged out real fast, gave a quick wave, and stood next to his boys. He could have done without this. All he wanted to do was play the game.

"Also from Hillside High School, Number 6, Earl Paxton Jr."

Earl ran out and acted like he was dribbling. His father, Earl Paxton Sr., jumped up and said, "Yessss!!!! Y'all know what time it is now."

"And last but not least is Number 55, Mario Lincoln, all the way from Charleston, Mississippi's Morgan Freeman High School."

When the team was on court, they all knelt, locked hands, whispered a quiet victory prayer, and then broke hands with an "In Jesus's name."

All of Jubilee Temple shouted out, "Hallelujah!!!"

"Those new uniforms, Yvonne?" Jeanette asked her daughter. Lately, when folks wanted the 411 on the team, they asked Yvonne, figuring she was the second-best source for some info.

"Yeah. They are nice. Markayla worked with Metro over at Yeah Yeah to get them in on time for this game."

"That Markayla is so talented, Marquita," Jeanette said.

"Yeah, she is," Marquita replied, trying not to look up at the president's box where her husband was sitting. She could not believe that Rico had thrown a full-blown temper tantrum in the car over Curtis and this game. She was glad the kids had decided to ride with their great-grandparents. They did not need to hear all that, and especially before going to a basketball game.

The team looked good in black athletic suits trimmed in red and silver, with a panther on the back of the jacket that was surrounded by red and then silver to make it more visible. The actual uniforms were almost identical to the suits, only the panther was on the front instead of the back. They were some high-quality uniforms that Markayla had been able to order from the same distributor who supplied many NBA teams.

The warm-up period had ended. Curtis and Sonny Todd shook hands and moved off the court. Sherron faced Bouclair's forward Jincintaye Lewis, and waited for the ref to throw the ball in the air. As soon as the buzzer went off, Sherron hopped in the air and slapped that ball over to where Kaylo was waiting to make his move. Jincintaye wasn't prepared for this new and improved Sherron. He tried to knock him out of the way and fouled during the first few seconds of the game.

Sonny Todd wasn't pressed, though. He had done some serious lining of referee pockets for this game. He tried to look miffed while he waited for the ref to make the right call. Charles, Pierre, and Bay were practically sitting on the edge of their seats, anticipating what Sonny Todd was going to do when he heard "FOUL."

At first he stood perfectly still, as if his ears were playing tricks on him. Then it dawned on him that he had heard what he thought he heard. In that moment Sonny Todd turned a deep red, snatched his coat off, and ran and chased the ref he'd paid off. When the ref turned and said, "You can forfeit this game, you know," he backed off and beat the floor with his coat.

The team went to the basket and Sherron prayed a quick prayer that he'd make this basket. Free throws were not his strength. He lifted the ball up, relaxed his wrists the way Coach Fountain had shown him, and threw the ball right in the center of the basket. It was a pretty shot. But not as pretty as the second one—which glided through the air as if it were being carried by an angel.

The buzzer sounded again, the ref threw out the ball, LeDarius slipped up under one of Bouclair's meanest players, Timmy Mays, and stole that ball like it was nothing. Timmy Mays was so outdone, he didn't even move when LeDarius ran down that court, passed the ball to Kaylo, and watched that boy slam the ball in the basket to make another score.

By now Sonny Todd was pissed. He knew he had paid those refs off and couldn't for the life of him figure out what was going on. He glanced up at Sam Redmond and Gilead Jackson, who stood up and lifted their hands in the air as if to say, "What . . . the . . . ?"

The first half was moving at the speed of lightning, and the Panthers were spanking some serious Bouclair College tail. Even though the actual halves are not that long, basketball minutes are really quite lengthy when being played out. And in this brief yet lengthy expanse of time the Panthers had pushed their score up to twenty-eight against Bouclair's pitiful two points.

Curtis and Maurice called out a time out. The team was moving so fast on the court, they were concerned about them wearing themselves out. They gathered in a huddle and Curtis squatted down in the middle of them. He said in a low voice, "You all all right? Y'all moving real fast out there."

"We're okay, Coach," Kaylo said, not even out of breath.

The rest of the players nodded and looked anxious to get back in the game.

"Anything we need to do, Coach?" Sherron asked.

Curtis and Maurice just looked at each other and shook their heads. It was kind of funny. They had never come to a point where the team didn't need to hear a thing from them. This was a game like nothing they'd seen or played before.

The buzzer sounded and they went back on court. The ref threw the ball and this time Mario Lincoln leaped up, snatched it in mid-air from Jincintaye, and ran just fast enough not to get called on traveling. He passed the ball to Earl, who tossed it to Kaylo, who did a three-point shot from across the court that was so sweet, it brought tears to Curtis's eyes. Maurice sniffled. He looked up in the stands and saw Reverend Quincey, Reverend Flowers, and Reverend Cousin pulling out their handkerchiefs.

But Kaylo was not done with them. He leaped up and snatched that ball, dunked it in midair, stole it one more time, and dunked it again. The crowd went crazy, and the band started playing Donald Lawrence's gospel song: "Giants do die, the bigger they are, the harder they fall."

Kaylo backed off after the last shot and let his other teammates get them a little taste of this good stuff. He dribbled just enough to entice Timmy his way, let Timmy take the ball, and then watched as LeDarius stole it so fast it took Timmy a second to realize that the ball was gone. LeDarius made his way over to Mario, passed that ball, and watched as Mario passed it to Earl, who made a sweet shot of his own.

By now Sonny Todd was losing his mind, and called out a time out. When the team got over to *their* huddle, he cussed them clean out, and then went on to say, "You dumb, gangbanging, low-SAT-scoring negroes better do this right if you know what is good for you."

The buzzer sounded and Sonny Todd put in his most hateful and dirty player, Chavez Jones. Chavez ran out on the court and right over to where Sherron was. He waited until Sherron had the ball and bore into him like they were on a football field. Sherron fell, was still a moment, and then hopped up like nothing had even touched him, and Chavez had to weigh a good 315 pounds.

"FOUL!"

"WHAT!" Sonny Todd screamed, and then started kicking the bench and knocking over stuff.

The team went to the basket and once more Sherron made his baskets effortlessly.

By now the score was so disparate that a few folks thought that they could just end it now. The chances of Bouclair making their current score of two points catch up to Eva T.'s 56 were slim at best.

Sonny Todd called another time out and instructed Chavez to hurt Sherron so bad he would have to go to the hospital. Chavez ran back on the court and made his way over to Sherron. As soon as Chavez saw Sherron with the ball, he bore into him and sent the poor baby sliding across the court. Again, Sherron hopped up and dusted himself off, now quoting Psalm 91.

"For they will hold you with their hands to keep you from striking your foot on a stone."

The members of Jubilee Temple started praising God in their seats, and the band started playing the shouting music. Sherron's grandmother left her seat and did the Holy Dance right on that basketball court. A few of her fellow church mothers came down and joined her. One mother fell out, and Linda, Sherron's mother, hurried down with a lap cloth she brought from the church to throw over her knees.

Linda shook her head. Just a few days before this game she had met with the church mothers and told them to wear pants, and then suggested culottes for the super-saved women in the group. But some of these old ladies were hardheaded. And the one lying on the floor, slain in the spirit at a college basketball game, was the worst. Mother Davis was always going against the grain and trying to do her own thing. Now here she was on the floor of a gymnasium with a lap cloth thrown across her knees because she didn't have sense enough to do what the First Lady had asked her to do in Christian love and wear some culottes to this game.

"Lawd, we are having church in the middle of a basketball game," Lena whispered to Obadiah, who whispered back, "Baby, you know black people can throw down some church just about anywhere."

"FOUL!"

"WHAT?" Sonny Todd said again. Only this time the fool ran out on that court and chased the ref down. When he caught up with him, he took a swing at the man, and then practically passed out when the man said, "*GAME FORFEITED*! Eva T. wins the game, and they are going to the play-offs. Praise the Lord!!!!"

Folks went wild! They were crying and laughing and shouting and jumping up and down all over the place. Nobody had ever seen a game like this. Because nobody had ever really taken note of a game where the real ref was God.

Yvonne and her people ran onto the court where Curtis, Maurice, and the team were. Curtis scooped her up in his arms and kissed that girl until he made her toes curl.

He said, "What a mighty God we serve," in the midst of all of those hallelujahs, praise the Lords, and amens.

Bay followed everybody to the floor to join in on the celebration, and then paused and held out his hand to Charles and Pierre. He started singing Jonathan Nelson's "My Name Is Victory."

Curtis looked up, not caring that tears were streaming down his cheeks. Victory that came from the Lord was so sweet.

READING GROUP GUIDE

1.) What is Kingdom Living, and how do the characters in *Up at the College* exemplify this way of life for the saints?

2.) Which characters best represent Kingdom Living? Which characters are the antithesis of this way of life?

3.) Coach Curtis Parker couldn't understand how God needed to be central to his life and his work as a head basketball coach. Do you understand how he could arrive at such a conclusion? And why was it so necessary for Curtis to alter this way of thinking?

4.) Yvonne Fountain is a woman in transition both naturally and in her walk with the Lord. How did Yvonne regain her confidence in herself? More importantly, how did Yvonne grow and mature in her faith walk and confidence in the Lord?

5.) Why did Yvonne and Curtis need saved and Holy-Ghost-filled friends in their lives? Why are those kinds of friends important in all of our lives? And how did these friends make a difference in their burgeoning faith walks?

6.) There were characters in this story who were struggling with letting go of the world and giving their lives over to Christ. Who were they? Why do you believe that they were having such a difficult time making this transition for both spiritual and natural reasons?

7.) Throughout the Bible, God has used the most unlikely people to carry out His will: Samson, Gideon, David, Jael (the wife of Heber the Kenite in the book of Judges), Rahab (the prostitute in the book of Joshua), Peter, and Paul, just to name a few. Who were the unlikely folks God worked through in *Up at the College* to help push things through for Coach Parker when faced with the works of the enemy?

8.) Who were your favorite characters and why?

9.) Who were your least favorite characters and why?

10.) What scripture spoken by or thought of by the characters touched you? And did any additional scriptures not mentioned in the novel come to mind, and why?